SOUTH BY SOUTHWEST
24 Stories from Modern Texas

SOUTH BY SOUTHWEST
24 Stories from Modern Texas

Edited by DON GRAHAM

University of Texas Press ◁▽▷ Austin

Copyright © 1986 by the University of Texas Press
Printed in the United States of America

First Edition, 1986

Requests for permission to reproduce material from this work
should be sent to Permissions, University of Texas Press, Box 7819,
Austin, Texas 78713.

LIBRARY OF CONGRESS CATALOGING-IN-PUBLICATION DATA
Main entry under title:
South by Southwest.
   1. Short stories, American—Texas.   2. Texas—
Fiction.   3. American fiction—20th century.
I. Graham, Don, 1940–
PS558.T4S68   1986   813'.01'089764   85-20227
ISBN: 978-0-292-77601-2

This one is for Elizabeth

Contents

CONTENTS

Acknowledgments

This collection of short stories began one day with a telephone conversation between Carolyn Osborn, a writer, and Suzanne Comer, humanities editor at the University of Texas Press. Suzanne deserves enormous credit for following through on that conversation. She brought the idea to me and worked hard with me to find the best stories we could. Indeed, she kept unearthing writers new to me and stories I did not know. We read and evaluated scores of stories and found ourselves in agreement an astonishingly high percentage of the time.

Besides Suzanne, a number of others offered valuable advice and opinions. Tom Zigal and Dave Oliphant, who together probably know more about small-press and little-magazine publishing than anybody else in the state, offered much sound advice. Several writers in this book are here because of their knowledge. Tom Pilkington and Jim Lee, with whom I have talked about Texas writing for a long time, were helpful as usual.

Barbara Rodriguez, another favorite editor of mine, gave me a good lead, and there were doubtless others who mentioned a writer or a story that sent me in directions I might not have gone. Special thanks are due Karen McCormick, who with her usual wit and efficiency did some essential word processing for me when time was short. My wife, Lois, helped me sort out conflicting impressions about a number of stories, and as always I am grateful to her.

Since I live in a state where the word *sabbatical* is a foreign concept, I am doubly indebted to the University Research Institute of the University of Texas for providing me with a Faculty Research Assignment, during which time this book was completed.

My only regrets are for anybody's favorite story that didn't wind up in the final selection.

The Short Story in Texas

The short story has enjoyed a resurgence in our time, a surprising turn of events for those who care about the form. Not so long ago it was being dismissed, another casualty of the mass media. Popular magazine markets dried up; audiences stopped reading short stories; the glory days of the 1920s, '30s, and '40s were gone forever. Mindless sit-coms, crash-and-burn TV adventure shows, and magazines peddling trashy gossip were what people wanted, not short stories, for god's sake. By the mid-1970s the short story looked like a literary auk. A critic in the *Southwest Review* (1975) was moved to melancholy: "To many of us, writers, editors, teachers, and aficionados of the short story, the future of the form looks bleak."

The short story might have been down, but it wasn't out. In the next decade it came roaring back. Following the best-seller success of *The Stories of John Cheever* in 1978, national publishers began to treat collections by old and new stars—Saul Bellow, Raymond Carver, Bobbie Ann Mason—with the respect usually reserved for celebrity diet books. Now things are so jolly on the short story front that such annual collections as *Prize Stories/The O. Henry Awards* and *Best American Short Stories* preen themselves on the revival of the form. Listen to William Abrahams, editor of the O. Henry award winners for the past eighteen years: "Marvelous stories are being written every day." Where are all of these stories appearing if they aren't to be found in the pages of mass-circulation magazines? In little magazines mostly, and there are hundreds of little magazines around the country. In them the short story flourishes and finds its readership, small compared to the classic days when everybody rode trains and had time to read a story and knew how. Small but vital.

What's true at the national level is also true in Texas. The short story here has never been more vibrantly alive than at the present time. Several little magazines in the state devote generous space to regional stories, though, again mirroring national trends, Texas' slick magazines fail to do their part. The lack of remunerative markets doesn't faze short story writers; they're a stubborn lot. One of the many pleasures of undertaking this collection was to discover just how many short story writers there are, both within the state and without. None of them make a living out of short fiction. How could they, when the appearance of a story in print may take anywhere from a few months to a few years, and the payment is a couple of copies of the journal. You could name on one hand the number of Texas writers who've made a dime from their short stories. Still they write, undaunted, often unheralded, but never, one hopes, unread.

It may seem presumptuous to bring together only Texas stories. Couldn't the volume have been expanded to include all of the Southwest, someone must be muttering. Is it necessary to remind anybody at this late date that Texas is a big country? Everybody from Zane Grey to George Sessions Perry has proclaimed Texas a world-in-itself. Russell Martin's recent anthology of Western fiction, *Writers of the Purple Sage*, omits Texas writers for the same reason: "Texas writers are excluded from this collection because Texas, for all its internal diversity, and for all that it stubbornly shares of the West's enduring cowboy culture, is a region unto itself."

Even so, many Texas writers reject the label just as serious writers of the West reject being labeled "Western." Western writers don't want to be L'amourized, and Texas writers don't want to be tied too closely to the old myths or their glossy updates. The presence of Texas in the national imagination, solidly entrenched since World War II but strongly present much earlier, starting with Alamo poems, novels, and plays and marching through the years in dime novels, old shoot-em-up movies about Texas rangers and cattle drives, and into the best little whorehouses, urban cowboys, and dallases of our time—this flood of trashy images of the Lone Star State poses something of a problem for serious writers. They get itchy at being fenced in. After he'd gotten semirich and famous, Larry L. King expressed a sentiment shared, I suspect, by many Texas writers when he said, "I had become weary of being labeled a Texas writer." Others have accepted the label with surprising equanimity. Katherine Anne Porter, writing to George Sessions Perry in 1943, said that she didn't mind in the least being thought of as a Southern or Texas writer.

Decades of stereotyping have hardened audience expectations, and those Texas writers who want to write about something besides good old boys, the ultra rich, blind heifers, and cowboys in Cadillacs, must do so at the risk of alienating mass-market literary consumers. Consumers are wooed with stereotypes of such crudeness that one stands in awe of Yankee benightedness. Here is a blurb from the back of a recent anthology of Southwestern fiction: "Some were born among the sagebrush and the mesquite trees. Others traveled here from the soot-choked cities of the East. But all write with their feet dusty from the mesas or with fingers greasy from chicken-fried steak." Pity the poor Southwestern writer! The pen skids off the slick roadway of his Big Chief pad; the keys on her word processor congeal in a glop of grease.

Audience expectations about Texas and the Southwest are scarcely a new problem, though. Earlier anthologists of Southwestern fiction felt the pressure of local-color imperatives. Hilton Greer, who edited *Best Short Stories of the Southwest* back in 1928, defined the familiar pattern in the first sentence of his introduction: "The typical short story of the Southwest wears the colors of sun and sand and saddle-leather." To escape these limitations, Greer included stories written *by* Southwesterners, which meant the locales might be anywhere.

George Sessions Perry, in his 1943 anthology, *Round Up*, reflects another side of the problem. Perry locates the Southwestern story within a tradition that, like the land, is "virile and strong." He goes on to place Southwestern writing in a false and unnecessary opposition to culture: "There has been more of cows and horses and thirst and violence and guns than there has of the self-conscious discussion of letters and salons and whatever is effete, and possibly decadent; for physical toughness, vitality, and stamina have been necessary attributes of our daily lives." This is the lusty-men or red-blooded school of Southwestern thought, understandable in its day but too simplistic to provide a perspective on the work of contemporary Texas writers.

Certainly the first Texas short story writer of note, O. Henry, fulfilled all of Perry's criteria. No one could accuse O. Henry of effeteness; his stories set in Texas dealt with outlaws and gunmen who didn't mind killing a man, usually a Mexican, whether he needed killing or not. Today O. Henry's Texas stories are still read, but few claims for their literary merit are forthcoming. After O. Henry there followed a number of Texas writers in the 1920s and 1930s who published Texas short stories and who, on occasion, were read beyond the borders of the state. Hilton Greer's 1928 anthology contains stories by Texas writers Dorothy Scarborough, Winifred Sanford, John W. Thomason, Jr., Norma Patterson, Horace McCoy, and Ted Dealey. Sanford was the only one of these who wrote first-rate stories. From 1925 to 1931 she published twelve stories, most of them in H. L. Mencken's *American Mercury*. The oft-anthologized "Windfall" and other stories, such as "Luck," are truly effective examples of ironic realism. But the best Texas short story writer of the era was Katherine Anne Porter, who by the late 1920s had already begun to achieve national recognition. In the next three decades Porter continued to add major and minor masterpieces to Texas and American literature. Porter's contemporaries among Texas short story writers accomplished much less. George Sessions Perry, John W. Thomason, Jr., Edward Anderson, Barry Benefield, and others, many of whom appear in William Peery's *21 Texas Stories*, all produced short fiction of mostly indifferent quality.

But even as that generation was completing its work, new writers came on the scene. *South by Southwest: 24 Stories from Modern Texas* reaches back to the World War II era and brings the short story in Texas up to the eve of the Sesquicentennial. In this gathering of recent work by several generations of Texas writers, a few definitions are in order. *Modern* in my title means since 1940, the earliest date of publication among the twenty-four stories. It also means this century; none of the stories is set in the nineteenth-century frontier past. *Texas* means that the story is set in Texas or in some way draws its essential spirit from a Texas background.

All the writers in this volume skirt the perils of stereotyping. No long-legged galoots gunning down varmints, no wheeler-dealers of oil patch fame, no Sue Ellen southern belles in crinoline and turquoise. Yet all the stories are thoroughly "Texas stories" because they grow out of either a Texas real and observed and lived in or a Texas made up and not lived in but real nonetheless in that compelling way the imagination has of shaping an image of a time and place. In some of the stories Texas is an overwhelming presence; in others it is more of an implicit subtext. Some of the authors are native Texans who live in the state; some are natives who haven't lived here for many years; some are newcomers; some are on loan from Eastern centers of culture.

In selecting the stories, I tried to cast a wide net. I read extensively in the back issues of prominent and obscure journals that publish regional Southwest fiction. But since short stories about Texas are likely to pop up in all sorts of places, I am certain that there were stories I missed. The stories are drawn from a large variety of magazine and book publications. Several appeared first in well-known national magazines, such as *Atlantic Monthly*, and several have been reprinted or cited in prestigious annual collections, such as *Best American Short Stories* and *Pushcart Prize*. A few appear here for the first time in print. All are independent short stories; none are excerpted from novels. They were selected, first of all, for their artistic merit, their narrative mastery. But they were also selected to give a vital picture of the Southwest in microcosm, the Southwest as revealed in its largest state.

South by Southwest attempts to mark the indeterminate boundaries within Texas itself. Texas began as a Southern state and did not cease to be one until the 1960s when Lyndon Johnson's ascendancy to the presidency redefined the national perception of Texas. First seen as a Southern pol, Johnson quickly became celebrated as a Texas cowboy and wheeler-dealer. His wide-sweeping Civil Rights reforms did much substantively to shift the focus from Deep South to Southwest, and his exuberant style, enhanced by television's fondness for Western imagery—Lyndon feeding the cattle, Lyndon speeding across ranchland in his Lincoln—sealed the identification.

In literature Texas found its first flowering on the Southern side of the invisible line separating East Texas from West Texas. James W. Lee has argued convincingly that "throughout most of this century, the mainstream of Texas literature was southern, not western."

The stories in this volume from the East Texas or Southern tradition represent the work of both older writers and younger ones. William Humphrey, William A. Owens, and William Goyen—the three East Texas Williams—began their careers long before many of the writers in this volume were born. Humphrey's "A Voice from the Woods," though set in New England, evokes a Bonnie-and-Clyde-like legend of Texas in the Depression years. Owens' "Hangerman John," a grim story of a lynching in Northeast Texas, published in 1947, reminds us of Texas' ties to the Deep South at a time when racism was the ugliest manifestation of the Dixie region. Goyen's "Bridge of Music, River of Sand" is a typically Goyenesque tale of mystery and transformation set in a vanishing pastoral world eclipsed by industrialism. Three other stories are also shaded with a Southern ambience. Bill Brett's "Justice" is a throwback to the old tradition of Southwest humor. Told in a letter-perfect folk vernacular, "Justice" comes out of a deeply observed, deeply felt rural East Texas landscape. Like many comic stories, it is deadly serious. Hughes Rudd's "The Shores of Schizophrenia" is probably the definitive account of those awful field trips one had to take in school. Rudd, a Waco native and nationally known network news correspondent, locates the materials of his hilarious story in a provincial world where cotton is king. "Pact," written by Vassar Miller, Texas' most acclaimed contemporary poet, demonstrates the author's skills in another genre. The story of a white child's visit to a black church, "Pact" depicts Houston as a Southern city long before it became the sprawling oil capital of the Sun Belt.

J. Frank Dobie, folklorist, and Walter P. Webb, historian, did the most to define literary Texas in Western terms. Neither wrote fiction. In short fiction O. Henry and scores of formula writers in pulp magazines painted Texas in the lurid colors of the Wild West. Texas has some fine novelists of the Old West, chief among them Benjamin Capps and Elmer Kelton, but their work, like that of any number of writers not represented in this volume, finds its best expression in novels, not short stories. The Western side of the South-by-Southwest equation is well represented here, though none of the stories are powderburners.

I have preferred stories of the modern West, in keeping with my desire to reflect Texas modernity, and in this vein belong all of the stories with a Western flavor. Paul Horgan's elegant "In Summer's Name" is a study of sexual and religious mores in small-town West Texas written twenty-six years before Larry McMurtry's much better known *The Last Picture Show*. Three stories are set on ranches. Linda West Eckhardt's "Christmas 1918: Sennicot Place" is a warm evocation of hard times and sturdy family loyalties reminiscent of the work of an earlier generation of Texas writers of the soil. A. C. Greene's "The Girl at Cabe Ranch" reworks familiar materials, too, and explores the tension between love of and attachment to place and the desire to experience a wider world. Dave Hickey's "I'm Bound to Follow the Longhorn Cows," unearthed at a friend's nudging from the forgotten issues of a defunct university student literary magazine, is a startlingly original story of a tough old cowboy's trail drive memories recollected while marooned in a bathtub, an old man undone by age but fiercely alive. Larry McMurtry's "There Will Be Peace in Korea" is a story that I had remembered vividly for twenty years, one of a very small number published by the prolific and best known of Texas' contemporary novelists. Readers familiar with *The Last Picture Show* will recognize in this account of two friends' farewell in Fort Worth beer joints an early version of one of the chapters in the novel. But the story stands alone and is an example of McMurtry at his disciplined best.

Any attempt to place a grid on the field of fiction is likely to be frustrated at some point, and probably rightly so. In any case, I have included a number of stories that defy easy regional classification. Robert Flynn's "The Savior of the Bees" is a deft story of strains in a marriage, narrated from a child's perspective and set on a small farm somewhere near Fort Worth. Carolyn Osborn's "Reversals" is a richly comic work arising out of family kinships and differences. Its setting, the fictional town of Leon, takes its name from the Leon River, which flows through North Central Texas near Gatesville, the town upon which Leon is loosely based. Amado Muro's "Cecilia Rosas," set in El Paso and Juarez, explores Chicano life through the vicissitudes of a love-stricken adolescent narrator. Muro, long thought to be a Chicano himself, was actually the Anglo writer Chester Seltzer. "Cecilia Rosas" is widely regarded as his best piece of work. Mary Gray Hughes' "The Judge" is set in the Valley and employs the classic short story device of the epiphany to reveal a profound disjuncture between Anglo assumptions and Mexican reality. "Whores," by James Crumley, is another story set in South Texas. Crumley, author of several successful detective novels, uses the familiar Anglo arrogance of bordertown sexual imperialism as the basis for a kind of Fitzgeraldian dissection of moral degeneration. "The Gift Horse's Mouth," by R. E. Smith, is a remarkable story of a female character created by a male author. Smith turns the heroine's desire to escape Houston and spend a quiet weekend in the country into a nightmarish but instructive encounter with nature. Thomas Zigal's "Orphan of the West" takes a familiar American hero— the movie cowboy—and pits the make-believe Westerner against a Vietnamese child refugee who interprets American violence in highly literal and convincing terms. Zigal's sidekick narrator provides a fine ironic dimension.

Three stories by women writers also form a kind of grouping in that each is set in a modern Texas city and each presents characters who in some sense are "outsiders." Harryette Mullen, who is primarily a poet, explores the once taboo subject of miscegenation in her story "What Can't Be Measured." This tale of a white woman in the grip of an erotic obsession with a black man unfolds in the black section of contemporary Austin. Naomi Shihab Nye, another poet who occasionally writes short fiction, depicts in her story "Pablo Tamayo" the warm intimacy of an old-fashioned neighborhood against a background of rapid change in booming San Antonio. Nye's hero is an engaging old Mexican man who, though victimized by rapacious development, refuses with good humor to act the part of a victim. Pat Ellis Taylor's comic and graphic story of East Dallas, "Leaping Leo," is another story of a survivor. Contrary to popular myth, there is poverty in Texas; there are people living in urban slums in the bitter shadow of high-rises and billboards trumpeting the American dream, Texas-style. Taylor's story is about a woman with a 1960s hippie consciousness holding things together in another era.

Since 82 percent of Texans live in cities, it should not be surprising to find that a number of Texas writers are exploring this urban environment in their short stories. In the mid-1970s Texas demonstrated once again its regional elasticity, its ability to adapt itself to changing economic imperatives. A popular coinage appeared in the national press, the Sun Belt, to describe the phenomenon of boom economies, rapid growth, and population increases stretching from Florida through Georgia to Texas, Arizona, and Southern California. Postindustrial America found its most buoyant expression in the sun-scorched Southwest. The Sun Belt phenomenon centered on Texas, or at any rate the media thought it did. Texas seized the national imagination with a new intensity. TV's *Dallas*, premiering in 1978, and the film *Urban Cowboy* (1980) exploited that sense of boom, prosperity, and hedonism that characterized American life in the early 1980s.

Serious, thoughtful, and reflective writers, the kind collected in this volume, cast a cold eye on Sun Belt bliss. Peter LaSalle's "Life in the Sun Belt," as its title implies, confronts the reality of modern-day Texas head on. LaSalle's tale of ambition, eroding values, and betrayal is set in Midland amidst a world of high-pressure salesmanship and cutthroat competition. This story is a kind of trial run for the novel that

LaSalle published in 1984, *Strange Sunlight*. Other stories approach the Texas urban scene more obliquely.

"Living in the Desert," by Doug Crowell, is a version of absurdist philosophy and experimental technique applied to the mundane materials of bourgeois life. Crowell's desert is located somewhere in West Texas—Lubbock is as good a guess as any—and his off-beat, comic slant gives to this story a hard-edged sensibility that renders the commonplace in a strange new light. The last of the Sun Belt stories is William Harrison's "Roller Ball Murder." It was written in 1973 before the term Sun Belt was invented. Harrison's futuristic tale, set in Houston, depicts a time when sports and capitalism are the opiates of the entire world, itself a kind of vast corporation. "Roller Ball Murder" seems to me a fitting prophetic end to a volume that shows how much Texas has changed in just forty-five years, the exact span of one anthologist's life.

DON GRAHAM
Austin, 1985

SOUTH BY SOUTHWEST
24 Stories from Modern Texas

WILLIAM HUMPHREY
A Voice from the Woods

Ssh! Listen," says my wife. "You hear? Listen."

"What?" says my mother.

"Hear what?" say I.

"Ssh! There. Hear it? An owl. Hooting in the daytime."

Then I do hear: a soft hollow note, like someone blowing across the lip of a jug: *hoo-oo, hoo-hoo-hoo; hoo-oo, hoo-hoo-hoo* . . .

A ghostly sound, defying location, seeming in successive calls to come out of the woods from all points of the compass. Near at hand one moment, far away and faint the next, barely audible, the echo of an echo. It is not an owl. Yet it cannot be what it is. Not here. So far from home. It comes again, this time seeming to sound not outside me but inside myself, like my own name uttered in a once-familiar, long-dead voice, and my mother says, "Owl? That's no owl. Why, it's a—"

"A mourning dove!" say I.

It is the sound, the solitary sound, save for the occasional buzz, like an unheeded alarm clock, of a locust, of the long hot somnolent summer afternoons of my Texas boyhood, when the cotton fields shimmered white-hot and in the black shade of the pecan trees bordering the fields the Negro pickers lay napping on their sacks and I alone of all the world was astir, out with my air rifle hunting doves I never killed, gray elusive ghosts I never could locate. I would mark one down as it settled in

1

a tree (I remember the finicking way they had of alighting, as if afraid of soiling their feet), and would sneak there and stand listening, looking up into the branches until I grew dizzy and confused. I would give up and move on, and at my back the bird would come crashing out of the branches sounding its other note, a pained squeak, and wobble away in drunken flight and alight in another tree and resume its plaint. They favored cedars, at least in my memory, and cedars in turn favored burial grounds, so that I think of the dove's whispered dirge as the voice of that funereal tree. It would be one of those breathless afternoons when the sun cooked the resin from the trunks of pines and sweet gums and the air was heavy, almost soporific with the scent. Heat waves throbbed behind the eyes. The fields were empty, desolate. High overhead a buzzard wheeled. The world seemed to have died, and in the silence the dove crooned its ceaseless inconsolable lament: *hoo-oo, hoo-hoo-hoo; hoo-oo, hoo-hoo-hoo* . . .

"A what? Mourning dove?" my wife says. "I never knew we had them here." *Here* being among the budding sugar maples and the prim starched white paper birches in the bustle and thaw of a crisp New England spring.

"I never knew you did either," says my mother. "What is a mourning dove doing way off up here?"

"What are you doing way off up here?" I say.

For my mother, too, has left Texas, lives out in Indianapolis. Now she has come on her annual visit to us. We sit on the sun porch, rushing the season a bit. As always, we two have fallen to reminiscing of Blossom Prairie and our life there before my father's death, telling stories by the hour which both of us have heard and told so often now that it is the rhythm which stirs us more than the words, our tongues thickening steadily until the accent is barely intelligible to my Yankee wife, who listens amused, amazed, bewildered, bored, and sometimes appalled.

"Son, do you remember," my mother says, "the time the bank was held up?"

I am still listening to the dove, and I have to ask her what she said. But now she is listening to the dove and does not hear me.

"The time the bank was held up? No, I don't remember that. First time I ever heard of it."

"Hmm? What did you say? First time you ever heard of what?"

"Of the bank being held up. The bank in Blossom Prairie?"

"Really? Oh, you remember such funny things! Old Finus, that used to come around to the house every afternoon selling hot tamales. Why anybody should clutter up their memory with him, I don't know! Lord, I would never have given him another thought this side of the grave. And not remember the great bank robbery! You were old enough. You remember lots of things that happened long before that. I took you with me, and we saw the dead men lying on the sidewalk on the square. You've forgotten that?"

"Dead men? Lying on the sidewalk? On the square? What dead men?"

"The bank robbers. All shot dead as they came out of the bank. You don't remember?"

"What!" says my wife. "You took a child to see a sight like—"

"That's the kind of thing I remember! Not an old boy who used to come around crying, 'Hot tamales!' Why, that was just about the biggest thing that ever happened in Blossom Prairie, I should think."

I open more cans of beer, and she drinks and sets down the can and wipes her lips and says, "Well, it was back in the bad old days. When lots of men were out of work and some of the young ones, who had all cut their teeth on a gun, took to living by it. The age of the great outlaws, when we had Public Enemy Number One, Two, Three. In our parts Pretty Boy Floyd was carrying on. And Clyde Barrow and Bonnie Parker."

"Did Clyde and Bonnie stick up the bank in Blossom Prairie?"

"No, no, it wasn't them. But it was in those days and times. No, the ones that stuck up the bank in Blossom Prairie—"

"Wait. Who was Pretty Boy Floyd?" asks my wife. "Who were Clyde Barrow and Bonnie Parker?"

"You never heard of them?" asks my mother, wiping away her mustache of suds.

"Now we will never get the story of the Blossom Prairie bank robbery," say I.

"Never heard of Clyde Barrow and Bonnie Parker? Never even heard of Pretty Boy Floyd?"

"Pretty Boy!" my wife laughs. "Pretty Boy!"

"Clyde Barrow," I say, "was a notorious outlaw, and Bonnie Parker his gun moll. They came out of West Dallas, the real low-down tough section of the town. They tore around sticking up banks and filling stations and honkey-tonks, and between them shot and killed any number of bank tellers and gas-pump operators and law officers in Texas in the

3

early thirties. We used to follow the exploits of Clyde and Bonnie in the newspapers every day, like keeping up with the baseball scores. We really cannot claim Pretty Boy Floyd. He was an Oklahoma hero."

"You're making fun," says my mother. "Well, no doubt they did a lot of bad things, but let me tell you, hon"—this to her daughter-in-law—"you can go back down there and out in the country and to this day you'll find a many an old farmer will tell you he was proud to give Pretty Boy Floyd a night's lodging when the law was hounding him down like a poor hunted animal, and more than likely they found a twenty-dollar bill under his breakfast plate after he had left the next morning. And he never got that nickname for nothing. Oh, he was a good-looking boy!"

"Well, what about the ones that held up the bank in Blossom Prairie?"

"He was a good-looking boy, too. All three of them were."

"She just never could resist an outlaw," I say.

The dove calls again, and my wife says, "What a sad, lonesome sound. I hope she doesn't come to nest around here. I wouldn't like to listen to that all day."

"As a matter of fact," says my mother, "as a matter of fact, I knew one of them. Travis Winfield, his name was. He was the leader of the gang. You wouldn't remember the Winfields, I don't suppose? Lived in that big old yellow frame house beyond the bridge out on the old Mc-Coy road? A wild bunch, all of those Winfields, the girls as well as the boys, but good-looking, all of them, and Travis was the best looking, and the wildest, of the lot. Well, anyway. One day when you were—oh, let's see, you must have been six or seven, which would make it—how old are you now, hon, thirty-eight?"

"Seven."

"Thirty-seven?"

"Yes'm."

"Are you sure?"

"I *was*. Aren't you?"

"Oh, you! Well, anyway, it was during the summer that you had your tonsils and adenoids out. Remember? We were living at the time in Mr. Early Ellender's little cottage out on College Avenue. I had that little old Model-A Ford coupé that your daddy had bought me."

"Was there a college in Blossom Prairie?" my wife asks.

"No!"

"Well, you were just getting over that operation, and that's how you happened to be at home at the time and not off somewhere or other out of call. I remember I was fixing dinner when the telephone rang. . . . No, honey, there wasn't any college in Blossom Prairie. It was just a little bitty old place—though it was the county seat, and we all thought we were really coming up in the world when we left the farm and moved into town. It was so little that his daddy used to come home for his dinner every day. What you call lunch. . . . Well, the telephone rang and it was Phil. 'Hop in your car and come right down!' he said. 'They've just shot and killed three men robbing the bank!'"

"Then why was it called College Avenue? That doesn't make much sense."

"Don't ask me. I just grew up there."

"Well, but didn't it ever occur to you to wonder why they would call it that when there wasn't any—"

"Now, here is what had happened. These four men—"

"Three, you just a minute ago said."

"I said three were killed. These four men had been camping out down in Red River Bottom and— However, I better start with the woman. There was this woman, see. She had come into town about a month before. A stranger. She took a house, and she gave herself out to be a widow woman interested in maybe settling in the town and opening some kind of business with the money her husband had left her. And she had had a husband, all right, but she was no widow, nor even a grass widow. That came out at the trial. In fact, her husband showed up at the trial. When the judge sentenced her to eighteen years in the penitentiary this man stood up in the courtroom and said, 'Mildred! I'll still be waiting for you!' And she said, 'You'll wait a lot longer than any eighteen years!' And as they were taking her away he yelled, 'Mildred! Darling! I forgive you!' Meaning he forgave her for leaving him and running off with Travis. And that she-devil turned and told him I-can't-tell-you-what that he could do with his such-and-such forgiveness, right there in front of the judge and jury and the whole town and county. And still the poor fool did not give up but went round to the jailhouse and yelled up at the window of her cell until finally she came to the bars. And do you know what she told him was the one thing he could do that might win her back?—and this, you understand, would be after waiting for her to come out of the penitentiary for eighteen years. To get a gun and go shoot the one that had told on them to the law and had got the lover that she had run off with killed. However, it was not him that did it."

"That did what? Wait. I don't—"

"She was a cutter! Well, shortly after coming to town she went to the bank one day and opened an account. The very next day she was back and said she had changed her mind and wanted to draw her money out. They asked her why, and she said she had had her money in a bank once that had been held up, and she seemed to imply that that bank had looked a lot stronger than what she saw of ours. This piqued the manager, and he took her on a tour of the place to convince her that her money was safe with them, showing her all the strong vaults and the time locks and the burglar-alarm system and how it worked and whatnot. Besides, he said, there had never been any bank robberies in Blossom Prairie. So he convinced her, and she said she would let her money stay. After that she would come in every so often and make a deposit or a withdrawal, and she got to know the layout of the bank. She was making a map of it at home, and after each trip she would go and fill it in some more and correct any mistakes she had made in it. That way, too, she came to know when the big deposits were made by the business firms and the big-scale farmers and when there was always the most cash on hand in the bank.

"Meanwhile, she wasn't spending much time in that house in town. She told her neighbors—and of course they told everybody and his dog—that she still hadn't made up her mind to settle in Blossom Prairie and was looking over other spots around the county before deciding. She was seen on the road a lot, and she was a demon at the wheel. I was a pretty hot driver my own self, but—"

"Was! You still are. You scare me half to death."

"Well, that redheaded woman handled a car like no other woman and few men that I ever saw. In town she would spread her shopping over all the grocery stores so it wouldn't look like she was buying more food than a lone woman could eat, and she bought a good deal of bootleg liquor too, it came out later, and she would fill up the car and slip off down to Red River Bottom where Travis and his gang were camped out, though of course nobody knew that at the time. Whenever any squirrel hunter would happen to come up on them Travis kept out of sight, as he was the only local boy among them, and the other three made out that they were a hunting party too.

"Travis had been gone from home for some years, and everybody had pretty well forgotten him, except for maybe a couple of dozen girls who would have liked to but couldn't. Word would get back every now and again of some trouble he had gotten into and gotten himself out of. Now he had rounded up this gang and come back to rob the bank in his old home town. But though he had grown up there, he had to have that woman, or somebody, to draw him a map of the bank, for I don't suppose poor Travis had ever set foot in it in his life.

"All the while that he was holing up down there in the woods laying his plans Travis had living with him in that tent, and eating and drinking with him, one man who was in constant touch with the sheriff. He had told him all about that woman and about that map she was drawing of the bank and every little detail and switch in their plans. Imagine it? Living with three men for a whole month and letting on to be their friend, listening to them plan how they'll do this and do that to get the money and make their getaway, and knowing all the while that they were walking into a death trap that he himself had set, for pay, and that they were doomed to die as surely as if he himself had pulled the trigger on them? I'm not saying that what they were meaning to do was right, you understand. But can you just feature a skunk like that?

"I and Phil must have been just about the only people in town that didn't know the bank was set to be robbed that Monday morning. The sheriff had gone out and hired eight extra deputies, old country boys, good shots, squirrel hunters, and had them waiting, each with a thirty-thirty rifle, on the roofs of the buildings on each corner across the street from the bank, the old Ben Milam Hotel and the other, well, office buildings, stores downstairs on the street and doctors' and lawyers' offices upstairs, four stories high. The tellers in the bank had all been told not to put up any resistance but to give them what they asked for, to fill up their sacks for them, they'd have it all right back. The tip-off man was to wear something special. I seem to recall he wore a sailor straw hat, so they would recognize him and not shoot him.

"You remember, the bank in Blossom Prairie sits on the northwest corner of the square. The street that goes out to the north, Depot Street, goes past the cotton compress and over the tracks and past the ice house and toward the river. That would be the street they would come in on. The one going out to the west went past your daddy's shop and over the creek and on out of town in the direction of Paris. Down this street that morning, headed toward the square, came a wagon loaded high with baled hay. On the wagon seat, dressed up in overalls and a twenty-five-cent hardware-store straw hat, sat Sheriff Ross Shirley, and under the seat lay a sawed-off pump shotgun. At twenty minutes to eleven he set his team in motion with a flick of the reins. A moment later a car came round the corner and pulled up alongside the curb, and four men got out and ducked into the bank. As soon as they were inside, the sheriff says 'Come up' to his team, and up on the roof-tops the rifle barrels poke over the walls and point down, followed by the heads of those eight deputies. The woman was driving, and she stayed in the car, keeping the engine idling. The wagon came down the street toward her, rattling over those old *bois-d'arc* paving bricks, un-til it got to just a little ways in front of the car. There suddenly the left rear wheel flew off the axle, the load of hay came tumbling down, scat-tering clear across the street, bales bouncing and breaking apart, the street completely blocked. The woman in the car made a sudden change in plans. She threw into reverse and backed around the corner into Depot Street, thinking that now, instead of going out by the Paris road, they would have to cross the square and go out by the southwest. Then she sees ahead of her a man fixing a flat tire on a big delivery van out in the middle of the street halfway down the block. This meant, she thought, that she would have to cut diagonally across the square, through the traffic and around the plaza and out by the southeast cor-ner. She didn't know it, but they had her cut off there, too. In another minute or so the men burst out of the bank carrying the sacks.

"The moment they stepped out the door it began to rain bullets on them. Those that were on the square at the time said it sounded like a thunderclap had broken overhead. You couldn't count the separate shots, they said. The bullets chewed holes in the cement sidewalk. The men must have all died in the first volley, but the deputies poured an-other round and then another into them as they went down. The fourth man had fallen a step behind, deciding not to trust everything to that sailor straw hat, maybe thinking they would just as soon not pay that reward, and when the noise broke he dove back into the bank. He had cast a quick look up above as he came out, and that woman in the car must have seen it. In any case, when he didn't come out with the rest a thousand things that she must have noticed at the time and shaken off suddenly added up like a column of figures in her mind. She didn't even try to run. She jumped out of the car and up onto the curb, swooped down and pried the pistol from the still-clutching hand of one of the bandits, and stepped over the body into the bank. By then the sheriff was one step behind her. He grabbed her and took the gun away from her and held her until help came. She was more than he could manage alone. They said it was all four big strong men could do to keep her from getting at that one and clawing his eyes out, and then when they dragged her outside she broke away and threw herself on the body in the doorway, crying, 'Travis! Travis! Speak to me, Travis!' They had taken her away, and taken away the informer too and locked him up for his own protection by the time we got there, but the bodies were still lying on the sidewalk where they had fallen."

"Taking a little six-year-old child to see a sight like that!" my wife says, shaking her head.

"It was a terrible sight to see. Three strong young men cut off in the very Maytime of life, shot down like mad dogs before they even knew what was happening to them. I was sorry I had come. I wasn't going to look any closer. I tried to back out of the crowd. Then Phil said, 'My Lord! Why, ain't that one there that Winfield boy, Travis?' Oh, what a funny feeling came over me when I heard Phil say that!"

"Why, had you known him pretty well?"

"Yes. In fact—well, in fact, I had gone with Travis Winfield for a time, before I married your daddy."

"You had!"

"In fact, Travis Winfield had once asked me to marry him. He was not a bad boy then. Wild, yes, but not mean, not any gangster. I—I thought about it awhile before I turned him down. That stung him, and he didn't ask me a second time. I was just as glad. Oh, he was a good-looking boy! I don't know what I might have said a second time. Well, he had quickly forgotten about me and I had gone out with other boys and in time had met and married Phil, your daddy, and wasn't ever sorry that I had. But I want you to know I felt mighty queer standing there looking down at poor Travis—he was still handsome, even there in the dirt and all bloodied—lying on the common sidewalk with people staring at him, and thinking of that wild woman who had loved him so and had shared his wild life and now been dragged off to prison, and I was glad to have you there to hold on to. It was a comfort to me then to have my own child to hold on to his hand."

Silence falls, and in it the dove utters again its dolorous refrain.

"My daddy and my brothers disapproved of Travis Winfield. I think —apart from the fact that I was infatuated with his reputation for wildness, and his good looks—I think I probably went with him mainly just to devil my brothers a bit, let them all worry over me a little maybe, at least give them some reason for all that concern over my reputation. I don't believe I was ever really serious about him, and I never thought he was serious about me, partly because there were already lots of stories of other girls he hadn't been serious over. So I was taken by surprise when he asked me that day to marry him. I told him I would give him my answer next week. I knew then what it would be, but I suppose I wanted a week of thinking of accepting what I knew I was going to turn down.

"You remember, honey, out back of my old home that little family graveyard where all my folks are buried? It was there that Travis Winfield proposed to me. I said to meet me there again next Sunday and I would give him my answer. I remember waiting for him to come. You know how still it can be on a farm on a Sunday afternoon. The only sound for miles around as I sat there waiting for him was the cooing of a dove. I sat there thinking, I'm going to turn him down, of course, but what if I was not to? What if I was to say yes? What would my life be like?

"There are people just born for trouble, you know; Travis Winfield was one of them. It was written all over him in letters like headlines. Wild. Stubborn. Headstrong. Full of resentment against those who had all the things he didn't have. Proud. Vain. Believing the world owed him a living for the sake of his pretty face. No one woman could ever hope to hold him for long. After a while she wouldn't even want to keep on trying, unless she was an utter fool. But certainly life with Travis wouldn't be dull. It would be different from life on the farm, or in Blossom Prairie in a bungalow that had to be swept out and dusted every day.

"But I knew what I was going to say, and I said it. And maybe Travis wasn't sorry to hear it. Maybe during the week he had begun to wish he hadn't asked me. Most likely it was just his pride. He wasn't used to having a girl say no to anything he wanted. In any case, he didn't ask me again, and I was glad he didn't. He just gave me a hot look and turned and left. After he was gone I sat there a long time listening to the mourning dove. I never saw him again until that day on the square. It's years now since I even thought of Travis Winfield. It was hearing that mourning dove that brought it all back to my mind."

We sit listening for some time to its call. Then something alarms it, and though we do not see it, we hear the thrashing of its wings among the branches and its departing cry.

"Who did shoot the one who told?" I ask.

"Oh, yes, him. The trustees of the bank voted him a big reward, but he never got to spend it. They found him a week later floating in the river, though it was a wonder, with all the lead he had in him. It was generally known to be the work of that Winfield tribe, but they could never prove it. Never tried any too hard, I don't suppose."

I make a move to rise, but seeing her face I sit down again. Brushing back a strand of her cotton-white hair, my mother says, "Aren't people funny? There in his blood lay Travis, whom I had forgotten, dead, and deservedly so, I suppose, if any man deserves it. There was I, happy, with a good, loving husband and a decent home and a smooth, even life ahead of me and my own child's hand in mine. And yet, thinking of that redheaded woman—even then on her way to prison—I felt, well, I don't know what else to call it if not jealousy. Isn't that crazy? What did she have? Nothing, less than nothing, and I had everything. It only lasted a moment, you understand, yet it comes back to me even now, and if it wasn't jealousy, then I don't know what else to call it."

1963

WILLIAM A. OWENS
Hangerman John

When I was a child we lived on a small sandyland farm about two miles from town. To the front of us was a broad flat field, where we worked the year round plowing, planting, hoeing, or picking cotton. My father being dead, my mother worked the days through with us, putting hand to hoe or plow with all the strength of a man. Beyond the field was the road from town. At the lower corner of our farm it branched. One branch led through sandy hills and flats to the river; the other turned back to the blackland. Mr. Rodgers, the chicken peddler, lived with his family in shouting distance on the river road. They were our nearest neighbors. A Negro family lived on the other side of the woods, but we did not count them as neighbors, though their son George sometimes roamed the woods with us.

These woods lay to the back of our farm. From the road our little house looked like a mound or a haystack against the tall dark trees. My three brothers and I were in the woods as many hours as we could be, hunting rabbits and possums, cutting wood, gathering poke sallet and sheep sorrel for early spring greens. John, the oldest, was a tall slender lad of seventeen, eight years older than I. Herbert and Edward were between us. John led us in work and play. He led us in the game of dare. In the spring, when the tall thin red oaks were full of sap and bent easily, he would swing from the top of one to the next—so fast that his blue overalls and shirt made a blur against the light green of

---

the budding branches. Herbert and Edward followed him from tree to tree, but never with as daring a swing. I followed on the ground, watching him excitedly, waiting for him to come to the last tree in a grove. When he would reach this one he would swing out as far as the branches would bend and then drop lightly to earth. I was always there to help brush the twigs and leaves from his clothes. Then he would roach his yellow hair out of his eyes.

"Next year, Bud," he would say, "you'll be big enough to swing trees. I'll show you how." Then we'd tussle on the earth till Herbert and Edward caught up with us. Sometimes he brought his hand down my face and up again, saying, "Down come a limb, up jumped a rabbit." It was a game I liked. If he was fast enough he tipped the end of my nose with his hand. More often I dodged his hand and sheltered my face under his arm.

When we met George, the Negro boy, in the woods he was glad to join us in play. He was the age of John, but taller and heavier. He could hoist things that John couldn't; but he was not clever at swinging his body through the trees. He was slow at learning our games, but cunning in the ways of woods and animals. Sometimes we went on cold clear nights to the persimmon trees looking for possums. As darkness came on we would leave our house. John would blow a signal on his cupped fists. George would answer, and come running along the path in the forest to meet us. When we found a possum, John climbed the tree and brought him down by the tail, sulled. John held the possum to the ground with an ax handle across his neck, while George pulled him by the tail. There would be a faint sigh and sound of breaking bones. Then the possum was dead. By the light of a fire we would skin him, keeping the hide for ourselves and giving the meat to George.

On warm fall nights we sometimes played "nigger uprising," using stories told us by our mother about times when white men had to go out and "put niggers in their place." Nearly all these stories took place at night. In most of them nigger cabins were burned. We would build up a great bonfire with dry leaves and branches and pretend that it was a nigger cabin on fire. Then we would run about the fire and shout and scream at imaginary niggers. After the niggers were all killed or frightened away we would throw burning sticks at the black sky, laughing with delight at the shower of sparks and arc of falling light. In these games no one would play the part of a nigger. And we never played this game when George was with us.

One night my brothers and I were playing hide-and-seek in the forest. It was a warm moist night the week before Christmas. Being the youngest and smallest, I was nearly always "it" in the game. The other three could outrun me to home base. When I refused to run any more, John took my place.

"I'll count for you this time, Bud," he told me. "I'll count to a hundred by ones . . . you hide good . . . if you hide so good I cain't find you, I'll call for you to come in free . . . we'll make Herbert or Edward be it . . ."

He leaned against the trunk of the red oak that was our base and began counting slowly.

"Cover your eyes," I ordered.

When he had covered his eyes I ran into the woods. I was afraid of the blackness among the trees, but I had to go. I had to be able to come in free. John was helping me. He counted to a hundred. His voice was clear in the night air. Then he was giving the warnings he had to give before he could start seeking.

Bushel o' wheat,
Bushel o' cotton,
All ain't hid
Better be a-trottin'.

I found a fallen tree top where we had cut wood in the summer. Dry leaves still clung to the branches. Dead leaves had swirled knee deep on the ground around it. I followed the branches until I found the trunk. I crawled in beside it. The outer leaves were damp. I scooped them away and pressed myself against the log. The smell of wet and dry leaves was about me. I hugged the log and trembled with excitement. I concentrated on lying still. Any move in the dry leaves might betray me. John finished counting.

Bushel o' wheat,
Bushel o' clover,
All ain't hid
Cain't hide over.

As I lay listening to John searching near the base I heard a wagon coming along the dirt road. By the way the wheels knocked on their thimbles I knew it was Mr. Rodgers' wagon. He had gone to town, to the county seat, that morning to sell a load of chickens. I thought of the things he had brought for Christmas: oranges, apples, firecrackers . . .

The blast of a shotgun rocked the night and drowned out the sounds of the wagon. I jumped to my feet in fright.

"Oh, my life!"

The voice of a man in agony came from the direction of the wagon. The wagon rattled on for a moment, and then stopped, but the man's voice repeated the terrifying cry over and over. I ran as fast as I could to the house. My brothers were ahead of me. They were standing around Mother on the porch when I got there.

"It's Mr. Rodgers," Mother whispered in horror. "He's been shot."

"I'm going to him," John said. "He needs help."

"You may get in trouble yourself," Mother warned him.

"Cain't help it if I do. He needs a man to help him."

We listened to the bare cotton stalks whipping against his duckings as he ran across the field.

"John ain't scared of nothing, is he?" I boasted.

The wagon started again. Mr. Rodgers repeated "Oh, my life" again and again, growing fainter each time. After a while the wagon stopped. We could tell by the sound that it had stopped at Mr. Rodgers' house. Then there was stillness. We stood on the porch and shivered. It was getting colder. We went in and sat by the fireplace, waiting for John to come back.

Within an hour John was with us again. There was a patch of blood on his knee. Bloodstains were on his hands.

"Mr. Rodgers was shot by a nigger," he said. "I got his blood on my hands and clothes lifting him out of the wagon."

"Is he bad hurt?" Mother asked.

"Awful bad. I'm afraid he'll die. He was shot in cold blood and robbed of forty dollars."

"Who's the nigger?" Mother asked.

"He didn't know. Said it was too dark for him to get a good look. Then he fainted and couldn't talk no more."

John moved over in front of the fire and turned the back of his duckings to the heat. He picked at the blood on his hand with a fingernail.

"They've gone for Ky Johnson and the bloodhounds," he said. "They're going to run that nigger down tonight. I'm going back and help them."

"Will there be a lynching?" Herbert asked.

"Maybe. If we catch him."

"You going to help them?" I asked, frightened.

John looked at Mother, sitting in her chair by the lamp with the Bible in her hands for the evening reading.

"I've got to take Pa's place," he said.

"When your Pa was living," Mother said, looking at the pages of the Bible, "he always took his part in everything that had to be done. Tonight a nigger's got out of his place. It is the duty of white men to put him back. If they don't, white women won't be safe. I'm a widow woman here with you boys. I won't be safe."

The look on her face sobered all of us.

"My son," she said, looking into John's eyes, "you have been taught right and wrong. You will know what to do."

Again John was gone into the night.

Mother went to the organ in the corner and sat down on the stool. She pressed the pedals lightly with her feet. A sound like the hissing part of the Lord's Prayer came from the bellows. Herbert held the lamp for her to read the notes in the hymnbook.

"Come, all you souls by sin oppressed," she sang in her high soprano. We sang with her, ". . . and He will surely give you rest." It was difficult for me to sing. I was thinking about Mr. Rodgers and the bloodhounds and the nigger. Then we sang, "I will arise and go to Jesus." If Mr. Rodgers should die, I thought, he would arise and go to Jesus . . .

We knelt by our chairs while Mother read from the Bible. "O Lord our Lord, how excellent is Thy name . . . What is man that Thou art mindful of him . . . Thou hast made him a little lower than the angels, and hast crowned him with glory and honor . . . O Lord our Lord . . ." Then she prayed—prayed for Mr. Rodgers' recovery, John's safety, protection for widows and orphans, justice and peace on earth, and for heaven "where thieves neither break through nor steal." My face was pressed close against the cowhide chair bottom. Its leathery smell was sharply unpleasant.

Before the last amen was over we heard men and horses on the road from town. We went to the porch to listen. A chill wind blew from the east and I was afraid. I clung to Mother's rough worsted skirt. Its gore seams chafed my cheeks. When the men reached the place of the shooting they dismounted and lighted lanterns. The lanterns were moving balls of fire as the men walked. They were like jack o' lanterns bouncing in some dark swampy place in the woods.

One of the bloodhounds opened up with a clear strong voice.

"There they go," Edward screamed excitedly. "Listen to them yelp."

The second hound had joined the first. Deep tones, light tones. Deep tones, light tones. They seemed to be circling. Then they ran to the southward. The men on horseback followed at a gallop.

"They're heading toward the lake," Herbert said, "and traveling fast."

"Run, nigger, run, paterollers'll catch you," Edward sang. He grabbed my hand and then Herbert's. We danced a circle on the porch singing, "Nigger run, nigger flew, nigger lost his wedding shoe." Herbert changed the words to "Run, nigger, run, Ky Johnson'll catch you." We laughed at the thought of the nigger running through the night with the bloodhounds at his heels. Above our laughing their yelping sounded.

They seemed to be circling again. Their barking was no longer that of hounds hot on the trail. It was the confused howling of hounds that had lost their quarry. Among us was the feeling we had when our own hounds lost the scent on the trail of a raccoon.

"They've lost him," Herbert exclaimed. "Lost him at the lake. What'll they do?"

"Go around the lake till they pick up the scent again," Mother told him. "Bloodhounds can get nigger smell a mile off."

There was silence for a few minutes. We went out in the yard to hear better. We cupped our hands over our ears and leaned on the paling fence. The hounds opened up again. They were in the open and running at breakneck speed. Occasionally we could hear one of the riders, urging his horse along to keep up. When the hounds came to the railroad they turned toward town. We followed the sounds and knew when they reached nigger town. There was a moment of silence, and then they began baying exultantly. They had found their quarry. Then there was silence.

"Wonder what nigger it is?" Edward asked, as we went into the house.

"Must be one of the town niggers," Mother answered. "They're a bad lot."

It was long past bedtime, but we stayed up, waiting for John to come home with the news. Mother spread my pallet by the fire, but did not tell me to go to bed. She sat by the lamp and read the Bible. We dug out hollows in the piles of ashes on the hearth and put sweet potatoes

17

in them to roast. Herbert brought out an ear of red corn he'd been saving. We parched the grains on the shovel and cracked them with our teeth, pretending all the time we were redskins.

Herbert raked the ashes away from one of the potatoes on the hearth. A warm, sweet fragrance rose from the ashes. We stopped to listen. A horse was galloping along the road. The rider pulled up long enough for someone to dismount.

"Thanks for the ride," we heard John call. "See you at the shindig. We got to show these niggers—"

I did not know what he meant. Before I could ask the others, he was running up the path through the field.

"Did you catch the nigger?" we all yelled as he came in the door.

"Sure, we got him," he bragged.

"Who was it?"

"George."

"George?" Our voices were sharp, disbelieving.

"Sure. I knew it was him all the time."

"How'd you know?" Herbert challenged.

"From what Mr. Rodgers said. Couldn't a been nobody else."

His voice was assured but unconvincing.

"How'd you catch him?" Mother asked.

"It was easy. Ky Johnson let the bloodhounds get one smell of his tracks. They took out as hard as they could go, like foxhounds with a brush in sight. We had a hard time keeping up. Ky Johnson let me ride behind him on his horse because of Pa. He said I favored Pa most every way."

"Didn't they lose him once?"

"At the lake. He waded it. But as soon as Ky Johnson saw what had happened, he tolled the hounds around the edge till they picked up the scent again. We trailed him up the railroad and into nigger town. The hounds went right into Uncle Wash's cabin. We found George in bed with his muddy clothes on and with the covers pulled up over his head. Ky Johnson had a hard time keeping the dogs from chewing him up when they found him. I nearly died laughing watching how scared George was with the dogs snapping at him and him digging deeper under the covers."

"Did he confess?" Mother asked.

"He had to. He still had Mr. Rodgers' pocketbook in his overalls."

"Why did he do it?"

18

"He said he wanted money for Christmas—to buy firecrackers and oranges. He said he ain't never had a orange for Christmas."

"He probably hasn't," Mother said, "but that's no reason for him to rob or kill anybody. You cain't tell what a nigger'll do, though. That's why we have to protect ourselves against them."

At the mention of oranges I remembered that George had ventured into our yard the Christmas before to see what we had for presents. When I showed him the two oranges in my stocking he grinned with pleasure and asked me for one. I was unable to part with an orange, but I did give him the peel from one of them. He left with the orange peel wrapped tight around his fingers.

"Where is he now?" Edward asked.

"Ky Johnson locked him up in the calaboose tonight . . . says the high sheriff from the county seat will come and get him tomorrow."

"What if he escapes?"

"He won't. They put a ball and chains on his legs so he cain't walk."

"Will they lynch him?" Herbert asked in a low voice, almost a whisper.

John walked back and forth in front of the fireplace with a boastful swagger I had never seen in him before.

"Maybe so, maybe not," he answered. He and Mother exchanged glances across the room.

"How about a baked potato, John?" Mother asked.

Herbert dug the potatoes from the ashes and handed us each one. Mine was soft and juicy, but I could not eat it. It was like soft warm clay in my throat. Mother spread another quilt on my pallet and I went to bed. After a while Herbert and Edward went off to bed in the shed room. Mother put out the lamp and she and John sat talking by the light of the fire. I could not hear what they were saying. My mind was full of the sound of bloodhounds on the trail . . .

A crowd of men was around the calaboose the next morning when we went to school. John, who had walked ahead of us, was among them. They were still there when the noon recess came. I went to the calaboose looking for John. Some other boys my size trailed after me. Most of the men in the crowd were silent. A few stayed with the horses tied along the railing. John saw me and caught me by the shoulders. His hard fingers made tears come to my eyes.

"Go back to school," he commanded me. He had never spoken so

19

harshly to me before. I was frightened, but I did not leave at once. I wanted to see George.

The calaboose door was open. I worked my way among the men until I was in front of the door. George was cringing against the back wall. He still had on the overalls and jumper he had worn when he waded the lake. They were crusted with black mud. He was bare-headed. His hair was cut short all over except for the tuft in front that stood up like a spur. His legs were bound with a chain shackle. A heavy ball lay at his feet. When he looked at me I could see that he had been crying. Brine had crusted in white streaks on his black face. He looked at me a moment, but hung his head when I tried to make signs to him.

Last week George had been at our house to help mark hogs. It was a job he enjoyed. I remembered how he laughed and sang as he caught and held hogs for John to mark. "Underbit in the right, crop off the lef'," he called as John cut our mark in the pigs' ears. Then George held their tails for John to snip off with his sharp knife. George took the tails and bits of ears home for a stew. That was last week. Now he was in the calaboose—a robber, maybe a killer. He might be lynched. This was a silent group of men around him. I recalled a song George had sung for us in the woods, "Hangerman, hangerman, slack yo' rope, and slack it for a while . . ."

Ky Johnson closed the calaboose door and hooked the lock in the chain. He did not close the lock.

"You fellers gonna be around for a while?" he asked.

Several nodded at him. I moved out of the way of his rough boots. The pistols on his hips were near enough for me to touch them.

"I'm looking for the high sheriff to come git this coon," Ky Johnson said. "If he comes while I am at the house eating, tell him I'll be back in a few minutes."

He galloped away on his roan stallion.

"Now's the time we been waiting for," one of the men said.

"Johnson's giving us a chance," another man agreed.

"Better git them kids away," a bearded man in a white hat said. 'We cain't do nothing with them around. They'll tell everything."

"You kids git back to school," one of the men ordered. "Recess is over."

John came through the crowd and caught me by the shoulders. He pinched so hard that I cried out. He threatened to beat me if I did not leave. They drove us from the crowd and started us up the main road toward school. As we neared the school we met the high sheriff and two of his deputies on their fine horses. They led another horse behind them. George would ride that horse back to the county jail, where he would be safe from the lynchers' rope.

That afternoon after school I went to the woods to gather sticks for the fireplace. It was gray cold and I shivered in my thin jumper. I put the sticks on a slide John had built for me. Before it was half full John came to the woods calling my name. I ran to meet him, but stopped when I saw the look on his face.

"You little fool," he said bitterly, "you kept us from lynching George today."

"How?" I asked, surprised.

"By hanging around the calaboose when you did. Ky Johnson give us our chance, but you ruined it. If it hadn't been for you George would be swinging from a white oak limb right now. Now he's in the hands of the high sheriff . . . he'll be behind heavy bars at the county jail . . . we cain't do nothing . . ."

He came closer to me. His face was white. His blue eyes looked straight at me.

"Fool," he said, and slapped me across the face with his hand. Then he went back to the house.

I went on picking up sticks until the slide was full. After it was piled high I still lingered in the woods, waiting until I could stop crying.

After dark Ernest, the tiehacker, came by and called John to the front yard. I went to the front window to eavesdrop on them.

"Better come along," Ernest said to John. "There'll be things happening tonight."

"What's up?"

"Mr. Rodgers died this afternoon late. Us vigilantes're getting ready to lynch George. Going to make it a real shindig."

"Ain't he in the county jail?"

"No. He's still in the calaboose. The high sheriff left him there long enough to go out and talk to Mr. Rodgers. Mr. Rodgers died, and the sheriff's still out there. Ky Johnson's with him now. Ain't nobody guarding the calaboose. Seems like they want us to lynch him. You want to go?"

"Sure," John replied.

"Get your stuff."

John went inside for a few minutes, but he did not speak to mother. He came out again with his cap on and a bundle under his jumper.

"Let's go," he said.

I was sleeping on my pallet near the fireplace when John came in. He stirred the smoldering chunks of fire and laid some fresh sticks on. They blazed up in yellow-red flames. John stood before the fire to dry the dampness from his clothes. I thought he was sick. From the look of his face and eyes I thought he had come through a malarial chill and the fever was beginning to rise. I sat up on my pallet.

"We lynched George tonight," he boasted in a voice pale as the ashes on the hearth.

"Lynched him?" I asked in horror. "George is dead?"

"Dead as a doornail."

John knelt on the pallet beside me, compelled to talk and glad to have me to talk to. He had forgot striking me in the woods that afternoon.

"Can you keep a secret?" he asked.

"Yes."

"You'd better keep this one. If you tell it, the Ku Kluxers'll get you."

He took a sheet from under his jumper and draped it over his body. He put a pillowcase mask over his head.

"This is the way we looked," he said. "Eight of us looking just like this."

I shivered as if I were looking at a real ghost. It was John under the sheet, but not the John I knew. I drew away from him, fearing he would strike me again. I did not want to hear more of the story, but he made me listen.

"Do you know the big white oak where we get persimmons?" he asked.

I nodded.

"George is hanging from it tonight. It was a tough job."

"Did you do the hanging?"

"Most of it. I nearly got hung myself."

"How?"

"We put a lariat rope over a limb. Then we tied one end around George's neck and the other to the horn of a saddle."

"What did Goerge do?"

"He bellered like a bull calf. They told me to get on the horse and make him run as hard as he would go. They said they would grab the rope and tie it tight when George was pulled up against the limb."

The robe hid all of John except his eyes. I dreaded to look at them as he talked. The fever in them was still rising.

"I got on the horse and spurred him as hard as I could. He started bucking and running. When George was about twenty feet in the air my saddle girt broke. The horse kept going but I swung back. I was swinging from the same limb with George. He was over me and thrashing around hard. I was still clinging to the saddle. I was scared, but I held on till the other men could tie the rope. Then they let me down. They said I was a good man and made me drink some whiskey."

"You left George hanging there?"

"Had to. He's a good example for other niggers. This'll keep them in their place for a while."

"But the buzzards—"

"Let the buzzards have him. He was a bad nigger—a killer. Come here."

John led me to the porch and pointed to the woods. Two great fires were burning. The sky above the forest was red and yellow with their light. Tree tops between us and the sky were like black lace.

"That fire to the west," John said, "is the one we built to hang George by. The other is George's cabin. Ain't nothing like fire and hanging to scare niggers . . ."

John put his arm around my shoulders to lead me into the house, but I moved away from him. He took off the mask and robe. I still did not recognize him as my brother. There was something in his eyes—more than whiskey or fever. He smiled a bit and brought his hand down my face, saying "Down come a limb, up—"

I jerked away from the touch of his hand. I lay down on my pallet and pulled the quilts over my face. He tucked the covers around me and stooped over me quietly for a moment. When I did not speak or move, he went off to bed.

I was warm in my covers but could not sleep. I was thinking of George . . . and hangerman John.

1947

WILLIAM GOYEN
Bridge of Music, River of Sand

Do you remember the bridge that we crossed over the river to get to Riverside? And if you looked over yonder you saw the railroad trestle? High and narrow? Well that's what he jumped off of. Into a nothing river. "River"! I could laugh. I can spit more than runs in that dry bed. In some places it's just a little damp, but that's it. That's your grand and rolling river: a damp spot. That's your remains of the grand old Trinity. Where can so much water go? I at least wish they'd do something about it. But what can they do? What can anybody do? You can't replace a *river*.

Anyway, if there'd been water, maybe he'd have made it, the naked diver. As it was, diving into the river as though there were water in it, he went head first into moist sand and drove into it like an arrow into flesh and was found in a position of somebody on their knees, headless, bent over looking for something. Looking for where the river vanished to? I was driving across the old river bridge when I said to myself, wait a minute I believe I see something. I almost ran into the bridge railing. I felt a chill come over me.

What I did when I got off the bridge was to draw my car off to the side of the road and get out and run down the river bank around a rattlesnake that seemed to be placed there as a deterrent (the banks are crawling with them in July), and down; and what I came upon was a kind of avenue that the river had made and paved with gleaming white

---

sand, wide and grand and empty. I crossed this ghostly thoroughfare of the river halfway, and when I got closer, my Lord Jesus God Almighty damn if I didn't see that it was half a naked human body in what would have been mid-stream were there water. I was scared to death. What ought I to do? Try to pull it out? I was scared to touch it. It was a heat-stunned afternoon. The July heat throbbed. The blue, steaming air waved like a veil. The feeling of something missing haunted me: it was the lost life of the river—something so powerful that it had haunted the countryside for miles around; you could feel it a long time before you came to it. In a landscape that was unnatural—flowing water was missing—everything else seemed unnatural. The river's vegetation was thin and starved-looking; it lived on the edge of sand instead of water; it seemed out of place.

If only I hadn't taken the old bridge. I was already open to a fine of five thousand dollars for driving across it, according to the sign, and I understood why. (Over yonder arched the shining new bridge. There was no traffic on it.) The flapping of loose boards and the quaking of the iron beams was terrifying. I almost panicked in the middle when the whole construction swayed and made such a sound of crackling and clanking. I was surprised the feeble structure hadn't more than a sign to prohibit passage over it—it should have been barricaded. At any rate, it was when I was in the middle of this rocking vehicle that seemed like some mad carnival ride that I saw the naked figure diving from the old railroad trestle. It was as though the diver were making a flamboyant leap into the deep river below—until to my horror I realized that the river was dry. I dared not stop my car and so I maneuvered my way on, mechanical with terror, enchanted by the melodies that rose from the instruments of the melodious bridge that played like some orchestra of xylophones and drums and cellos as I moved over it. Who would have known that the dead bridge, condemned and closed away from human touch, had such music in it? I was on the nother side now. Behind me the music was quieter now, lowering into something like chime sounds and harness sounds and wagons; it shook like bells and tolled like soft, deep gongs.

His hands must have cut through the wet sand, carving a path for his head and shoulders. He was sunk up to his mid-waist and had fallen to a kneeling position: a figure on its knees with its head buried in the sand, as if it had decided not to look at the world any more. And then the figure began to sink as if someone underground were pulling it

25

under. Slowly the stomach, lean and hairy, vanished; then the loins, thighs. The river, which had swallowed half this body, now seemed to be eating the rest of it. For a while the feet lay, soles up, on the sand. And then they went down, arched like a dancer's.

Who was the man drowned in a dry river? eaten by a dry river? devoured by sand? How would I explain, describe what had happened? I'd be judged to be out of my senses. And why would I tell somebody— the police or—anybody? There was nothing to be done, the diver was gone, the naked leaper was swallowed up. Unless somebody had pushed him over the bridge and he'd assumed a diving position to try to save himself. But what evidence was there? Well, I *had* to report what I'd seen, what I'd witnessed. Witness? To what? Would anybody believe me? There was no evidence anywhere. Well, I'd look, I'd search for evidence. I'd go up on the railroad trestle.

I climbed up. The trestle was perilously narrow and high. I could see a long ways out over Texas, green and steaming in July. I could see the scar of the river, I could see the healed-looking patches that were the orphaned bottomlands. I could see the tornado-shaped funnel of bilious smoke that twisted out of the mill in Riverside, enriching the owner and poisoning him, his family, and his neighbors. And I could see the old bridge which I'd just passed over and still trembling under my touch, arching perfect and precious, golden in the sunlight. The music I had wrought out of it was now stilled except, it seemed, for a low, deep hum that rose from it. It seemed impossible that a train could move on these narrow tracks now grown over with weeds. As I walked, grasshoppers flared up in the dry heat.

I saw no footprints in the weeds, no sign of anybody having walked on the trestle—unless they walked on the rails or the ties. Where were the man's clothes? Unless he'd left them on the bank and run out naked onto the trestle. This meant searching on both sides of the trestle— Christ, what was I caught up in? It could also mean that he was a suicide, my mind went on dogging me; or insane; it could also mean that nobody else was involved. Or could it mean that I was suffering a kind of bridge madness, or the vision that sometimes comes from going home again, of going back to places haunted by deep feeling?

Had anyone ever told me the story of a man jumping into the river from the trestle? Could this be some tormented spirit doomed forever to re-enact his suicide? And if so, must he continue it, now that the river was gone? This thought struck me as rather pitiful.

How high the trestle was! It made me giddy to look down at the riverbed. I tried to find the spot where the diver had hit the dry river. There was absolutely no sign. The mouth of sand that had sucked him down before my very eyes had closed and sealed itself. The story was over, so far as I was concerned. Whatever had happened would be my secret. I had to give it up, let it go. You can understand that I had no choice, that that was the only thing I could do.

That was the summer I was making a sentimental trip through home regions, after fifteen years away. The bridge over the beloved old river had been one of my most touching memories—an object that hung in my memory of childhood like a precious ornament. It was a fragile creation, of iron and wood, and so poetically arched, so slender, half a bracelet (the other half underground) through which the green river ran. The superstructure was made more for a minaret than a bridge. From a distance it looked like an ornate pier, in Brighton or early Santa Monica; or, in the summer heat haze, a palace tower, a creation of gold. Closer, of course, it was an iron and wooden bridge of unusual beauty, shape, and design. It had always been an imperfect bridge, awry from the start. It had been built wrong—an engineering mistake: the ascent was too steep and the descent too sharp. But its beauty endured. And despite its irregularity, traffic had used the bridge at Riverside, without serious mishap, for many years. It was just an uncomfortable trip, and always somewhat disturbing, this awkward, surprising, and somehow mysterious crossing.

Some real things happened on this practical, if magical, device for crossing water. For one thing, since it swayed, my mother, in our childhood days, would refuse to ride across it. She would remove herself from the auto and walk across, holding onto the railing, while my father, cursing, drove the rest of us across. My sister and I peered back at the small figure of our mother laboring darkly and utterly alone on the infernal contraption which was her torment. I remember my father getting out of the car, on the other side, waiting at the side of the road, looking toward the bridge, watching my mother's creeping progress. When she arrived, pale, she declared, as she did each time, "I vow to the Lord if my sister Sarah didn't live in Riverside I'd never to my soul come near this place." "Well you could lie down in the back seat, put the cotton in your ears that you always bring, and never know it, as I keep telling you," said my father. "I'd still know it," my mother came back.

"I'd still know we was on this infernal bridge." "Well then take the god-dam train from Palestine. Train trestle's flat." And, getting in the car and slamming the door, "Or stay home and just *write* to your damned sister Sarah. Married to a horse's ass, anyway."

"Mama," said my sister, trying to pacify the situation. "Tell us about the time you almost drowned in the river and Daddy had to jump in and pull you out."

"Well, it was just right over yonder. We'd been fishing all morning, and . . ."

"Aw for Christ's sake," my father said.

On the other side of the bridge, after a crossing of hazards and challenges, there was nothing more than a plain little town of mud streets and weather-faded shacks. The town of poor people lived around an ugly mill that puffed out like talcum something called Fuller's Earth over it. This substance lay on rooftops, on the ground, and in lungs. It smelled sour and bit the eyes.

As I drove away toward that town, haunted by the vision of the leaping man and now so shaken in my very spirit, lost to fact but brought to some odd truth which I could not yet clear for myself, I saw in the mirror the still image of the river bridge that had such hidden music in it, girdling the ghost of what it had been created for, that lost river that held in its bosom of sand the diving figure of the trestle that I was sure I had seen. I was coming in to Riverside and already the stinging fumes of the mill brought tears to my eyes.

1975

BILL BRETT
Justice

I t seems to me if justice is done properly it ought to be done immediately after the deed. That way there can't be no pleasure took, which would be pay for doing it, nor remorse felt, which would be extra punishment. I never seen it happen that sudden but once.

Me and the two Nichols boys had been gathering cattle for Mr. Jordan up to Batson and had got through and stopped at Mr. J. G. Price's store to get some dinner on the way home. John Clendennin was there getting a bill of groceries and had a mule hooked to his wagon we hadn't none of us seen before. He'd drove up to where the mule's head was close to a big sweet gum that growed close in front and had tied him to it with a piece of half-inch rope. We all knowed when we seen that that John had got aholt of another outlaw. He was the dangdest feller I ever seen about buying or swapping for work stock that had been spoilt by mishandling, and trying to make them fit for using. We all set down on the front porch, and while we was eating our sardines and cheese and crackers, John told us about this black mule.

"I heard about that mule nearly killing a couple of men in the logging woods up to Saratoga, and rode up there to see about buying him. I located the feller that owned him, and he told me the mule could be bought for thirty dollars, which is less than half price for a good mule, but any examining I done was at my own risk. Immediate I crawled

"Justice" from *There Ain't No Such Animal and Other East Texas Tales*, by Bill Brett. Published by Texas A&M University Press. Copyright © 1979 by Bill Brett.

over in the pen I knowed that mule had a special feeling for me from the way he come meeting me.

"I seen right off I couldn't stand all the affection that mule had for me, me being a bachelor and not used to it, so I just went right back over the fence. I was afeered I'd hurt his feelings by leaving so abrupt, but he'd got close enough to give me a little love bite and help hisself to a good portion of my shirt and seemed contented with that. After I'd got two or three fellers that was there awatching to confirm that I wasn't bleeding too bad, I told the owner I'd buy that mule, that I believed I could give him the love and affection he seemed to have been deprived of. After I'd paid him, I got my whip off my saddle and climbed back in the pen, and time I hit the ground here come that mule again, ears laid back, head out, and them big teeth popping. I had come prepared with love and kisses of my own this time, though. I took a chunk out of that soft nose the first lick with that bullwhip and slowed him down and tried to take a ear off the next lick. Well, sir, that was two weeks ago, and I ain't never worked a better mule in my life than that one. Gentle, willing, and so sweet it's sickening, just abiding his time till he can catch me off guard and kick my brains out. Ever' time something moves in back of him, be it fish, meat, or fowl, you can tell he just automatically calculates range, elevation, and windage. If either one of you boys is feeling bored with life, I'll be glad to swap you that mule. I guarantee he'll overcome that for you."

About then we heard a wagon coming and Big Nick stood up and looked and said it was Frank Pearson and his boy. Said Frank looked happy so he must have whipped his wife before he left home. This was just his way of passing an opinion on Frank Pearson, but it pegged the man to a T. He was the kind who kicks dogs, if they don't growl at him, whips and slaps his womenfolk around, if they don't threaten to take a skillet to him, and keeps his children scared half to death till they're half as big as him, but wouldn't say boo to a man if he spit in his face. By any measure, a bully. Mrs. Pearson had a ol' bachelor brother, lived in Houston, who'd tried to get her and the kids to come live with him, but she was so scared of Frank, said he'd kill her and the kids both, she wouldn't go. They had a little girl about four or five and the boy, about nine, that was with Frank. Frank was cussing and threatening the boy when he stopped the wagon and climbed down over a wheel.

All of us already had a bellyful of him, but when he howdied us we howdied back. None of us made a move till he turned around and seen the boy hadn't got down off the wagon and grabbed him and jerked the little feller like a bundle of fodder. When he done that, John Clendennin mumbled something about "another spoilt 'un" and reached and got his whip and started to get up. Little Nick was setting on the edge of the porch carving his initials in the floor, and I seen him close the little blade in his knife and open the big one, getting redder in the face all the time. It weren't setting a dang bit better with me and Big Nick than it was them, but we knowed either one of the two would kill Pearson if they ever started on him, and we didn't want it to go that far. I'd been setting by Little Nick and I just slid off the porch and pulled up a sleeve on my brush jumper and said how about him digging a black locust thorn out of my arm, since he had his knife out. About the same time Big Nick jerked a piece of binder twine out of his leggings pocket and ask' to see John's whip a minute so's he could twist a popper like was on it. Before Pearson had his team tied and him and the boy went in the store, I wished to hell Little Nick was cutting on him instead of me, mad as he was. Big Nick had kept on at John Clendennin about that popper, and then slid his hands on up the whip and looked at the way it went from eight plait to four plait, and then gathered it in to where it went from sixteen plait to eight plait, and then went to admiring the way it was plaited on the stock, and Pearson went in just in time, Nick was dang near out of whip.

Well, it was about ten minutes before Pearson got his trading done and come out, and John and Little Nick had calmed down enough that I thought maybe he might get away before there was any trouble.

The boy came out first, toting a jug of kerosene and working on a stick of candy I knowed Mr. Price had give him. Frank come out right behind him with his arms full of groceries, and just as he went off the steps on the ground, he stepped on the boy's heel. 'Course the boy stumbled, and his daddy went to cussing and hollering watch where he was going and if he spilt that coal oil he'd take his hide off, and all of a sudden he just hauled off and kicked the boy with the inside of his boot. The young'un went sprawling in the side of John's wagon and dropped the jug and just stood there, about half stunned-like. Frank went to cussing louder and threatening worse and jumped and throwed his armload in his wagon and went to pulling his belt off. About then he noticed the kerosene jug where it had rolled up behind John's black mule, and made for it, still raving and cussing. Just as he bent over to pick it up, John Clendennin's black mule reached back with his right hind foot and kicked Frank Pearson's damn brains out.

That was the finest example of justice I've ever seen.

1971

HUGHES RUDD

The Shores of Schizophrenia

I started spouting off the other night about how I'd always wanted to have a conducted tour through a mortuary, with somebody along to explain what it was all about, exactly how they do it and so forth, when I remembered that I did take a tour like that once, although it didn't turn out too well. I'd forgotten all about it, it just shows you how useless everything is, how absurd it is to try and tell kids anything. You give them an experience like that, something you'd think they could never forget, and within a week they don't know what you're talking about.

I had to shut up when I thought of it, I was sitting in the garden behind the Peanut at one of the tin tables, swilling beer and working up to a good speech, really getting ready to insult somebody, but it plugged me right up. The other people at the table decided I hated them, they couldn't understand it, it wasn't like me at all. I just sat there, I couldn't tell them about it because they wouldn't have understood it, it would have meant a lot of babbling and shouting, before it was all over we'd have been down on the gravel, rolling around and beating each other with beer bottles while the fat rats skipped back and forth, trying to stay out of range. That's the way it is out at the Peanut, sometimes, the place attracts that sort. You can curse and shout and belch all you want, as long as you don't pull anything funny, anything unusual. If you do—blooey! out you go.

That mortuary trip was just one of several we had at that time. We were in the fourth grade, somewhere around there, at Dean Highland school in Waco, Texas, a building stuck out on the muddy edge of town like an unsuccessful factory, with two mulberry trees in the front yard.

The teacher was absolutely the meanest bitch I have ever known in my life, nothing pleased her, she snarled and slapped and snorted until everybody in the class was terrified, we worked like dogs. But we didn't seem to learn anything, we just went through the motions, almost hysterical, so of course things got worse and worse. Nothing did any good, you could have cut your throat to please her and she still would have hated your guts. An average schoolteacher, in fact.

And then she started those damn trips of hers. As I remember it, at first we thought it was a terrific idea, anything to get out of that gloomy, hideous building, with its smell of cedar sawdust and stale, infantile pee, we couldn't wait for the first outing. Everybody had to show up in their best clothes that day, washed and combed and buttoned up to the eyeballs, like a Sunday school class. The kids from the other rooms nearly split themselves laughing at us, they thought we were out of our minds and you know nothing gives you such a belly laugh as a real loony walking around in your everyday world. They got a real kick out of it. But for once we didn't give a damn, we were the ones who were getting out, and we piled aboard the bus like we were headed for the Crystal Theater or a calf cutting.

Well, teacher soon fixed that. It was slap, slap, slap, up and down the aisle, pulling ears and twisting cowlicks until we were almost in a panic, ready to kick the windows out. For some reason it never occurred to us to gang her. By the time we pulled up in front of German's Funeral Home everybody's clean clothes had all gone to hell and we were covered with dirt, there was chewing gum in hair and eyebrows and two or three of the more timid souls had wet their pants, including little Robert, of course, he never failed us. We looked like a wild-eyed rabble lined up on the grass in front of the funeral home, like we'd broken out of prison and crawled through a hundred miles of dust to get there, to be on time for the guided tour through the mortuary.

The first thing, of course, was to explain what the hell it was all about. In school we had been reading about the Egyptians and their mummies, the King Tut tomb business happened about that time and it set everybody off, I never knew why. The teacher started brooding about what a stupid bunch we were, I suppose, not understanding embalming and so on, she was sick and tired of trying to explain what it was all about so she decided the hell with it, we'd go to the source. And, too, she probably was just as happy to get out of that damned building as we were, I don't know. Anyway, she lined us up on the grass and tried to make it clear what was about to happen, which was a mistake. Up till then I don't think anybody had any idea what was going on, but as soon as she put it across that we were going in there and look at a lot of dead people the ranks faltered, then broke, and in a split second most of the girls and some of the boys were squawling like turpentined cats. She had a nimble time for a few minutes, running all over the lawn after kids who wanted to go home, hopping around the house, plunging through the canna beds, dodging around among the iron deer and sundials that Mr. German had all over the place. The people passing by must have thought one of our little classmates had kicked off and we had turned up in a group at the funeral, unable to contain our grief. It was lively, but it wasn't getting things done, and pretty soon Mr. German's son came out in his black suit and helped her round up the strays. Little Robert got away, though, he wandered around downtown all that day, wetting his pants every fifteen minutes, until somebody recognized him and took him home. So he missed it.

It was cool inside, but you really couldn't see much. Mr. German's place had been just a house to begin with, the mortuary stuff was all in the basement and the upstairs was pretty much like our own houses, only darker and a good deal tidier, and somehow that made it seem even worse. We trailed around in the gloom in a chorus of little moans, everywhere you looked you could see eyeballs shining. We held on to each other for dear life, and there were squeaks and grunts and sighs and other nervous noises while we were led around through the rooms, completely aimlessly. It was really senseless. Finally the teacher started arguing with Mr. German about letting us go down in the basement where the meat of the matter was, but he refused to do it, he was against the whole idea, in fact, and they had a real go-round while we stood there looking on, waiting for our fate like a bunch of pigs. After a while the teacher gave up and led us back to the bus and we reloaded and went back to school. All we had seen that was unusual was the portable organ and an empty casket, unlined. The rest of it was just rooms and folding chairs, we couldn't understand what the hell it was all about. A field trip!

The next thing was the compress. Naturally we were involved with cotton all the time, no matter what you were studying they always managed to drag cotton into it somehow, and with the Egyptians it was a cinch. As usual, we had to bring bolls of it to school, and we made little speeches about it, the way it had been in every class since we had started school, but you couldn't keep coasting along on your old speeches. Oh, no. Some jerk would snitch if you did that. You had to come up with new facts every year and you had to have a novel way of presenting your cotton boll to the collection, too. We pasted the damn things on cards, we wired them into little trees, we made leis out of them, we dyed them with watercolors, we did every damn thing you can think of with cotton before it was over. Well, of course there was no pleasing this bitch, she didn't think much of our efforts. She flung the silly things back in our faces, she ranted and howled and redoubled her pinching and slapping. We were a spineless bunch, we just took it. She wasn't even reported to the school board by an outraged mother, as far as I know. Of course, she had a lot on her mind, a lot of worries, as it turned out, she probably expected the ax to fall at any minute, but apparently that just made her bear down harder on this cotton business. We'd never had such a siege of it, it made us shudder to think what must be ahead of us in the grades to come. If it was this bad here, what would they expect in junior high school? Would you have to go out and pick the stuff, gin the Goddamned cotton yourself? For Christ's sake! We worried our little heads about it, I can tell you. Little Robert was soaked, every day.

Well, after we'd done everything possible with our bedraggled cotton bolls and had brought in tons of newspaper clippings about it, all smeared around and pasted on cards and in scrapbooks, we had to show up in our best clothes again to go to the compress. The compress! There's not a damned thing to see in one of those places and every kid in town knew it. They pile the cotton in a hopper and a big weight comes down and packs it into a bale. That's all, and you can't even see that, there's always so much dust and lint in the air, and the machinery isn't out where you can stick your finger in it, anyway. A hell of an uproar, but you can't see what they're doing, and if you don't look out one of those tough bastards will knock you on your ear, clear off the loading dock. We all knew that, but we packed ourselves into that stinking bus, a little troop of smelly martyrs, and off we went. We had no guts at all.

The compress manager thought everybody had gone nuts. They'd told him we were coming, all right, but Jesus! A busload, piling out all over the joint! What a day for the compress manager! And the terrible thing for him, of course, was that he couldn't figure out what the hell we were doing there. He'd been around compresses all his life, he didn't see anything unusual about it at all. What else did we expect him to do with the cotton, for God's sake, tie it up with string? Of course they baled it, of course the plunger came down and packed it tight, of course, of course, and we agreed with him. What the hell, we knew all that as well as he did, we weren't idiots, you know. We just stood around and looked at the poor devil, getting filthier by the minute, dirt and lint settling all over us, in our ears, in our nostrils, we could hardly breathe. It was like the rope factory in a prison, and the noise! You couldn't hear yourself scream, so of course we did, we opened our little mouths and bellowed like maddened bulls, looking at the compress manager. To that poor sod it looked like our mouths were hanging open in astonishment at his machine, he couldn't hear a thing. We were all hoarse when we got out of there and nobody had heard us make a sound. That was getting even, all right! That was one up the teacher's nose! We enjoyed that, but it wasn't over yet. She lined us up, the usual business, out in the road this time in dust deeper than our sweaty little ankles, and everybody had to describe what he had just seen. Not just, "They bale cotton." Hell, no! The first one tried that and got a real wallop. You had to go into ecstasies over the crumby place, really tear your heart out about that compress. To be successful at it you needed a degree in hydraulic engineering and a steam boiler operator whispering in your ear. We stood there in the dust and took it, we were absolutely no damned good to Dean Highland school whatsoever. We thought any minute she was going to give us the order to go hop in the compress bin, under the plunger, it was the only honorable way out and we knew it. We were ready, it was tough, but that's the way it was, so what the hell. Let's get it over with. But no, back in the bus, slap, smack, pinch, somebody puking on the floor, a splendid little outing, the teacher behaving like a drunk storm trooper. Well, we've seen the compress, now what. Mass suicide? Why not, what else? There's nothing left, is there? Come on, we'll all do it together, out on the playground. We can hang ourselves from the swing supports, in relays of ten.

Well, that took care of cotton. Let's see, what's next, now. Oh, yes, coffee, of course. Is there anybody here who doesn't know what coffee is? Of course there isn't, we have it all over the house, we practically live on the stuff. Well, that doesn't make a Goddamned bit of difference, you little slobs! What a filthy bunch! What parents you must have! Wipe your noses and get into that bus, or I'll wring every one of your grimy necks! We're going to the coffeeworks.

If anybody else had told us there was a place in town where they ground coffee we wouldn't have believed it. They'd drummed it into us that the stuff came from South America, we knew what the score was. We'd seen a thousand pictures of it growing down there, or over there, or wherever the hell South America was, we'd even seen pictures of it lying on the ground, with people walking around on it barefooted. What the hell! You didn't have to tell us about coffee, we'd all had nightmares about it at some time or other, at one point we had to go around to the grocery stores, begging for a coffee bean to take to class, just to show some teacher we knew what she was talking about. Coffee! Why bother! We weren't even allowed to drink it, yet here it was, coffee, coffee, and still more coffee, you heard nothing else. What a world!

They were waiting for us at the coffeeworks, I suppose they were more accustomed to the screwballs in town than the compress manager was, they were a high-class bunch. You'd have thought we were little movie stars, for the first five minutes. There we were, all cleaned up again, they thought it was downright sweet. Sweet! Jesus, why didn't they put us to work digging sewers, we were getting a little sick of all this idiocy by now, we were beginning to figure maybe all this wasn't in the contract, that they were putting one over on us, in fact. We hadn't been idle, we'd been asking around.

Well, there it was, the coffee! Now what? There were tons of it, in all stages, and that was all right, we had nothing against it, but so what? Sure, it was coffee, we admitted that, didn't we? What did they want us to do, throw ourselves in it? What good would that do anybody? What was all the fuss about, anyway?

Well, here's the kind they drink New Orleans, somebody said. See? It's ground up finer than the rest, like powder. New Orleans? What the hell are they talking about? Sure, we supposed they drank coffee in New Orleans, why not, when you think of it? And we dawdled around, an impossible scene. It's really hell in a coffee mill, you know, especially if you don't drink it. Instead of dust in the air you have little motes of coffee, I suppose from the batch those New Orleanians had to have, trying to be different. We figured that out, and we began to hate New Orleans' guts. We breathed the stuff, that powdered coffee filled up our lungs and passed into our bloodstreams until we were as hopped up as if we'd gotten bugged on cocaine. We didn't know what the hell we were doing, it was a colossal coffee jag. Our nerves were shot, we almost got bags under our little eyes, and not one of us slept a wink that night. It upset the whole west end of town. For a week we puked every time we saw a cup of the nasty stuff. We were feverish with caffeine.

Well, that was another one under our belts. Live and let live, that was us, we could stand anything, Powder River, let 'er buck! We hadn't lost anybody yet, we were a damned tough crowd. They were going to have trouble polishing us off, all right. We were ready to go back to the mortuary and start all over again, we'd drag the damn stiffs out in the front yard if we had to, if that was what they wanted. A hardy little class!

We could've kept it up forever, we were just hitting our stride when the whole thing blew up. I got on the streetcar one afternoon and who was sitting in front of me but the teacher, with some woman I'd never seen before. I was on my way down to the Crystal and I didn't want to miss any more of the show than I had already, I just sat there scared stiff, afraid she'd see me and start grilling me about streetcars or electricity or some damn thing. But I got by, she just bawled on the other woman's neck all the way downtown, it was quite a scene, everybody was disgusted, and after that I never saw her again.

The next day we had a new teacher and she had to break the bad news. The old bitch had pinched our little savings, the dough she'd extorted from us a dime at a time so our room would look good on the chart out in the hall, she'd blown the whole seven bucks! Jesus, no! We set up quite an uproar, but there it was, nothing anybody could do about it, we'd just have to lump it. They'd found out about it and fired her, but that didn't get our money back. We wanted her arrested, we wanted the cops to beat the hell out of her, but they let her go, of course. That's always the way it is. If *we'd* hooked the seven bucks— brother! They'd have taken us down in the coal bin and buried us alive. But we finally figured, what the hell, you know, at least those idiotic tours were finished with, and just in time. She'd been raving about dragging us out to the cement factory, just before the roof fell in. God knows what would have happened out there, it was a rugged place.

1961

VASSAR MILLER

Pact

The Church of the Healing Waters wasn't an impressive sight, nothing like my own St. Timothy's Episcopal. It was just a little frame building with cracked and peeling paint on the edge of niggertown.

Anna, the maid, puffing and panting, carried me into the church. I wasn't very heavy for seven years old, but the braces on my legs were.

"I want to get up front where we can be the first in line for Brother Betz. He can put his hands on you and the Lord Jesus, bless His holy name, can heal you."

Anna was stout and breathed hard. My stomach turned inside me. Would the Lord Jesus really do it? And would Daddy be mad at the Lord Jesus if he did? Daddy would be mad if he knew Anna was taking me to her church, and for *healing* of all things, after none of the doctors Daddy had taken me to could cure me. Guilty, I knew it was wrong. But, guilty also, I loved her just the same, and I had promised to tell Daddy she was taking me to the movies. This was my most important moment, except for Christmas and Santa Claus.

People crowded around us.

"Bless her little heart," one old woman said. "Is that the little girl you take care of?"

"This is my baby," Anna said.

That made me feel good. Daddy was always reminding me that I was a poor motherless child. Anna's words made me feel better, though I wouldn't have told him for the world.

"Pact" was previously published in *Shenandoah* 14, no. 2 (Winter 1963): 41–47. Copyright © by Vassar Miller.

"I'm hoping the Lord Jesus will heal her tonight when Brother Betz lays hands on her."

"Brother Betz can do wonders for the Lord," a young woman said.

"Yes! Yes! Praise His holy name!" several people said ecstatically.

"You have faith, don't you, darlin'?" somebody asked me.

I nodded and made a strangled sound.

"*Awww* . . . She can't talk."

"Yeah she can talk," Anna said. "It just takes a while to get used to her. Now you folks let me and Velma get a front seat so we can be the first in line."

"Let me carry this poor child for you," a man said.

He lifted me out of her arms. He was soft and flabby and smelled of sweat. I didn't much like him calling me a poor child.

Anna and I finally got seated on the front row. The seats were wooden folding chairs with places on the backs for yellow, paper hymnals. Not at all like our pews, all shiny and smooth with their backs holding neat little red and black books. There were no kneelers either. Everybody was chattering along just as if we *really were* in the picture show waiting for the movie to begin. I smelled sweat instead of candle wax and flame, and the windows were just like the windows at home, only dirtier. They had no soft bright pictures for the panes. There was no carpet down the aisle, no carpet anywhere, only the scrape of chairs and feet on bare, dusty floor.

I didn't exactly like it, but Anna had said that here in this strange ugly place the Lord Jesus would heal me if I had faith. It was the whole mysterious idea of being "healed" that drew me, more than the idea of being able to speak like anybody else or walk. I had been "that way" all my life and I could not imagine being any other way. But whenever Anna spoke of the Lord Jesus and His healing power, she became changed and charged with wonder and marvel. And her talk filled my mind and body with a strange lawless elation.

There was a low platform just in front of us. No sign of altar or cross. Only a bare wooden table, which might have been in a kitchen, with a Bible on it. There was an old upright piano. A woman came in and sat down at it and started a fast tinkling melody on the keys. Still everybody went right on talking. Everything seemed strange, as in a dream. I was afraid I was going to wake up in my own bed with no chance of being healed at all.

I asked Anna why her church was so different from mine.

"Hush, never mind," she told me. "The Holy Spirit ain't in your church the way He is here."

In my church nobody ever said anything about healing. They just asked Daddy what was wrong with me and made him mad. I guessed Anna was right.

The woman kept on playing. Then a man came onto the stage and stood behind the table. He was a tall skinny man and his long face was like a knife blade seeming to cut the air in two when he moved his head. His eyes were like two bright blue marbles. When he cried out, his voice was shrill and piercing and made me jump.

"Is everybody happy? Everybody that is say Amen!"

It seemed like a strange question coming from such a thin, sad-looking man, but everybody said Amen.

This surely was different from my church, but I kept hoping that if all the noise didn't turn into a slamming door or a power mower crashing into my dream, then it would be real.

"That's Brother Betz," Anna said, beaming.

"Is everybody happy in the Lord, I mean?" Brother Betz asked. "You can't just be happy. You gotta be happy in *Him!*"

"Amen!" roared the congregation.

"Everybody have faith?"

"Amen!"

"Everybody have faith in the *Lord*, I mean?" Brother Betz insisted. "You can't just have faith. You gotta have faith in *Him*!

"Amen!" everybody agreed.

"Everybody have faith that the Lord Jesus can heal?"

"Amen!"

"Everybody have faith that the Lord Jesus can heal *you*? Not just your brother or your sister, but *you*?"

"Amen!"

Anna squeezed my hand so hard it hurt. "Hear that, honey? You gotta say Amen too. You gotta have faith."

I nodded, dry-mouthed and weak inside me. I hadn't been saying Amen because it hadn't seemed that Brother Betz was talking to me. But now I could join in. But there weren't any more Amens. Nobody needed a prayerbook to know when to start and stop. Everybody began singing hymns out of the paper hymn books. They were jazzy, foot-tapping tunes, and I began swinging my leg until somebody noticed the noise my brace was making against the chair and stared at me.

Brother Betz opened the big Bible on the table.

"Tonight," he said, "we're going to have a great healing service. Yes, praise God, a great healing service! But first I'm going to speak to you out of Acts."

He read what I learned much later was the story of the impotent man laid by the Gate Beautiful, the man who was healed by Peter and John. Even if I could have understood, I didn't hear the words. He spoke softly, but soon was speaking in a shrill voice. I paid so much attention to the way he talked that I didn't hear what he said.

Everybody there seemed happy in the Lord. Amens came from all around the room, Praise the Lord and Glory Hallelujah. I listened open-mouthed.

"Amen!" Anna would say, squeezing my hand. "Oh, honey, He's gonna heal you. I know it! I know it!"

Won't Daddy be surprised? I thought. I hoped it would be a pleasant surprise. I wondered, though, if maybe he wouldn't feel a little disappointed if I got healed for free after he had gone and spent so much money on me. I was getting excited, but not enough to try and yell with the rest.

"You can throw away your glasses!" Brother Betz shouted. "Your crutches, your hearing aids . . .!"

Should I throw away my braces when I got healed? They were very expensive. I heard Daddy say so. I was still puzzling about all this when Anna nudged me.

"Get ready," she said. "We wanna be first."

I felt myself tighten, my stomach quiver.

"Come all you sick and infirm and be healed of the Lord . . ."

Brother Betz was talking more softly now. I could hear people back of us getting up, scraping their chairs. Anna rose and took me firmly in her arms and started toward the platform. A man stepped up and offered to hold me for her.

"No, thanks," Anna whispered. "I'm going to take my baby to the Lord by myself."

Tense in her arms, I looked up into the long lean face of Brother Betz.

"Well, bless your heart, honey," he said. "Do you believe the Lord Jesus can heal you?"

Speechless, I nodded.

"How old are you?"

"Seven," Anna answered.

"Look here, everybody," he told the congregation. "If the faith of any of you is weak, this child's should put yours to shame. Just seven years old and she knows the Lord can heal her!"

Every eye on me, I felt pinned by the stares of the congregation. It *was* all different from St. Timothy's where Daddy always sat with me in the very back so nobody would see us.

"I get so damned sick of their curiosity," he would say. "If only your mother was still alive!"

Now I longed to hide myself in Anna's arms.

"Now, folks, help me to pray for this little child."

I could hear a quiet descend, a hush that was like sound itself. Reaching forth his slender hands, he clasped them around my forehead in a firm grip. He closed his eyes and lifted his face toward the ceiling.

"O Lord Jesus," he prayed, "may this child upon whom I lay my hands be freed from the devil's power and be healed by Thy mercy. Amen."

"Amen!" echoed the congregation in a soft rumble. I could hear Anna breathing hard again.

Suddenly I felt snug and safe, no longer pinned upon their stares. I was enveloped in a gaze of loving concern. Was *this* what being healed meant? The same feeling I so often had with Anna's fat arms around me, only more of it . . . .

"Sister Anna," Brother Betz said. "You can take off her braces. Praise the Lord, she can throw 'em away."

The congregation praised the Lord.

"Yessir," Anna whispered.

But when she carried me back to my seat she said we'd better wait until we got home. Daddy might not like it if we threw the braces away, not just yet. I nodded. I was glad to be back in my seat. But for a moment the light of all their eyes had become a glow of warmth. I could play with it in my mind later. I could make it grow. I could do all kinds of things with that moment and that feeling, because it was mine.

After me came a line of the sick and the infirm. An old woman with a nasty boil on her face. A thin, sickly, middle-aged woman. A baby blind in one eye. A boy with T.B. One man told Brother Betz he couldn't afford a pair of glasses and he wanted his poor eyesight cured. Then another old woman came limping. None of them, except maybe the one-eyed baby, looked as interesting as my case. So, after watching them a little while, I was lulled to sleep by Hallelujahs and slept in Anna's arms.

After a while she carried me out, caught the bus, and so we went home.

On the way home I wondered, half-asleep, whether I had been healed.

"Do I talk better?"

"Wait and see, honey," she said. She sounded worried. "Just wait and see."

Daddy met us at the front door with his angry look.

"You know it's way past Velma's bedtime," he told Anna. "You should never have kept her out so late. Coming home on a bus! Why didn't you just call me to pick you up?"

"We had streetlights all the way," Anna said. "It was a double feature at the picture show and Velma seemed to be enjoying it so much."

"You mean *you* were enjoying it so much," Daddy said.

He sounded so cold and mean I almost hated him. It made me love Anna that much more. I tightened my hold around Anna's neck. I didn't want Daddy to fire Anna the way he fired Mary, the maid before her, because she was late coming back from her afternoon off.

"Stop crying, Velma," he said. "You know I just want what's best for you."

I bawled louder.

"All right, all right, all *right!*" Daddy said. "Get her to bed right now, Anna."

When Anna undressed me and took off my braces, we found that I was going to need them the next day. And Anna admitted that, no, I didn't talk any better. I was a little disappointed.

"Sometimes it takes a while to build up enough faith," she told me. "Sometimes you have to keep going back."

"Take me back, Anna," I begged.

"We'll have to figure some way to get around your Daddy," she said. Then: "What's the matter, honey?"

"You might get fired. I don't want you to get fired."

Anna hugged me tight. "Bless your heart, honey. Anna won't get fired. Anna won't leave her baby."

I didn't know how Anna was going to hold out against Daddy, but for the time being I clung to her reassurances as to a new treasure. Anna would stay with me. And I could go back with her to the Church of the Healing Waters.

1963

45

PAUL HORGAN
In Summer's Name

Because as a doctor I was abroad in the streets at such frequent and irregular times of the day and night, I think I saw more of the town's temper than anybody else. I mean the weather on the vast Texas plain where the town sat, and what the weather in its season did to the gracious hood of cottonwood trees that stood up and down all the streets. Coming to town from far down the plain, I would see the little mound of light-crowned green haze, the trees locating the town for me. In summer, especially, I loved those towering cushions of glittering leaves. In daytime, when the heat tried to press everybody to the earth, the trees breathed forth some fragrant essence that was refreshing; and at night, with chance bloom from the few remote street lamps of the little town, the leaves looked cool and delicious.

In the summer evenings all life was lived out of doors.

I came to know it as a seasonal symptom when the summer afternoon was spent at dusty hot sunset on the yellow plains, and the evening came, and cars moved out along the streets, and in one way or another the whole town was moved by the spirit and yielded to it whatever contribution its people could make.

The revival meetings began in May and continued until late August.

I used to see them as I drove on my rounds. Sometimes I stopped in the dark, and turned off my car lights, and watched and listened to those working souls who tried the summer night with their calls and cries, their rude apprehensions of beauty and their clamorous denunciations of fear.

I came to realize that the town went as two classes to the meetings: one was the class of the earnest, poor, plain people to whom this kind of thing was theater; it was opera, and ballet, and poetry. It took the lame knowledge that so hindered their lives and, by the infusion of several dozen human spirits with the same belief, lifted that knowledge up into a dizzy and golden certainty that raced the blood, and made the heart powerful, for a little while. People who lived violent lives, in the sense of unease and grapple with the very forces of the earth, needed to alleviate their trials as violently.

The other class I supposed I belonged to: the ones who went to observe; but in observing I always felt too a responsibility somehow, some share in this ecstatic devotion to those powers in life which rise and fall as mysteriously as the droughts on the plains where we lived. Mostly, the others, like LaVerne Dicely, the banker's son, and his crowd, simply came to make soft catcalls, daring to see how soon they'd be caught or chased off by outraged Christians.

At one time during the summer several revivals would be going on at once.

On an empty corner near the business blocks they had erected poles and a skeleton roof, over which they laid pine and cottonwood boughs, making a great arbor. When the light was burning in the gasoline lamps under the leafy roof, and the men and women and children were working in their chairs, it made some sight, I can tell you.

There was another which I always thought of as the Tree and Lantern. In an empty lot by the railroad tracks there stood a single venerable cottonwood, and from its lowest branch an electric light of great power had been strung; and beneath the tree, in the open field, under the ice-bright stars of the West, humbles came and called and bent, so that an unconscious poetry seemed to rise from their worship of whatever it was before the great tree.

On the outskirts of town a wooden tabernacle had been built. Here in the summer nights the air was boxed and stifling. People sweated and steamed, lost themselves and sang.

Late every summer a professional revival troupe came and set up an enormous tent with cherry-colored rope lacings, and a trombone quartet, and a jingle harness worn by a pretty plump blonde girl whom the revivalist drove through the tent shouting a pious sentiment about

"Trotting Home in Glory." They all looked like vaudeville actors; they preached God and sang Jesus and made cajoling sounds, winning their audiences with familiar sentiments, but delivered by clever boys and pretty girls and distinguished middle-aged men who looked anything but Godly: which made the hearts of the hearers sink and then rise; first, because these visitors looked so smart and seemed so rich; and, second, because, with all those worldly qualities, they should still shout and praise the Lord God of the plains . . .

One of the most extraordinary things, I always thought, was the way boys and girls from the high school used to get caught up in the emotional tug that fetched the town.

Many of them came to me in panic-stricken privacy for the usual re-assurances or, if those were not possible, then the proper care. I knew that young people anywhere were open and eager before any emotion whatever. Yet I was always a little chagrined for my faith in the old blind gods of the body when boys and girls I knew would skulk on the edge of the revivals and now and then enter into the arena with shouts in a hymn, and then retreat in pairs or threes or fours to the shadowy outskirts of the spirit's circle and there taste the fruits of conversion, so easily plucked when the daily presence was dropped and the exalted promise of glory raced in the blood, and filled every head . . .

Some youngsters even in a fairly large town become personages at early ages.

Some achieve this by some physical brilliance which they properly cultivate; like the boy, whose name I never knew, who because of his hair like the whitest corn silk, which grew off his forehead like a plume, was recognizable everywhere.

And some were individuals by sanction of circumstance, like LaVerne Dicely, the son of the banker.

And some, like Trillie Dee Spelzer, received the public homage which is given beauty everywhere. She was a junior in high school and, like most of our high school children, rather old for her class. She was dark haired. She was brilliant with the loveliest colors of earth in their loveliest and likeliest places—eyes like the little precious pools of blue water on the plains, full of sky; skin like the skin of fruit protected by shade. Her body was wieldy and she could afford to pretend she was awkward, which she frequently did. I suppose mostly what she had was vitality, properly expressed in physical ways; but it was quite enough.

Her father was very poor, a carpenter and cabinetmaker. Her mother was dead. She used to work after school as a house servant. I knew the people who employed her from time to time. One of them was the high school principal, a patient of mine. He used to shake his head over her, and screw up his eyes which felt hot and smarting at the precious dangers he detected everywhere.

"I'll be glad when she graduates and gets out," he said. "She's hard on the boys."

This was clear to anyone who ever saw her.

I talked with her several times, casually, and she was instinctively gifted as a flirt. She had but one vehicle for her relation to life. It often happens so. Great loveliness, great poetry, fine music, a good painting sometimes result from it. But the custodians of the power of love most often end worse off for it. Perhaps Trillie Dee was an exception here, as in so much else.

She was not stupid; she made average grades in school; she was clever and careful at her housework; but she was a half-wit in appetite and love, an emotional fool.

It was a thing you never could remember when you looked at her.

And during the summer I am speaking of, all these things were demonstrated.

It was a contest between religion and boys, for Trillie Dee.

The drugstore was a sort of forum or club for the younger leaders of the town. There I would see them, gathered about the soda fountain, where Martha Rooks, the druggist's girl, presided like a charming hostess with all the authoritative graces which the position required anywhere. Martha had the quizzical prettiness of any young creature, without any suggestion of what she would turn into as a woman. She blushed easily; her father watched her in sullen suspicion, down the length of his glass showcases or as he came from the back room bringing me my prescription. He was conscious of his family's place in the town; the Rookses were nearly as "leading" as the Dicelys. It was typical of his fatherly conscience that when Martha went out with LaVerne Dicely all he had ever heard about the boy disappeared from his memory.

Martha and Trillie Dee each had the power of symbolism; for the one, propriety and charm; for the other, adventure and furious beauty.

And now it is time to describe the stuff on which these symbols worked. LaVerne Dicely was a tall boy, with a rather small head on which there sat tight yellow curls always highly lustered. He must have used brilliantine. His clothes came from Fort Worth, and in consequence were masterpieces of inventiveness and novelty. He always looked too long for them, in arm and leg, and the buttons were strained across his bony chest. But he had three suits to other boys' one, and was highly complacent over it. He kept talking about going away to college.

He was the acknowledged leader of the high school set. Nobody liked him very much, really; but he boasted a certain power which was effective, the power of riches and skepticism among people who were mostly poor and credulous.

Martha Rooks worked at the drugstore all that summer. The boys and girls dropped in and out. The town was tired and empty looking all the hot days. Trillie Dee worked for some people I knew all day long until after the early supper which was customary in summer. Then as the dusty light of the day failed under the clarifying stars, life began to move. The movie theater sign came alive, and red light chased white light around and around the frame of the sign. Rooks' drugstore took on the life of a smart café where friends met and the day was redone. And in wafts of silence during the evening, a vagrant breeze would bring the thump and whinny, the scrape and bellow, of the herded worshippers making noise unto their aspirations. The revival meetings sounded over the plains.

Trillie Dee Spelzer went one night with LaVerne Dicely to sit in his car and watch, and kid, and carry on, and wisecrack, and use what others did as clumsy and joking references for their own usage of each other. LaVerne smoked and roved her with his hand and she kept pushing him away, saying it was too hot. The music from the Tree and Lantern, where they were parked, had an animal beat to it. The next thing you knew, Trillie Dee was out of the parked Ford and scampering into the area of light from the blazing electric bulb in the lower branches, her arms raised and her fingers quivering, her mouth slack and happy, her eyes almost milky with inner light, her voice wailing in the bleat of the pitiful, her lovely breasts rigid with intention and excitement—until she fell forward on the plain plank mourners' bench directly before the great trunk of the cottonwood, crying to be saved, to be taken up, to know Jesus, oh, yes!

LaVerne was dumfounded.

He was suddenly aware of his delicate position, and thought how humiliating it might be to be invited in with his girl friend to know God.

He started his car and backed away from the trodden lot, and went downtown, smoking gloomily.

He could hear the cry and bump of the congregation singing and stamping.

He turned around the block and left his car in an alley under the shadow of a lumber shed and sneaked down the tracks until he came within sight and sound of the Tree and Lantern again.

There she was.

She was white and startling in the fascinating light, the blazing globe that hypnotized and revealed. She was in a tight dress. She stood on the bench whimpering loudly and straining her arms upward. He could see people's faces shining from sweat in the heat of the night and the soul's labor. She was crying words. The benched people moved with her; they confirmed her with glad yet suffering cries, "Oh yes . . . isn't it so! . . . Know me, God! . . . Hear the tongues!" and she was saying, "Anna-ballie-shillalioh! Bally-annie-shall-ibanny-oh! Oh, sha-mallay-ash-a-malley-she-nannie-oh!" over and over again, with the same limited variations. It was received as revelation.

She was alive in another world; and, lying in the dusty and coal-smoky grass between the tracks and the live area of light, LaVerne Dicely was quivered alive by the animal possession of all the listeners.

He watched and waited until the spell was broken, and Trillie Dee had sat down among the washed. When the meeting ended, he watched for her and he believed in an excitement of certainty that he would take her in his car to his will.

But she went away with another young man, who had played the guitar during the meeting. They looked sober and earnest, going up the street toward Main, with the great shadow of the guitar box between them.

LaVerne was disgusted.

For several days he let Trillie Dee alone.

He would go and sit for hours at Martha Rooks' soda fountain and stare at himself in the big mirror behind it, where the soft drink menu was written in rose-colored washable paint. He could turn his head without losing sight of himself in the glass. Martha served him sundaes and Cokes until he was drowsy. They hardly ever conversed; sometimes he offered his attention by becoming a jazz orchestra, all by himself, making poop and beep noises with his mouth, and tapping with his feet on the fake marble floor of the fixture, and scraping one hand on his corduroy leg, and jazzing the other hand with loose change on the counter top. It was an authentic representation of his feelings, and at such times Martha really felt intimate with him. She would make up her mouth and kiss the air in the accepted idiom of her time.

They were silent and comfortable together.

Sometimes they kissed, in the back room, while Martha blushed. She began to have a mental picture of him that was wholly different from what he really was. The heartless chemistry of love was effecting its delusive changes in her very view.

Then LaVerne heard that Trillie Dee was making a great success as a convert, at all the other revival meetings. She went the rounds, pounding her heart and confessing her wickedness as often as they would let her. It was always a ravishing performance; and she achieved a tiny little fame, and brought tears to old eyes and hot breath to young mouths among her listeners.

The Fords were parked under the cottonwoods every night.

Trillie Dee worked all day and took her wages to her father, who was silent, and looked wry, and had a legend, as any "eccentric" is likely to have in a small town. Somehow, long ago, the word had gone around that he was a German baron. The town absently believed it. He gave himself no airs, unless that of being remote in a small and teeming town were one.

In the evenings LaVerne and his crowd ranged the streets, the revivals, the countryside roads where cars stopped in the dark. It was the old repetition of the roving blood, LaVerne and his gang like the rascals of the Renaissance in Paris, exacting pleasure from the historic sense of privilege. They had privy knowledges. They got drunk together and stretched the boundaries of their permitted license. They dumped produce trucks that were parked near the trackside warehouses. They toured the revivals and mocked and cheered.

And they all knew that Trillie Dee was having a summer in which her stars compelled her strangely.

In her triumphs as a convert she found for the exhausting floodwaters of her emotions a way to burst. Her fantastic loveliness went very well with the role of the pleading sinner.

She came to look upon herself as the theater of a war between Christ and Satan.

She told about it in her strange tongue and with dancings of her beautiful body.

When LaVerne heard from one of his gang that Trillie Dee was going off after the meetin's with a new man every night, he felt a private strike of rage and renewal in his breast; but he pretended that he'd known it all along, and whistled an experienced tune.

But the next night he was alone and watching, outside the North Hill tabernacle, whose plain pine walls clapped and rang with the high doings within. It was so hot that he had to wipe his face now and then. He could see Trillie Dee inside, working and at love with her spirit; her face gleaming with silvery lights in the heat and the hard light of gasoline lamps; dancing the people with her into the state that would spell freedom from torment, whether about body, or soul, or love, or death.

A fat girl sat down at a piano without any front to it, and began banging a rapid rhythm out in primitive chords.

The listeners began to sing.

Trillie Dee swayed before them and shouted, with her eyes closed:

There'll be pastures bright with clover
  When He comes;
There'll be pastures bright with clover
  When He comes;
There'll be pastures bright with clover
When the long hard day is over
And Lord Jesus is my lover
  When He comes.

The piano tongued along, *bung*-bung-bung-bung, and the voices sounded like those of herded spirits in tired joy at the end of the hot hard work of life. The song dealt in terms of their earthly wants with the bright destinies of their desires. Another song said:

My heart is like a red, red rose,
My heart is like a living rose,
  Just like anyone's heart is
  That the good Lord knows!
My soul is like a big white bird,

My soul is like a flying bird,
  Just like anyone's soul is
That has heard the Word.

Now and then a hollow trumpeted fume of glee arose from some man's throat, confirming above the sound what they all believed.

LaVerne, in the shadows outside, smoking nervously, felt a lump in his throat at the possession within.

He was prickling with the impatience of lust.

He, like all the rest, was a creature of the hot, hot summer, and the eternally youthful trial toward God and life which knew so many different terms.

The high school principal and I had agreed several times that Trillie Dee was a complete fool in one direction. Now we had to add LaVerne Dicely to the category. He had recaptured her; and they were locked by all the pressures that overwhelmed them that summer, and for which they were essentially ready. Weeks went by and he never went to see Martha Rooks. Trillie Dee lost her job with my friends because if she came to work at all it was with such sleepy resentful eyes, such sluttish ways of laziness and pretension that she was insufferable. La-Verne revealed a cruel streak; took to bullying littler boys on the corner of Main and Arroyo streets; became glossy in some new snakelike way, his yellow tight curls oiled under the sunlight. Days long he and Trillie Dee would cruise slowly around town in his Ford "job" with the top down, stopping for Coke, under the immense old tree at the eastern edge of town where the summer sang in the leaves and the wings of bugs droned; or, again, pulling up in front of the movie theater on Main and merely sitting to watch the people go by at their hot duties of commerce and meager prosperity. The movie theater was two doors down from Rooks' Pharmacy.

Everybody saw what went on. LaVerne's own gang sneered at him.

So he couldn't take it when someone else went out with his girl, eh? So he had to monopolize her and snub everybody else?

They were envious and hated his easy powers.

They thought bitterly, "Let his old man's bank go phooey, and see what happens to him then! Nobody'll look at him!"

But Martha would still.

Her face became actually grayish, from ill health in her thoughts; she served her young public at the soda fountain and matched their wits with the proper wisecracks. But she had no rich sway over her own heart. Several boys dutifully flirted with her and took the conventional liberties with her when they were alone. Her agony made her honestly angry at them for it. They told her LaVerne wasn't worth all that. She admitted to herself for the first time in her life, but not the last, that this was perfectly true; and that it made no difference.

At the proper time in August the professional revival troupe arrived, set up their tent on the same corner, out north of the business blocks, a large empty lot with a towering hedge of salt cedar and many trees; rather a picnic ground, it looked. Just beyond it to the east, the open country began, though the town continued north and west for several blocks.

Trillie Dee and LaVerne went the first night. A huge crowd came.

The show was glorious. I sat there myself for a while. The star was a white-haired man with a kind face and merry blue eyes and a snappy suit. He laughed between every two or three words he uttered. His assistants were several young women made up prettily, and several young men, with slicked hair, confident baritone voices, and all the physical unity of cheerleaders in college. That's what they were, in effect. They played harmonicas, trombones, accordions, and one did a novelty number with a jazzy tin whistle, a child's toy, while one of the girls sang, in a baby voice, a semi-sacred verse about "Baby's First Prayer." It wasn't until the second hour of clever speeches and smooth harmony numbers that the devotional quality received release; but then the actors skillfully drew the audience into the performance; and in less than half an hour the whole tent was an orgy. Everybody making some odd sound of remorse, resolve, or desire; women wailing and fluttering their hands; men sitting with closed eyes, slumped bodies, and making lowing sounds like the hungry kine; while down in the mourners' space, the scented, slick boys tugged and yearned at the poor bleating sinners who sought something beyond their powers of recognition. The slick young men embraced and murmured, and winked, and stroked. The pretty girls of the troupe made noises of rejoicing. The kindly boss evangelist went from one to another, laughing hollowly and alight in his eye at the powerful miracle he was performing—the turn of a population from its daily sense into this scene of abandon and collapse. His power was sincere. At the moment when the ice in people's hearts began to melt, he always felt some surge of restatement, his life bloomed anew, he fed on its results. His eyes flared and glittered. His hollow laugh continued. I had seen possessions like it in hospitals. I didn't like it. I got up to leave.

Just then Trillie Dee stood up and began to go down the aisle between the circus chairs yelling and waving. I saw LaVerne reach out to hold her back, blushing in a rage. But he was too late. She was down there, and the handsomest and glossiest of the young men received her into Glory.

There was no denying the superb liveliness of the child, the lavish scatter of sparkling vitality she made; most of all at these, her idiot moments.

I felt very gloomy, almost like LaVerne, I suppose, at the odd combination that dwelled in her.

I drove off on some routine calls of the early night; and later, coming back, I saw the tent emptied and only one light burning.

A faint warm night wind was going through it. The salt cedar hedge was whispering warmly. The tent sides were not yet rolled down for the night. The hedge had received much of what had been generated inside the tent, I knew. There was a precise tapping of people's wells, in all the work by the troupe. Young men and women found the shadows discreetly enough, going out of the tent which was open all around. The hedge was a long whispering shadow far enough away, and not too far. Beyond that was the country of the open plains. Beyond that was our oldest mystery.

When you are a medical man, you are apt to think of everything that happens each day in terms of the consequences it might have.

After a while the consequences spring to mind, and carry no opinion, no sense of shock or judgment, simply recognition.

When fall came, and school opened, and the nights were a little cooler, and the summer's possession relaxed, and life turned more willingly to work, all these factors were reflected in the lives I have been talking about. It was as if a normal rhythm returned to the pulse, after a period of febrile agitation. You might say the town was well again.

Trillie Dee returned to school, and so did Martha, and LaVerne, and the gang.

The proper hours, the lessons, the pleasure in organization which young people feel, the worried love of the principal, a keen new show that everybody looked forward to at the movie theater, most of all the inexorable demands of contingency as against those of memory brought everybody back to normal ways.

Trillie Dee got her job back.

She worked soberly and worried about losing the heavy tan the summer had left on her, and which made her blazingly beautiful.

But now formal society was in force, with the school going, and La-Verne could not go with a girl who worked as a servant and who went to his same school; so he pleaded his need for her to Martha Rooks, in his own odd way, and she paid attention. He gave a little show for her in assembly one day, with his purple felt hat, with the half-inch brim. He made it into funny shapes, and put it on for her, each time with a new face. She finally had to smile at him. He pulled out his pocket comb and combed his hard yellow hair in triumph. Later he skidded his Ford to a stop by the sidewalk as she went down to the store to finish out the afternoon. She got in, and once at the soda fountain she had a chance to see him again as she *knew* he really was: his eyes not hazed with pink veins, but clear and loving; his face not buckled at the mouth in an insecure sneer, but cleverly smiling; his body not long and animal-frank, but graceful and modest.

They fell in with the autumnal mood, and had together a superior air of virtue and security.

Trillie Dee smoldered at them from the distance they preserved.

She said to anybody who would listen that she was dying to get to Dallas.

There was somebody in Dallas who would make them all sit up and take notice around here. He was just waiting for her. Let them look out!

But these fiery sentiments went oddly or not at all with her actions. Trillie Dee was claimed by normality again, and the early autumn went along through its cooling tempers; the plains were clear and exhalant of some sweet breath; the little town, or city as it called itself, prospered spiritually under the well-being of the weather; I had the sense of people happy, as we do receive that sense in the intervals of trouble and pain.

This is where it would be comfortable to end my story.

But one day in late September, Trillie Dee came to see me at my office. She had the tragic tact of a human being forced to utter the most painful realities. Her dignity was astonishing. She was bitter, underneath; but rather than show it to me at first, she assumed a face of social charm, smiling and posing as if to reassure *me*, when the roles were actually reversed. She confessed her suspicions, and only too readily was I able to confirm them.

We sat staring in silence at each other, and I feel sure the pulse of the spent summer was revived in her memory as it was in mine.

Then she began to talk, and told me in flat, curious eloquence of the things I have already set down; and my mind filled out the details when she talked.

She declared that her father would kill her if he ever found out about this.

She said he had one passion in life and that was his independence. If his daughter fell into disgrace, then the whole town would "have something on" him. She said quite soberly that she had nowhere to go. Then she snapped her fingers and licked her lips, looking infantile and exquisite, and declared that if she could only get to Dallas: the evangelist young man had left her his address; and she got to know him pretty well here, and she felt pretty sure that he . . .

Her cheeks began to redden at another thought; and she spoke of LaVerne Dicely, with the utmost hatred now. She also mentioned Martha Rooks, and, so to speak, spat upon her virtue.

"I think I'll know what to do now," she said, and stood up to go. Her eyes had a yellowish cat gleam and she was breathing deeply, consciously looking superb and making me want to laugh at this clumsy imitation of a movie star, which yet had its flashing style and physical loveliness.

I told her to be a sensible girl, and make her decisions slowly and carefully.

She asked if she might come back for advice when she had made up her mind. I said of course. She held out two dollar bills to me—a week's wages, I imagine. She had that sort of propriety—the only thing of her father in her character, I imagine; the pride of a poor person who insists upon paying for indispensable services. I handed the money back to her and said, "I'll send you a bill when the case is finished."

She squinted suspiciously, then snickered.

The next thing she did was that evening.

At half past six, when all families in town had got up from the supper table, Trillie Dee, in her finest clothes, strolled up to the house of the Dicely family, rang the bell beside the screen door, and demanded to see the banker himself.

The man's wife received her and fetched her husband. Mr. Dicely was more like an undertaker than a banker. He wore starched collars that stood away from his yellow neck, and his face was gray where he shaved, and his eyes were hollow with some permanent misery in shadows about them. His mouth was like a fold of skin over a skull, without the life. When he spoke it was oddly soft, and he cleared his throat often. I often thought he had a tubercular larynx.

He took Trillie Dee into his den.

He stared out the window at the front yard, where no grass grew, only wind-raked throws of gravel.

He never opened a conversation: part of his cheap and sinister strategy as a man of affairs.

Trillie Dee told him, first, that she was pregnant; second, that his son was responsible; third, that she wouldn't marry him if he had good sense; fourth, that she only wanted one thing.

Mr. Dicely looked at her and shivered. I could imagine the rattling dusty blow of the dried leaves of life which might go through him at any reference to passion.

In a very few minutes Trillie Dee left the room on her way out in triumph. In the hall Mrs. Dicely was waiting. She was a tall woman resembling her son—yellow hair, long spare bones, a cheek that burned quickly with hysterical flush. She detained the girl now with her pale hand and demanded to know what was up.

Mr. Dicely told her in a few ashen words, burdened with contempt that mocked the very pattern of a family.

Mrs. Dicely turned and clutched at Trillie Dee with her sharp fingers and nails.

They were fixed in a tableau of impotent furies when a noise on the stair landing made them turn.

It was LaVerne, trying to back upstairs without being seen or heard. He had been listening all the time. He couldn't get away without knocking into a mahogany pedestal that stood there with nothing on it.

His mother called upon him to come down and deny this horrible story.

This is just what he did.

But his father's dark and rubescent eyes pierced him like a bird's, a creature which with all its selfish pursuit of function still and without a sense of virtue recognizes a threatening circumstance.

The boy gangled and blushed and tried to wisecrack his way to safety.

But his mother perceived the hollowness of his efforts.

She turned and slapped Trillie Dee and began to cry and ran up the dustily carpeted stairs. It was one of the few two-story houses in town—white wood with stone corners, an unroofed porch, a shingled cupola, a short driveway bordered with stone cairns between which black chains were stretched; the whole sitting on a wide corner lot where there was no grass, and looming over that end of town on the very edge of the dwelling section. Behind the house, the grand, fair plains stretched away.

Trillie Dee came to see me late that night, and told me all this.

She exhibited money which Mr. Dicely had given her to go to Dallas on.

"And I'm going."

"Have you told your father?"

"No, I'll write him."

"Do you want me to tell him after you leave?"

"I guess so. . . . Say, that'd be keen!"

"All right, I will."

The train went shortly after midnight.

She was on it.

I heard it.

It gave me some catch of feeling. There was a certain bravery about it, though perhaps I'd be hard pushed to say exactly how. Perhaps to take the burdens of your very quality as simply as she did was the point. Anyway, the train whistled a long faint windy chord through the dark and I thought of the lighted windows and the silent spacious land; and Trillie Dee Spelzer setting out for Dallas, where she would seek and find and undertake further folly, without a doubt; and I thought again of how pretty she was.

But hardly that obvious quality of hers was remembered in the next few days, when the town was thoroughly sure of her flight.

She was damned and scolded everywhere.

People drove slowly by the gray board shacklike building on East Arroyo Street where Spelzer had his shop, and where Trillie Dee had lived with him. They looked to see if anything of this extraordinary performance were somehow *visible* about the premises, or in his face, chanced he to show for a moment.

I wondered where the truth leaked out, and was dumfounded to discover that Mrs. Dicely had gone clacking to her friends with it, not mentioning her own son, of course, simply saying that Trillie Dee had been caught *doing* with a high school boy, and run out of town for it. She had a withering wryness about her, an instrument of strength, some decadent current alive in her, a desperate and miserable woman.

I went to see her and told her that I knew the truth, and that it was not fair to go around with a half-truth to the damage of only one of the parties implicated.

"The surest way to save my family's name," she said, "is to be the first to tell the facts, without telling the circumstances."

"But if you must know, Mrs. Dicely, the whole town knows it is LaVerne."

"Yes, but they aren't admitting it."

There was some truth in this.

The older people were simply not agreeing with the truth: that a son of Banker Dicely (to whom they all owed so much, in both cash and power for their small concerns) had created a scandal.

"There isn't anything anybody can tell me about my relatives, doctor," said Mrs. Dicely, with hot spots on her cheekbones. There were tears in her eyes. She seemed to pour at me all the unsatiety of her womanly dreams and their crude half-fulfillments.

She was wry and starved and difficult.

I went off and left her.

I didn't know then that she had cancer.

I contrasted the way she behaved with Spelzer's behavior the morning after his daughter left for Dallas on the night train.

He heard what I had to tell him with a critical smile on his face, his teeth gently chewing a pencil, his head nodding.

If he really were a German baron in unexplained exile, he could not have more clearly disdained showing his sentiments to a stranger with unpleasant news.

But a night or two later his shop began to burn.

The town was stirred and summoned by the light in the sky and the noise of the fire truck.

Spelzer wasn't around. The gray boards of the shop, the decades of shavings inside, the very dryness of the life it reflected seemed to blow upward in the strenuous relief of flames. In the crack of the wood and the calling of the firemen and the glasslike break of the hose water in the blackening walls, everybody kept looking for Spelzer. But he was gone. The next day it was understood that the fire was his *congé*.

The acts proceeded to their ends.

A year or so later LaVerne and Martha Rooks married. It was jubilantly understood in the town that the boy had decided to give up his college career and not wait any longer for the girl he had been in love with since they both learned to toddle. A sentimental seizure followed. The happy proprieties were indulged to an almost hysterical degree. There were showers for the bride, and vestigially obscene festivals for the groom; and on their return from the honeymoon (which they'd spent in Galveston, seeing for the first time the mystery of the sea and the communion of two human spirits, and understanding neither, like many a better man or woman), the "younger married set" set upon their brick bungalow at ten at night with flashlights, tin pans to beat, rattlers to whirl, and ticktocks to fasten on window frames: a shivaree, in which all the crude impulses of savage and naïve society are formalized, given sanction by numbers, and license to make sport of the generative act, without violating any local laws. The newly married couple had their lights out; but somebody cried in the street: "They're there; I saw them drive in and go to bed; don't give up!"

It was a very important occasion in their communal life.

The crowd went on making noise and peering.

Inside, LaVerne and Martha whispered in humorous terror. He was all for pretending they were not home; hiding his head, as he always did in danger. But she, who felt secretly outraged by the vulgar nuisance and its instinctive meaning, yet saw how it was meant in friendship, and that to refuse the shivareers' entry would be hostile and even ungracious. So, blushing and hanging her plump head, which was so pretty and still maidenly, she got out of bed and shivered, put up her hair and threw an overcoat of LaVerne's on, and went out to the little cement stoop, reached up, and turned on the amber coach lantern that was their "porch light," and called: "Come in!—I'll make coffee for us all!"

They surged in, dropping their bushmen's implements on the bald little lawn.

It was a tribal union.

Everybody spoke of how sweet Martha was, and, once you got La-Verne over his odd and fumbling bravado, how nice he was.

He retired with some of the men and produced a gallon of bootleg corn. The girls and Martha had coffee until the drunkest husband came back to the front room with its tinted wrought-iron and sponged-color walls, and they all decided to "make whoopee." Martha drank too, and it made her weep. But somehow it seemed like a night of nights, and the scheme included so much that was reassuring and proper because it was always done to honeymooners; so she tried not to think of the noisy and unattractive part of it, but only of the confirmatory part of it; and she thought of Trillie Dee, knowing a great deal more than anyone thought she knew; and the evening seemed to become a triumph of goodness, in Martha's eyes, for this was the thing, the way of life, that poor Trillie Dee could never know.

The first winter passed, and everyone spoke of how gay the town was that year.

When spring came, it got around that LaVerne Dicely's wife was going to have her first baby, and that he himself was drinking heavily. I knew (as I knew so many unutterable pieces of news) that he was consorting with the prostitutes on South Ranger Street. He would go off to Fort Worth and Dallas, too, on "business," and come back looking ill and resentful. He worked at managing his father's cotton gin west of town.

In summer the season of the Holy Ghost broke over the town as it always did.

Memories were revived now and then by the tokens of emotion which had had such visible results the previous summer.

In the march of the seasons this coming of holy men and the lofting of their obsessions and voices resembled some perfectly natural phenomenon, the heat which brought forth desert creatures, the song of the locust, the cry of the prophet in the plains.

Martha had her baby, a boy.

I took care of them, and both were brave and everything was quite usual.

The generations stretched away in the future, and the grandparents on both sides tried to possess what they could of it through the favor of the baby.

But he was like his mother, sober, yet simple; questing with his eyes, and uncomplaining at finding so little.

The years came along.

There was another baby at the younger Dicelys.

The winters were windy and full of loneliness for those who stopped to listen to those great travels of hurrying air across the plains.

The summers were hot and needful and dry.

One day at the movie theater the town was amazed and stirred by a face on the screen.

The heroine of a serial film was perfectly and unmistakably Trillie Dee Spelzer.

I hurried to see it as soon as the news reached me.

There she was, under the name of Laura Marsh, performing those breathless antics with all her old zest and childlike intensity, all her liveliness magnified and yet somehow made stony by the odd light of the photograph. She rode horses and avoided cliffs and was swept down canyons, and she wrecked railroad trains and saved lives and shot a man and stabbed a mad dog and performed countless other fascinating stunts through the duration of the serial. When she looked out into the theater of her hometown during one of her silent soliloquies (this was before talkies) and stared right at us, many people were heard to say it gave them quite a turn!

There was a tremendous amount of speculation about the actress.

What do you suppose she makes?

How did *she* get into pictures?

"Where does she *get* that?" wondered many a mother with a daughter of her own.

So, revisiting us, Trillie Dee had perhaps one further set of consequences for our lives.

LaVerne now showed much of his mother's spirit. It was the winter she died, and it took her months of wretched agony to do it.

LaVerne drank more and more heavily, and had gradually been eased into the role of the town bum by the very people in whose "social set" he moved.

Mrs. Dicely had insisted on going to see one installment of Trillie Dee's serial.

This was the supreme tribute, we all felt.

It dramatized the dying woman's will, and was the peg upon which many appeals were hung and presented to her son: to stop drinking and doing all the other things that distressed his sweet little wife so, his lovely children, his aging father. They *knew* he didn't *have* to work for a living, like everyone else. But if he went on he'd kill himself . . .

He was so uncertain of his wants and his desires that he would agree readily with the last person he talked with, and then go on his way.

He was fattening at the belly, though his arms and legs were still gaunt, and his face and yellow curls foolishly young.

Mrs. Dicely died in April.

One of her last utterances had some fierce grandeur in it, I felt, and I've never forgotten it; for even to a doctor, there is sometimes a prophetic and terrible weight about words that come from the last burning in the human intelligence. She said, "*You'd* never've admitted a thing, *either*."

She looked at me straight, after this, and her face was pathetic and dreadful, the effort to communicate.

There was no use telling LaVerne the defensive words which confessed so much. He came to the funeral weeping and drunk.

Martha had her third baby a little later.

Warm weather, and the hot heaven of summer.

The tents and the lanterns, the cry and the bellow, the prayer and the kiss, all the summer possession returned.

So did Trillie Dee, or rather, Laura Marsh, in another movie. I said to myself, seeing it, that in the film she was just like the old Trillie Dee of the revivals: the same emotional sprees, done with the same artful and commonplace genius for projecting her body, bearing the very same results; only, as her movie popularity grew, the results affected a million men and women, perhaps, where in my town and in my time it affected some one only.

For LaVerne went that summer drunkenly down to Jesus at the mourners' bench.

It might have been in memory of Trillie Dee.

He was a violent convert.

He moaned and sang and smashed all the liquor bottles he could find, anywhere.

He was now a terror in his house, instead of a familiar, disgusting responsibility.

So the bitter seed of Trillie Dee's planting so long ago meant something strong, now that it had grown in them; even though it meant something different to each.

To LaVerne, was it all the beauty he had once touched, not in recognition but in lust, and had now lost?

Was this a reminder, this convergent return of her likeness, and the shoutin' of the preachers?

Was Trillie Dee right, all this time?

Whose virtue?

Martha Rooks loved her children and cared for them and hoped for them until she felt sometimes her breast would open under the weight of her image of a proper life for them. She *knew* that everything she had was a synonym for the proper life. She would tell them over so often—a lovely home; three dear little children, so clever and so pretty, so promising; a devoted circle of friends; a husband who was everything everybody said he was, but still a man whom she knew in humility and perhaps that was really the core of love . . .

But a haggard sense of guilty judgment always came alive behind these proper beliefs.

Martha had a lot of character, at last, if not much of the grander and more spectacular style in people. I remember thinking when she was a high school girl that I couldn't have imagined what she'd turn into. That now seems unintelligent of me. For life had written down its facts upon her and her spirit had illuminated each one as it came. I suppose she was the one person in town who might have understood poor Mrs. Dicely's valedictory sentiments, but I never told her what that bitterly faithful sentence was. Martha was a proof of the real goodness there is in people. It is best undisturbed by the mysterious intelligence of bitterness, such as her late mother-in-law's.

And if everybody felt, even Martha, that Trillie Dee had cheated them, had broken all the rules, and had received no penalties, this was still another way in which her destiny wielded its influence.

What they felt was that Trillie Dee had seized life, and condemned them to existence.

It is so easy to console people, if they really know what troubles them.

But as for me, though it wouldn't have made sense to tell anyone so, I remembered the vanity of blame and the words of Socrates, who, when informed that his fellow citizens had condemned him to death, replied, "And Nature, them."

1940

LINDA WEST ECKHARDT
Christmas 1918: Sennicot Place

I f good times could be measured in jars, the summer of 1917 was bliss. Dazzling jars of tomatoes stacked up all across the east window of my mother's kitchen, reflecting a garden that had outdone itself. The earth had yielded up its bounty in such abundance that our kitchen was a frenzy of activity. Tomatoes, beans, corn. With every lid my mother snapped down, she knew the winter would pass by painlessly.

Deefy, our cook and gardener, returned again and again, laden with bushels of vegetables. He would be whistling. A strange, unearthly tune. Deefy had lost his hearing to smallpox as a child and his memory for sound had faded over time until the music he made while he picked beans was as strange as the songs of angels. But since he had come, two years before, our garden had flourished. Down on his knees, watering each plant from a coffee can, Deefy could sing each seed into flower and fruit. We were very nearly overwhelmed with produce that summer.

Everyone in the household except my father was pressed into service. I, at eight years old, standing on a stool, scrubbed jars with hot soapy water. My younger brother, Alfred, who was only five, was kept on the jump, bringing coal for the stove, then taking the clinkers to the ash heap. Even Irish Maureen, the hired girl who cleaned house and usually stayed out of the kitchen both by custom and by some unreasoning fear of the sound of Deefy's voice, was soon seated in the kitchen, a paring knife in her hand and a big bowl of plump ripe

---

tomatoes in her lap. At the helm, like a captain of a great sailing ship, stood my mother.

She was swaddled from head to foot in white. The fine lawn dress that she had painstakingly embroidered that spring was covered by a full white apron. Her long, luxurious hair she caught up in a white headkerchief until you could only see dark damp curls at the nape of her neck. She seemed to be everywhere at once. She could get more work out of you than anyone I have ever known. She had a vibrant energy that equaled the force of the garden and she could charge those under her supervision to work as hard as the earth itself. She was such a driving force in our family that father used to say he believed she could turn a stampede with only a look.

We worked like Turks that summer, fusing our own efforts with that of the soil to provide for ourselves a winter of comfort. With every jar put up, we gained a kind of peace. The kind of peace that prosperity brings. We had a faith in the future that could be measured in mason jars. We were happy in the summer of 1917. All of us. Mother. Father. Alfred and I.

We had lived on the Banner Ranch in the Texas Panhandle as long as I could remember. The ranch was owned by a British holding company and my father was foreman. He had improved the herd in the same way my mother and Deefy had improved the garden soil, so that we had, in the summer of 1917, more cows and calves than anyone could ever have imagined being produced on that sea of grass. Stepping out the kitchen door to catch the cool evening breeze, you could look in any direction and see flat green pastures dotted with peacefully grazing mother cows and calves.

And, for once, nature and fortune were in harmony. Not only did we have a bumper crop of calves and yearlings, but the market prices were higher than ever. Black Jack Pershing, whom my father had met the year before in the bar of the Menger Hotel, had landed the first troops of the American Expeditionary Force on the shores of France in June of that year. The great gnawing hunger of an army had driven cattle prices to unprecedented heights.

My father worked on a kind of commission basis, so that the bounteous herd of that year, when sent to the generous market, yielded up an inordinate amount of money for a thirty-four–year–old cowboy to hold. My father knew that the time had come. He could buy his own place. He could take this seed money and begin to husband his own herd. He was a tall, lean, taciturn man with skin as brown as a saddle. He had the bearing of a prince. He had light-blue eyes that could, by turn, be as opaque as a milk-glass bowl or as dazzling as aquamarine.

The very idea of being his own boss had charged my father and his eyes became an electric blue. Such blue eyes that when they turned on me—I can see them right this very moment—a kind of transparent blue flame shining out from his very soul, it quite took my breath away.

He had met Pershing the year before in the bar of the Menger Hotel. Pershing knew then, fresh from his own battle with Pancho Villa, that we would soon be in the war. He told my father so. And we'll be counting on you boys, he had said to my father, to give us good Texas beefsteak. We can lick those Boches. I know we can. Why, with the help of fellows like yourself, we'll clean up that mess in Europe right away. And you will make yourself quite a little mint of money in the process. It takes a lot of meat to move an army. You'll see. It will be good for your business. He had clapped my father on the back and moved on, a charismatic man attracting younger men to himself like filings to a magnet.

My father thought Black Jack Pershing was a prophet. He had told this story a hundred times. He believed what Pershing said. And he knew he stood on the brink of an opportunity that might not come again in his lifetime. It's an ill wind that blows no good, he told my mother. I believe this war is going to blow us right into the possibility of owning our own ranch.

They were sitting at the dining room table. Father had stacks of gold pieces from the sale rising before him. I tell you what, mother, he began, pushing one short stack of gold in her direction. I will take this, he waved at the rest of the money before him, and make a down payment, and you keep the rest, and I'll just bet you that by next Christmas, what with the market prices holding, the war and so on, we can all go to San Antonio and visit your mother. How would you like that? You just take that money and put it away and it will be your Christmas present. He waved a finger of admonishment toward her. Not the first year. Not this year. But next year. I promise you. We buy that place. Work real hard. And by next year, we'll all get on the train and go to San Antonio for Christmas. How would you like that?

But my mother was afraid. She wanted us to stay put. We had security. We had a salary. My mother's people had been dreamers and she had suffered from the excesses of fantasy with a father who pushed life out in front of him like a torch. He had always been able to spit a tale of grandeur and riches that were just over the next hill. He had been able to ignore the hardships his family endured at the moment. In fact, my mother told me later that one of the things that had attracted her to my father was that he seemed to be just the opposite from her dreamy, fantastic father who had dragged his family from pillar to post. My father, the prudent parsimonious cowboy, working for a corporation and doing a good job of it, had seemed just the ticket to my mother. To discover, ten years into the marriage, that, once opportunity beckoned, he might risk everything they had for real estate scared my mother. She knew about bankruptcy. She knew about shame. She was frankly terrified at the prospect.

She sat, staring at that stack of gold coins he held out to her. It was a fact that she hadn't seen her own mother since before Alfred was born. She looked from father, to Alfred, to me. She was weakening.

In looking back on it, I can sympathize with her position. We had a big old comfortable house filled with heavy dark furniture. The kind of furniture with legs like those of a very fat woman planted firmly and holding her ground. There were big dark rugs that my mother and Maureen would roll up twice a year and transfer to the clothesline, where they beat them violently to discharge the dirt. Keeping dirt and disorder out of life was a passion with my mother. It was as if the outside world, with its unpredictable weather and ever-present capacity for calamity, could only be endured by living in an orderly immaculate house. Between my mother and Maureen they kept that tall, narrow house as clean as a crystal.

Whenever one of the owners would come out, he would stay in the front bedroom that was reserved for that purpose. This bedroom was as well set up as any you'd find at the Menger, the furniture all poised to spring on ball-and-claw feet. The owners liked my mother. She kept a good house. She managed the inside as well as my father managed the outside, and between them they had made the Banner the showpiece of the properties owned by the holding company. My mother liked her role as manager. When the owners would come, bringing guests, my mother could fire Deefy and Maureen to such excesses that the food and lodgings were better than a five-star hotel. She hated to give that up. She was a born executive.

But my father preferred animal husbandry to corporate management. Paradoxically, he was much less ambitious than my mother. Give him a little place, his own string of cows and calves, and maybe one hired man, and he could be happy. It was my mother who had the grand designs.

But in the end, he convinced her. Even though she had never heard Black Jack Pershing talking intimately into her ear, she began to imagine that he had whispered to her and she began to dream the dream with my father. Her own secret desires spun out to a fine home and fine guests of her own. She could envision herself, stepping off the train next Christmas, the wife of a cattleman not simply a cowboy. She agreed to go along with his plan to buy his own place.

The XIT had been broken up by that time and my father was able to make a down payment on a parcel he called the Sennicot Place. I was fully grown before I ever called it anything else. Before I ever understood that the word *Sennicot* was, in fact, Syndicate and referred to the original ownership of the XIT. The deal was to close the end of September and we made preparations to move on the first day of October.

There was a great flurry of excitement. My mother supervised the packing as efficiently as she supervised everything else. Every jar of tomatoes, every can of beans was packed as carefully as if it had been bone china. She set aside the dining room for our things, and boxes and barrels began to stack up. By the time moving day arrived, we were ready. Deefy and Maureen and two or three cowboys came to help and we began loading our things onto the wagons.

Our true situation soon became apparent, for when we had loaded all our things onto the wagons, the house looked little different than it had before. Most of the stolid furniture and fine china belonged to the company. Maureen, whose only filial tie in America had been with my mother, was sniffling and weeping the whole day. Once we had removed all the boxes from the dining room, Maureen began rolling the rug. That stays, my mother snapped. And dry it up right now, she continued. My mother knew that if Maureen kept crying she would soon join her. Once we had everything loaded, my mother took a final turn through the house. She came to the wagon, her face as long as a fence line in flat country and boarded the seat beside my father. We struck out leaving the big gracious Banner, unchanged except for the improved garden, and felt as small and vulnerable as a calf on its first day of life.

It took three days to get there. We moved due west, cross country, cutting and mending fences as we went along. My father was as joyful as if it had been a vacation. My mother was guarded, only allowing him to infuse her with hope at odd moments. Alfred and I thought it was quite a lark. We had both longed to go on roundup and traveling along, riding in the chuck wagon we had borrowed from the Banner, trying to sing along with Deefy's odd songs—we had borrowed him too—it all seemed quite the holiday to us.

At last, we arrived. The house was nothing more than a line shack, used previously for cowboys who simply camped out here to avoid the exigencies of weather. There were two rough rooms besides the original dugout. I remember my father turning to my mother as if he'd just presented her with the Taj Mahal and saying, here it is. Our very own. My mother looked as if she had just been struck by a rattler. At last she regained her composure and replied, well we won't need much furniture here.

For the first three days we camped out because the house was knee deep in old cans, rotting tack, yellowed dime novels, and dirt. My mother and Deefy cleaned that house with a vengeance. Deefy even gave the walls a coat of whitewash, inside and out, so that by the time we were ready to move in, the house seemed purified, purged of its former purpose, and ready to receive a family, here to make a home.

Mother supervised the unpacking, taking her final opportunity for executive action by ordering Deefy around until he, who could hear little and tended to do his thinking out loud on the mistaken assumption that no one else could hear either, took to calling her Old Bossy. My father thought this was vastly amusing and for months after, whenever mother would seem to swell with a desire for her former managerial status, would tweak her just a little by repeating the phrase.

The single most important aspect to the unpacking was the careful stacking of the home-canned vegetables on open shelves in the room that was to serve as both kitchen and living room. By the time those white walls were lined with red and green and yellow jars, the place took on quite a cozy look. Finally, Deefy brought in an overflowing bucket of coal for the stove. We were all set. We had food for the winter, we had coal for the stove. The beds were piled high with mother's handmade quilts. Everything was in readiness for our new life.

Deefy and my father struck out for the Banner on the morning of the fourth day to move the cattle my father had purchased from the company. We were left alone in the little house. Mother, Alfred, and I. Until we heard the sound of lowing cattle shuffling across the prairie about a week later, the three of us were struck as dumb as Deefy. We spoke in whispers. We were suddenly shy in the presence of that immutable silence which is the plains country.

As the sound of those cattle shuffling across the grass came nearer, the three of us hung on the fence. It was as if time had suddenly stretched out beyond bearing, but at last my father and two cowboys came into view, gently prodding the newly purchased seed herd into our pasture. These were cattle that had been carefully bred up from the Banner stock and my father looked at them as contentedly as if they had been his own children. Father even purchased a bull from the Banner. Not the best one they had, but a good one. He was a fine, heavy limbed animal with a dark-red coat, as soft and curly as a baby's hair. Even my mother got excited when she saw this fine bull being coaxed into the pen beside the house. Their bull. Their pasture. Their pen. She looked over at my father and gave him a fond, proud look.

My mother named the bull Brewster after the banker who had loaned my father the money to buy the Sennicot Place. Brewster the banker had said to my father, I am doing this against my better judgment, Mr. Edmonds. Your string is too short and we both know it. But I have a hunch, if there's ever a man who could make it, it's you. I'll back your bet. Yes, I will. We were grateful to Brewster the banker. He knew the caliber of my father. He did.

Within the pen where the bull was kept was a pothole overflowing with water, for the rains had been plentiful that summer. We called the pothole a lake after the fashion of Panhandle folk who identified anything more than three teacups of water a lake. My brother, Alfred, and I trapped tiny frogs that hopped in the mud at the edges of the lake. The frogs were a very good sign, my father said. They were a late hatch and signified the long growing season that was still in effect.

We soon settled into a routine. I started to school, riding our old dappled mare, Dixie, to the one-room schoolhouse that was just on the next section. Alfred and mother bought some chickens and built them a chicken house, nothing more than a lean-to, really. Father was kept busy with the cattle. We had a good many calves that year. The market prices were holding.

For fourteen months things went along so. But as time passed, you would have thought we were standing in a downpour for the talk turned more and more to rain. During that fourteen months, a cloud never once even cleared the horizon. The sky paled and shrank back from the hot dry winds that blew across the prairie. The lake evaporated until it was little more than a mudhole with a small glassy center. The grass withered and browned. The cattle ranged every inch of our place, taking more and more grass. By the time the second autumn came, my father was getting worried.

Our resources were limited and father and mother had to make some hard decisions. They were huddled around the table. Mother kept the books and she had a double entry ledger open before her. The situation was that, although cattle prices were up and holding, our herd was poor because of the dwindling grass. Mother wanted to sell. Father wanted to hold. He looked like a gambler at a poker game, his eyes gazing off into the distance, considering the odds.

The way I figure it, he began, this drought can't hold out forever. If we get some moisture over the winter, the cattle will put on weight and we'll make out better next year. But what if the prices don't hold up? my mother asked. With this war? my father snorted. They're likely to be higher than ever. Perhaps, she said. Perhaps.

But how will we get by? she asked, staring at the ledger. My father cleared his throat and squirmed in his chair. You remember that Christmas money I gave you? he asked.

Yes, she said.

We'll just have to borrow from ourselves. He began talking faster and faster as if he could overtake her thoughts. We can buy some cottonseed cake to hold the cattle until the rains break, and some stores for the kitchen, and some coal oil for the lamps and we'll be just fine.

Christmas? she asked.

He looked at her, his blue eyes suddenly cold. That will have to wait.

The decision wasn't difficult. It was just hard. My mother went to fetch the sock that she had kept under the mattress. She dropped it before him. What about coal? she asked.

He was untying the knot. We'll have to see, mother, we'll just have to see.

Once father returned from town the results were clear. Mother and Alfred and I would have to take over the job of gathering fuel for the stove. And so began a search that was as relentless as the wind. Mother, Alfred, and I would drive the wagon to a pasture and comb it clean for cowchips. We threw them into the wagon. Once my brother, Alfred, complained and my mother slapped him hard, leaving a red mark on his cheek. This was a slow, relentless task. My mother no longer wore starched lace-trimmed dresses. She now covered herself with layers of rough gray wool. Her face became as expressionless and gray as her clothing. Silently, bitterly, she gathered cow chips. The situation was now plain. Although my father's life had changed but little coming from the Banner, my mother's life had changed drastically. She missed coal.

Sometimes, at night, I would catch a glimpse of my mother, sitting before the fire, examining her hands. Hands that had in the past been most skillful at fine needlework and tatting. Hands that now were grimy and growing with blisters that resolved themselves into calluses.

Almost as serious as the loss of grass had been the failure of our first garden. Without Deefy, without rain, and without a plot of ground that had been improved from its original clay structure by the patient addition of manure, we literally had no garden that year. Not that we hadn't tried. We had all worked, and hauled water from the lake, and done our best. But the hot droughty winds had withered whatever seedlings we had managed to coax from the ground. We were left, at the end of the first summer, with a dwindling number of jars we had brought from the Banner. Father bought a hundred-pound sack of pinto beans, cornmeal, and cases of canned tomatoes from the store on his trip using mother's Christmas money. That would have to suffice.

Indian summer held and held. Even into the middle of October it was so warm that we were sleeping on cots, out in the yard. But one night, when the moon was full, we heard the mournful honking of geese, in search of a resting place. We sat up in our beds and watched, as motionless as statues so as not to disturb the wild things. They circled and called and conferred and decided that the tiny mirror they saw in the earth was, indeed, a viable resting place for the night.

Guests, my father whispered out into the night. As the geese circled lower and lower we could hear the powerful beating of their wings. They churned the air downward, settling on the surface of the water with a gentle whoosh. Within moments the little body of water was covered with graceful long-necked Greater Canadians, Speckled Bellies, and Snows. Weary travelers indeed, they soon had their heads tucked under their wings and were fast asleep. We lay back in our beds, dazzled by the company. There was a long silence yet each of us was wide awake, stirred deeply and in a way we couldn't explain by the presence of these wild things. At last my father spoke out into the night. It means an early winter, he said. Not one of us replied, for the tone of his voice carried such a warning that there was no appropriate answer.

Even before dawn, the wind changed and the first dry norther of the year slammed into the yard. Quickly, quickly we all dragged our beds into the house. Mother stoked the fire and we were soon warming ourselves. Outside the wind rushed in as if it abhorred the still warm air that had stood in its place. The little house groaned and leaked. Cold air seeped in faster than we could stoke the fire.

But the first norther blew through and the weather warmed again. It had been, it seemed, a false alarm. However, every day more birds flew south, over our house. Sand Hill Cranes, Curlews, ducks, and geese. My mother and father became silent. There was a kind of hush over our house. As if each one of us, from some unspeakable preliterate part of ourselves, knew that the worst was yet to come.

On the tenth day of November, a few innocent-looking fleecy clouds passed across the sun. Well, maybe at last, my father said, we'll get a little moisture. If we'd get just one good, wet snow, the grass would flourish in the spring. We watched the clouds gather and coalesce until the enormous sky was a sleet-gray bell clamped over the earth. A few flakes of snow began to fall lazily and melted as soon as they hit the ground.

My mother had lit the lamp, even though it was only four o'clock in the afternoon. She was picking beans. We ate beans morning noon and night now and she was at her regular chore, sitting in a circle of yellow light, hunting through the stack for rocks, twigs, and broken beans. Outside the snow was drifting down, as silent as death and beginning to stick. By seven o'clock the wind had picked up and by midnight it was blowing a gale.

We awakened the next day to a solid-white world. There was no horizon line. No landmarks. White ground. White air. We couldn't even see the chicken yard. Against my mother's wishes, my father began pulling on his heaviest clothes to go out and tend the cattle. He had an old bearskin coat, stiff with age, that he pulled on over layers that seemed to include every garment he owned. His face was grim with determination as he opened the door and plunged into the swirling white snow. That was, I expect, the longest day of my life. With nothing but the howling wind and the swirling white beating against the windows, the three of us waited in the house, unable to see anything, feeling smothered by the snow.

Long about 5:30 we heard a stamping at the door. My mother rushed to open it and there stood my father, sheathed from head to foot in ice. He came in stiffly as if his very joints had frozen. His leather-brown cheeks had brilliant red patches of frostbite on them. He was armored in ice and it took all three of us to peel off his gloves, his boots, that coat rigid as steel. His eyes were like pale marbles in a field of red. He was so cold he could hardly speak.

He had managed to drive Brewster into the chicken house. He had located two mother cows who had chosen this day to calve. Dead, he said. But the bulk of the herd, he had never found.

Well, there's nothing to do now but wait, my mother said, pouring another cup of hot coffee for him. Nothing to do but wait. For three days and three nights the wind raged and the blizzard blew. Snow piled up against the north side of our house until the cold seeped through, wet and penetrating. The wall sweated and wept until Alfred and I were kept busy, wiping up the gathering pools of moisture.

Father took a rope from the house and staggered out to search for the lean-to. The wind shifted and changed until the snow seemed to blow from all directions at once, but at last he returned, following the rope. Brewster was safe, he said. Taking his cottonseed cake and content.

On the morning of the fourth day the wind stopped as suddenly as it began. There was a stillness beyond all stillness. The earth was blanketed in white. The sky was blue. At least four feet of snow lay on the earth, sometimes stopped by a fencepost, drifted into mountains to which we were unaccustomed. The entire landscape had changed.

Father ventured out to check on the cattle. When he returned that evening, he was buoyed. Not too bad, he kept saying. Not too bad. About a 10 percent loss and with all this moisture we'll make that up in the spring.

Snow in the Panhandle rarely stayed on the ground long and this moisture would do nothing but help. It's an ill wind that blows no good, he said again to my mother. We've got plenty of cottonseed cake to make it through. It will be all right, mother. Mother was tending to his face, covering the angry red frostbite with Sloan's liniment and lard, a treatment that soothed and comforted my father.

What we couldn't know, living through this bout with nature, was that fortune had turned in an unexpected way, for on November 11 the

Germans had signed an armistice at Compiègne. The war was over. The cattle market, right at the moment we were in the process of fighting the weather to save the cattle, was collapsing. By spring, the market was in such disarray that it would hardly be worth it to drive cattle to market. But we knew none of this, huddled in our little snow-bound house on the fourteenth day of November.

Even though the blizzard had passed, the temperature hovered around zero and the snow stayed on the ground. Right into December. Father was living with the cattle. Feeding them, rounding them up to bring them closer to the house. Shepherding his flock and gathering his resources.

On the fifteenth day of December, it began to rain. A freezing, silent, solid rain that fell and formed sheaths of white ice on the backs of cattle. We could see them now, they were mostly herded into the pasture beside the house. They turned their backs to the north, huddled up against the fence, and tried to stay warm. My father was moving among them, tall on his white horse, feeding them, taking calves to the shed and back again to nurse. He knew, in every case, which calf belonged to which mother. He worked from dawn to dark. Once the night fell, the rain turned to outright sleet, icy razors that pelted the cattle, and by morning at least half of them were dead. Dead from exposure. Some frozen in their tracks. Some with their mouths frozen shut. Some with their feet frozen in place.

Father was working like some sort of mechanical man by this time. He never slowed down. Tying the dead cattle's feet together, he used the team to drag them out of sight. He butchered two and he and my mother managed to put up the meat so that we would have something to eat from it—at least. They both worked furiously. I, left in the house with Alfred, was in charge of cooking the beans and keeping the fire stoked. That was the time I learned to make coffee. It seemed as if the work was the only thing that kept my father going. He never stopped moving. My mother never stopped moving. There was more activity than I had ever seen since we had put up vegetables from the garden.

Brewster, who had weathered the storms in relative comfort, being tied up in the lean-to, developed a nose that ran with thick yellow mucous. My mother discovered this one morning when she went to tend the chickens. She came back to the house, pale with fright. It was as if Brewster were our last hope. Mother boiled water, father applied poultices, but nothing could reverse the pneumonia. Despite their best efforts, Brewster sickened and died.

At last the weather broke. Christmas Eve no wind and no snow on the ground. There would be no presents that year. There would be no Christmas tree that year. There would be no train trip to San Antonio. There would only be two days' respite from the work. That was to be our gift.

Long about one o'clock in the afternoon we heard the sounds of a team approaching. It had been seven weeks since we had seen another living soul and we all watched as the speck grew larger and larger until it became clear who was coming to call.

It was the Baptist preacher along with a deacon and two ladies of the church in Plainview. Townfolk, they came into the yard all smiles and concern. Mother rushed out, glad for company, and invited them to step down. Father shook hands with the preacher. The outside world had at last reached us. About that time the ladies began reaching into the back of the buggy and hauling out baskets of food. There was fresh-baked bread and turkey and cranberry sauce and pies and I never knew what all. When it came to my father what they were doing—bringing baskets of food to the poor—he turned as white as a dead man. It was the last straw. He had worked and labored and kept up the good fight and had lived through the tortures of nature. This was more than he could bear. He was no candidate for charity.

This usually taciturn stoic man turned and bounded into the house. He returned with the shotgun drawn and shouting hoarsely at the top of his lungs. You take your dad-burned food to somebody that needs it. Why I've got more beef hung than you ever saw from one Christmas to the next. Get off my place. Get off my place. He was shucking the shotgun.

The ladies of the church were stricken. The preacher was sputtering, Brother Edmonds, Brother Edmonds. But father menaced those Baptists back into the buggy. They left quickly, the preacher lashing the team furiously.

We sat down that night to our usual dinner. Pinto beans and corn pone. I looked at the empty shelves that had once groaned with home-canned produce. How I longed for a real Christmas dinner. Why didn't you fry me some meat? my father asked my mother. He was at the end of his rope. We've got meat to burn and you know it. My mother was too exhausted to reply.

It took the preacher to make us see how truly vulnerable we were. Although nothing was said, we knew we couldn't hold out much longer. Our time on the Sennicot Place was running out.

Christmas Day dawned bright and clear. A day of such exquisite beauty that it took your breath away. As if Nature itself, guilty for its caprice, was bestowing a gift on our little family. The ground was spongy with moisture. Moisture that would, no doubt, produce a bumper crop of Buffalo grass by spring.

Shy as a bridegroom, the most self-effacing Santa Claus that you ever saw, my father produced from some secret place presents he had bought at the store, way back in the fall, with mother's Christmas money. Toy trucks, a tiny doll, and horehound candy for Alfred and me. Yard goods for my mother, some brown velveteen. We'll get you to San Antonio for Christmas, Mother, I swear it. We will, he said. My mother began to cry. She hugged the cloth to her breast and sobbed.

Next year will be better. You'll see, said my father.

My mother cooked a great haunch of beef for dinner that day. She even produced three jars of vegetables from the Banner that she had saved. Beans, corn, and tomatoes. We ate them all. It was the grandest feast I ever had. And for dessert, we sat around the fire sucking on horehound drops. I have never had a Christmas dinner to equal that one.

Sometime along about March, the Banner offered my father a job as foreman of a spread in Kansas. He managed to dump what few cattle we had on the market, getting back ten cents on the dollar. He leased out the place, telling himself and my mother that the job with the Banner was only a temporary thing. And we took ourselves back to the comfort of the company.

We loaded our few possessions on the train in Hereford. Mother, Alfred, and I rode in the coach. Father rode in the boxcar with the horses and goods. I looked over at my mother. Her head was resting on the back of the chair. Her eyes were closed. She had on her new brown velveteen dress. For the first time since the summer of 1917, she looked relaxed.

The next winter, the company sent my father to San Antonio to a sale. We all went along, visiting our grandmother and having a merry old time. But my father had changed. He had retreated within himself and was now more silent than ever. The frostbite scars on his face were a reminder of the winter of 1918. Whenever one of our San Antonio cousins would comment on the scars, he would seem to withdraw, to a place where no one could reach him. He would not speak of his time on the Sennicot. He had taken a long shot. He had gambled on nature and fortune. He had lost the bet. He bore himself with a new humility that was excruciating to see.

My father continued to work for the company for eight more years. He and my mother turned the Kansas spread into the pride of the properties. Then, suddenly, he contracted undulant fever and died. He was forty-three years old. I was called home from college at West Texas State. Alfred dropped out of high school. The company was understanding. They gave us plenty of time to clear out. The new fore-man was a single fellow and he bunked with the cowboys while we helped mother to pack. Once more on the train we returned. Returned to the Sennicot Place. Our home. Our only home. The home that our father had provided for us. Where we have lived ever since. Mother, Alfred, and I.

1984

A. C. GREENE

The Girl at Cabe Ranch

T he road turned into a puzzle of trails going off left and right. I asked the boy, Harris, if he knew which was which and he shook his head, yes.

The woman at the Chamber of Commerce back in Toller said Harris knew the country better than anybody except Uncle Bartlett, whoever that was.

"I don't see how you can tell these ruts apart," I said to the boy as we bounced along in the pickup.

"Just know 'em," he said.

I had picked a bad day in a bad month in a bad season to make the trip. Fifteenth of July. It couldn't have been hotter and it couldn't have been drier. One of the ranchers in Toller said if it rained now all the cows would die from fright. Why had Uncle Sam picked such places for western history, or why had I picked western history as my field when there are so many more timely and relevant disciplines?

After the Chamber of Commerce woman recommended him I found Harris and we made a deal. He said we'd better go in his old pickup truck, the roads might be a little hard on my Chrysler. I thought about the Chrysler now, parked at the courthouse square, its air conditioner doing me no good.

We went north out of Toller on the state highway, across a wide, hot mesquite prairie. The tires on the concrete highway sounded to me like sizzling flesh and went bumpity-bump, bumpity-bump as they hit the

"The Girl at Cabe Ranch" is from *The Highland Park Woman*, by A. C. Greene (Shearer Publishing Co., 1983). Copyright © 1983 by A. C. Greene.

tar-filled joints. The sound took the place of the conversation I wasn't having with Harris.

The ranch road turned off the highway ten miles out of town, and now we had driven another five or so over Cabe ranch land.

"I don't see any cattle," I said.

The boy didn't answer but kept glaring down the road like that old picture of the heroic railroad engineer in a storm you used to see.

I hadn't been told the boy's full name. Just Harris. Something Harris or Harris Something; the woman at the Chamber of Commerce didn't say and neither did Harris.

He looked to be about twenty. He might have been a little older. The older I get the less I can tell ages, especially younger ages.

"Any of the Cabes live out here?" I asked.

"Mart Cabe does," he said.

"I don't think I'd want to live out here, even if I owned it all," I said.

"He doesn't own it all. He's got two brothers own part of it."

"Well, I wouldn't want to live on it if I had ten brothers."

"He's just got two."

I told myself I had asked for that comeback, but I knew Harris hadn't meant it as a retort. There was no need for me to be so damned contemptuous of this country. It was mine, too, or I was its. I was born less than fifty miles from the Cabe ranch.

But something had gone different in me, and where boys like Harris whoever-he-was had taken up 4H clubs and horses, I'd taken up history and books. Pretty soon they couldn't understand me and my history books, and I didn't try to understand them and their horses. So I left. That had been a long time ago. Twenty-five years ago, at least. A long time to be away and come back.

The sun was shining from all directions. The ground was red and dusty, the grass was brown and dusty; but then, "brown is the natural condition of the grass," an old emigrants' guide once said of this country.

The land rolled away in hills which fell into breaks and draws. You could see for miles. It was all rocks and grass and red clay dirt and the only trees were mesquite bushes, seldom taller than a man—and the ranchers killed even those because they kept the brown grass from growing.

But I found myself settling into an excited sort of contentment as I rode with the boy, letting him pick out the way from among these twisting, all-alike trails. I breathed deep, feeling the hot, dry air going down into my lungs. The air is the best thing about that country, to me.

The boy was wearing an old Stetson Double X with the wings folded up rodeo style. When I was a boy a rancher wouldn't have been caught dead wearing his Stetson that way. Television even tells the cowboys how to dress. Harris was nice looking, neat around the neck, and his hair clean. He had to have some pride to keep his hair washed, working on the ranches away from everybody like he did.

"Is that the Cabe house over there?" I pointed to a gray, wooden structure, needing paint, with a lone tree beside it.

"That's the Mulkeys'. Mr. Mulkey's the foreman." The boy looked over at the Mulkey house. "The Cabe house is a lot nicer."

We drove around the gray house. A television aerial rose above it and a red Ford was parked in the carport. With a few neighbors and a coat of paint the whole scene would have fit neatly in a suburb. A woman waved at us.

"We going to stop?" I asked as the boy slowed down.

"Not unless you want to," he said.

I laughed. "You're the boss, Harris. You're taking me where we're going."

We didn't stop. The road, if you want to call it that, circled the house and went into a big pasture behind it. We came out of the pasture through a cattle guard, then dropped down the side of a hill and were alone again. Hot it was, but magnificent it was, too. You could turn in any direction and see no trace of the hand of man—except for our pickup truck.

About two miles from the foreman's house the ruts parted like railroad tracks at a switch. One set went right, through a tall gate with a sign on it: Horsetail Ranch. We took that one.

"The name sounds like a dude ranch," I commented as we started down this new branch of the road. Once again my humor failed to reach Harris.

"Horsetail's a big outfit. The Cabes've got land all the way into Young County."

Sometimes I would lose all traces of the road as the entire landscape turned into a brown panorama. Here and there another set of tracks would spill off, disappearing into the grass like a ship's wake. Then we came to a level stretch and I could see tall, green trees about a mile ahead.

"That must be the river," I said, more or less to myself.

"That's the Clear Fork," the boy said. "It runs all year."

"Is it drinkable?"

"Reckon so. I've done it enough. Gets gyppy when it's low. Drains from the gyp beds out on the Plains." He paused, then asked, "You thirsty?"

Before I could answer he said, "We'll stop by the house and get a drink. They've got a good well."

The Cabe ranch house surprised me. I was prepared for something like the foreman's house or possibly something huge and Victorian out of a western movie. It was neither. It had age and dignity and that unexpected beauty one finds now and then left from the frontier. It was tall and stood high off the ground. It was built of rock, old and carefully masoned. A square cupola surmounted the roof, and there were six tall, slender chimneys, three on the east, three on the west, standing in rows. A white, wooden fence was around the yard and four lines of old, big trees outlined the rectangle of land where the house stood.

"That is tremendous," I said in admiration.

Harris drove the pickup to the back door and honked the horn, then got out. "We'll go in," he said.

An old brown hound yelped and barked at us from inside the fence as we walked up to the gate. The boy leaned over and unlatched the gate from the inside and said something to the old hound. He waited to snap the latch on the gate after I went through as though I wouldn't know how.

We walked up to the big, deep porch along the back side of the house. The door opened and a blonde-headed girl came out, looked at me, then at the boy.

"Hello," she said.

"Hello, Sid," he said back. "How about some water?"

She looked at me without answering him.

"Oh. This is Dr. Powell." He made a motion toward me.

"I'm Sidonie Cabe," she said, deciding to hold out her hand. It wasn't hard and dry like some country hands are from work and weather. But then, it wasn't soft and moist either.

She was a good-looking girl. About eighteen, I guessed. She had on shorts, and her long, slim legs were brown. She was barefooted and her toenails were painted bright red. It looked freshly done.

"Come in," she said. "Mother and Sis are over at the Fultons'. I'm here by myself."

"Where's your dad?" the boy asked.

"He's gone to Denver to an auction. He and Zene Mulkey flew."

"It's a little lonesome out here by yourself, isn't it?" I asked.

"She doesn't mind," Harris said to me, then to her, "Dr. Powell's from California. He's come out to see the fort."

"Are you a history teacher?" she asked.

"Sometimes," I said. "Right now I'm writing a book on some of the old outposts in this part of the country. Doing research."

"Oh," she said, and gave a little shrug. "I'll fix some cold water."

We went into a big room that opened off the kitchen. There was a well at one end of the room and the wall of the kitchen was rock.

"This used to be the sleeping porch a long time ago. Before air conditioning," the boy said. "Mr. Cabe says the well was enclosed because of the Indians."

I doubted this but didn't say anything. You learn not to disturb family legends when you're a historian. It looked to me as if the well had been dug close to the house for convenience and whoever added the porch room enclosed it for the same reason.

The girl brought out a big enamel pitcher of ice water with some glasses. Suddenly I felt as if I could drink it all.

"I've lost my hump," I said, over my third glass.

"Your hump?" the girl looked toward me.

"That's what we used to say when I was a kid. Your hump was what kept you from getting thirsty. We thought a camel's hump was full of water."

"Did you live out here?"

"I was born in Taylor county."

"You don't live there now though, do you?"

"No. I left to go to college and never moved back."

"Mr. Cabe says the stone for this house came from the old fort," the boy interjected.

"I was wondering if it didn't," I said.

"There's some frosted glass around the front door that's supposed to be from the fort, too," the girl said.

"How far is the fort from here?" I asked.

87

"Not far. Just across the river over there," the girl said, pointing out the direction of the back door.

"Can we drive it?" I asked.

The boy answered. "No, you've got to wade the river. Road's been washed out for years."

The girl turned to him coldly. "You can drive there, too. You can go through the Lambert and drive there. You just came the wrong way to get there in an automobile."

The boy grinned. "We're not in an 'auto-mobile.' We're in a pickup."

"All right, or in a pickup either." She reached out a bare, red-toed foot and kicked at a magazine. She must have been reading it when we drove up.

"It's pretty over there," she said, not looking at either of us but concentrating on the movement of the magazine with her toe. "I go there all the time. Ride over. Especially the graveyard. Down where Spring Creek runs into the Clear Fork. Daddy says it's dangerous because of the copperheads but I go there anyway."

"It's too hot," the boy said. "Too hot and muggy." He looked toward me. "The fort's on a flat that backs up against the hill. It's a lot lower than it is here. It doesn't get any breeze."

"Yes," I smiled in historical superiority, "General Pomeroy used to complain in his letters to his wife about how hot it got. 'Sweaty as a well,' he wrote to her."

The girl looked up. "Was General Pomeroy really at this fort . . . the famous one?"

"He was commander here just before the Civil War. Spent nearly two years."

"Well, good," she smiled. "I've lived here all my life and I never have known for sure. I thought it was just a kind of legend."

"I knew it," the boy said, without looking at her.

"General Pomeroy might have spent a lot of his time right where we're sitting," I said. "He wrote his wife that when the nights were too hot, he'd take his gear to what he called 'the Red Bluff beyond the River' and sleep."

"I know where that is," the girl said. 'It's the place around behind the cowsheds. It's real high above the river."

"That may be the spot," I told her. "Of course, in a hundred and some-odd years things can change a lot. The river may have cut the bluff down years ago."

"It doesn't change that much around here," she said. "Nothing does."

"I don't think that's the bluff," the boy said.

"Why?" she turned toward him fiercely. "You don't know anything about it. Dr. Powell said it was. He knows a lot more about it than you do. You're just an . . . an ignorant cowboy," she bit her lower lip, "that's all you are. You don't want to be anything else."

"I still don't think that's the bluff," the boy said, not looking at her. "General Pomeroy would have had to come plumb around to the shallows to get across. He wouldn't have walked that far just for a cool place to sleep."

"He had a horse," she said tautly.

"He wouldn't have saddled up a horse just for that."

"Things were different then. He had aides and servants to saddle his horse. You heard what Dr. Powell said. The river might have been different."

She looked at me as if she were demanding I support her statement.

I ducked out. "All he wrote his wife was that he oftentimes took his bedroll and spent the night on the red bluff beyond the river. I just assumed it might be here, if the fort lies below this land."

The girl looked at the boy sullenly. When she turned back to me I could see tears gathering on the bottom rims of her deep blue eyes.

"Do you write for the movies or TV, Dr. Powell?" she asked.

"No, just history books. I don't even write historical novels."

"And you've come all the way out here just to write a history book?"

"Partly. It's sort of a homecoming for me, coming from near here. I've got to go other places, too."

"If I left here I'd never come back," she said. "I wouldn't come back to write a book or do anything else. I'd go away and I'd stay wherever it was I went."

"Why, this is wonderful country, Miss Cabe," I said. "The old fort over there, just across the river . . . it has a lot of romance connected to it. General Pomeroy's son Catlett brought his beautiful young bride here on their honeymoon. She was daughter of the governor of Virginia."

"He brought her here to live?" the girl asked.

"Yes, and she was just about your age. Cat Pomeroy was a soldier, too. A lieutenant under his father."

"I'd die before I'd let a man bring me to a place like this," she said.

"Well, I'll admit, she didn't stay long. She went back to Virginia."

"Did she divorce him?"

"Oh, no. She just went back there to have a baby and live while her husband was on frontier duty."

"I'd have divorced him," the girl said firmly.

"You wouldn't have done any such thing," the boy said suddenly. "You'd have come out here and lived at that fort with him and liked it, heat and all. And you wouldn't have run back to Virginia just to have a baby, neither."

She shook her head violently. "I would have, and someday when I leave I'll show you. I'll never set foot here again."

The boy watched her. "You couldn't do that. You can't even spend a weekend in Dallas without wanting to come back. Your daddy told me so. He said, 'I can't get a room on the west side of the hotel or old Sid'll spent all her time gazing out the window tryin' to see home.'"

She was crying. "That's a lie you made up. Every word of it. It's daddy wants to come back early. Not me."

"And you wait," the boy continued, "when you go off to that girls' college this fall, you'll be home Christmas and you'll say, 'Oh, Harris, I don't want to go back.' You'll flat hate it, being gone from here."

"I won't!" she was crying hard. "I'll go away and get married to somebody in another place. Anywhere but here."

The boy watched her. They acted as if they were going to do something more, but finally the boy stood up and grinned.

"Well, I guess we better get going."

"I suppose we'd better," I said, standing also. I felt to blame for the little domestic quarrel, as it were. "Thanks again for the water, Miss Cabe," I said. "You saved our lives."

Harris stood there running his tongue over his lips. "All right," he said, then turned to me and motioned, "come on," and walked out the door.

"I'm sorry, Sid," I said. "I didn't mean to start a fuss between you and Harris."

She shook her head, and her hair fell golden around her face. She wiped her tears away with her bare hand, pushing her hair back at the same time.

"You didn't start anything, Dr. Powell. You just got in on something. You better go on before he runs off and leaves you." She tossed her head and looked at me. "He's just a cowboy. All he thinks about is land and cattle. That's all he wants out of life. Just like my daddy. He won't

90

even get any more education. Thinks he knows everything he needs to know." She looked at me sadly. "I'd marry him if he was different."

I took her hand, "Goodbye, Sid."

"Come back again sometime," she said, sniffing.

The boy was seated in the pickup when I walked out. His rodeo hat was pushed down on his forehead.

"Why don't we wade across from here?" I asked.

"Naw. Get in. We'll drive."

"I thought you couldn't get there driving?"

"You can if you go through the Lambert."

"Have we got time?"

"It's not far. It's no further than through the Cabe if you start for there in the first place."

I smiled. "There must not be any cute girls at the Lambert ranch."

My humor failed again. "There isn't anything at the Lambert but cattle and cowmen," he said. "It's a big spread. A genuine ranch, not anything TV dreamed up. I'll guarantee you, I'd like to think I'd ever run something just half as big as the Lambert."

I decided I'd better make my amends to the boy, too.

"Harris," I said, "I apologize for what happened. I didn't realize I would bring up a sore subject, telling about the old fort."

"You didn't. We go through it all the time. In fact, you might have done her some good. That story about the general's son bringing his bride out here . . . she'll go to thinking about it and next time I see her, she'll be telling me how much tougher she is than some Virginia aristocrat." He nodded his head in a strong affirmative. "And, by God, she is."

He wheeled the pickup around and we bounced down another gravelly hill to take up the pursuit of a pair of faint creases in the dry grass. It didn't look like a road to me. But the boy knew where he was going. I leaned back and let him drive.

1983

DAVE HICKEY

I'm Bound to Follow the Longhorn Cows

"I'm bound to follow the longhorn cows until I get too old;
It's well I work for wages boys, I get my pay in gold.
My girl must cheer up courage and choose some other one,
For I'm bound to follow the longhorn cows til my race is run."

—A Cowboy Song

When the white sun had spun into the pupil of the sky, as it hung at the top of its trajectory between the two horizons and then began to fall into early afternoon, the old man found himself trapped in a bathtub of tepid water on the second floor of his ancient house. He flailed about for a few moments and then he became quiet and listened to the long winds shushing through the empty corridors and rooms of his house, which was Victorian in design, having two stories, an attic, a storm cellar, spires, lightning rods, weather vanes, cupolas, traceries, and an occasional leaded window; it rested on the plain like a child's block dropped on an immense crazy quilt, patched with green and yellow, an old house, but the interior had been completely modernized, and the bathroom in which the old man sat was paneled with cool blue tile.

He had seen ninety summers, as the Comanches, who were gone now, would say, and he was the only person in the surrounding country who was older than the house. On the old man's first birthday his father had driven four stakes into a bald ridge on the prairie, and began to lay the foundation, and the old man had grown up with the house. It was part of all his memories, the nucleus of his childhood, the point of departure and the point of return for the many journeys of his youth and manhood, for, during his first half-century, the old man had been a rambler and a heller. But unfortunately, unlike his house, the old man

---

"I'm Bound to Follow the Longhorn Cows" was previously published in *Riata*, Spring 1963, pp. 12–23. Copyright © by Dave Hickey.

could not be modernized, except by the use of what he called "contraptions," his false teeth, his electric wheelchair.

He was just a shriveled man with gray eyes whose sight was still keen, with a yellowish-white mustache drooping below a swollen pock-marked nose that still smelled well enough. He had only a few fringes of white hair on his head, and there was more growing out of his ears than around them, but his hearing was still better than most since he knew what to listen for. He still had the use of his senses, but ninety is an age when senses can be a burden, for your body no longer responds to them. It would have been a blessing if the old man had been a little deaf, or a little blind: then he could not hear the hooves clopping beside the stable, or see the Mexican cowboys ride out toward the pastures where the white-faced cattle dipped their heads slowly in the heat.

At the age of sixty-five he had lost his teeth and his virility, and hadn't mourned his teeth for an hour; he put them in a bottle on his desk. At the age of eighty his right arm was crippled with arthritis, and at the age of eighty-six his legs gave out. They refused once and forever to clench a horse's side, or even to support his weight, though he was a small man. When this happened, his son, who was born when the old man was fifty, bought an electric wheelchair for his father, and, after several interviews, hired a pretty blonde nurse with heavy breasts and a slow smile to care for him. For the next four years the old man spent most of his time resting on a couch in his second-floor bedroom, watching his land, watching the seasons and the sun change its face. Sometimes the nurse, whose name was Berta May Kuykendall, would read the newspaper to him, and once a week she bathed him. . . .

Berta May had left the old man's face covered with a lather of soap, and it dried into a crust in the first few minutes, while he sat there, immobile, not knowing what to do. Finally he decided to remove the soap by lifting his knees and sliding down into the clear water. His buoyant heels and buttocks leisurely rose and fell as he let the water creep over his chin and climb in a prickly line across his cheeks. He lifted his good arm and freed the dried soap by rubbing his sand-grained face. His skin felt better, but the taste of soap still hung about his gums. Berta May had let one soapy finger slip into the old man's mouth as she fell. He sucked his saliva into a cud and spat vehemently into the bath water.

Berta May lay where she had fallen. She had been scrubbing the old man's neck when her eyes had widened. Her hand jumped, a soapy finger slipped into the old man's mouth, and she had collapsed. She sat for a moment shaking convulsively. She had cried something in surprise and then fallen back, her head striking the tile like a clay jar. And she had died, so quickly it wasn't even sad, sprawled on the blue tile with her blue eyes looking upward, her skirt caught up around her thighs, and one white arm extended so that the hand rested on a crumpled pile of clothes.

The clothes belonged to the old man's son. As Berta May had wheeled him down the hall they had met him coming out of the bath. "I have to fly to Dallas, Pa. I'll see you tomorrow afternoon," he had said and run down the steps three at a time. Now his jeans, his denim work shirt, and his wide-brimmed straw hat lay in a little pile between the toilet and the bathtub, and the girl's hand seemed to be pointing to them. A scrap of a breeze lifted Berta May's skirt, revealing another inch of her thigh.

The bathroom curtains billowed white above the old man's head, and the smell of alfalfa, incredibly sweet, swam into his nostrils, only to be cut by the lingering fumes of the soap. The alfalfa wind died quickly, like a breath sucked in, and becalmed the curtains. The old man heard the starched linen crackle faintly as it collapsed. Then he became aware of grasshoppers clicking in the hot grass of the lawn. Outside the window the lawn sloped down to a barbed-wire fence where the hay fields and pastures began and continued into the horizon, but the sill was two feet above the old man's head. All he could see by looking upward was a rectangle of blue sky.

It irritated him to be able to move with such relative freedom in the buoyancy of the water, and yet not be able to climb out of the tub and into the wheelchair which stood by the bathroom door, but he knew he couldn't. He pulled in his lower lip and clamped it with his gum. Before him the pale image of his body undulated on the surface of the water. His legs were thin and hairless, and the skin on his ankles and thighs had a yellowish cast; his narrow chest was covered with white hair that bristled in patches out of the water, creating little patterns of surface tension. His body (which in its time had mounted many good horses, and many women as good as Berta May) was just a stringy bag of flesh. He glanced at Berta May's nylon-sheathed legs, and then slowly looked away.

Just a few minutes before she died, they had heard the Estansas'

94

Chevrolet clatter by the house, had heard Manuel's special honk which he gave every Saturday when he and Señora Estansa headed for town.

"I can tell you two Mesicans gonna be drunk tonight," the old man said.

"Oh, Mr. Cotton," Berta May said. "Now how do you know that?"

"Well, I'll tell you little girl, I done a little cowboyin' in my time, and whenever *I* got to town, it sure wasn't for no tea party."

"Mr. Cotton, I bet you were a wild one."

"That I was, in my way. I drank a little whiskey, and chased me a few girls might near as pretty as you," he had winked at her. "I ain't gonna tell you if I caught 'em or not."

Berta May had laughed as she bent over and scrubbed the old man's neck. He looked down the V of her blouse and watched her hanging breasts quiver as she laughed. What a sweet hussy you would have been, he thought, and cast a furtive glance down into the water where everything was still. And if the old man had ever cried, which he hadn't, he would have then; he would have clenched his fists and let the hateful tears, squeezed like vinegar from his clenched eyelids, crash down over his cheekbones; he would have dropped his toothless jaws and howled, then or any of a thousand times when Berta May with her soft hands was bathing him or changing his clothes. He would watch her narrowly as she went about her business, as a newly broken horse will watch the wrangler approaching with the bridle dangling from one hand, trailing in the dust. He would decide that she was teasing him, that she was flaunting herself, but closeted in the back of his mind he marked a secret calendar from Saturday to Saturday, when he was bathed by Berta May Kuykendall, who bent forward so casually. Then he would try to convince himself that it was a good thing, nature's law, that old men and young girls could not get together, but never did. And *now* the heart beneath those breasts had stopped, the valves had sucked closed, stopping the surge of blood that flushed her cheeks and made little patterns of red on her neck, and the darkness in her veins, where her blood eddied into stillness, closed around her sight. She had fallen very heavily, not at all as a girl should fall, onto the blue tile, with her blonde hair sprayed around her head. . . .

And so he sat there for a long time, not thinking anything, knowing all along that the day was Saturday, and that the Estansas had gone to town to get drunk, that his son was relaxing in flight somewhere between Sonora and Dallas, in the blue air, and that he, like some god-damned relic, had been left in Berta May's care and that she was stiffening on the chilly tile, but not formulating these thoughts in his mind, not admitting their consequences, until the room began to fill with golden light that poured through the bright window like water from a sluice. It was only then, when he knew the sun was falling, that he accepted the fact that the tub was his prison. Its white slick sides described his boundaries and confined him. He, who owned three hundred sections, who had ridden to Montana and back, might as well have been in a life raft in the middle of a golden ocean, or in a coffin.

But deep in his marrow it was not fear that the old man felt, it was inconvenience; the habits of his last four years, the last fifteen hundred days, plucked at him more urgently than any terror: More than anything on God's green earth he wanted, *desired* even, to be on his couch by the window, dry, in soft pajamas, his knees covered with a Navajo blanket. He wanted Berta May to rise up and read him the newspaper while he watched the prairie change colors, or he wanted his son to come into the room and talk to him, a little dully, about a new cattle deal, or oil deal, or the prospects for the cotton crop. For his warm bedroom was twenty steps away from the bathtub. Behind the blue-tiled wall, one door down the upstairs hall was his couch being warmed by the falling sunlight with the Navajo blanket folded at its foot. He shivered. . . .

It startled him for a moment because he thought he was afraid of dying there, ending his century in the bathtub, but it just irritated him; the whole idea filled him with indignation: to have to spend the night in the *bathtub*! He wasn't afraid, but he was very nearly mad. He lifted his good hand and twisted his mustache, twisting the damp hairs and poking the end into his mouth. "Crap!" he said aloud.

Then, when he dropped his hand, making a little splash, he realized that the water had become chilled. Three hours. With a little effort he lifted his left leg, watched it appear like a continent bursting from the sea, draining, and with his toe he turned on the hot water faucet. The burst of water burned his heel, and so, maneuvering his foot, he turned on the cold faucet and settled back to enjoy the warm surge of water around his feet and up his legs, the tingling when it reached his crotch.

When the edge of the water's surface began to sting like the touch of a hot razor, he turned off the water, and no sooner had the last drop pinged into the tub than a muffling silence settled around him. It pressed against his eardrums and drew sweat from his bald scalp. But the silence, in itself, wouldn't have bothered him, for he had spent a large portion of his life in silence. But it was the noiselessness, the noiselessness of an empty house, and different from the silence of the high plains. Out there, there were distances in the silence, crystalline depths; it had size, magnitude, but it didn't make a man, or a man on a horse anyway, feel small. Somehow the two feet between the stirrup and the ground put a man's head among the stars, if he was young and made the silence right. But in the house where the silence was cut into dusty cubes, divided into a thousand little silences . . .

He grasped the side of the tub, pulled himself into a sitting position, and to the golden room, the dead girl, and the cavernous house he shouted:

"I'm big and I'm bold, boys, and I was big and bold when I was but nine days old. I'm the meanest son of a bitch north, south, east, and west of *Sonora*, Texus. I've rode everything with hair on it and a few things that was too tough to grow any hair. I've rode bull moose on the prod, she-grizzlies, and *long* bolts of lightning. I got nine rows of jaw teeth and holes bored for more, and whenever I get hungry, I eat stick dynamite cut with alkali, and when I get thirsty, I can drink a risin' creek after a goose-drowner plum dry and still have a thirst for a little Texas whiskey cut with cyanide. Why when I'm cold and lonesome, I nestle down in a den of rattlers cause they make me feel so nice and warm!"

He took a long breath and continued at the top of his lungs. "And when I'm tired, I pillow my head on the Big Horn Mountains, and stretch out from the upper Grey Bull River clean over to the Crazy Woman Fork. I set my boots in Montana and my hat in Colorada. My bed tarp covers half of Texus and all of old Mesico. The Grand Canyon ain't nothin' but my bean pole. But boys, there's one thing for sure and certain, and if you want to know, I'll tell ya: that I'm a long way short of being the Daddy of em all. Cause he's full growed. And as any fool can plainly see, why boys, I ain't nothin' but a young un!"

Ho! Drunk in Tascosa or Abilene with your hands behind you holding to the bar, bellied out and hellraisin', stinking of two weeks' sweat, bad whiskey, Bull Durham, and cowdung, with a whole skillet of mountain oysters under your belt. . . . The echoes of his voice wandered for a few moments down the halls and into some of the empty rooms of the old house; then, one after another, like pebbles falling into a stream, they dropped into silence. (Shards and flecks of the yellow light glittered in Berta May's eyes.) There was the silence again, but the old man felt better for having shouted.

He had composed that brag, and a lot more of it he couldn't remember, when he was a boy, seventeen, nineteen, he couldn't remember now, but when he had followed the last of the big herds up the trail through the Indian Territory into Wyoming and Montana. It was something to do while you rode in the drag and chewed on the cloud of dust that billowed from the herd of long-striding cattle who walked steadily with their heads down and their wide horns dipping rhythmically. But most of all it passed the time on night watch after the herd had been thrown off the trail. The old man could remember himself, young Jerry Cotton, sitting in the saddle, there in the tall darkness, feeling his pony breathing, its barrel expanding and contracting regularly between his thighs, listening to the sleeping cattle snort and bluster in their dreams of new grass. There was nothing to do but lean on the saddle horn and compose brags, or rather compile them, adding an occasional flourish of your own, putting them in the order in which the words fell right. It was the kind of thing to do in silence. Or he could count the stars which hung like diamonds on fire around his head. (And he counted the stars so often, and in such detail, that he used to tell his wife: "Judy, I got so I could tell you the date, tomorrow's weather, and who your grandmother was, just by looking at the stars." And she would always say: "What if it was cloudy?" "Then I could only tell you tomorrow's weather and let you worry about the date and your grandmother, which you ought to know anyway.") Or he could sing songs, which he did, in a thin voice that was a little unsteady, but good enough for himself and the cattle. In his prime he had known eighty-five verses to *The Texas Rangers*, some of which he had composed himself.

And so, as the surface of the water grew placid around him, old Jerome Cotton shuttled these memories through his mind, selecting the ones he liked and discarding those he didn't—(and also those dealing with women, in respect for, or at least because of, Berta May, whose feet encased in sandals stood up awkwardly at the ends of her exposed legs). He reflected that he liked these memories, but he was not such a damn fool as to say that there was anything good about those days except that they were the days when he was a young bull and on the prod. He had sold his longhorns and bought white-faced cattle when they produced more beef, and when the railroads came, and hadn't wept one tear for the old rangy cattle who could live on anything and tasted like it. He and his wife had nearly starved when the drought came and the Depression on top of it. He had taken Mr. Roosevelt's money, gladly. When the oil came, he found some, more or less on his property, a good deal of it, and when irrigation was practical he irrigated and planted cotton and alfalfa, but by then George was running the land. But his son didn't get excited about leaving land fallow and taking Mr. Truman's money, or, though he was a Republican, Mr. Eisenhower's, or Mr. Kennedy's.

Whenever some old coot would get to talking about the "good old days" around the table, Jerome Cotton would lean forward out of his wheelchair and say: "I'll tell you what, sir, there is not one good thing about eating dust all day and gettin' rained on at night unless you're young." But by damned if you were young . . .

It became dark in a moment, as it always does when the air is clear, and a square of moonlight appeared on the door opposite the window as if a switch had been snapped. The wreath of white hair around the back of his skull dripped onto his neck, and little droplets traced cold paths down onto his narrow shoulders. He slid again down into the tepid water and, resting his chin on his shoulders, he watched the square of moonlight on the door until he could perceive it moving downward toward Berta May who was stretched in the shadows.

It was an exercise in patience. It kept his mind off his stomach which was tightening painfully, excreting unusable acid, waiting for food, wanting food. He watched the square moving and finally he thought about food: *enchiladas covered with cheese, frijoles, tortillas with steam rising from them, which you picked up gingerly, smeared with butter, salted, poured hot sauce on, folded, bent so the sauce would not run out, and stuffed into your mouth while they were still hot. There was an art to folding tortillas, you had to do it quickly or the thin circles of corn meal would cool, and dextrously or the hot sauce would pour into your lap. And when the sauce burned your throat, when you could feel it burning all the way down to your stomach . . . He could see Señora Estansa silhouetted in the kitchen door holding a big plate of enchiladas and chili con queso . . .* His chin fell forward into the water and awakened him. It frightened him a little that he had fallen asleep, so he reached up with his toe and flipped the handle which let the water out of the tub.

This amused him for a few minutes: listening to the gurgling water and watching his dark body appear like islands growing out of a sea of mercury. But then he felt his weight returning to press him into the bottom of the tub. His head became hard to manage; it seemed to roll erratically on his white shoulders, and his good arm, when he reached up to pull three towels from the rack above his head, was as heavy as a log. But he laboriously dried himself and the inside of the tub as well as possible. His elbows and knees made thumping and clanging noises as they collided awkwardly with the porcelain, sometimes causing little pinches of pain and making red flowers bloom and fade before his eyes. But as he worked in the darkness he was not altogether unhappy; he enjoyed being without his contraptions, controlling what he did, even if it was only drying a bathtub from which he might never escape, in which he might wake up dead. "This is a hell of a thing for a man ninety years old!" he said to the dark, and a hilarious vision of himself being buried in the tub built itself before his eyes: there he was, arms folded, in a blue suit, resting in the tub. He chuckled.

When the tub was as dry as he could get it, he folded a towel and placed it beneath his head. As he closed his eyes he reflected that the towel was a damn sight softer than some saddles. But it was no good. There is no one in the world, he realized, as naked as a naked man in a damp empty bathtub, and there is no place which is more uncomfortable to sleep in, when you are naked. His shoulder began to ache, as did his arthritic arm. His hip bone was thrust cruelly against the stone-hard bottom of the tub. But worst of all, his manhood (his "gentleman" his Granny had called it). *It ain't no gentleman now*, he thought, *wouldn't stand up for nobody*. It lay damply against his leg. When he rolled over, if it touched the porcelain, he awoke with a start; if he rolled the other way it became uncomfortably wedged between his legs. *If he could only get out!* He grasped one side of the tub with both hands and, with a wrenching movement, began to lift the dead weight of his body. Flares of pain pulsed through his bad arm and the flowers returned whirling before his eyes. But he was almost up, he had almost raised himself high enough to flop forward out of the tub, when he saw dead Berta May Kuykendall, and his bad arm slipped. He fell, striking his chin on the edge of the tub and slithering and squeaking back into its dark maw. He curled in the bottom of the tub with his eyes closed and his breath coming in cries. He knew the side of his chin would be black with a bruise in the morning. *On the other side of the white wall, Berta May rested with her white face framed in the moonlight, lips slightly parted. Her hair flared out to one side, as if windblown, and her eyes flickered in the silver light.*

In an hour he moved; he held his bad arm to his side and rolled over onto his back; then with his toes, he turned on the water full force, and closed the drain. The roar of the water laughed in his ears; it laughed down the halls of the empty house and out into the climbing night. The water was fine; it brought heat, buoyancy, freedom, everything a man could want. He arranged a wet towel around his neck so he would not drown himself, turned off the water and relaxed. Involuntarily he glanced at Berta May. The moonlight had moved again and now it fell across her breasts. Only her chin and her half smiling mouth were visible above the V of her blouse. Her brassiere held the breasts upright and they flowed together on her bare neck. But the old man pushed thoughts of the dead girl behind curtains in his ancient mind. Before he went to sleep, he lowered his chin and quenched his thirst, then he leaned his head back comfortably, his "gentleman" floating blessedly free . . .

In his dream the old man was a part of a story which he hadn't believed when he had heard it: Marsh, who had had his nose cut off, squatted just inside the circle of light thrown by the bitter-smelling mesquite fire and spoke with a Colorado twang. "By God it was raining, catfish and nigger babies, and we was so drunk you would have had to sober us up to kill us . . ." They were all drunk and running through the back streets of Tascosa in the rain. Jerome Cotton could feel the deep mud gurgling over the instep of his boot every time he took a step. They ran past bright windows whose light bled in his vision like yellow paint. There were four or two of them running together, and he could see Marsh's noseless profile rising and falling beside him as they ran through the downpour. Finally, after hours it seemed, he realized that they were looking for a special whore.

Suddenly Marsh, without saying a word, dodged into a lighted doorway, and Jerry followed. He burst into dryness and light just in time to see Marsh draw his pistol and shoot a Mexican who was climbing out of a high window. (I don't believe this story, the old man thought, but the Mexican fell with a splash outside the window.) Then Marsh, the two nostrils on his face bubbling because he had a cold, turned the pistols on the whore, who was curled on the bed staring at them. She was a tall black-headed woman, slightly pretty. Marsh lowered the barrel of his pistol, as if he were shooting a bottle off a fence post, and shot her.

"You want her in here or out in the street?"

"Out in the street," Jerome Cotton heard himself say in a young voice.

"Good enough," Marsh said, and slung the whore over his shoulder and carried her into the rain. Jerome Cotton heard the splash as Marsh threw her into the mud, but it seemed to come from down on the river . . .

But then it was daylight, dry beautiful daylight, and they were on the trail. He was sitting on his pony on a grassy slope overlooking the Platte River; its wide sandy bed twined away into green distance. Down on the river the boys were trying to free about ten head of cattle who were being sucked down into a bed of quicksand. He noticed one particular steer who was caught near the bank. A cowboy had waded out and slipped a rope around one of the steer's hind legs. The rope was tied to the saddle horn of another cowboy, who was trying to pull the steer free, and the steer was bawling to the sky. In a moment there was a sucking noise as the leg to which the rope was tied popped up out of the sand and lay at an odd angle in the water. The man on the horse continued to pull but he couldn't free the other three legs. Two men were with the steer in the water now.

Jerry Cotton took off his hat and swatted a fly. There was a nice breeze and it was a pretty day. He seemed to be hearing the shouts of the cowboys and the bawling of the cattle from a great distance. When he looked again down into the river bed, the boys had tied the rope which was attached to the steer to the chuck wagon, and the grub-spoiler was trying to drive the team up the slope, and out of the river bed. There was a clatter of harness and a shout from the cookie as the wagon shot forward. Young Jerry Cotton had to look very closely to see that the steer's hind leg was bouncing behind the wagon, trailing water and blood . . .

The old man was awake during the last few seconds of this dream, but he didn't open his eyes; he let the phantasma play itself out on the back of his eyelids until the team and the driver disappeared behind a melting bluff, but still he did not open his eyes. He knew that the room was lit by the gray gallows-light that crept like smoke before the dawn. He lowered his chin and took some of the bitter water into his mouth and spat it out. He had relieved himself during the night. His face itched with its damp morning bristle which Berta May would—which Berta May used to shave with his electric razor. Still without opening his eyes, he raised his foot and let the polluted water out of the tub; then, feeling with his feet, he turned on the faucets, admitting fresh water. The water crackled like new fire as it spattered on the porcelain. "Just like a goddamn goldfish," he mumbled to himself, but he drank great quantities of the new water.

He opened his eyes, looking straight ahead. His hands were grotesquely shriveled, and his entire floating body was logged and puckered. The old man felt that he could grasp his arthritic arm tightly, and slide the skin right off the bone. All of his joints ached and hunger sent pains sliding up under his ribs. *Ninety years old*, he thought and found the dangling tip of his mustache with his tongue and sucked on it. To avoid looking at the girl he closed his eyes again and waited for the sunlight; Sunday morning.

But even after the light shone dark red through the blood vessels in his eyelids, and an occasional flash fell through his lashes like dawn through a forest, the old man kept his eyes clenched against it. He lifted his hand from the water and pressed two fingers into his eyesockets until they hurt; but finally he had to; it became, in the darkness of his morning thoughts, a test of courage. He opened his eyes and deliberately looked at the body stretched on the tile. He stared at her for a moment and then, strangely, the vision liquefied. He blinked his eyes fiercely to clear his vision only to discover that there were tears in them. Children, women, cowards, and men in pain may cry, but the old man who had nearly turned a century wept . . .

He wept because during the night some immodest wind had blown her skirt completely up, exposing her legs, her blue garters, and her blue panties; wept for the silliest thing: a heart sewn on the panties just above the left leg, and *Saturday* embroidered just below it. He wept because he had desired her so overtly and called her the names of his frustration. But most of all, and this is why he wept and didn't cry, the tears topped his lower lids and streamed down because she was dead. His own life had only been a furious explosion of days, a mad clock which ran the seasons round, a flash in the eye of time; what a flicker hers must have been, who had touched, and seen, and tasted only one year for his five. And he wept because he was ashamed and brave enough, or old enough, to be.

But he didn't weep for long at all with his forehead pressed to the side of the tub. His sobbing stopped and his throat relaxed. His eyes dried quickly as he stared down into the turquoise water. He was ninety years old, and it seemed to him a little sacrilegious for a man ninety years old to weep for very long, and a little silly for anyone to be weeping in a bathtub where he was preserved like a snake in a fruit jar; too much weeping renounces too many things. And so he raised his head and looked at the girl again, giving her the respect which, perhaps, is due the dead. He looked at her closely and dispassionately, wishing the body could be taken to a funeral home, noticing again her hand which seemed to be pointing to his son's clothing which lay between the toilet and the bathtub. With his good hand the old man reached over . . .

George Cotton arrived from Dallas in the late afternoon. He entered the front door and called, and when he heard the muffled answer he ran up the stairs three at a time. He threw open the bathroom door and saw his father sitting in the bathtub pulling at his mustache, wearing the wide-brimmed hat he had left on the floor.

"You take care of that poor dead girl," his father said.

"Here, Pa, let me get you out of that tub," George Cotton said, and he started to step over Berta May Kuykendall.

"You get that girl," his father said. "I just may never get out."

1963

LARRY MC MURTRY
There Will Be Peace in Korea

About half an hour before dark there was a bad norther struck, but I figured since it was Bud's last night we ought to go someplace anyway. He'd been home two weeks on leave, but we hadn't gone no place —I hadn't even been to see him. Since him and Laveta broke up and we had that fight and Bud put out my eye we hadn't run around much together. I didn't know if he'd want to go nowhere with me, but I thought whether he did or not I'd go over and see him. His Mercury was parked in front of the rooming house—Bud never even had the top up. I parked my pickup behind it and went up on the porch and knocked. I thought Old Lady Mullins never would get to the door. The porch was on the north side of the house and the norther was really singing in off the plains. She finally come and opened the door, but she never unlatched the screen.

"Hello, Miss Mullins," I said. "Bud home?"

"That's his car there, ain't it?" she said. "I guess he's here if he ain't walked off."

She was still dipping snuff. The reason she never asked me in, my Daddy killed himself in one of her rooms. He wasn't even living there, it was my room, but I was off on a roughnecking tower and I guess the room was the best place he could find. Old Lady Mullins hardly ever let me in after that. I wished I'd worn my football jacket—the Levi didn't

"There Will Be Peace in Korea" was previously published in *Texas Quarterly* 7 (Winter 1964): 166–170. Copyright © 1964 by the University of Texas at Austin.

have no pockets and my hands were about to freeze. Ever time I turned into the wind my eye started watering.

When Bud come to the door he acted kinda surprised but I believe he was glad to see me. Anyhow, he stepped out on the porch. He had on his home clothes, just some Levis and a shirt and his rodeo boots. I didn't know what to say to him.

"Goddamn that wind's getting cold," he said. "Why didn't you come inside?"

"She never unlatched the door," I said. "You know her better than that. I just come by to see what you were doing."

"Nothing," he said. "I was intending to work on my car, but it's turned off too cold."

"I thought we might take off and go someplace," I said. "Maybe to Fort Worth. It might be a good night to drink beer."

"I believe it might," he said. "Only trouble, I got to be back by six in the morning. Bus leaves at six forty-five."

"Aw go get your coat," I said. "We can make that in a walk."

"All right. You might as well get in that pickup and keep warm."

I did, and started the motor. The heater sure felt good. Ever once in awhile the wind would rock the pickup, it was blowing so hard. Some dust was coming with it, too. It wasn't three minutes till Bud came running out. He was a notch smarter than me—he had on his football jacket.

"Wanta go in mine?" he asked. "Might as well get some good out of it."

"Naw, this one's warm and I got a full tank of gas. You might want to sleep on the way back and I'd be afraid to drive yours."

"No reason for you to," he said. "Only trouble, this one's got such a cold back seat. If we was to scare up something we couldn't take advantage of it."

"We could take advantage of it in a motel," I said. I saw Bud was in a good humor and I drove on off. I was glad he felt good—I never intended to fight with Bud nohow. We was best friends all through high school.

"You be over there eighteen months?" I said.

"I reckon." Bud yawned and scratched his cheek. "If I don't get killed first."

We never talked much on the way down. The pickup cab got warm and cozy and Bud had to crack his window to keep from going to sleep.

I figured he was thinking about Laveta and all that, but if he was he never brought it up. We had the road to ourselves and the norther for a tail wind besides—I made nearly as good a time as we would have in Bud's Mercury. A cop stopped us outside of Azle, but we didn't offer him any talk and he let us go without a ticket.

"He wasn't so bad," Bud said. "You ought to see them goddam army cops. Meanest bastards on earth."

Pretty soon we crossed Lake Worth and gunned up the hill above the big Convair plant. We topped it, and all the city lights were spread out below us. I always liked to come over that hill. You never get to see that many lights nowhere around Thalia.

"Let's have a beer," I said.

"Let's have about a case."

I pulled off at the first little honky-tonk I came to and we went in and drank a couple of bottles of Pearl. There were some pretty rough-looking old boys working the shuffleboard, so it was probably a good thing Bud didn't wear his army clothes.

"This end of town ain't changed," Bud said. "Could get in a fight awful easy out here."

"Or anywhere else," I said. I wished I hadn't. Bud took it wrong and thought I was talking about us.

"Yeah, you can," he said, and stood up.

We went on up the road and hit two or three more beer joints before we decided to head into town. Bud got blue and really swigged down the Pearl.

"Let's hit the south-end," he said. "Then if we don't scare up nothing we can make the Old Jackson."

We went on down to South Main and parked the pickup in front of the Mountaineer Tavern. The wind was blowing right down Main Street about sixty miles an hour, and I mean cold—cold and dusty too, blowing off them old brick streets. There weren't many people moving around. The winos were all in the Mission staying warm. We saw a few country boys standing in front of the Old Jackson with their coat collars turned up. It looked like they just had enough money for one piece of pussy and were flipping to see which one got it. We went into a bar but there didn't no stag women come our way so we just drank a beer and moved on. We went into the Penny Arcade and shot ducks awhile and Bud outshot me eight to five. The man that ran the guns never noticed my eye.

"I ain't been practicing ever day, like you have," I said.

"You ain't gonna have to shoot no goddam Japs, either," he said.

Then we went in a place called the Cozy Inn, where they had a three-piece hillbilly band. It wasn't much of a band and we never paid no attention to the music till the intermission. Then the musicians went off to pee and get themselves a beer and they made the old lady who was working tables go up to the stand and play the guitar while they were gone. I don't know why they made her, because there wasn't but Bud and me and one couple and a few tired-looking old boys at the bar, but when the woman went to singing she sure took a hold of everbody. She was just an ordinary looking old worn-out woman, I guess she musta been fifty years old and Bud said fifty-five, but she could outsing those musicians three to one. She sang "Faded Love" and "Jambalaya," and "Walking the Floor over You," and a couple more I don't remember. She sang like she really meant the words. We all clapped when she quit, and Bud liked her so much he made me go up to the bandstand with him to talk to her. I guess she thought she had sung enough—she was tying her apron on.

"Hello, boys," she said. "What are you'all up to?"

"Oh, trying to find some meanness," Bud said. "Say, my name's Bud Farrow. This is Sonny. Say, I'm going off to Korea tomorrow and sure would like it if you'd sing me another song or two."

"Why I sure will, Bud," she said. "All my boys was in the service. I can't sing but one or two, though—I ain't no regular singer." She grinned at us and picked up her guitar and went back and sat down.

"Folks, these next two songs are for the soldier boys," she said, and that made me feel good because I knew she thought I was in the army too. Only when she got to singing it made me feel pretty bad, because I wasn't in it and Bud was going off anyway. She sang "Dust on the Bible" and "Peace in the Valley," and we all clapped big for her, but then the musicians came back and she handed over the guitar and went to draw some beer.

"Let's get on," I said.

That cold wind hit us right in the face when we stepped out on the street. It felt like it was coming right off the north pole.

"We ain't gonna scare up nothing," Bud said. "Let's go to the Old Jackson."

"I'm game," I said. "I want off this cold-ass street."

We went up and got introduced. Bud's was a little better looking in the face, but mine was a better size and she was real nice. Her name was Penny. It was a nice place, the Old Jackson—it was warm and had good rugs and about the best beds I ever saw, and nobody gave you any static one way or the other. Only thing, it took a rich man to make it last, and it didn't seem like no time till we were back out in the street, cold as ever.

"Well, how do you feel now?" I asked him.

"Horny," he said. "It was worth the money, though."

"It's right at two o'clock," I said. "We've got two hundred miles to make, we better hit the road."

We hit it, and Bud went right to sleep. He always does that coming back from Fort Worth—I seldom seen him fail. One time when he still had his Chevvy he done it when he was driving and rolled us over three times. It didn't hurt us, but after that I was glad enough to drive and let him sleep. I got to thinking about all the times me and Bud had made that run from Thalia to Fort Worth and back—I guess about a hundred, anyway. We done an awful lot of running around together before we had the fight. Used to, when we were in high school, we'd make it to the Old Jackson about ever three weeks. I wish the damn army had left Bud alone. It was dead enough in Thalia, anyway, without them shipping him off to Korea.

I never slowed down but one time going home. Just this side of Jacksboro I got to needing to pee and stopped and got out. Bud woke up and needed to too so we both turned our backs to the norther and peed on the highway and then got back in and went on. Bud went right back to sleep. The wind was whipping the old pickup all over the road, and I didn't make very good time. But I drove through the stop sign in Thalia just before six and got Bud to his rooming house right on the dot.

"Wake up, Bud," I said. "We're home."

He looked pretty gloopy, but he got out. I slipped in the house with him and waited while he washed his face and got his army stuff on. He looked a lot different in uniform. He just left most of his other stuff in the room—Old Lady Mullins could put it away if she accidentally found a renter. He put the top up on his Mercury and locked the doors and we went up to the coffee shop and ate some breakfast. Then we drove on over to the drugstore where the bus was supposed to stop, and we waited. We never said much. I knew what Bud was thinking about, but I didn't have no business mentioning it. The wind was blowing paper sacks and sand and once in awhile a tumbleweed across the empty street.

"You don't have to wait if you got some business, Sonny," Bud said. "I can get in the café out of the wind."

"Aw, I got nothing to do this early," I said. "I might as well see you off. Unless you got something you need to do by yourself."

"No, I don't have nothing," Bud said.

Then we seen the Greyhound coming and we got Bud's duffelbag out of the back and stood there in the wind in front of the pickup, waiting for the bus driver to drink his cup of coffee and get his business done in the drugstore. Bud fished around in his pocket and got out both sets of keys to the Mercury and handed them out to me.

"Sonny, you better take care of that car for me," he said. "I was about to go off and forget that. I mean if you don't mind doing it. I may want you to sell it and I may not, I guess I can write and let you know."

"Why I'll be glad to take care of it, Bud," I said. "I can put it in my garage. It don't hurt this old pickup to sit out."

I put the keys in my pocket and Bud picked up his duffelbag.

"I heard it's pussy for the asking over there," I said. "I guess that's one good thing about it."

"Maybe so, if you live to enjoy it," Bud said. "I never did get to ask about you and Laveta."

I had to turn my back on the wind before I could answer him—the wind took my breath.

"Well, I guess it's too bad you never got to go see her, Bud," I said. "Her old man made us get the marriage annulled. He never thought I was rich enough for Laveta, or you either. I think she's going to marry some boy from Dallas."

"I knew she would," Bud said. The wind was so cold it would burn your face, but Bud was looking right into it.

"I think she would have liked to see you," I said. "She never liked getting it annulled no better than I did, at first. I guess she might be liking it a little better now. They sent her off to Dallas to that school."

Bud set his duffelbag down and rubbed his hands together. "I ain't over her yet, Sonny," he said. "After all of this, I ain't over her yet."

"Well, I wish I never had got into it, Bud," I said. "I should have just let you'all make it up."

"Aw, didn't make no difference, he'd of annulled me too," Bud said. "Only I wouldn't a hit you with that bottle, maybe. I never intended to do that. I don't know how come me to do that. Did you'all get to spend the night?"

"Naw we never even done that, Bud. They caught us that night, about ten miles from the J.P.'s. Her old man had the Highway Patrol out looking for us."

"I done that, anyway," he said. "She's a sure sweet girl."

The bus driver came out of the drugstore then and Bud picked up his duffelbag with one hand and me and him shook.

"I enjoyed the visit, Sonny," Bud said. "Watch after this town. I'll see you."

"Bud, take it easy," I said. "I'll be seeing you."

He gave the driver the ticket and got on the bus and it drove away. There wasn't a car on the street, or a person, just that bus. I knew Bud would put off talking about it as long as he could, he always done things that way. I stood there in front of the pickup in the wind, trying to see. A lot of things happened when me and Bud and Laveta was in high school. There were some dust and paper scraps whirling down the street toward me but when the bus was out of sight it seemed like Bud and Laveta were gone for good and I was standing there by myself, in the wind.

1964

ROBERT FLYNN

The Savior of the Bees

The summer I was 13 I was the savior of the bees. At least that's what I called myself. Dad called me his little farmer, especially when he was pleased with the way I did my chores. Mother called me "Granddaddy Long-legs" because I was always hanging around thinking, and because I was all arms and legs and tall like her side of the family. Dad was dark and thick shouldered and stocky. Mother once bought him a pair of high-heeled cowboy boots to make him look taller but Dad wouldn't wear them. Dad had once been a cowboy but said he had outgrown it.

It was the third summer in a row my mother had planned a trip we did not take. The first had been to Fort Worth so I could see the zoo, the second to Carlsbad so I could see the caverns, the third to Corpus Christi because Mother wanted me to see the ocean.

Mother made careful plans and enlisted my support. "Tell your father that the other children have all seen the zoo." "Tell your father that your teacher went to Carlsbad Caverns and said it was something you should see." "Tell your father that you'd do better in geography if you could see the ocean." I told him but we never got caught up enough with the farm work to be able to go.

It was the summer Dad gave Mother a new pressure cooker for her birthday. Because of the war a lot of things were rationed, but we raised our own beef, pork, and chickens and had an orchard and a garden besides the field crops. The pressure cooker would make it easier for Mother to can fruits and vegetables for the winter. Dad said no matter what fool thing Roosevelt did we were self-sufficient.

Dad and I picked out the cooker and I distracted Mother while Dad hid it, and I placed it in the kitchen the night before her birthday, after he and Mother had gone to bed.

The morning of her birthday, Dad and I sat at the table passing looks, waiting to hear Mother's gasp of surprise when she discovered the cooker. I was trying not to laugh, and then Dad saw something that made his face change. I looked too. Mother was standing at the stove frying our eggs, and she was crying, the tears sizzling when they hit the hot skillet.

I thought Mother must be crying because Dad was sitting at the table in his low quarter shoes with no socks. Dad didn't wear socks in the summertime, not even to town, because they made his ankles hot. Mother said it made him look loose and spiritless. Mother was younger than Dad, she said he had married as an afterthought, and was from the city where folks wore socks all year round and were Democrats.

"Why are you crying?" I asked her.

"It does seem to me that sometimes I could be something besides a farm hand," she said, speaking to Dad, not to me.

The wives of Dad's friends talked about how young and pretty Mother was, but Mother didn't feel pretty. "Do you think my face is getting leathery?" she asked me sometimes. "Do you think my hair looks tired?" Now I knew what the words meant. Her eyes were puffy, her dark hair was damp and stringy. I noticed how hot and red her hands were, and the little lines around her mouth, and the way her shoulders sagged, making her neck look long. Mother felt old.

"Maybe if I were one of your cows you'd appreciate me," she said to Dad, looking at him now, her eyes hard and angry. "Maybe you'd do nice things for me."

Dad did do nice things for his cows, and he had the look he had when Beulah tried to hook him when he picked up her new calf. Beulah was his favorite cow, the one he bragged on, and he wasn't so much angry, because a man had to expect that kind of thing from a cow, as puzzled and disappointed that it was Beulah, after all he had done for her.

"We got the pressure cooker to make things better for you," Dad said. "The man said it would save you lots of time."

"Time is all I have. All I do is work so what am I saving time for?" Mother asked. "We never go anywhere. We never do anything." Tears were still rolling down her face and her mouth was pinched and ugly. "Did you ever think that I might like something pretty?" She put the plates of bacon and eggs before us and left the room.

I remembered then how carefully she had shown me the rings, bracelets, watches, earrings in the catalogue. "When you get married," she said, "these are the kinds of things you should give your wife." But I wasn't even thinking about getting married, and I was impatient to show her the .22 rifle I wanted for my birthday.

After Mother went into her room, closing the door, Dad and I ate quickly, wanting to be out of the house, and knowing there was a lot of work to do before we ate again. "I don't know what she wants," Dad said, taking his hat from the nail beside the door before he left the house. "I gave her the prettiest place in the county."

It was the summer Dad began sleeping in my room because he had to be up early and Mother stayed up late reading books she checked out of the county library. They were romances and mysteries, mostly. She said it was to fill up all the time the pressure cooker saved her.

I thought Dad was trying to make up to Mother because he spent so much time in the fields I was sure we would get caught up with the farm work and go to Corpus Christi. The only time he came in the house was when it was time to eat or go to bed.

He and Mother didn't talk much at the table anymore, and when they did I wished they didn't. "Do you think you might get through today in time for me to go to town and get groceries?" Mother asked one morning. Her face had that stiff, tight look that made her eyes and mouth look small. The only time she could get books from the library was when we went to town to get groceries.

"What do we need from town?" Dad asked. His face was swollen. Dad had a short, thick neck, and when he was mad he didn't seem to have any neck at all. Dad didn't like the idea that Mother needed something he couldn't provide.

"Salt and sugar if I'm going to do any canning with the pretty new pressure cooker you bought me."

I stayed away from the house as much as I could. When I finished my chores I went down to the corral and watched the bees trying to get water. I liked to watch the bees. They worked so hard. They had worn the opening to the hive smooth with their coming and going to the honeysuckle and lilac bushes Mother had planted to hide the wire fence that kept the chickens out of the yard. Mother said that people had to be removed from animals. "Decent distance," she called it.

I had never noticed how many bees drowned in the water tank. They scrambled around the sides of the tank, climbing over one another. When the cows stuck their muzzles in the water, the water came up over the bees and they floated around in little circles until they drowned. Wasps floated on top of the water like they thought they were gods.

One morning at the table I asked Dad why wasps floated while bees drowned. Dad knew everything about animals. He could just look at an animal and tell what was wrong with it and what it needed. "Bees have little hairs on their legs," he said. "That's how they gather pollen to make honey. The hairs break the surface tension of the water and they drown. Wasps don't have hairs because they don't make honey, so they can float."

"But that's not fair," I said, appalled that bees were doomed by the very thing that made them valuable, while wasps that did nothing but wound floated on the water, safe because they didn't make honey or anything else that people could use. "Wasps don't do anything but make nests for themselves."

"Why did you have to tell him that?" Mother demanded. "You have to make everything so ugly."

Dad was not normally a violent man but he appeared about to explode. His neck had disappeared and his head was swollen. "Everything in life is not pretty," he said.

"When you're young it can be," Mother said. "For a little while."

Mother looked at me like she was going to read to me from the Bible. Mother didn't study the Bible the way some folks did, she read it for answers, the way others read the advice columns in the newspaper. And when she read it to me she took on a look that said, you don't have to understand this, you just have to believe that it is for the best.

"Jimmy," she said. Her voice was low and thoughtful, not the way she talked to Dad. "Jimmy, wouldn't you rather be a bee and make something beautiful like honey, even if it made you liable to drowning, than to be a wasp and be hated and feared by everybody?"

"What good is it telling him things like that?" Dad asked. "Bees don't have any choice in the matter, or wasps either."

"People do," Mother said. "We can choose whether we want to do something beautiful with our lives or just think of ourselves."

"Wasps make nests just like bees," Dad said, "and they defend them."

"They don't sacrifice their lives the way a bee does, because when a bee stings you it dies."

They had forgotten all about me and the bees, too. I slipped out of the house with Dad describing the difference between a bald, frayed-wing worker and a sleek and useless drone.

"I thought the drones were all males," Mother said.

I went down to the corral and dipped the bees out of the water. It wasn't fair that bees drowned and wasps floated, and the only thing I knew to do was put myself on the side of the bees.

I started making regular rounds each day, rescuing the bees, placing them on the corral fence to dry their wings, taking care not to be the cause of their self-destruction. It was frustrating saving the bees as they never seemed to learn. I took broken shingles from the barn and made little rafts for them to climb on while I was away at work. Sometimes I splashed water at the wasps trying to make them liable too, but they just flew away.

One day Mother came down to the tank and put her arm around me. She had on her Bible-reading face. "Jimmy, I'm going to leave your father," she said, "and I want you to go with me. Don't you want to go with me?"

She wanted me to look at her but I couldn't. I couldn't look at the house either because I knew Dad was watching. I just looked at the bees, drowning in the water.

"I don't want you to hate your father," she said. "He's a good man, he works hard, he loves this place. He likes plowing and taking care of the cattle. He doesn't want anything else. But there's so much more. Jimmy, if you stay here you'll be buried just like I am. You'll just be a farm hand taking care of his place, feeding his cattle, raising his crops. Come with me."

She waited for me to say something but I didn't. I couldn't. I couldn't get my breath.

"I'm going to the house to get my things," she said. "If you want to go with me, go to the car. Your father won't try to stop you."

I wasn't sure when she started to the house but I was sure when Dad was there beside me. I could feel him standing there, like at night when it was so dark I couldn't see the barn but I could feel it there, towering over me.

"I know your mother talked to you," he said, "but I don't want you to go. I don't want you to have hard feelings about your mother. She is a good woman and she loves you, but she doesn't love this place the way you and I do. She wants things for herself, things she can put back there in that room of hers with the big bed and the fancy dresser, and all her pretty things. I know she wants what she thinks is best for you, but she'll just smother you in prettiness."

They wanted me to choose, but I couldn't help one and hurt the other. After a while, Dad left too, went into the barn I guess. Then I heard Mother come out of the house and get in the car. I don't know what she was taking with her but it seemed like she slammed every door on the car. Then she got in and started it. I could hear the drone of the car for a long time after she left.

I thought about drowning myself in the tank. I thought about running away. I didn't know what to do. After a while Dad told me he had to go to town for a while.

It was almost dark when he came back and I had already started the milking. "Your mother and I decided to stay together until you're grown," was all he said. Then I heard Mother drive in and slam all the car doors again, and go into the house and start cooking supper. It wasn't until we sat down at the table that I realized that Dad had put on socks before going to town.

Dad's face wasn't swollen but his head seemed sunk down into his shoulders so that he didn't have a neck. He looked pleased with himself and ashamed at the same time. Mother looked pretty. She looked like she felt pretty, and she kept pushing at her hair to put life in it.

We talked about Corpus Christi, and the ocean, and seeing sharks, and picking up sea shells. Supper seemed to last a long time as they kept talking and talking. Dad said, "Jimmy, go on to bed, you're about to fall out of your chair. I'm going to stay up for a while."

Mother said to Dad, "Why don't you sleep in my room and that way you won't wake Jimmy up when you get up in the morning."

I don't know what happened after that but we didn't go to Corpus Christi that summer. We didn't go to Grand Canyon the next summer either. Mother planned it and talked about it, and I drove a tractor all summer. Mother said I did the work of a man. Dad said he might as well sleep in my room since we both had to get up early, and since Mother stayed up late reading.

I guess the bees took care of themselves. I didn't have any time that summer to save them. And when Dad bought a new cook stove for Mother's birthday I didn't help him pick it out. I didn't help him hide it either.

1983

CAROLYN OSBORN

Reversals

Tutankhamun returning from battle in his chariot, preceded by two captives. . . . The scene is symbolic of the king's dominion over foreign lands, for Tutankhamun himself is not known to have taken part in any military exploit. [Metropolitan Museum description of a gold buckle]

My father, a field artillery officer during World War II, was the man who stayed behind. He trained soldiers, but he never went to battle, a source of lifelong guilt. He reaped the rewards— promotion, salary, good assignments—yet proving himself under fire was impossible. After the war he went civilian, gathered his family, and settled near his last post in Texas, the most foreign place he'd ever lived. In mind he held the most stereotypical and, therefore, the most satisfying vision of peace—a house surrounded by a white picket fence with hollyhocks nodding over the top. My mother convinced him that hollyhocks would not grow in our soil and a white fence would need repainting every year. So he built an eight-foot cinder-block wall where ivy and honeysuckle crawled and choked each other prettily. The wall enclosed only the house's back side, containing a patio and a small yard. The front remained vulnerable to any passing stranger.

More than the realization of this fantasy, he wanted evidence that some of the men he'd trained had survived, especially when Korea began. He read the lists provided by old army friends at Fort Hood. There were too many names to remember; he went by battalion numbers. If someone was missing, he mourned privately.

His public reaction was to collect eccentrics; the lost, the forlorn, even the resolute who were so marked by their experiences they were hopelessly displaced from conventional paths. During Korea, God's measure of these people found their way to our door. There was a colonel, an ex-prisoner of a Japanese concentration camp who'd escaped, returned to his ranch in South Texas, and built a tall barbed-wire fence around his house, where he assigned himself guard duty on his front porch. All day he shot a 30-30 at nothing. A major showed up who'd survived Guam then drank himself into alcoholism and retired to a forgotten mountain in Arkansas. This one decided to move to Leon to be nearer to my father as well as to a veteran's hospital forty miles away. Father also magnetized a wealthy father's wizened son who'd retired from the service too early and lived in what his harsh-voiced wife called "the dog house," a little room tacked onto their garage. An old doctor who had done time in the air force came to visit. This one would not wear his false teeth and would not buy another set. He was incoherent most days.

Though he had other friends—people who sold real estate, ran cotton gins, were presidents of local banks—he saw more of the disturbed ones. He listened to them, drank with them. Gradually there were minor changes.

The major who'd lived on a mountaintop found himself a remote collection of hilly pastures and began raising goats. For six months my father had driven him to the VA hospital every Friday. The rifleman returned to his ranch, put his gun away, rolled up the barbed-wire fence which barricaded his house and used it plus hundreds of reels more for a deer fence around his land. The colonel went to see him for a two-week hunt in November.

Mother, after patiently serving cases of liquor to my father and his friends, said, "The atmosphere is healthier. He's always tried to cure everybody. He's helped some."

She'd say things like that even when the man who lived in "the dog house" was still dropping by every Saturday and the toothless doctor still wouldn't wear his newest set of teeth. But Korea was over; my father was no longer a list reader.

Feeling optimistic, she went to Galveston to see her sister, leaving me home to do the cooking. I had been away in college for a year and was going to summer school in mid-July. It was my turn.

"Everything will be okay," Mother said.

"Of course." I reassured her though I knew I could never be as efficient as she was, nor would I know what to do if my father expanded his pack of loonies.

"It really will be."

I nodded and waved, remembering the time she went to Dallas on a shopping trip. The sink stopped up, my bed fell in, and my brother got expelled from school. At least I was older now, and only my father and I were home.

We were by ourselves three days before the twins appeared. Cousins, they called themselves, sons of my father's first cousin's son, hardly kin, even by Southern standards. The last time I'd seen them, they were two little boys in droopy drawers chasing each other around the house with bullwhips. The years hadn't improved them. Warren and Wallie zoomed up on matching Harley-Davidsons the Fourth of July. They were outfitted in filthy Levis, black leather vests, and the obligatory scuffed leather boots. Warren had a mermaid tattoo on his left arm; Wallie had one on his right. The mermaids' tails wriggled when the boys revved their motors.

"You know who we are?" Two narrow, clever-looking faces stared at a spot somewhere above my eyes.

"Yes."

They lounged on their cycles, letting them rumble.

"Which is which?"

"You're both the same except for the mermaids. Kenyon told me." I stood in the side door leading to the driveway. In my right hand I held a cooking fork, no use at all against Warren and Wallie, but holding it made me feel better.

"Where's your brother?"

"Jumping out of airplanes."

"Aww."

"It's the truth. He joined the paratroopers. Things have been a lot quieter since he left." Which was also true, since my brother had been in nearly every kind of trouble. Without anyone's permission, he'd ridden bulls in rodeos. Then he got involved in a one-man war against the entire football team—he stood on the roof of the stadium with a bucket of horse apples and shied them at the team below when they finished afternoon practice. He also printed DEATH IS $ in three-foot letters on the pavement leading to the funeral home, and he went AWOL from the military school my parents finally sent him to. Sometimes I think my father collected loonies partially because he missed Kenyon so much.

"Is your daddy at home?"

"The colonel is taking a nap. I wouldn't disturb him if I were you."

Who could sleep with two Harley-Davidsons sputtering outside, two male voices rasping questions, and me shouting against them all?

My father hollered out his door, "Turn those damn things off, boys."

He commanded as usual, and the twins obeyed because, I suppose, they needed someone to obey.

"Who in the hell are they?"

I recited our long line of weak relationship like an amateur genealogist who's wandered too far out on a branch of a family tree. My father's loyalty to his kin prevailed. The twins swaggered through the back gate.

It was a long, hot afternoon, full of the noise of cicadas buzzing and glasses clinking on top of metal patio tables. Beer was all my father would give them; they drank all we had. Inside, out of sight, I overheard bits of their stumbling confessions:

"Never did get back to school."

"Yeah. We both got married too young."

"Naw. I don't think. . . . Was yours, Wallie?"

"I don't know. She never said she was pregnant."

"Mama didn't like . . ."

"Daddy gone since we was three."

"Rode over here."

Warren said "over here" like it was the next town. They lived in Arizona.

After I fixed all of them supper, a steak and beans miracle, dinner for one stretched over one man and two wolves, I went to a family fish fry with Royal Jimson. We'd known each other since we were in high school and provided each other company when we were in Leon, a place we were equally ready to leave. He had to work on his father's farm that summer; I had to work in my father's kitchen.

The colonel called out after us, "Celia, I told the boys they could stay out in the empty apartment." Behind the cinder-block wall he'd built a duplex which faced the next street.

"All right." What else was there to say? I was thankful one of the apartments was empty. He could have asked them to move into Kenyon's room.

Warren and Wallie ripped out of the drive and flashed down the block before we reached the corner.

"Those are my out-law cousins," I told Royal. "I believe they think they're going downtown to buy more beer."

We both laughed. Leon is the county seat of a dry county.

Fauntleroys' Crossing is a big bend in the Leon River. Almost an island, it's still connected to somebody's cornfield by a road and to an opposite bank by the Fauntleroys' rotting wooden footbridge. The Fauntleroys themselves are long gone, leaving only their name and a picnic and parking spot.

We had to speak first to Grandpa Jimson, who was sitting, as he sat every year, in a slat-backed chair under a pecan tree. When somebody wasn't there paying respects, he told stories to children, sent messages to the men who were frying fish, or talked to the women who were unpacking bowls of coleslaw, slicing homemade bread, cutting up red onions, and showing off this year's pickles. They were all perfectly occupied, and I was perfectly happy to watch them. Other families' rituals are always impressive.

Grandpa Jimson was the nearest to Abraham I've ever seen, and, like Abraham, he was interested in expansion. He asked, as he did every July Fourth, "Well, Royal, what's wrong with marrying this one?"

Royal had his answer ready. "I would, but she's too pretty." ("Too rich" or "too smart" were other acceptable variations.)

Grandpa Jimson laughed, showing a mouthful of his own teeth, and sent us off to the beer keg.

Sitting at a picnic table, surrounded by Jimsons, all of them eating fresh fried fish and drinking beer, I let Warren and Wallie sink slowly out of mind. My father might entertain every species of wildman who walked, my brother might be one, and my mother, who'd endured them all, might stay in Galveston all summer. For a while I was in a nest of peaceful folk who wouldn't even shoot firecrackers on the Fourth.

"Too dry." They said.

"Might start a grass fire."

"We can always ride over to Fort Hood and watch the army display."

That was where my father was going. He hated war, yet he loved guns, hunting, and fireworks.

After supper Royal had arranged a lazy boat ride on the river. The

Leon is nothing much to look at. It's small, twisty, and full of sandbars, wicked currents, and water moccasins. On a hot July evening in the long twilight, it's a pleasant place to be in a small rowboat.

Royal and I were talking about places we planned to be later in the summer. I was going south to Cuernavaca to learn Spanish, which had swirled about me in a mystifying way ever since we moved to Texas. He was headed north to an uncle's wheat farm in Canada. Both of us were trying to imagine Canada—so immense, so far away, so cool, so full of European influences.

"Not that I'll ever get to see anything. I'm going to be tied to a combine until late August."

"Run away to Quebec," I suggested.

"I can't do that. I wish I could. I've never run away in my life. Have you?"

"No."

We were both silent; there was so much we hadn't done. Drifting under the Fauntleroys' footbridge, I looked up to see the Harley-Davidsons sitting on it, and not far downstream, slithering naked in the water, were those two overgrown toads, my cousins.

"Get out of the river you idiots. It's full of snakes and quicksand."

"Aww." Warren held onto one side of the boat. Wallie clung to the other. Both their mermaids were gleaming.

"Haven't seen one yet." Warren rocked us over to his side.

Royal knelt on the bottom of the boat to keep us from tipping.

"Don't do that!" I shouted. "Don't turn this boat over. You may need us." Self-preservation was the only angle I could think of that might appeal to the twins.

They did it anyway.

With only a halter, shorts, and tennis shoes on, I made it to shore downriver pretty fast. Royal took longer. He was wearing jeans. And he wouldn't pull off his almost new handmade boots in the Leon. The boat, upright and empty, caught by the current running round the bend, slid past us near the opposite shore.

"Maybe it'll catch on the bank. Why did they want to do that?" Royal stood in the mud beside me offering his hand.

"Because I told them not to. I'm sorry."

"Do they always do what you tell them not to?"

"I don't know how they work." I smelled like a corner of a dank closet. Dusk was drawing in; mosquitoes attacked. I felt low, mean, vicious. Slapping bugs and kicking vines aside, we crawled out. In the distance I could hear two motorcycles creaking over the footbridge. I hoped it would break, but it didn't. The fools' luck held.

Once we reached higher ground, Royal poured water out of his boots. He bit the edge of his lower lip as he pulled off the second one.

"Jealous bastards! They saw us having a good time."

I leaned over and kissed him. I don't know why. Maybe it was because I'd never seen him so frustrated before, or was it the way river water curled his hair around his forehead?

We sat on top of an old picnic table kissing sweetly and tentatively while blindly aiming at mosquitoes in the dusk until Royal said, "The boat! I've got to get it before dark."

He and three or four of his younger cousins went back to the river. The hard-core beer drinkers were at the keg finishing it off. I stood with them, paper cup in hand. Someone said, "Howdy!" in a foreign accent. It was Warren wearing a straw cowboy hat.

"Yes sir, I be-lieve I'll jes' have some of that."

Wallie was at the keg pumping up two beers. His disguise was a green baseball cap with John Deere printed on the back strap.

Both the hats were Kenyon's. He had a collection hanging off the antlers of a buck he'd shot.

"Get out of here," I hissed.

"A man can get mighty dry in this here part of Texas," Warren drawled.

"Now, don't we look like all those other thirsty men?"

It was so dark now it was hard to distinguish Warren and Wallie. I kept my mouth shut and let them infiltrate. The Jimsons' company never hurt anybody. When Royal appeared again, he caught me by one hand and led me to the pickup.

Just as we parked in front of my house and Royal raised one half-dry arm to pull me toward him, and just as I was about to complain about my own sogginess, we heard two motorcycles.

"Are they going to follow us everywhere?"

"I guess they don't have anything else to do."

A fist rapped on the rear window.

Warren poked his head in my side of the cab. "Y'all seem to have carried off the rest of the beer."

"Stingy!" Wallie sang from the back.

Royal looked around. "Now they've stolen the damn beer! It was supposed to go in Grandpa's truck." He stepped out to negotiate with the twins. The keg belonged to a distributor twenty miles away in McGregor, the nearest town in a wet county.

I ran inside, grabbed two big pitchers, and carried them back to the pickup. Royal was leaning on the tailgate looking unconcerned. The twins were both leaning against the beer keg looking equally unconcerned.

"Here." I shoved a pitcher toward each one. "Fill them up and let Royal return that keg."

They gave me two half-drunk, arrogant winks.

"If you don't, you're going to be out of bed, out of board, and out of town by tomorrow."

They drew off the beer, then stumbled down the drive, wheeling their cycles and carrying a pitcher apiece.

Royal was embarrassed. "You didn't have to do that."

"What could you have done? There were two of them."

"I wouldn't have minded getting beat up if I could have just hit both of them at least once."

"Well, I would have minded. My father would have minded, and all the Jimsons would have too."

"We get in fights sometimes."

"This one wasn't worth getting into."

"You should have let me decide that."

"They are my depraved cousins. We're in front of my house."

He stared straight through the windshield.

"Goodnight, Royal." I opened my door and stepped out. If that was all the thanks I got for getting rid of the twins, he could go home and hug his hurt pride. Walking across the front porch, I stepped on a June bug on purpose.

Royal sat in his truck for about five minutes before he started the motor.

Early July fifth, the twins were still asleep, both on their sides curved toward each other. Under Mother's clean white sheets they looked like choir boys until I noticed the mermaids wriggling against the percale.

126

After gathering their clothes off the floor, I dropped them each a pair of my brother's old jeans and a shirt. On the way out I banged the front door, where I'd already tacked a note: NO EATS SERVED TO THE UNWASHED.

The colonel was up making coffee when I came in to start the washing machine.

"You're in a huffy mood this morning."

Why didn't I tell him they'd dumped Royal and me in the Leon, made us their stupid confederates in a beer heist, and followed us all over the county? Partially because he'd suffered through so many of Kenyon's pranks, partially because I needed his help.

"Can you get them jobs?"

"Sure, but they won't like them."

"Why not?"

"Celia, those boys don't like work . . . not the kind they'll have to do around here."

"Let's try anyway."

They wanted to ride their motorcycles. The colonel insisted on driving them to a service station, where they pumped gas, washed cars, and tinkered with other people's engines happily for five days. On the sixth day they tore down the engine of a Chevy belonging to the postmaster. They said they could have put it together again, but their boss wasn't interested in what the twins might do next.

"Why did you have to take that engine completely apart?"

Warren grinned. "We never saw one so old in such good condition. We thought if we could find out what made it run so good, we'd—"

"We'd know something," Wallie added. They had the irritating habit of finishing each other's sentences.

The colonel said, "They can work on a fencing crew. Those boys will be safer out in the country."

When I brought up natural dangers, he assured me, "Warren and Wallie will know what to do with a rattlesnake."

From Monday till Friday their clothes were full of dust and grass-burs instead of oil and grease. They demanded salami sandwiches, pickles, and a quart of iced tea apiece for lunch. When he gave me the order, Warren rolled his eyes like an aborigine who's just arrived at a salt lick. "Hot out there. We sweat all day long."

Of course I added hard-boiled eggs, cherry tomatoes, celery in mason jars with ice like Mother packed it for family picnics, salt twisted in waxed paper, and brownies or cake. I baked three times a week now.

The second Friday when they got home, Wallie wanted to know if it would be all right to stretch a rattlesnake skin in the garage. When I said sure, he reached in his lunch sack and handed me the rattle. I'd lived in Texas eight years, and no one had ever offered me such a gift, nor had I been sitting around crying for one. Appalled at first, I stared at Wallie's expectant face. He was giving away a trophy. I counted the buttons.

"Eleven. Must have been a big snake."

"Yep." Wallie looked up at me. Both of them had light, light blue eyes, the sort that make a person appear a little crazy.

"Well . . . thank you."

"Welcome."

Then Warren, who'd been standing slightly behind him in the shadowy dusk, leaned into the light and placed a small obsidian arrowhead in my hand.

"How beautiful. Where did you find it?"

"Out there—" Warren gestured toward the west with his bulging lunch sack. As he swung it, a lot of little metal pieces dribbled all over the ground.

"What's that, Warren?"

"The post-hole digger. The foreman says we can come back to work when we put it back together again."

I sat down on the doorstep. The twins hunkered in the grass. At that moment I hoped the redbugs were chewing on them both, then I remembered that was impossible because I'd dosed them with flowers of sulphur every morning of the week.

"How long are you-all going to play this Humpty-Dumpty game? First it was a car, now a post-hole digger. If my father gets you a job where you have to ride horseback, are you going to take the saddles apart?"

"We don't know how to ride horses, Cousin."

"Your daddy . . . he's got these ideas about what we're supposed to do—"

"If the colonel's ideas don't suit you, find your own jobs."

"We will."

"Yeah . . . only, Cousin Celia, don't tell him about this old post-hole digger, please."

128

"All right." How many people have been bribed with a rattlesnake rattle and an arrowhead? "But he's going to find out anyway."

"We know. We just don't want to hurt his feelings. Maybe it'll take a few days. And maybe we'll find something else by then."

I agreed to keep quiet. As long as they were doing something, my father would be content, and so would I. For a week I saw the twins only at supper. They were morose, sunburned, and usually dusty. I assumed they were riding around the county looking for other jobs.

I was wrong. That summer I almost got used to being wrong. Royal came by the house one night before going to Canada. I hadn't seen him since July Fourth. After our one attempt, neither of us had made a move. We were too much alike in some ways, too different in others, and both of us were more interested in leaving than in sorting anything out. I was glad he came to say good-bye, though.

"There's something I ought to tell you. Do you know what those two idiots are doing now?"

Royal leaned toward me. We were sitting next to each other on the front porch steps, and this was as close as he got all evening. "They're bootlegging beer. They've got carryalls on those motorcycles. Two or three times a day they go over to McGregor and haul it back."

"How do you know?" It was a ridiculous question. We were both experts on how small-town gossip travels, yet I asked, hoping it wasn't true.

"Haven't you noticed how the traffic's picked up back there at night? Everybody calls it the Pleasant Street Bar. You know the sheriff will be out to check on them pretty soon."

Royal and I shook hands. The minute he drove off, I ran down the drive toward the apartments. Two Harley-Davidsons were neatly tucked into the carport. In front, five cars loitered. Some others were circling the block. I threw the front door open so fast I could have been a member of a raiding party. Warren was holding onto the open refrigerator door handle. Behind him cans of Lone Star, Pearl, and Bud solidly covered the shelves. Wallie sat on three cases of something. I didn't know what. I was too mad to read anymore. Altogether there were seven men in the room, more men than I'd seen in a kitchen all summer.

"Would you like—?" Warren stretched out his hand toward the beer.

Wallie shook his head sadly.

"I would like the premises cleared."

Five men shuffled out muttering, "Later." "Okay, Lady." "Haw!" "I done paid already."

When they were gone, I locked the front door and told the boys, "Your business is closed."

"What are we going to do with all this beer?" Wallie wailed. He didn't waste a minute looking contrite.

"We are going to take it back where it came from." I couldn't wait till the twins made twenty more trips to and from McGregor on their motorcycles. I couldn't trust them to get to the liquor store with the goods. They would be selling it to assorted customers all up and down the highway, roaring into farmhouse drives peddling beer door-to-door, spilling it in bowls belonging to miscellaneous puppydogs, baptizing startled armadillos by moonlight. They had no discretion and all the time in the world. My own time was running short. Mother was returning the next day. Father and I might be captivated by any number of loonies, but my mother was not going to like these two. She was patient. She would oversee and overlook the colonel's counseling sessions. But he was dealing with grown men who were war ruins, and they took themselves home or to a motel every night. Warren and Wallie had moved into our tent. All this came to mind when I went back to the house to tell my father I needed to use his pickup. He didn't ask what for, so I didn't tell him.

I drove both ways with the twins sitting next to me. On the way home, a can of beer in both shirt pockets, two in hand, and his blue eyes going almost yellow in the approaching headlights, Warren said, "Cousin Celia, what are we going to do now?" I suggested they learn horse-shoeing or some other nonmechanical trade that would sop up their energies. Then Wallie began talking about weighted shoes, dope, and other crooked methods of fixing horse races. I was sorry I'd mentioned it.

Wallie offered to drive.

"I'd be lucky to scrape myself off a hackberry tree if either of you were driving. I've seen you riding those motorcycles—weaving around like two Comanches on a war party. I'm leaving town in two days, and I plan on going with all bones intact."

It was 6:30 when we rolled into Leon. I hadn't had time to cook. On the outskirts of town I stopped and got half a dozen hamburgers to go. My father was pleased with the beer the twins provided. He told me

130

after supper he thought they might even be learning a little about the conventions of hospitality.

"At least they're sharing."

So I had to tell him the six packs were the last of many cases they had sold at our back door.

"Celia, why have you been trying so hard with those boys?"

"Somebody's got to."

"Lots of people have. I called their mother right after they came. She couldn't deal with them any longer. They've been in reform schools, in jail, in everything but the army, and the army wouldn't have them now. They stole over five hundred dollars' worth of guitars from a pawn shop. That's a felony. They pawned their own guitars, honey, then stole them. They pawned some of their mother's silver, too. She had to redeem that."

"Well, why do you try to help hopeless people?"

"Most of them aren't so hopeless. They're only confused by what has happened to them—by wars, bad marriages, bad health, reversals of various kinds."

"So are the twins—no father, too much freedom."

"And an inclination to daredevilment. They make their own disasters. My friends are only suffering from natural disorders."

There was no sense in going on though I could have. An inclination toward trouble seemed as natural to me as my father's list of his friends' turmoils. He was a strict line drawer, though, and if he made one, all you could do was either step over it and go or stay within his boundaries.

The twins were gone before breakfast the next morning. They left a note on the door saying, "Thanx. Warren and Wallie." And they left the dried snakeskin on the garage wall.

Mother drove in that afternoon just in time to unpack and advise me about what to pack, which she couldn't help doing although I'd been packing my own suitcase since I was ten. She looked rested, tanned, unworried. I was glad to have her back. There had been too many men around, too many of them needing attention. Mother attended to me and to the colonel for the rest of the day. We told her about the twins.

She laughed. "I'm sorry I didn't get to see them, but it's probably best they moved on."

"Yes," my father said.

The next afternoon, flying over the green valley of Central Mexico, I looked down at all the roads left by various civilizations—the Aztecs, the Spaniards, the Mexicans—and wondered if Wallie and Warren might one day weave over those curves on their motorcycles. What would happen to them? Anything could, for the world is full of dangers, and Warren and Wallie often went out to meet them. I hoped their luck would hold.

Except for a postcard from Zihuatanejo, an isolated Mexican town on the west coast and a collecting point for beach bums, dope lovers, and other escapists, I never heard from the twins again. The card was a familiar one, a palm-thatched roof on a pole, beneath the pole, a hammock, and behind these a calm sea meeting a blue sky. On the back were three lines: "Dear Cossin Celia, We are not workin. Yrs. Warren and Wallie." I kept the card.

1979

AMADO MURO

Cecilia Rosas

When I was in the ninth grade at Bowie High School in El Paso, I got a job hanging up women's coats at La Feria Department Store on Saturdays. It wasn't the kind of a job that had much appeal for a Mexican boy or for boys of any other nationality either. But the work wasn't hard, only boring. Wearing a smock, I stood around the Ladies' Wear Department all day long waiting for women customers to finish trying on coats so I could hang them up.

Having to wear a smock was worse than the work itself. It was an agonizing ordeal. To me it was a loathsome stigma of unmanly toil that made an already degrading job even more so. The work itself I looked on as onerous and effeminate for a boy from a family of miners, shepherds, and ditchdiggers. But working in Ladies' Wear had two compensations: earning three dollars every Saturday was one; being close to the Señorita Cecilia Rosas was the other.

This alluring young woman, the most beautiful I had ever seen, more than made up my mollycoddle labor and the smock that symbolized it. My chances of looking at her were almost limitless. And like a good Mexican, I made the most of them. But I was only too painfully aware that I wasn't the only one who thought this saleslady gorgeous.

La Feria had water fountains on every one of its eight floors. But men liked best the one on the floor where Miss Rosas worked. So they made special trips to Ladies' Wear all day long to drink water and look at her.

Since I was only fourteen and in love for the first time, I looked at her more chastely than most. The way her romantic lashes fringed her obsidian eyes was especially enthralling to me. Then, too, I never tired of admiring her shining raven hair, her Cupid's-bow lips, the warmth of her gleaming white smile. Her rich olive skin was almost as dark as mine. Sometimes she wore a San Juan rose in her hair. When she did, she looked so very lovely I forgot all about what La Feria was paying me to do and stood gaping at her instead. My admiration was decorous but complete. I admired her hourglass figure as well as her wonderfully radiant face.

Other men admired her too. They inspected her from the water fountain. Some stared at her boldly, watching her trimly rhythmic hips sway. Others, less frank and open, gazed furtively at her swelling bosom or her shapely calves. Their effrontery made me indignant. I, too, looked at these details of Miss Rosas. But I prided myself on doing so more romantically, far more poetically than they did, with much more love than desire.

Then, too, Miss Rosas was the friendliest as well as the most beautiful saleslady in Ladies' Wear. But the other salesladies, Mexican girls all, didn't like her. She was so nice to them all they were hard put to justify their dislike. They couldn't very well admit they disliked her because she was pretty. So they all said she was haughty and imperious. Their claim was partly true. Her beauty was Miss Rosas' only obvious vanity. But she had still another. She prided herself on being more American than Mexican because she was born in El Paso. And she did her best to act, dress, and talk the way Americans do. She hated to speak Spanish, disliked her Mexican name. She called herself Cecile Roses instead of Cecilia Rosas. This made the other salesladies smile derisively. They called her La Americana or the Gringa from Xochimilco every time they mentioned her name.

Looking at this beautiful girl was more important than money to me. It was my greatest compensation for doing work that I hated. She was so lovely that a glance at her sweetly expressive face was enough to make me forget my shame at wearing a smock and my dislike for my job with its eternal waiting around.

Miss Rosas was an exemplary saleslady. She could be frivolous, serious, or demure, primly efficient too, molding herself to each customer's personality. Her voice matched her exotically mysterious eyes. It was the richest, the softest I had ever heard. Her husky whisper, gentle as a rain breeze, was like a tender caress. Hearing it made me want to dream and I did. Romantic thoughts burgeoned up in my mind like rosy billows of hope scented with Miss Rosas' perfume. These thoughts made me so languid at my work that the floor manager, Joe Apple, warned me to show some enthusiasm for it or else suffer the consequences.

But my dreams sapped my will to struggle, making me oblivious to admonitions. I had neither the desire nor the energy to respond to Joe Apple's warnings. Looking at Miss Rosas used up so much of my energy that I had little left for my work. Miss Rosas was twenty, much too old for me, everyone said. But what everyone said didn't matter. So I soldiered on the job and watched her, entranced by her beauty, her grace. While I watched I dreamed of being a hero. It hurt me to have her see me doing menial work. But there was no escape from it. I needed the job to stay in school. So more and more I took refuge in dreams.

When I had watched her as much, if not more, than I could safely do without attracting the attention of other alert Mexican salesladies, I slipped out of Ladies' Wear and walked up the stairs to the top floor. There I sat on a window ledge smoking Faro cigarettes, looking down at the city's canyons, and, best of all, thinking about Miss Rosas and myself.

They say Chihuahua Mexicans are good at dreaming because the mountains are so gigantic and the horizons so vast in Mexico's biggest state that men don't think pygmy thoughts there. I was no exception. Lolling on the ledge, I became what I wanted to be. And what I wanted to be was a handsome American Miss Rosas could love and marry. The dreams I dreamed were imaginative masterpieces, or so I thought. They transcended the insipid realities of a casual relationship, making it vibrantly thrilling and infinitely more romantic. They transformed me from a colorless Mexican boy who put women's coats away into the debonair American, handsome, dashing, and worldly, that I longed to be for her sake. For the first time in my life I revelled in the magic of fantasy. It brought happiness. Reality didn't.

But my window-ledge reveries left me bewildered and shaken. They had a narcotic quality. The more thrillingly romantic fantasies I created, the more I needed to create. It got so I couldn't get enough

135

dreaming time in Ladies' Wear. My kind of dreaming demanded disciplined concentration. And there was just too much hubbub, too much gossiping, too many coats to be put away there.

So I spent less time in Ladies' Wear. My flights to the window ledge became more recklessly frequent. Sometimes I got tired sitting there. When I did, I took the freight elevator down to the street floor and brazenly walked out of the store without so much as punching a time clock. Walking the streets quickened my imagination, gave form and color to my thoughts. It made my brain glow with impossible hopes that seemed incredibly easy to realize. So absorbed was I in thoughts of Miss Rosas and myself that I bumped into Americans, apologizing mechanically in Spanish instead of English, and wandered down South El Paso Street like a somnambulist, without really seeing its street vendors, cafés and arcades, tattoo shops, and shooting galleries at all.

But if there was confusion in these walks there was some serenity too. Something good did come from the dreams that prompted them. I found I could tramp the streets with a newly won tranquillity, no longer troubled by, or even aware of, girls in tight skirts, overflowing blouses, and drop-stitch stockings. My love for Miss Rosas was my shield against the furtive thoughts and indiscriminate desires that had made me so uneasy for a year or more before I met her.

Then, too, because of her, I no longer looked at the pictures of voluptuous women in the *Vea* and *Vodevil* magazines at Zomora's newstand. The piquant thoughts Mexicans call *malos deseos* were gone from my mind. I no longer thought about women as I did before I fell in love with Miss Rosas. Instead, I thought about a woman, only one. This clear-cut objective and the serenity that went with it made me understand something of one of the nicest things about love.

I treasured the walks, the window-ledge sittings, and the dreams that I had then. I clung to them just as long as I could. Drab realities closed in on me chokingly just as soon as I gave them up. My future was a time clock with an American Mister telling me what to do and this I knew only too well. A career as an ice-dock laborer stretched ahead of me. Better said, it dangled over me like a Veracruz machete. My uncle Rodolfo Avitia, a straw boss on the ice docks, was already training me for it. Every night he took me to the mile-long docks overhanging the Southern Pacific freight yards. There he handed me tongs and made me practice tripping three-hundred-pound ice blocks so I could learn how to unload an entire boxcar of ice blocks myself.

Thinking of this bleak future drove me back into my fantasies, made me want to prolong them forever. My imagination was taxed to the breaking point by the heavy strain I put on it.

I thought about every word Miss Rosas had ever said to me, making myself believe she looked at me with unmistakable tenderness when she said them. When she said: "Amado, please hang up this fur coat," I found special meaning in her tone. It was as though she had said: "Amadito, I love you."

When she gave these orders, I pushed into action like a man blazing with a desire to perform epically heroic feats. At such times I felt capable of putting away not one but a thousand fur coats, and would have done so joyously.

Sometimes on the street I caught myself murmuring: "Cecilia, *linda amorcita*, I love you." When these surges swept over me, I walked down empty streets so I could whisper: "Cecilia, *te quiero con toda mi alma*" as much as I wanted to and mumble everything else that I felt. And so I emptied my heart on the streets and window ledge while women's coats piled up in Ladies' Wear.

But my absences didn't go unnoticed. Once an executive-looking man, portly, gray, and efficiently brusque, confronted me while I sat on the window ledge with a Faro cigarette pasted to my lips, a cloud of tobacco smoke hanging over my head, and many perfumed dreams inside it. He had a no-nonsense approach that jibed with his austere mien. He asked me what my name was, jotted down my work number, and went off to make a report on what he called "sordid malingering."

Other reports followed this. Gruff warnings, stern admonitions, and blustery tirades developed from them. They came from both major and minor executives. These I was already inured to. They didn't matter anyway. My condition was far too advanced, already much too complex to be cleared up by mere lectures, fatherly or otherwise. All the threats and rebukes in the world couldn't have made me give up my window-ledge reveries or kept me from roaming city streets with Cecilia Rosas' name on my lips like a prayer.

The reports merely made me more cunning, more doggedly determined to city-slick La Feria out of work hours I owed it. The net result was that I timed my absences more precisely and contrived better lies to explain them. Sometimes I went to the men's room and looked at myself in the mirror for as long as ten minutes at a time. Such self-studies filled me with gloom. The mirror reflected an ordinary Mexican face, more homely than comely. Only my hair gave me hope. It was thick and wavy, deserving a better face to go with it. So I did the best I could with what I had, and combed it over my temples in ringlets just like the poets back in my hometown of Parral, Chihuahua, used to do.

My inefficiency, my dreams, my general lassitude could have gone on indefinitely, it seemed. My life at the store wavered between bright hope and leaden despair, unrelieved by Miss Rosas' acceptance or rejection of me. Then one day something happened that almost made my overstrained heart stop beating.

It happened on the day Miss Rosas stood behind me while I put a fur coat away. Her heady perfume, the fragrance of her warm healthy body, made me feel faint. She was so close to me I thought about putting my hands around her lissome waist and hugging her as hard as I could. But thoughts of subsequent disgrace deterred me, so instead of hugging her I smiled wanly and asked her in Spanish how she was feeling.

"Amado, speak English," she told me. "And pronounce the words slowly and carefully so you won't sound like a country Mexican."

Then she looked at me in a way that made me the happiest employee who ever punched La Feria's time clock.

"Amadito," she whispered the way I had always dreamed she would.

"Yes, Señorita Cecilia," I said expectantly.

Her smile was warmly intimate. "Amadito, when are you going to take me to the movies?" she asked.

Other salesladies watched us, all smiling. They made me so nervous I couldn't answer.

"Amadito, you haven't answered me," Miss Rosas said teasingly. "Either you're bashful as a village sweetheart or else you don't like me at all."

In voluble Spanish, I quickly assured her the latter wasn't the case. I was just getting ready to say "Señorita Cecilia, I more than like you, I love you" when she frowned and told me to speak English. So I slowed down and tried to smooth out my ruffled thoughts.

"Señorita Cecilia," I said. "I'd love to take you to the movies any time."

Miss Rosas smiled and patted my cheek. "Will you buy me candy and popcorn?" she said.

I nodded, putting my hand against the imprint her warm palm had left on my face.

"And hold my hand?"

I said "yes" so enthusiastically it made her laugh. Other salesladies laughed too. Dazed and numb with happiness, I watched Miss Rosas walk away. How proud and confident she was, how wholesomely clean and feminine. Other salesladies were looking at me and laughing.

Miss Sandoval came over to me. "*Ay papacito*," she said. "With women you're the divine tortilla."

Miss de la Rosa came over too. "When you take the Americana to the movies, remember not to speak Christian," she said. "And be sure you wear the pants that don't have any patches on them."

What they said made me blush and wonder how they knew what we had been talking about. Miss Arroyo came over to join them. So did Miss Torres.

"Amado, remember women are weak and men aren't made of sweet bread," Miss Arroyo said.

This embarrassed me but it wasn't altogether unpleasant. Miss Sandoval winked at Miss de la Rosa, then looked back at me.

"Don't go too fast with the Americana, Amado," she said. "Remember the procession is long and the candles are small."

They laughed and slapped me on the back. They all wanted to know when I was going to take Miss Rosas to the movies. "She didn't say," I blurted out without thinking.

This brought another burst of laughter. It drove me back up to the window ledge where I got out my package of Faros and thought about the wonderful thing that had happened. But I was too nervous to stay there. So I went to the men's room and looked at myself in the mirror again, wondering why Miss Rosas liked me so well. The mirror made it brutally clear that my looks hadn't influenced her. So it must have been something else, perhaps character. But that didn't seem likely either. Joe Apple had told me I didn't have much of that. And other store officials had bulwarked his opinion. Still, I had seen homely men walking the streets of El Paso's Little Chihuahua quarter with beautiful Mexican women and no one could explain that either. Anyway it was time for another walk. So I took one.

This time I trudged through Little Chihuahua, where both Miss Rosas and I lived. Little Chihuahua looked different to me that day. It was a broken-down Mexican quarter honeycombed with tenements, Mom and Pop groceries, herb shops, cafés, and spindly salt cedar trees; with howling children running its streets and old Mexican revolutionaries sunning themselves on its curbs like iguanas. But on that clear frosty day it was the world's most romantic place because Cecilia Rosas lived there.

While walking, I reasoned that Miss Rosas might want to go dancing after the movies. So I went to Professor Toribio Ortega's dance studio and made arrangements to take my first lesson. Some neighborhood boys saw me when I came out. They bawled "*Mariquita*" and made flutteringly effeminate motions, all vulgar if not obscene. It didn't matter. On my lunch hour I went back and took my first lesson anyway. Professor Ortega danced with me. Softened by weeks of dreaming, I went limp in his arms imagining he was Miss Rosas.

The rest of the day was the same as many others before it. As usual I spent most of it stealing glances at Miss Rosas and slipping up to the window ledge. She looked busy, efficient, not like a woman in love. Her many other admirers trooped to the water fountain to look at the way her black silk dress fitted her curves. Their profane admiration made me scowl even more than I usually did at such times.

When the day's work was done, I plodded home from the store just as dreamily as I had gone to it. Since I had no one else to confide in, I invited my oldest sister, Dulce Nombre de María, to go to the movies with me. They were showing Jorge Negrete and María Felix in *El Rapto* at the Colon Theater. It was a romantic movie, just the kind I wanted to see.

After it was over, I bought Dulce Nombre *churros* and hot *champurrado* at the Golden Taco Café. And I told my sister all about what had happened to me. She looked at me thoughtfully, then combed my hair back with her fingertips as though trying to soothe me. "Manito," she said, softly. "I wouldn't . . ." Then she looked away and shrugged her shoulders.

On Monday I borrowed three dollars from my Uncle Rodolfo without telling him what it was for. Miss Rosas hadn't told me what night she wanted me to take her to the movies. But the way she had looked at me made me think that almost any night would do. So I decided on Friday. Waiting for it to come was hard. But I had to keep my mind occupied. So I went to Zamora's newsstand to get the Alma Nortena songbook. Poring through it for the most romantic song I could find, I decided on *La Cecilia*.

All week long I practiced singing it on my way to school and in the shower after basketball practice with the Little Chihuahua Tigers at the Sagrado Corazon gym. But, except for singing this song, I tried not to speak Spanish at all. At home I made my mother mad by saying in English, "Please pass the sugar."

My mother looked at me as though she couldn't believe what she had heard. Since my Uncle Rodolfo couldn't say anything more than "hello" and "goodbye" in English, he couldn't tell what I had said. So my sister Consuelo did.

"May the Dark Virgin with the benign look make this boy well enough to speak Christian again," my mother whispered.

This I refused to do. I went on speaking English even though my mother and uncle didn't understand it. This shocked my sisters as well. When they asked me to explain my behavior, I parroted Miss Rosas, saying, "We're living in the United States now."

My rebellion against being a Mexican created an uproar. Such conduct was unorthodox, if not scandalous, in a neighborhood where names like Burgiaga, Rodriguez, and Castillo predominated. But it wasn't only the Spanish language that I lashed out against.

"Mother, why do we always have to eat *sopa, frijoles, refritos, mondongo,* and *pozole*?" I complained. "Can't we ever eat roast beef or ham and eggs like Americans do?"

My mother didn't speak to me for two days after that. My Uncle Rodolfo grimaced and mumbled something about renegade Mexicans who want to eat ham and eggs even though the Montes Packing Company turned out the best *chorizo* this side of Toluca. My sister Consuelo giggled and called me a Rio Grande Irishman, an American Mister, a gringo, and a *bolillo*. Dulce Nombre looked at me worriedly.

Life at home was almost intolerable. Cruel jokes and mocking laughter made it so. I moped around looking sad as a day without bread. My sister Consuelo suggested I go to the courthouse and change my name to Beloved Wall, which is English for Amado Muro. My mother didn't agree. "If *Nuestro Señor* had meant for Amadito to be an American he would have given him a name like Smeeth or Jonesy," she said. My family was unsympathetic. With a family like mine, how could I ever hope to become an American and win Miss Rosas?

Friday came at last. I put on my only suit, slicked my hair down with liquid vaseline, and doused myself with Dulce Nombre's perfume.

"Amado's going to serenade that pretty girl everyone calls La Americana," my sister Consuelo told my mother and uncle when I sat down to eat. "Then he's going to take her to the movies."

141

This made my uncle laugh and my mother scowl.

"*Qué pantalones tiene* (what nerve that boy's got)," my uncle said, "to serenade a twenty-year-old woman."

"La Americana," my mother said derisively. "That one's Mexican as pulque cured with celery."

They made me so nervous I forgot to take off my cap when I sat down to eat.

"Amado, take off your cap," my mother said. "You're not in La Lagunilla Market."

My uncle frowned. "All this boy thinks about is kissing girls," he said gruffly.

"But my boy's never kissed one," my mother said proudly.

My sister Consuelo laughed. "That's because they won't let him," she said.

This wasn't true. But I couldn't say so in front of my mother. I had already kissed Emalina Uribe from Porfirio Díaz Street not once but twice. Both times I'd kissed her in a darkened doorway less than a block from her home. But the kisses were over so soon we hardly had time to enjoy them. This was because Ema was afraid her big brother, the husky one nicknamed Toro, would see us. But if we'd had more time it would have been better, I knew.

Along about six o'clock the three musicians who called themselves the Mariachis of Tecalitlán came by and whistled for me, just as they had said they would. They never looked better than they did on that night. They had on black-and-silver charro uniforms and big, black Zapata sombreros.

My mother shook her head when she saw them. "Son, who ever heard of serenading a girl at six o'clock in the evening," she said. "When your father had the mariachis sing for me it was always two o'clock in the morning—the only proper time for a six-song *gallo*."

But I got out my Ramirez guitar anyway. I put on my cap and rushed out to give the mariachis the money without even kissing my mother's hand or waiting for her to bless me. Then we headed for Miss Rosas' home. Some boys and girls I knew were out in the street. This made me uncomfortable. They looked at me wonderingly as I led the mariachi band to Miss Rosas' home.

A block away from Miss Rosas' home I could see her father, a grizzled veteran who fought for Pancho Villa, sitting on the curb reading the Juarez newspaper, *El Fronterizo*.

The sight of him made me slow down for a moment. But I got back in stride when I saw Miss Rosas herself.

She smiled and waved at me. "Hello, Amadito," she said.

"Hello, Señorita Cecilia," I said.

She looked at the mariachis, then back to me.

"Ay, Amado, you're going to serenade your girl," she said. I didn't reply right away. Then when I was getting ready to say "Señorita Cecilia, I came to serenade you," I saw the American man sitting in the sports roadster at the curb.

Miss Rosas turned to him. "I'll be right there, Johnny," she said.

She patted my cheek. "I've got to run now, Amado," she said. "Have a real nice time, darling."

I looked at her silken legs as she got into the car. Everything had happened so fast I was dazed. Broken dreams made my head spin. The contrast between myself and the poised American in the sports roadster was so cruel it made me wince.

She was happy with him. That was obvious. She was smiling and laughing, looking forward to a good time. Why had she asked me to take her to the movies if she already had a boyfriend? Then I remembered how the other salesladies had laughed, how I had wondered why they were laughing when they couldn't even hear what we were saying. And I realized it had all been a joke, everyone had known it but me. Neither Miss Rosas nor the other salesladies had ever dreamed I would think she was serious about wanting me to take her to the movies.

The American and Miss Rosas drove off. Gloomy thoughts oppressed me. They made me want to cry. To get rid of them I thought of going to one of the "bad death" cantinas in Juárez where tequila starts fights and knives finish them—to one of the cantinas where the panders, whom Mexicans call *burros*, stand outside shouting "It's just like Paris, only not so many people" was where I wanted to go. There I could forget her in Jalisco-state style with mariachis, tequila, and night-life women. Then I remembered I was so young that night-life women would shun me and *cantineros* wouldn't serve me tequila.

So I thought some more. Emalina Uribe was the only other alternative. If we went over to Porfirio Díaz Street and serenaded her I could go back to being a Mexican again. She was just as Mexican as I was, Mexican as *chicharrones*. I thought about smiling, freckle-faced Ema.

Ema wasn't like the Americana at all. She wore wash dresses that fitted loosely and even ate the *melcocha* candies Mexicans liked so well on the street. On Sundays she wore a Zamora shawl to church and her mother wouldn't let her use lipstick or let her put on high heels.

But with a brother like Toro who didn't like me anyway, such a serenade might be more dangerous than romantic. Besides that, my faith in my looks, my character, or whatever it was that made women fall in love with men was so undermined I could already picture her getting into a car with a handsome American just like Miss Rosas had done.

The Mariachis of Tecalitlán were getting impatient. They had been paid to sing six songs and they wanted to sing them. But they were all sympathetic. None of them laughed at me.

"Amado, don't look sad as I did the day I learned I'd never be a millionaire," the mariachi captain said, putting his arm around me. "If not that girl, then another."

But without Miss Rosas there was no one we could sing *La Cecilia* to. The street seemed bleak and empty now that she was gone. And I didn't want to serenade Ema Uribe even though she hadn't been faithless as Miss Rosas had been. It was true she hadn't been faithless, but only lack of opportunity would keep her from getting into a car with an American, I reasoned cynically.

Just about then Miss Rosas' father looked up from his newspaper. He asked the mariachis if they knew how to sing *Cananea Jail*. They told him they did. Then they looked at me. I thought it over for a moment. Then I nodded and started strumming the bass strings of my guitar. What had happened made it only too plain I could never trust Miss Rosas again. So we serenaded her father instead.

1964

144

MARY GRAY HUGHES
The Judge

The Mexican's name was Baille. "Pronounced 'Buy-ye,'" the Judge liked to explain with amusement, and for the past three months now, at least once every week, the Judge had driven out through the flat countryside to where the Mexican lived to try to make him sign some papers. So far the Mexican would not do it.

"You'd think I was trying to sell him snake oil," the Judge said. "The old charlatan. I can't help liking him. Last time he came out with the statement that he didn't even have any rights in the claim at all. Just after I had shown him, with genealogical charts, how I had traced him. He says he's Basque, but that's nonsense. The name is pure Spanish. You find it all over this part of the state and in northern Mexico, going back, with a few orthographic variations, for two hundred years. There were never any Basques around here."

The Judge would know. He knew about languages and races and the origins of people and their names. He had made a study of such things. He could speak five languages and read two more. He knew Baille personally, too, though it was only in the last year that he had come to know the Mexican well.

"It's not that he's an important claimant," the Judge said. "His portion is one of the smaller ones. But when it is a question of the heirs in a petition against the States, then it looks better to have all the heirs

file. He's the only one who won't sign. One hundred and twenty-seven depositions I've got, two of them from as far away as the state of Oaxaca, and a brief that is easily the most complicated ever submitted in this jurisdiction, and I'm held up by a country school janitor. It's good I can appreciate the humor of it. Nonetheless, time is getting short. I must try to move him along this Sunday. I'll tell you one thing, if I have to drive out to that place of his many more times, I'm going to get the county to do something about that road."

Not the highway. The Judge did not mean that. The highway was fine; laid flat and dead straight on the ground, it fell before him across the countryside like a clap of thunder, splitting the gray brush in two. On Sunday afternoons it was usually empty, and the Judge's solitary car hummed along at the fifty miles an hour advised by the instruction book as best for breaking in a new car. They had offered to let him keep a state car when he resigned. "No, no," the Judge had said, "you know me better than that."

The first turn off the highway to Baille's came just beyond the railroad crossing. From there the Judge's car followed a gravel road past the country school where the Mexican was janitor. Beyond that there was a bend crowded by willow trees and then a sharp right turn onto a narrow dirt road. Dust spilled out under the wheels and rose up beside the car like a giant gray dog and ran around the curves with it, brushing against the bushes in the narrow places. When the Judge stopped at last before the Mexican's house, dust poured up and over and through the car and on ahead down the road before collapsing back down into the ground again.

The Judge spat out the window to clear his mouth and honked the horn once, then again. Nothing happened. He knew Baille would not come out. He honked again, longer.

"Baille," the Judge yelled out the car window. "Hey, Baille."

"You know, I took a Sears catalog out there to him once. And a big black pencil in case he didn't have one. I told him to put a check by all the things in the catalog he wanted, just go ahead and mark everything he would like to have, anything and everything, and to keep on marking, and I would tell him to stop when he had used up the money I could make for him in one single year. He wouldn't do it. He wouldn't even look at the catalog. Wouldn't even open it."

The Judge sat in the car staring at the shack and rubbing his nose, which he did in a very distinctive way. He held his hand still and moved his head gently up and down, sliding his nose between his thumb and forefinger. It was occurring to the Judge that it would all be a great deal easier if the Mexican had more of the world's goods, for then there would be more places where pressure could be applied.

The Judge honked again, and called "Baille" louder, but without really expecting any result. He got out of the car and started over to the gate. A short man, with most of his height from the waist up, the Judge walked with his back rigid and his big powerful stomach firmly leading so that he looked in profile like a chair being pushed steadily forward.

Around his feet two bulbs of dust spouted onto his shoelaces and his trouser legs and then settled back down on the tops and sides of his shoes when he stopped before the fence. It was a fence made of barbed wire and mesquite. The wire was a dull color, with rust exploding around the base of each barb, and the untrimmed mesquite posts were knobbed and twisted and so dried up that the old shallow, hand-dug postholes gaped open around them.

The Judge established himself by the main gate post to wait. He lifted a foot to rest it comfortably on one of the lower strands, but the wire twanged loose onto the ground, throwing the Judge forward.

"Damn," the Judge swore. And yelled "Baille!"

"It's true that it is not precisely flattering to be kept cooling my heels outside his fence until it suits him to come out. I need my old bailiff to hail him for me. Still, they have a sense of dignity and pride, these Mexicans. It denies our tempo of doing things. They insist on time, they respect it. And let me make one other point: he has some strange, absolutely prefect sense of just when it is the right time to come out."

The Judge pressed his stomach against the gate, moving it back on the tripled loops of wire that served as hinges. His hand eased along toward the latch. From around a corner of the shack the Mexican appeared, walking quickly with little low steps that moved him over the bare ground with no up-and-down movement at all but simply a fast unbroken propulsion forward as steadily efficient as the towing along of rakes or harrows after tractors, or the dragging of dead things behind the low rear bumpers of cars.

He was a man in his fifties, and so short he was forced to tip his head back to look up at the Judge. When he did, the Mexican showed his face with all the flattest angles exposed, showed his quick blinking eyes and soft squashed nose.

147

"How can you stand the heat out here?" the Judge said in a friendly tone.

The Mexican stared at him with the wild surprise the Judge's lisping Castilian always brought to him, for how was it this man could go on sounding like a drunken bird every time he spoke?

"Doesn't it bother you?" the Judge said again.

"You don't like the heat?" the Mexican said finally, hopefully.

"I can take the heat. It's the dust I really don't like. I swear, if you don't start acting sensibly, Baille, I'm going to get this road blacktopped."

The Mexican peered in amazement at the thin dirt road running along his fence and beneath the Judge's car, for the Judge had just announced that he intended to take an oath to do away with the road in darkness with a coating of perpetual obscurity.

"You don't like the dust then?" the Mexican said, trying again. "There is certainly much dust here. Much dust. You should stay in town. You stay in town, and I will come to visit you there."

"There is an innocence, or rather an obviousness that reminds one of innocence, in some of his ploys. At times it is terribly poignant. A touch . . . not of childishness, they are not childish, these people, he's a grown and very tough man, but a touch of the basic, unconcealed, open human being that can be very moving. Would any of you believe that I feel I have actually learned from him?"

"I think not," the Judge said to the Mexican. "I think not. You might forget to come. But I never forget, do I?" And the Judge began to fan himself slowly, swinging his hat in wide arcs. His clothing was sweated through. "Listen," the Judge said, "why won't you trust me? All I want is to make some money for you. Why won't you do what I tell you?"

"Don't think the irony of it has escaped me. Mrs. Easterbury reminded me only the other night that I was the one who got him his job. Otherwise he might not even be around here. Well, I don't regret it. He came to me for help about two years ago. I'd hardly spoken to him before, but he knew who I was, so of course I had to help him. His wife had just left him, and he had some scheme in mind, some absurd plan for getting her back. I got him the job as janitor. I told the school board he would never steal. I took the responsibility for that and gave them my assurance, and he never has stolen a thing."

"No papers," the Mexican said, shaking his head. "No papers for signing. Absolutely no."

"You can sign your name," the Judge said. "I've seen it written down at the courthouse."

The Mexican neither moved nor spoke, but the Judge became instantly alert, for he knew, just as he would have in a courtroom, that the Mexican was running inside, running and running while he was standing still. The Judge was sure of it.

"What's the matter with your name on the records?" the Judge said. "Hm? What's wrong with it?"

"Nothing, nothing," the Mexican said. "It's my mother's name for me, why not? So if you don't like it, what will you do? Shoot me?" And he burst into a fit of giggles snuffled out against the back of his hand. For the phrase in Spanish was *Fuegame*, and it could mean either "fire me," as from a job, or "shoot me," as with a gun. Months ago when the Mexican had first said it, the Judge had been so delighted he had laughed out loud, and after a few seconds of uncertainty, Baille had joined in, laughing harder and harder.

"Their humor. Even when used as the most pathetically obvious smoke screen, still it is always appealing. Superb, poised, and proud. It's dour and simple, yet with sophistication, too, and with that special cast of appreciating language. That's what I relish most of all, the gift of language that they have. You see it right from the earliest days of the nation's history and down through all the major shifts in the language itself. They have a racial genius for language. Do you realize that even the poorest, most uneducated Mexican uses the subjunctive mood?"

"Fuegame," the Mexican said again, giggling behind his hand.

"Maybe, maybe," the Judge said. "Or better than that, if you don't act sensibly, I might have a look at those records in the courthouse. The ones with your name." He said it pleasantly, and aware that the expression on his face was one of brightness and humor, with his eyes twinkling, yet he wanted a threat in his words, and there was. The Mexican was running again inside.

"How old are you?" the Judge asked suddenly, trusting it was the right question.

Intelligence flicked and vanished in the Mexican's face the way a lizard's tail slips away between sun-baked rocks, and the Judge was left gazing at the place where understanding had been. And slowly, with exquisite precision, the Judge's mind eased open and gave up to him his secrets in the order in which he needed them: the Mexican's age did not match his name. This Mexican's age was decades short of what was

149

needed to match those yellowing, smudged courthouse records. He had "bought his name," as the Mexicans put it, and his papers were forged.

The Judge was home free.

"I was reminded of the last will and testament of one of the first Spanish conquistadores. 'Before us,' he had written, 'there was no evil, now there is no good.' A moving sentiment, but is it history? The Aztecs could not have been conquered if the majority of the Indians in the Valley of Mexico had not joined Cortez's crew precisely because the Aztec rule had been so cruel; so evil, indeed, that they were willing to follow anyone else in order to overthrow that rule. Our Spanish testator erred in the way we all do—what we do not understand, we always simplify."

"Has the Sheriff ever looked at those records of yours in the courthouse?"

There was no more running now inside the Mexican, just the quick blinking of his eyes, the rabbit caught and waiting.

"You look to me, Baille," the Judge said, "like a man who may have himself some trouble."

The Mexican waited.

"Listen," the Judge said, "I could go on away from here right now without any signature of yours on any papers. I don't need it. I can prove from the records in the courthouse that I don't need it. But I'm not going to do that. I've made up my mind to help you. I know all about you, and you'll have to do what I say. Do you understand?"

"It would be all right if you went away from here now," the Mexican said. "You can do that."

"Don't think it is just altruism on my part," the Judge said. "If I don't get your signature on the papers, it will not look right, because there are people who know your name should be in this case. So if you do not sign, I will have to explain why you did not, and I will have to tell about your records. Do you see? I will have to tell, and then the Sheriff will know about you, and then he would come for you. Understand?"

The Judge set himself to sound absolutely commanding, and it was easy because he had come to that key moment when he knew he was winning and was enjoying his skill at closing a case.

"Now, you go on in there and change your clothes," the Judge said firmly. He knew better than to give the Mexican any time. "I am going to take you with me into town to sign those papers." The Mexican's fast-blinking eyes kept wavering away, glancing off toward the road and the brush around. "Oh, yes," the Judge said, "yes, right now. You go put on something else, something cleaner that you can wear to the courthouse. Go on. Now. And while you're changing, I'll go take a look at your lake."

"Mud pond—that's what I usually call these unimproved water holes when I'm not trying to be nice to the people living near them. Little indentations in the ground they are, no deeper than the hollow in a beggar's palm and filled with thick brownish water evaporating away from the muddy banks. Often one end will go deeper, keeping a permanent water supply, and willows grow up all around it. Any of you noticed these little ponds? Ah, you should. These sites are going to be worth good money one of these days."

The Judge crossed the road and walked alongside it, and the soles of his shoes snapped down the brittle grass that grew and burned and grew again out in the sun beside the road. Once in the shade of the willow trees the grass thickened and made a soft cushion under the Judge's feet. He went straight to the deep part of the pond. As he went he kicked in the reeds and fallen tree limbs for frogs or turtles or any signs of the small animals that exist in the banks near water. Just at the end of the pond there was a little rise of ground. It was not more than three feet high, but in the midst of the violent flatness of the countryside around it seemed higher, and the Judge, coming out from the fringe of willows and putting aside their frail branch tips with the side of his hand, pulled himself up onto it with his short legs and felt he could see a long way, felt he could see for miles. He looked across the pool to the low brush beyond and the dense trees of pale green and gray on the other side. He would have been embarrassed to say how stirred he was by the countryside, or how much beauty he saw in the tangle of mesquite trees growing in a solid cloud on their thin, crooked trunks. He would not have wanted to tell of a game he played, when he was out in the country, of letting his eyes rise only slowly, slowly along the low line of brush and small mesquite, and inch by half-inch go along the solid mass, then slowly lift to the first few broken spaces in between, and moving faster, a little faster and rising again, up and farther along, and going with joy now, joy, up and faster and off over mesquite and willow to the horizon and the dumb unbelievable idiot palm trees grinning like God, he told himself, over the long flat landscape running beneath them all the way to the sea.

"It wasn't easy. I tried just about everything on him. I made three trips out to the school to see the principal, and I made sure each time that Baille saw us together. That preyed on him. He would hang around in the hall pretending to sweep out but watching us. That fool principal spent all the time carrying tales to me against Baille. He told me the Mexican sneaks the lock shut on the boys' washroom once a week or so, and then hangs around in the hall to watch the fun. I was supposed to be shocked at this. Especially shocked because Baille thinks it's funny. The principal is naïve. He doesn't understand their humor. More than that, I think it bothers him that I like Baille. He can't understand why I want to help him. At heart, the principal has no feeling for them."

The Judge's attention was caught, by a sound? a smell? and he turned his head and the Mexican was there beside him. The Judge opened his mouth to speak, thinking to ask why the other was in the same clothes and had not changed, when all at once the whole of the Mexican—body, head, shoulders, arms, legs—came leaping onto the Judge and jolted him so hard that he hurt all through his body. The two of them fell, not backward and so down the slope of the little hill and into the shallow water as the Judge thought they would and the Mexican intended, but straight onto the muddy lip at the deep edge of the water, just below where the Judge had been standing. For the Judge had been felled absolutely, had had his short legs collapse right under him, and had fallen with the Mexican on top of him. They rolled from side to side on the muddy ground, and the willows shaded them some of the time, and the position of sky and lake and trees kept shifting in their line of vision.

All the time the Judge kept grunting and trying to get his breath to say something like: But this is an accident and I accept your apology for stupidly and clumsily and accidentally knocking into me; I understand; while the Mexican pulled at the Judge's head and shoulders trying to haul and shove him farther forward into the water, deep enough to cover his head and face entirely. Reeds at the water's edge snapped beneath the Judge's head, and a rock under his shoulder made him arch his back up in pain as he tried to roll free from the Mexican's hands, which fled from his head and face back to his arms and tugged and pushed at him again, moving him forward once more, farther into the water.

This time the Judge realized what was happening, and focused his eyes finally on the Mexican's face close above his own. The Judge's body jerked rigid and then turned frantic with terror. He grabbed at the Mexican's wrists, uselessly, then tried to get a hold anywhere on the skin that was thin and taut over muscle and bone, and not able to do that, clutched at the worn overalls, but he could not grasp hold of the Mexican in any way. "Knee him in the groin, knee him in the groin," yipped some part of the Judge's mind, delighting him with his own tough knowledge. But his legs thrashed foolishly and uselessly up and down, miles, it seemed, away from the Mexican straddling his chest. The Judge could not even kick the man in the back. The Judge pulled again, and again with no effect, at the Mexican's small hard wrists. With a hiss the Mexican shoved and slid him another few inches into the water and once more tried to submerge the heavy, golden head. There was not enough water, simply not enough water, and in a rage of despair the Mexican grabbed the Judge's head and pressed it deep into the mud. The shallow sludge filled the Judge's left ear and shut one eye, and the nostril on that side was plugged as solidly as by a finger. But the Judge's entire head would not go under. His free eye saw a reed inches in front of his face. It seemed gigantic, the strands that formed it long and beautifully green, and the edges of it the most incredible sharp yellow. The Judge strained toward it, moving with great effort, his head rising out of the mud and water. The Mexican hissed by his ear and got a different grip under the Judge's shoulders and hauled him forward again, deeper into the water. The Judge could feel mud under his shoulders now and dampness down to his waist, and water washed against his neck and up to his ears. With a deep grunt of satisfaction the Mexican pushed the Judge's head down again, hard, and this time the whole head and white face went beneath the water.

It was shocking. The Judge's eyes shut at first, but his ears heard all the sounds water takes in from the air but does not give back to it. He could hear hands thrashing in the water, and the sound of the Mexican's voice cursing. He opened his eyes, and he could see the Mexican, could see everything; it was there, but changed because of the layer of water over his face. The Judge went limp and the Mexican, too ignorant, too eager (*"Poor son of a gun. They're so often like that, defeat-*

ing themselves by lack of experience or lack of self-control"), pushed forward too fast, thinking it was over, thinking to finish it, rushing, and so rising up on the Judge's neck too high and getting himself off balance for just that instant (*"Timing has always been one of my greatest courtroom assets, you know"*), so the Judge gave a heave of his powerful stomach and short legs and rolled up and over his own shoulder, tossing the two of them backward, half-somersaulting, and crashing through the reeds and over the muddied lip of the pool and down into the clearer, deeper water. Wet now to hip, to chest, and at any minute over the head possibly, but the Judge was not to know, for the Mexican had turned and flung himself at the shore, crying out for it, lunging back to the bank with the Judge hanging on around his hips while the Mexican grasped and tugged on the reeds, pulling great, sucking chunks of them out of the mud and lunging back again at them and seizing thick sheaves of them in his hands. And all the time the Mexican kept making hoarse, gasping noises, steadily louder, until with a burst of strength he tugged the two of them out of the lake and plunged onto the muddy bank where they fell, crushing the reeds down into the mud.

The Judge propped himself on his knees but kept hard hold of the Mexican as they panted side by side. Streaks of mud curled down the sides of the Judge's face. "Listen," the Judge gasped. "Listen." But he could not get enough air for the words. He was bursting, bursting with joy. He had had a fight. He, the Judge, at his age, had had a fight, like any man, and with a Mexican.

"Listen," the Judge said, holding on to the Mexican's arm just under the shoulder, holding tight, lovingly. "Don't be frightened," the Judge said. "I understand. I am a man, too. I won't bring any charges against you for that. I know how you feel. I won't call the Sheriff. Understand? I know you had to fight."

"Have you ever seen a Mexican cry? A Mexican man, I mean? A grown man? Not the way we do, but with a little 'hee hee hee' noise. Sitting back on his heels with his head pressed against his knees and crying 'hee hee hee,' like that. Just like that."

"See here. Now, see here," the Judge said. "It's going to be all right. It's going to be fine. You can trust me."

The Mexican would not move or lift his head from his knees.

"I'll come out here tomorrow," the Judge said. "At ten. Ten in the

morning. And I'll take you to town. And I'll call the principal personally and explain to him that you won't be at work so you won't have any
trouble there. You be ready at ten sharp. Understand? Then you can
sign those papers. Look, it will be fine. Fine. Don't be scared. Don't
. . . don't make noises. Please. Don't. Why listen, listen, you may have
. . ." and he stopped. "Saved my life," the Judge wanted to say, but
inexcusably he could not remember the verb "to save" in that sense in
Spanish. "You may have kept me from drowning," he said. "Saved my
life," he remembered, "that's it. You may have saved my life."

The Mexican at least stopped making the noise. The Judge shook his
arm in comradely fashion.

"That's right. That's right," the Judge said. "See?"

*"No, of course we didn't shake hands. They don't make agreements
in that fashion. But by an old, mutually understood joke I became his
attorney. Yes, that's it, that's the truth, I was made his counselor by
humor, and, to be honest, I don't have a better contract, I can swear to
that. It was an extraordinary experience; he's an unusual man. All
the same, I think I may take up judo on the side if my practice con-
tinues in this way."*

"Of course you understand now," the Judge said. "Certainly. You
probably saved my life, and so I want to help you, too. I'll come out
here for you tomorrow at ten. Ten in the morning. You be ready. Hear?
You be ready, or I'll have to go get the Sheriff to shoot you. Our joke.
Right? Ha ha. Our joke."

In the morning the Judge changed his mind. It seemed to him the
best and most courteous thing would be to save the Mexican the trip
into town and to the courthouse. Instead, the Judge decided to take his
secretary, who could act as notary, and the necessary papers and go
out into the country and let the Mexican sign the papers there. The
Judge liked the idea of the gesture. He would meet the Mexican more
than halfway. And in any case, the Judge did not know how he and the
Mexican, with the closeness that they had between them now, would
manage in town, for the town was not ready for that yet.

The Judge went first thing, as he always did, to get his morning
newspaper. The newsstand attendant was waiting for him. An obese
man, he was squeezed into the narrow doorway of the shop with the
Judge's paper held folded and ready.

"You heard?" the attendant asked eagerly. The Judge, as was his custom, dropped a quarter into the brass bowl although the paper cost only ten cents. The attendant kept hold of the paper until he could finish his story. "Haven't you heard? Really? They's a Messgun drowned in the river. Sheriff says it's one you know. Says you know him for sure. I was the second one down to the bridge to see him. I could see him plain as I see you. He was washed up nearest the American side, and he still had a bundle with his things in it tied around his wrist. He was curled up and lying real funny, sort of right on his head and knees, like a little brown snail, and down back of him there was a trail going all the way he'd come out of the river. Everyone wondered where his hat was, but I told him any idiot would know a hat would be the first thing to float on off. Isn't that the truth, Judge? Any idiot ought to know that. But you know something I don't get, how come Messguns don' learn to swim since they keep crossing back and forth in that river all the time? You'd think they'd learn to swim, I say. Now, you take my sister's boy, he's learned to swim good and he's only fourteen. If they'd have learned to swim, them Messguns, none of them would have never drowned."

The Judge stood on the sidewalk with his feet planted square and carefully apart. He had a wide staring look on his face as if an arrow had shot straight through him from back to front going at a great speed and he was looking way off in the distance after it for some vital part of him that was being taken away faster and faster and faster over the long, flat Texas landscape. Then the Judge gave a sudden, violent jerk, as happens sometimes when falling asleep, or waking.

"So what I say," the attendant said, "is someone ought to teach them to swim. That's what I say."

The Judge turned and began walking away, stamping off with hard steps pounding on the sidewalk.

"Want your paper?" the attendant called after him. "Judge?"

The Judge did not answer. He was getting into his car. He turned it around in the middle of the street and started straight out into the country to the Mexican's home.

He drove the distance in the same way that he always did, at the same carefully restrained rate of speed. There were not even many other cars on the highway, and he got there in the same time that it took him on the quiet Sundays.

There was no sign of life from the shack or from the treeless area of dirt around it. The gate hung open, slanting crookedly onto the ground. The Judge turned off the engine of his car.

"Baille!" he yelled at the shack. "Baille!"

The Judge got out and slammed the door hard and began to walk through the sparse grass and the dust that heat and wind had worn to a powder. He walked cautiously, as if at any minute he expected to be struck lame by a stiffening in both knees, an affliction he had felt creeping up on him from a long time past and which he dreaded because he knew that, like old rusted locks, it was something no oil or ointment or paid-for expert he might hire was ever going to loosen for him again.

"Baille!" the Judge yelled.

There was no point in standing still before the open gate. The Judge went through it into the yard where he had never been before. He walked toward the corner of the shack around which he was used to seeing the Mexican come. He supposed there must be some sort of door on the other side. When he turned the corner he saw a square black opening in the wall before him. "Baille?" he called again, when he had reached the door, "Baille?" and, there being no reply, he lowered his head and plunged into the darkness inside.

There was no one there. The Mexican was gone. And the second shock was the size of the room. For somehow the Judge had always imagined rooms and rooms expanding within the small frame of the shack. In his mind, the Judge had thought of the Mexican waiting for him while sitting in a living room or small reading room, with a kitchen off to his left somewhere and at his back a bedroom. The Judge had placed the Mexican there, sitting comfortably, reading perhaps, or walking around at his ease while he waited for the Judge to come so he could match wits with him again. But there was instead a square of space marked off by gray wooden boards and covered with a tin roof and with the bare ground underfoot. There were not even windows cut in the walls. Threads of light spun themselves down through gaps in the roof, and a block of light fell through the doorway like a hunk of wall collapsed onto the floor.

The Judge's eyes adjusted to the dimness, and he could see every part of the room. Quite obviously the Mexican was gone, gone and had meant to go. He had left a coat the Judge had given him, and a pair of pants the Judge had given him, and two black shoes the Judge had given him. But all the rest was gone except the heavy things he could not carry, a table made of railroad ties and next to it a three-legged stool; an old kerosene stove that was thick with rust; a brass bedstead with no mattress.

A cup, still half-filled with coffee, was on the table, and the Judge put his palm against its side. It was cold.

"Damn him," the Judge said. He struck the cup a flat blow, lifting it up through the air to smash into the wall. "Damn, damn, damn him," and the Judge kicked the small three-legged stool. It rolled under the table. The Judge kicked one of the table legs, but the table stood firm on thick square legs. The Judge bent over and caught the edge of the table to upend it, but it would not move. He could not budge it. He tugged again, heaving on it, and when it still stood motionless he bent lower, his head just above its surface, and pulled harder, his mouth strained open with the effort and his face glazing with sweat as he pulled and pulled—and he was seeing through the bright sunlight his car just beyond the gate, and realized he had been seeing it for several seconds before he understood that it was possible, that he had been seeing it with that special clarity of vision given by a peephole, a tiny tear-shaped opening between two warped boards.

And he understood that the Mexican had seen him this way. The Mexican had sat there in the dark at this table and had seen him, the Judge; had watched and waited, all the time looking out through the little hole, and seen the car arrive and the Judge get out of it, and watched it all in a flood of garlic-smelling sweat and terror while his heart leaped and raced all over the place inside his frozen, terrified fraud's pose of stillness.

"Your simple Mexican has a grace of bearing and manner that is hard to believe if you have not seen it. Or experienced it, perhaps, is a better way of putting it. Let me give you an example. I drive up to his house, you see, and of course he hears the car, but first I have to sit and wait. There is to be no rushing. Finally, I get out and walk to the gate, and sometimes I call out to him. Nothing happens. Some ethnic formality of time has to be satisfied first, some proper amount of respect allowed for. Then he emerges and comes forward to meet me at the gate. But it is always just as I become restless and impatient, yet most receptive, that he appears. He comes when I am most alert, most open to meeting with him. He knows this somehow. Then he comes forward, and every time it is done with pride."

158

"Damn him." The Judge slammed his palms down on the table so hard his cheeks quivered with the blow. "Damn him for a rotten fraud. Damn him." He leaned forward over the table with his arms braced stiffly straight on it. "Damn him to hell, I swear if I could I'd kill him . . ."

He stared straight ahead at the empty air, and slowly his body sagged down onto the thick black table. His hands slid across the rough surface to the opposite side so that he was half lying on it, almost embracing the wood, with his heavy stomach pressed against the edge.

"I wonder when he started packing?" the Judge said. "I wonder what he used to make the bundle—a secondhand gunnysack and some old begged-for, handed-down rotten piece of twine?"

The Judge's cheek rested flush against the table. Suddenly he stretched out his tongue and licked across a section of the surface, violently hoping it was thick with germs.

He raised his head and, drawn irresistibly, put his eye to the peephole and looked out again through the bright sunlight that was another dimension of his country, and saw his new blue empty chrome-iced car winking and flashing back at him.

"St. John of the Cross," the Judge said, "as we know perfectly well from the writings of Alonso de la Madre de Dios and the dissertation of the brilliant medievalist Jean Baruzi, made a point of choosing for himself the smallest, meanest, darkest cell in the monastery because he knew that from there, when he looked through the tiny window out over the fields of Spain, he would see visions. Visions."

1971

JAMES CRUMLEY
Whores

I

O n long summer afternoons when our idle time lay as heavily upon our minds and lives as the torpid South Texas air, often my friend and colleague, Lacy Harris, and I would happen to glance across our narrow office into each other's eyes. Usually we simply stared at each other, like two strangers who have wandered into an empty room at a party, ashamed of solitude among mirth, then we turned back to the disorderly stacks of freshman themes, heaped uncorrected upon our desks. Occasionally, though, the stares held; one would shrug, the other suggest a beer, and in silence we would rise and go out, seeking a dark and calm beer joint.

Sometimes French's, a place south of town, where a cool high-yellow bartender, Raoul, let us bask in the breeze of his chatter, as ceaseless and pleasant as the damp draft roaring from the old-fashioned water-cooled window fan. Sometimes the Tropicana to joust with an obtuse pinball machine called the Merry Widow, while off-shift roughnecks slept drunk at the various tables scattered among the fake tropical greenery. Easy afternoons, more pleasant and possible than hiding in the air-conditioned cage of our office, where the silences had no meaning. Dusty air, dark bars. Outside, the sun, white hot upon the caliche or shell parking lots, reminding us how pleasant the idle afternoon. Dim bars, cold beers, our mutual silence for company. Harmless.

Or so they'd seem until I'd catch Lacy's hooded blue eyes slipping toward the heated doorway. His wife, Marsha, was already prowling the town like a lost tourist, looking for him in the bars. Almost always she found us. One moment the doorway would be empty, the next a slim shade stood quietly just inside, perhaps a glint of afternoon sunlight off her long blonde hair. Somehow I always saw her first. When I said "Lacy," he never moved, so I would walk to Marsha, welcome her with the frightened ebullience of a guilty drunk. She seldom spoke; when she did, in a hushed murmur, too quiet for words. She moved around me to Lacy's side, slipped her hand into the sweaty bend of his elbow, led him away. At the doorway, framed in heated light, his face would turn back to me, an apologetically arched eyebrow raised.

On those rare occasions when she didn't find us, we drank until midnight, but without frenzy or drunkenness, as if the evening were merely the shank of the afternoon. Then I drove Lacy home, let him out in the bright yellow glare of his porch light. As he sauntered up the front walk, his hands cocked in his pockets, his head tilted gently back, his tall frame seemed relaxed, easy. A tuneless whistle, like the repeated fragment of a birdsong, warbled around his head as he approached that yellow light. At the steps he'd stop, wave once as if to signal his safe arrival, then go inside the screened porch. Sometimes, glancing over my shoulders as I drove away, I'd see him sitting on the flowered pillows of the porch swing, head down, hands clasped before him, waiting.

On the mornings after, he never spoke of the evenings before, no hangover jokes shared, never hinted of those moments before sleep alone with Marsha in their marriage bed. And on the odd chance that I saw Marsha later, no matter how carefully I searched that lovely, composed face, no matter how hard I peered beneath her careful makeup, I caught no glimpse of anger. Unlike most of my married friends, the Harrises kept their marriage closed from view, as if secrecy were a vow. Aside from her sudden intrusions into our afternoons, his too-casual saunter toward the bug light, as casual as a man mounting a gallows, and a single generality he let slip one night—"Never marry a woman you love"—I knew nothing about their marriage.

On rare and infrequent summer afternoons, when the immense boredom that rules my life stroked me like a cat and the heavy stir of desire rose like a sleepy beast within me, when our eyes met, I would say *Mexico*, as if it were a charmed word, and Lacy would grin instead of greeting me with a wry smile, a boy's grin, and I could see his boy's face, damp and red after a basketball game, expectant. On those afternoons, we'd fill a thermos with gin and tonics, climb into my restored 1949 Cadillac, and head for the border, bordertown whorehouses, the afternoon promenade of Nuevo Laredo whores coming to work at the Rumba Casino or the Miramir or the Malibu, the Diamond Azul or Papagayo's.

Perhaps it was the gin, or the memory of his single trip to Nuevo Laredo after a state basketball tournament, whatever, he maintained that grin, as he did his silences, all the way across the dry brush country of South Texas, my old Caddy as smooth as a barge. Or perhaps it was the thought of Marsha driving from bar to bar, circling Knight until full dark, then going home without him. He never went intending to partake of the pleasures, just for the parade.

Sometimes it seemed the saddest part, sometimes the most pathetic, sometimes the most exciting: the dreadful normalcy of the giggling girls. Dressed in jeans and men's shirts knotted above their brown dimpled bellies, they carried their working clothes, ruffled froth or slimy satin, draped over their young and tender shoulders. Although they chattered in Spanish, they had the voices of Texas high school girls, the concerns of high school girls. Dreadfully normal, god love them, untouched by their work, innocent until dark.

Occasionally, because I knew the girls more intimately than Lacy— unlike him, I'd never married either the loved or unloved—I could convince one or two to sit with us a moment before they changed clothes. But not too often. They seemed shy, unprotected out of their whore dresses, like virgins caught naked. If the mood seemed right, the shyness touching instead of posed, I'd have one then, slaking my studied boredom on an afternoon whore as the sun slanted into the empty room. Afterward, Lacy often said, "I'll have to try that again. Someday." I always answered, as if wives were the antithesis of whores, "You've no need. You've a lovely wife at home." To which he replied, "Yes, that's true. But someday, some summer afternoon, I'll join you . . ." His soft East Texas accent would quaver like a mournful birdcall, and a longing so immense that even I felt it would move over him. Even then I knew he'd want more than money could buy.

Most whores in Nuevo Laredo are carefully cloistered in a section of the city called, appropriately, Boys Town, a shabby place with raucous bars spaced among the sidewalk cribs, but the better-class whores worked in the clubs we frequented, outside Boys Town. By *better-class* I don't mean more practiced. I mean more expensive, less sullied by the hard life. More often than not, they're just good old working girls, pleasant and unhurried in bed, not greedy, and sometimes willing to have fun, to talk seriously. Many were sold into the business as young girls, many are married, making the most of a bad life. And then there are the rare ones, girls a man can fall in love with, though I never did, never will. Whores help me avoid the complexities of love, for which I am justly grateful. But even I have been tempted by the rare ones. Tempted.

One afternoon in Papagayo's in the blessed stillness after the parade—the waterfall silent, the jukebox dead—Lacy and I sipped our Tecates. A moist heat had beaten the old air conditioners. Behind the bar one bartender sliced limes so slowly that he seemed hardly to move; the other slept at the end of the bar, his head propped on his upright arm. Lacy's whistle seemed to hover about us like a swarm of gnats. All of us composed, it seemed, for a tropical still life, or the opening act of a Tennessee Williams play. Absolute stasis. And when Elena came in, moving so slowly that she seemed not even to stir the hot air with her passing, she seemed to hold that moment with her lush body. As I turned my head, like some ancient sleepy turtle, she too turned hers toward me. A slack indifferent beauty, eyes always on the verge of sleep, the sort of soft full body over which frenzy would never leap. Otiosity sublime. Surely for a man to come in her would be to come already asleep.

I clicked my Tecate can lightly on the tile bar as she eased past us. The sleeping bartender, knowing my habits, looked up. I nodded, he asked her if she would join us for a drink. Halting like a tanker coming into dock, she nodded too, her eyes closing as she lowered her head. A life of indolence is really a search, I thought, a quest for that perfect place to place one's head, to sleep, to dream . . . but behind me, Lacy whispered, "This one, Walter." So I let her go. Walter Savage, perfect languor. Habits can be restrained; passions should not.

After the preliminaries, an overpriced weak brandy, an unbargained price—local airmen had ruined the tradition—Lacy left with his prize ship, walking away as casually as he wandered into the force of that yellow porch light, hands pocketed, loafers shuffling, head back, his aimless whistle. But as he held the door for Elena with one hand, the other cradled itself against her ample waist. I meant to warn him, but in the languorous moment all I could think was, "You've a lovely wife at home," and that seemed silly, the effort too much.

They were gone quite a time, longer than his money had purchased, so I knew it had to be an amazing passion, impotence, or death. Afternoon slipped into evening, the waterfall began flushing. Two students from the college came timidly in, then left when they recognized me. The girls returned in bright plumage. I took the gaudiest one, ruffled her as best I could, but when I came back, Lacy hadn't returned. The bartender cast me a slimy smile. I drank.

When Lacy finally came back, Papagayo's hummed with all the efficiency of a well-tuned engine, and I would have stayed to watch the dance, but Lacy said, "Let's go."

"Why?" Though I could guess.

Hesitating, unable to meet my eyes, he shook himself as if with anger, a flush troubling his pale face. Then he answered, "I don't want to see her working."

Not just impotence, but love, I thought, wanting to laugh.

More silent than usual on the trip back, he drank beer after beer, staring at the gray asphalt unwinding before us. Outside Falfurias, I ventured, "Impotent?" To which he answered, with hesitation, "Yes."

"It happens," I said. "Guilt before the deed. With whores and wives and random pieces . . ."

"Don't," he said, almost pleading.

"Hey, it doesn't matter."

"Yes," he whispered, "I know."

When I dropped him at his house, he said goodnight, then walked into that yellow haze quickly, as if he had unfinished business.

During the twenty years or so I've been beating love with border-town whoring, I've had it happen to me—drink or boredom or simple grief—and I knew most of the techniques with which whores handled the problem. Those who took simple pride in their work, those honest tradeswomen of the flesh, usually gave the customer his best chance, along with motherly comfort and no advice except to relax. Then they would try to laugh it off. Others, working just for the money and those few natively cruel, would pointedly ignore or even scoff at the flaccid gringo member. Or, as happened to me once, they would act terribly frightened, whimpering as if caged with a snake or a scorpion instead of a useless man, occasionally peeking out of the corners of their sly brown eyes to see if you'd left yet. Whatever the act was meant to do, it did. Perhaps because of my youth, when it happened to me, it kept me away from the whores for months, nearly caused me the grief of marriage with a rather chubby woman who taught Shakespeare very badly.

But Elena did none of those things. She was after all only a child, in spite of that woman's body, so she just started talking aimlessly, in her child's voice, winding her black hair with her fingers. What she did was, of course, more cruel: she talked to him, told him about her life. The dusty adobe on the Sonoran desert, the clutch of too many children, both alive and dead, the vast empty spaces of desert and poverty. When their time was up, he asked if he might pay for more, to which she shrugged, lifted a shoulder, cocked an eye at his member. And she answered, *why not*, she covered her breasts with a dingy sheet and smiled at him. God knows what she had in mind. When I told her, months later, of his death, she also shrugged at me, slipping into her dress.

Although Lacy and I were both in our thirties and both knew that, except for a miracle, we were going to ease out the rest of our academic careers at South Texas State trying to make them as painless as possible, I accepted my failure more gracefully than he. I'd been born in Knight, still lived in a converted garage behind my parents' house, and I taught because it was a respectable way to waste one's life. Unlike my mother's attachment to morphine and my father's to the American Conservative Party, teaching is respectable. The salary may be insulting, the intellectual rewards negligible, but when I tried doing nothing at all, the boredom drove me to drink. So I teach, my U.T. Ph.D. a ticket to a peaceful life.

But Lacy, like so many bright, energetic young men, once had a future. Articles published in proper journals, one short story in a prestigious quarterly, an eastern degree, that sort of thing. And he came to South Texas State for the money, just for the money. When he came, he thought that, like a boulder tumbling down a hillside, he had only lodged for a moment, a winter's rest perhaps, and when spring came with heavy rains, he would be on his way once again. By the time he realized that no more showers were going to fall, he had been captured by the stillness, the heavy subtropical heat, the endless unchanging days of sun and dust. He hadn't accepted his defeat, but it didn't matter. By the time of this last summer, he had stopped writing letters of inquiry, had ditched his current Blake article, replacing somehow his fiery vision with Elena.

II

They say the second acts of all boring plays take place at parties, where truth looms out of the drunkenness with all the relentless force of a tidal wave. But in Knight the parties were dull, deadly dull, and whatever shouted insults rose above the crowd like clenched fists, whatever wives were hotly fondled by whomever in dark closets or under the fluorescent glare of kitchen lights, was beside the point. The truth lay in the burnished dullness, not in the desperate cries of hands clutching at strangely familiar bodies. The last party at the Harrises' seemed no different, perhaps was no different, despite the death of our chairman.

Even Lacy had risen from his torpor long enough to become a bore. Each time he found me near enough to Marsha for her to overhear him, he would remind me loudly of our golf game the next day, suggesting earlier and earlier tee-offs. But he had El Papagayo's in mind, not golf. We had been back three or four times in less than a month, more often than was my habit, and his love remained unconsummated. He had passed through acceptance to sorrow to rage, and on quiet midnights in my apartment I had begun to think of Lacy and Marsha abed, he cursing his errant virility, she pliant upon their bed. His untoward passion had begun also to disturb the tranquillity of my life, and when he reminded me about our golf game the fifth or sixth time I answered querulously, "I don't think I'll play tomorrow, I think I'll go to Mexico and get fucked." Then I left him, his stricken face like a painted balloon above the crowd.

It was then I noticed our chairman, a pleasant old gentlemanly widower who asked no more of life than I did, leaving the party. He wore a tweed jacket, as if fall in South Texas were autumn in Ithaca, that smelled lightly of pipe smoke, paper, and burning leaves. We chatted a moment, the usual graceful nothing, then bid each other good-night. He suffered a coronary thrombosis just off the porch and crawled under the oleander bush at the corner of the Harrises' house; slipped away to die, I like to think, without disturbing anyone. The party continued, somewhat relieved by his absence, until those wee dumb hours of the morning. Shortly before noon the next day, Marsha found him as she worked in the flower beds. On his side, his head cradled upon his clenched hands, his knees lifted toward his chest, the rictus of a smile delicate across his stubbled face, the faint stink of decomposition already ripe among the dusty oleander leaves. She brushed bits of grass and dirt from his face as she knelt beside him; she began crying and did not stop.

In an ideal, orderly world, on this day Lacy would have performed his necessary act, a final act of passion before we went home to his mad wife, but the world is neither ideal nor orderly, as the life we forge from the chaos must be. Elena, who was I can attest a very dull girl despite her interesting beauty, decided that day to become interested in Lacy's failure. She no longer babbled about her past but promised to cure his problem, if not with her antics, then surely with a *curanderas potion*. Of course, neither worked, and Lacy's life was complicated for the next month with an infernal dose of diarrhea. Even now, even in my grief, I know he deserved no better.

When he returned that night, we both noticed the absence of the porch light. He took it as a favorable omen, I thought it an oversight. Even as I unlocked my apartment door—unlike most folk in Knight, I lock my door; I have a small fortune in medieval tapestries and Chinese porcelain, two original Orozco's—the telephone's shrill cry shattered the night. Lacy.

After the bodies had been disposed of, our chairman's beside his wife, Marsha into a Galveston hospital, instead of driving Lacy back to Knight, I made him stop with me in Houston, not so much to cheer him up as to hold him away from the scene of disaster for a few days. We stayed at the Warwick, drank at the nicest private clubs, where my father's money and name bought us privacy. Finally, on our third night, as we were sipping scotch at the Coronado Club, our nerves uneasy in their sheaths from seventy-two hours of waking and sleeping drunk, Lacy began to talk, to fill in the gaps, as if by breaking his silence he could restore his shattered life.

His mother, as she often said, had made only one mistake in her life, she'd fallen in love with a Texas man and followed him out of Georgia and into exile in East Texas. In exile her native gentility grew aggressive, proud. No girls in Tyler met her standards, none quite good enough for Lacy, so except for one wild trip after a basketball tournament his senior year, a single fling to the border, Lacy knew nothing of girls. Where he found the courage to remove his clothes before a strange dark woman in a dank cubicle behind the 1-2-3 Club, and how

167

he overcame his disgust long enough to place his anointed body upon hers, I'll never know. What guilt he suffered, those days he carried himself carefully around Tyler as if a sudden knock would unman him, he never said. I like to think of that first time, Lacy's body lean and as glossily hard as a basketball court, yet tender, vulnerable with innocence, a T-shirt as white as his buttocks, flapping as he humped, his wool athletic socks crumpled about his ankles, his soul focused on the dark, puffy belly of a middle-aged whore with an old-fashioned appendix scar like a gully upon the center of her stomach.

In college, his career as young-man-about-campus kept him so busy that girls were just another necessary accessory, like his diamond-chip KA pin, scuffed bucks, and chinos with a belt in the back, and it wasn't until he began graduate school at Duke, where all the other teaching assistants seemed to have thin, reposed women at their elbows, that he discovered the absence of women in his life. Then too he looked over a freshman composition class and mistook that dark quietness in Marsha Long's wide eyes for intelligence, mistook her silence for repose.

The brief courtship could only be described as whirlwind, the wind of his stifled passion whirling around her pliant young body. Surprised that she wasn't virgin, he forgave her nonetheless, then confessed his single transgression in Mexico. Marsha nodded wisely, just as she did when he suggested marriage, expecting her to hold out for magnolia blossoms and fourteen bridesmaids. But she didn't. They were married by a crossroads justice of the peace on the way to South Carolina to tell her parents.

They lived on the old family plantation on the Black River in a columned house right off a postcard, and as he drove up the circular way, Lacy thought how pleased his mother would be. But inside the house he found an old woman, perfumed and painted like a crinolined doll, who called him by any name but his own and confused Marsha with her long-dead sister. In Marsha's father's regal face he saw her beauty, larded with bourbon fat. Everywhere he turned, each face—black, white, or whitetrash—every face on the place had the same long straight nose, the broad mouth, the wide dark eyes. Only the blacks still carried enough viable intelligence in their genes to maintain some semblance of order. Marsha cried ten solid hours their first night, only shaking her head when he inquired as to why. By dawn he expected a black mammy to waddle in from the wings and comfort the both of them, but none came. At breakfast, Marsha had redrawn her face, and stare as he might through his own haggard eyes, he could see neither hint nor sign of whatever endless grief lay beneath her silence.

They left later that morning, since nobody seemed to mind. Mr. Long ran wildly out of the house, spilling whiskey, and Lacy, fearing now for both sanity and life, just drove on. But he heard the shouted, "Congratulations, son." He looked at this mad child, now his wife, seeing her now, dumb, painted, pliant. Perverse marriage vows followed; he made her silence his, vowed to love her.

"They were so old, old enough to be her grandparents, they didn't have her until they were in their forties. God knows what her childhood must have been like, locked on a movie set with those mad people, and every face she saw for ten miles in any direction, every club-foot, humpback, cross-eyed genetic disaster, was her face. She thought she was ugly. You know that, ugly. In all the years we were married I saw her without make-up just twice. Once, when she had the flu so badly that she couldn't even crawl to the mirror. I found her like that, on her goddamned hands and knees, mewling and crying and holding back the vomit with clenched teeth. When I tried to carry her back to bed, she fought me like a madwo . . . fought like a wildcat, hiding her face from me as if she'd die if I saw her . . . Listen, I shouldn't be here, I should be back in that room, room, shit, cage with her. She needs me, she needed me and I wasn't there . . . And all those niggers in that house, so goddamned servile, so smug butter wouldn't melt in their assholes. Listen, drive me back to Galveston, will you? This isn't helping."

I led him out of the club, holding his elbow as if he were an elderly uncle. And it had helped. In the car he slept, quiet, not mumbling or twisting or springing awake. Slept really for the first time in days. I checked us out of the Warwick, drove us back to Knight on benzedrine—bordertown whorehouses are filled with more vices than those of the flesh. When I woke him in front of his house, dawn flushed the unclouded sky as birds chittered in the mimosa trees of his yard. He mumbled a simple thanks, grabbed his grip, and went into this empty house, his toneless whistle faint among birdsong. I thought he'd be all right.

III

He seemed all right for the next few months, more silent perhaps, uninterested in afternoons at French's or jousting with the Merry Widow, but accepting his life on its own terms. I hadn't the heart to suggest a

169

trip to Nuevo Laredo, and Lacy didn't invite me to accompany him on the frequent weekends he spent in Galveston. So we began to see less of each other. He had his grief, I had a spurt of ambition and energy that threatened to destroy my wasted life. I handled it, as usual, by spending a great deal of my father's ill-gotten money. Christmas in Puerto Vallarta. An antique Edwardian sofa. Two Ung Cheng saucers in famille rose that made my father take notice of me and suggest that I was worse than worthless, expensively worthless. I even gave a party, a Sunday morning champagne breakfast, fresh strawberries, caviar, an excellent brie, and, although Lacy didn't come, those good folk who did, didn't make church services that morning, not even that night. For reasons beyond me, I made the mistake of resuming my affair with my chubby Shakespearian, an affair it took me until spring to resign.

Spring in South Texas lacks the verdant burst of those parts of the world that experience winter, lacks even the blatant flowering of the desert, but it has its moments. A gentle mist of yellow falls upon the thorned huisache; tiny blossoms, smaller than the hooked thorns of the catclaws, appear briefly; and the ripe flowers of the prickly pear, like bloody wounds, begin to emerge. And the bluebonnets, sown by a grim and greedy highway department, fill the flat roadside ditches.

On a Sunday when he hadn't gone to visit Marsha, I took Lacy out into the brush country north and east of Alice to show him the small clues of our slight season. But it only works for those who take pride in the narrowness of their vision, who stubbornly resist boredom, whatever the cost. By one o'clock we were drunk in the poolhall in Concepcion, by three, drinking margaritas at Dutch's across the border in Reynosa, at seven, stumbling into the waterfall hush of Papagayo's in Nuevo Laredo, giggling like schoolboys.

Lacy, standing straight, asked loudly for Elena, but she wasn't working that night, so he collapsed into his chair, morose and silent for the first time that day. I, ever-present nurse and shade, bought him the two most expensive girls in the place, sent him with them to find Elena's room. *Dos mujeres de la noche.* Where love had failed, some grand perversion might work.

And of course it did. When we met at the dry fountain in the courtyard afterward, Lacy had a bottle of Carta Blanca in each hand, a whore under each arm, his shirt open to the waist, and a wild grin smack on his face. "Hey, you old son-of-a-bitch, you set this whole fuckin' thing up, didn't you?"

I smiled in return, trying to look sly, but failing. My eyes wouldn't focus. "I'm responsible," I said. "How was it?"

"Ohhh, shit, wonderful," he said, stumbling sideways, his two ladies holding him up with a patient grace that my father's money hadn't purchased. "Listen," he said to them, "I want you to meet my best friend in the whole damned world, he's a good old boy." He lifted his arm from the right one's red satin shoulders, gathered me into his fierce grasp. "Stood by me, held me up, laid me down, introduced me to the woman I love . . ."

"We've met," I said, putting my arm around the abandoned whore. Her skin, warm and sweaty from the bed, smelled like all those things that men seek from whores: almonds and limes, dusty nights, cheap gin, anonymous love. I buried my face in her neck, had a moment's vision in which I bought both girls and fled south across the desert toward some other pleasantly idle life, a Yucatán beach, a mountain village, Egypt. But even as it came, it passed like a night wind. Lacy began to shout and shuffle our circle around.

"Ohhh, what a great fucking night." The girls slipped out of the circle, whores again, leaving the two of us. Lacy hugged me until my breath faltered, repeating, as if it were a litany, "Ol' buddy, Ol' buddy, little ol' buddy."

It had been years since I'd been frightened by a man's embrace, or ashamed, or, I must add in all honesty, aroused, but Lacy held me with such a fierce love, so much drunken power and love, that I clutched him, hugged him back, and for a few seconds we whirled, stumbling about the dark courtyard. Then—perhaps he thought it a disgusting revelation, perhaps he responded, I'll never know—he flung me from him as if I were a sack of dirty laundry. My knees hit the fountain wall, my head the fountain.

IV

The next morning I woke in the back seat of my car, not a great deal worse for the night. A bit stiff and sore, but no more. Because I am terribly responsible about the way I exhaust my life, I cleaned up, made a thermos of Bloody Mary's, and went to my office. Lacy was already there.

"Listen," he said as I sat down, "I'm sorry."

"Hey, it doesn't matter."

"I know, I know."

He smiled once, nearly grinned, then raised his hand and left the office, walking with a bounce and energy that I'd never seen, striding as he must have onto the hardwood courts of his youth. I never saw him again. Elena says he was drunk, but I doubt it. She thinks he was drunk because of the wad of bills he offered her to flee across the border with him, because of the wonderful grin on his face.

"Did he make it?" I asked.

She shrugged again, not knowing what I meant until I showed her. Then her whore's face brightened, like a cheerleader's welcoming home a winner. "*Bueno*," she said. "*Muy bueno*."

I tried to excuse her, telling myself that the craft of whoredom is lying; I tried to excuse myself, blaming my grief. But it didn't work. I paid her for another time, and as she slipped out of her yellow dress, she shrugged once again, as if to say *who knows about these gringo men*. Inside her, I slapped her dull face until she cried, until I came.

I don't go back to Nuevo Laredo anymore: I satisfy my needs up or down the border. Of late my needs are fewer. I visit Marsha occasionally. We sit in her room, I talk, she nods over the doll they've given her. Her parents would rather have her back than pay for her keep, so I pay; that is, my father pays. Even in her gray hospital robe, without a trace of makeup left on her face, she is still lovely, so lovely I know why men speak of the face of an angel. She neither ages nor speaks; she rocks, she nods, she clutches her painted doll. I believe she's happy. When I told her about Lacy, just about the accident, not the cause, she smiled, as if she knew he were happy too. I didn't tell her that it took a cutting torch to remove his body from the car.

As they say, the living must live. I don't know. From my parents' house I can hear them living: my mother's television tuned to an afternoon soap opera, the volume all the way up to penetrate her morphine haze; in the kitchen my father is shouting at a congressman over the telephone. I don't know.

I'll marry my chubby Shakespearean, or somebody so much like her that the slight differences won't matter. I'll still go bordertown whoring, and it will never occur to her to complain. And we'll avoid children like the plague.

1977

R. E. SMITH

The Gift Horse's Mouth

Are those hawks or buzzards?"

"I think, honey," Estelle said, "those are buzzards. Hawks fly alone."

I'm like a hawk, she thought, coming out here on my own. If Ed wants to come down in two weeks instead of now, fine, we can fly in. But I've had it with Houston, and I'm tired of him talking about nothing but that new building of his, and if I feel like getting some peace and quiet in the country with just Barbie, and I feel like driving, why then, that's just what I'll do.

"Rio Ancho thirty-two miles, Jackson's Creek seven," Barbie read.

Estelle thought Barbie had lost her case of the squirms after they had stopped for a hamburger in New Braunfels, but now she was back to reading every sign along the road. She liked best the long, wordy signs for film development, political candidates, and gala country music weekends, which she would try to read completely before the car was past.

Estelle thought again that it was strange to name a town "Rio Ancho" when it was the Sangre River that cut over the limestone along the west side of town before flowing into a broad pool below the plateau on which the town set.

"Welcome to Rio Ancho, Guest Ranch Capital of the World, Enjoy Yourself in the Beautiful Texas Hill Country," Barbie read. As they turned onto the main street, Barbie began reeling off "Circle R Trading Post, Horseshoe Bar, James Kelcy, Attorney at Law, NAPA Auto

---

Parts" until the signs came so quickly she gave up and lapsed into silence.

A pickup truck coming toward them suddenly made a U turn without signaling.

Estelle hit the brakes. Barbie pitched forward but awkwardly braced herself on the dash with her hands. Recovering, Barbie reached across the seat for the horn. Estelle pushed her hand away.

"Stupid old man," Barbie said. "Why don't you honk at him?"

"He may be right," Estelle said. "We're just too used to the big city. We need to calm down a little, get in tune with a slower pace. It's different out here. Besides, I'm kind of used to that. He drives the way my grandfather used to drive."

Estelle had read a condensed version of *Talking to Your Child* in one of her ladies' magazines. She didn't remember the fine points of the article, but she did recall that you don't argue with your child when the child is experiencing emotional difficulties.

"I know you feel frustrated at not being able to honk the horn," Estelle tried, "but we do things differently in the country than we do in town."

The truck turned left, again without signaling.

"He's still a stupid old man."

"I wish you had known my grandfather," Estelle went on. "Maybe you wouldn't feel that way. Some of the best times of my life were when I'd go visit him and Grandma in the summer. He'd take me with him when he went trading for cattle and horses, and he kept a horse for me to ride." Estelle became a little weepy. "In fact, he was killed driving his cattle truck."

"Ninety-seven," Barbie said, reading the time-temperature sign in front of the bank.

They stopped at the grocery store for supplies. Estelle thought it was silly of the cashier to ask for identification when she had been buying things there for years. Besides that, she was wearing her emerald ring, the big one, which should have been proof to anybody that she wasn't going to write a bad check for a few piddling groceries.

After a stop at Jed's Drive-In where Barbie had her Big Red soda, they went past the Watering Hole, now advertising cocktails, the Cedarcrest Nursing Home, and into the hilly country beyond. The Eldorado swooped across the low-water bridges where families, most of them Mexican, sat on bright-webbed aluminum chairs and splashed in the shallows.

Just as she rounded the bend before their turnoff, she noticed something in the road ahead. She braked and honked. Three buzzards took flight with laborious indignity and glided off to wait in the weeds.

"Gross," Barbie said, looking at the armadillo crushed on the pavement.

Topping a small hill on their road, Estelle saw a truck approaching and pulled over as far as she could. The truck stopped, and both waited for the dust to settle a little before lowering their windows.

"Hello, Mr. Wilson," she began.

"Hello, Mrs. Grady," the rancher returned. He lived on the ranch beyond theirs, and, for the privilege of running some of his cattle on their land, he kept an eye on their place and looked after their horses when they were gone. "Hot enough for you?" he asked.

"Certainly is warm, isn't it?" she replied. "Are the horses down?"

Wilson nodded.

"How are you getting along?" she asked.

"Can't complain," he said.

After a pause, Estelle said, "I guess we'd better be getting along. We'll see you later."

The electric window sealed out the heat and dust, and they eased down the hill. Off to the left, a deer stand stood like a sentinel tower.

The house was hot and stuffy. Estelle opened the windows and started the air conditioner to drive the heat out. She put the groceries away, turned on the water, made the beds, and then closed the windows, resealing the house.

"Well, what do you want to do?" she asked Barbie as she mixed a big pitcher of iced tea.

"I don't know," Barbie said.

"How about going riding?"

The summer before she had been so enthusiastic about riding they had bought her a horse plus a second one so somebody could ride with her.

"It's too hot."

"How about a walk then?"

"It's too hot for that, too."

Having driven the entire morning and then some so they could enjoy the ranch, Estelle was irritated at the nebulous refusal to utilize the opportunities.

"How about a swim? That'll cool you off."

"There're snakes down there."

"I know it's different from swimming in a pool like at home," Estelle said, "but it's very safe. Let's go get our suits on."

"All right," Barbie said and heaved herself off the couch.

They drove the half-mile to the river, the Eldorado bumping over the road, which was little more than two tracks through the grass. One reason Estelle had argued for buying the place was that the river made a big curve as it cut around a bank and provided an ideal swimming hole. Swimming in the clear water, Estelle thought for a moment of shucking her bathing suit. As long as she was out to enjoy nature, why not be totally natural? But then she would have to explain to Barbie why she was running around naked. In the end, she undid the straps on her top when she lay down to soak up the afternoon sun.

As they drove up to the house, she noticed that the horses had come up to the fence. She stopped and they got out to pet them. The bay was the one she usually rode, while Barbie or guests not used to horses rode the old sorrel mare. Both leaned against the fence and stretched out their heads.

Estelle scratched them behind the ears while Barbie climbed onto the top rung of the fence. As Barbie talked "nice horse" language to the animals, Estelle watched a solitary hawk rising above the hilltops in wide circles. She felt cleansed by the river. The warmth of the day radiating from the rocks and earth enveloped her.

She knew how to really enjoy the land, just like that hawk she was watching. Relax and get in tune with what was around you. Don't worry what you look like. Let the days float along. In the house behind her there was no schedule, no calendar crammed with appointments. It was rejuvenating to live without demands, and she always felt more alive and fresh when she returned to Houston.

Barbie's cry jerked her out of her reverie. Barbie looked on the verge of crying and was holding the upper part of her left arm. "She bit me," she said as if a trusted friend had suddenly hit her.

The mare shook her head slowly from side to side as if denying the accusation but, prying Barbie's hand away, Estelle saw the large red area and the imprint of the incisors. It looked as if the mare had twisted her head as she nipped so that the skin was pulled and broken in several spots.

Estelle weighed the seriousness of the wound and decided, "We'd better have the doctor look at it."

Barbie began to cry in earnest. "He'll give me a shot. I know he will."

"He may not. First, let's clean it up."

She drove the fifty yards to the house where she washed the arm and bandaged it to keep Barbie from massaging dirt into it. Estelle kept her bathing suit on but threw a bright patterned shift over it and ran a comb quickly through her hair. Thank goodness for blow-dry haircuts, she thought; otherwise I'd be a fright.

Estelle drove quickly, but as they passed the city limits, the digital clock in the dash indicated that it was well past closing time for offices. The doctor's office was a small brick building off the main street. Thank goodness, she was observant and noticed on an earlier trip or they'd have to drive all over town and really be late. As they arrived, a man in boots and checked, jean-cut slacks was coming down the steps. Estelle rushed up while Barbie climbed out of the car.

"Is the doctor still in?" she asked.

"He just left," the man said. He looked in his mid-fifties, but she really couldn't tell with the brim of his western straw pulled low on his forehead. "What's your problem?"

"A horse bit my little girl."

By this time, Barbie had come up, and the man could see her holding her arm. "Let me see," he said and peeled back the three band-aids Estelle had laid over the bite.

"Better go inside," he said, straightening up.

"But you said the doctor wasn't in," Estelle said.

"He's not," the man said, "but as soon as I unlock the door, he will be."

"Oh," Estelle said, but didn't go any further.

The man looked at her tolerantly. "My medical license is on the wall if you'd like to check it against my driver's license," he said.

Estelle smiled her best smile. "Let's just get Barbie fixed up," she said.

The doctor clumped across the waiting room and down the hall, turning on lights as he went. The floor was linoleum tile throughout with nondescript vinyl couches in the waiting room, above one couch a picture of a huge Santa Gertrudis bull. Estelle thought the office looked more like a veterinarian's than an M.D.'s. Still, if anybody was accustomed to treating horsebites a country doctor would be.

"Next time a horse does that," he said as he let them out, "you bite it right back."

Barbie grinned. She was feeling like a survived martyr with the gleaming bandage on her arm and the doctor's judgment that she didn't need a shot. She had had a tetanus booster a month before as part of her precamp physical. To perk her up further, Estelle took her to the Corral Restaurant to eat chalupas. Barbie ordered a hamburger instead.

After Barbie was asleep, Estelle took a walk. The afternoon had upset her, but the night calmed her once more. She walked toward the road until she was well beyond the circle of light cast by the mercury vapor lamp next to the garage. She could not see another light anywhere. She stood for a while, surveying the isolation, looking at the stars bright in the cloudless, moonless night. A gentle breeze came over the land, scattering the heat of the day. As she returned, skirting the fence, she could hear the horses moving quietly and see their dark shapes outlined against the paler earth.

When she woke the next morning, the sky was cloudless still, the sun harsh and bright. Squinting against the brightness, she stopped beating the eggs for omelets and tried to see what was moving in the pasture with the horses. Something or several somethings were on the ground, but she couldn't see clearly because the fence blocked her view.

She put the bowl down and went outside. Before she reached the fence, she had an idea of what she would see, but she forced herself on anyway. The bay was grazing calmly off to one side while straight ahead three or four black buzzards were walking around the mare stretched on the ground as if they were appraising merchandise.

She stood at the fence debating what to do. She climbed the fence and picked up a rock as she approached the group. The buzzards noted her approach and took to the air in an awkward flapping and fluttering before she was close enough to throw the rock. Once aloft, they glided to landings at a safe distance and turned back to watch.

The mare's eyes were open, her head stretched at the end of her neck as if she were reaching for something. Several flies buzzed around her loose, grizzled lips. Estelle looked at the mare's flanks. They remained sunken. Estelle started to nudge the horse with her foot but drew back. The animal was clearly and indisputably dead.

Barbie had been watching her from the den. "What's the matter with Bootsie?" she asked as soon as Estelle was inside.

Let's be honest, Estelle thought. "She's dead," she said.

"Serves her right for biting me," Barbie said. "Are those buzzards out there?"

Estelle nodded.

"Gross," Barbie said.

"Let's have some breakfast," Estelle suggested. Whatever the problem, she knew, you do better to face it with a full stomach.

"I don't want any breakfast," Barbie said. "A dead horse and buzzards, super gross!"

Estelle managed to coax Barbie into eating a bowl of Count Chocula cereal. As they got into the car and headed back toward town, Barbie said, "One of them's sitting on top of her. And three others are looking."

Estelle didn't look.

"Office Hours 1:00–5:00," the sign on the doctor's door said. She could have sworn the sign said something else when they were in the day before. Whoever heard of a doctor who didn't have morning office hours? She opted for staying in town rather than driving out to the ranch and back.

A Tab, a Diet Dr. Pepper, a Diet Pepsi, and a pair of shoes she really didn't want later, they returned to the doctor's office. He came in ten minutes late and began working his way through the pile of folders waiting for him.

"My horse died," Estelle told him as soon as he swept into the examining room.

He looked around the room for a brief moment as if he expected to find something lying on the floor.

"I'm sorry to hear that, ma'am," he said, "but I'm not a vet."

"I mean the horse that bit my daughter died."

"I doubt we have anything to worry about," he said. "You told me it was an old mare. Probably just old age. But we still ought to check to make sure nothing's really wrong."

"How do we do that?"

"Pretty simple," the doctor said. "Just cut off its head and take it or send it to the public health labs."

Estelle pictured the decapitated horse lying in the pasture.

"When could you do that?" she asked.

He looked at her as if she had failed to understand what he just said.

"I mean," she said, "you don't do anything in the mornings, do you? Doctors are used to cutting on things." Even thinking about it she could feel her stomach muscles contract, her throat tighten.

"In the mornings I make rounds of the nursing home and invalids. In the afternoons I have office hours, and in the evenings I drive thirty-five miles to see my patients in the hospital. I don't have time to tend to the people in this town, much less take care of that dead horse. Tell you what, go talk to Clyde Morris. He's the vet. You'll have to see him anyway to get the shipping box and forms. Or hire somebody to do it for you."

At the Rio Ancho Veterinary Clinic Estelle was met by a German Shorthaired Pointer and a twentyish young woman with a child.

"Clyde's out in the field," the woman said after Estelle asked to see the doctor.

Estelle looked around but didn't see anything but live oaks and cedars around the house. Maybe he farmed a little somewhere. "Could you go out in the field and call him?" she asked.

"I mean," the woman said, "he's out making calls. I can try to raise him on the radio."

Estelle and Barbie followed the woman through a back entryway stacked high with cartons of medicine.

"This is Pig Cutter One calling Pig Cutter Two," the woman intoned into the microphone. "Can you read me?"

How quaint, Estelle thought.

After several tries, a man's voice came over the speaker. "I read you. What do you need?"

"Lady here has an emergency."

"Put her on."

Estelle took the microphone gingerly from the woman. Estelle never used the CB her husband gave her for Christmas because she couldn't stand the static.

"Hello," she said.

180

"This is Morris," the voice came back. "What do you need?"

She wasn't going to make the same mistake with him that she had made with the doctor. "Our horse bit my little girl," she began.

No reply.

"And then the horse died," she added.

"What's the emergency then?" the voice asked.

"The horse might have had something wrong with it."

"If it died, I'd say that was a pretty sure bet."

Estelle thought she heard the wife snicker behind her, but she didn't turn to look.

"But I mean something bad." She could not bring herself to say "rabies."

"If you're worried about it being rabid," the vet said, "fill out the forms and ship the head off to Public Health in San Antonio."

"That's my emergency," Estelle said.

"My wife'll give you the forms and the address."

"But I can't cut off the animal's head."

"Neither can I," the voice said.

"But you're a vet."

"That's right, but I'm a vet with a sow that's ready for a caesarian and a call twenty miles away from a rancher with a sick stud bull. No way I'll be home until after dark. Tomorrow's the same thing. It's no big deal. Just get a sharp knife and have at it."

"But I can't," she protested.

"Try Phil Murphy. He might be willing to do it for you. I have to get back to this pig. I've taken almost too long already."

"Thank you," Estelle said automatically as she handed the microphone back to the wife.

She spent an hour trying to track down Phil Murphy but couldn't find him.

She filled up the car at the filling station she usually patronized, led up to the topic as easily as she could, and asked the owner if he knew anybody who might help her out.

"You do have a problem," he said and called over the boy who worked in the station. In between servicing cars, they conferred for ten minutes, one proposing a name, the other judging the nominee. "I'm sorry," the owner finally reported, "but I can't think of anybody right off who might do that kind of thing."

She stopped at the Watering Hole. She ordered a Coke for Barbie and a light beer for herself. Halfway through the beer she sauntered over to the group of men at a corner table.

They must have been occupying the table for a long time, judging from the piled-up ash trays and how loudly they guffawed at her story of the dead horse.

"Lady," one of them said, "I'd be happy to go out to your place."

"You would?" she said.

"But not for no dead horse."

She stopped short of throwing her beer in his face, whirled, and walked away, feeling their laughter hit her square between the shoulder blades.

On the way home she remembered her neighbor, Mr. Wilson, dependable Mr. Wilson who looked after everything for them.

"He's gone cattle buying," Mrs. Wilson told her. "Making the rounds of the auctions. Won't be back until Thursday."

Dinner was burritoes and canned chili microwaved back to life. Barbie took her plate to the TV and watched a rerun of "Gilligan's Island" while she ate. When she brought her plate back, she asked, "Am I going to die?"

"Of course not," Estelle said. "We just want to check and make sure Bootsie wasn't sick when she died."

"Will I have to get lots of shots?"

Where did she pick up all this business about shots, Estelle wondered. "I don't think so," she said.

Barbie showed instant relief. "What happens to the head when they're through with it?"

"I suppose they dispose of it some way or the other."

Barbie clouded up again.

"It's kind of bad," Estelle comforted, still following the article she had read, "thinking about an old friend like Bootsie dying and being worked on in a laboratory."

"It's not that," Barbie said.

"What is it then?" Estelle asked.

"I wanted to take it to school," Barbie said. "It'd be a lot neater than the bird's nest Billy brought in last week."

Estelle let Barbie stay up late and watch the movie on television to make up for the problems of the day. In bed, Estelle tried reading. The book's cover pictured a young woman in a pale dress fleeing from a de-

182

crepit mansion set on the cliff behind her, but the story didn't hold Estelle's attention. She thought of taking a walk to calm herself, but somehow she didn't want to go outside. She went to the bar and mixed a pitcher of martinis.

Halfway through the pitcher, she hit upon a solution. She would think of it just like packing a suitcase. They would get up, eat, pack to go home, she would pack the horse's head, and they would close up the house and leave.

She drifted off to sleep in the recliner chair. She dreamed she was having an affair with a friend of her husband. He took her to a discreetly located hotel with a luxurious decor. At the door to their room he kissed her passionately, then pushed open the door, and swept her inside. In the middle of the king-sized bed was a horse watching Johnny Carson and working a crossword puzzle. "Enjoy your stay," her lover said and left.

She woke up, staggered into the king-sized bed in the master bedroom, and fell asleep.

When she pulled the pillow off her head in the morning, she thought for a moment of ringing for room service instead of going down to breakfast. As the familiar items in the room focused, she remembered where she was. She felt nauseous.

She thought of just leaving, period.

But if anything happened to Barbie, she'd never forgive herself. Her husband would never forgive her. Barbie would never forgive her. Why did that stupid horse have to die?

She showered, dried her hair, and examined her wardrobe, trying to decide what she should wear for cutting off a horse's head. She finally put on a pair of jeans and a bandana blouse.

She did everything neatly and overly precisely. They had breakfast. They packed. She put things in the car.

Opening the knife drawer, she felt like a character in one of her novels presented with a case of dueling pistols and told to choose. Except none of the knives looked very efficient. You would think with all the deer that bunch of boozers slaughtered, they would keep a decent knife in the place, but then they all took their kill to the processing plant in town. The cost made a handy tax write-off since they donated the meat to the children's home outside town. She couldn't find a cord long enough to use the electric carving knife. Even though it didn't feel very sharp, she took the biggest one she could find, a butcher knife. She wanted to sharpen it, but the electric can opener with the sharpening attachment was in town. She put on her sunglasses, picked up the packing box in the garage, and started for the pasture.

It was hot already. Around her she could feel the land reflecting the heat it didn't absorb. The sky was cloudless. In the distance, she could see a hawk riding the air currents between two hills. The buzzards were riding the dead mare. One was perched on her flank while the others hopped off and on her. As Estelle approached, they turned, one by one, to watch her. Only when she was close enough to see their featherless heads in detail did they begin to move sullenly away from the horse. She beat on the box with the knife and shouted to hurry them away. They sailed off a short distance to watch her as if she were auditioning for a part.

The birds had begun working on the mare on the softest part of her body, her anus. They had torn the opening larger and were working down her stomach. Except for her ravished flesh, the mare looked as she had the day before but stiffer, duller. Her lips were pulled back from the yellow teeth, dried as stone. Her eyes were open and staring but covered with dust. Ants marched in and out of her nose.

Estelle thought she was going to pass out. She shut her eyes and gripped her stomach until the feeling passed. On second glance, the mare didn't look quite as bad as she had originally. The details seemed to have more distance to them. Estelle looked at the head where she was supposed to cut.

She couldn't do it.

She opened and shut her eyes several times more. The dead body by itself was not so revolting as the thought of touching it. She bent down and touched the neck and drew back immediately, shivering.

She poked the horse's neck again. She shut both eyes and lowered the knife until she felt it touch the horse. She squinted one eye to see where the blade lay.

Keeping her head turned away, she placed the knife behind the curve of the large cheekbone and pulled the knife toward her. Slowly she looked to see the rend in the flesh.

All she could see was a little disturbance in the dust on the horse's neck.

With both eyes open, she pushed the knife back and forth more, bearing down a little. The hair bristled up about the edge of the knife and went flat at one spot. The skin was parting.

184

She stopped, leaving the knife resting on the horse's neck, and covered her face with her hands.

Where were *they*?

She was not supposed to be out in a rocky pasture, getting her pants filthy dirty, sweating through her blouse, getting sick at her stomach, cutting off the head of a horse that did something as stupid as bite her daughter and then die. She cursed her husband who hadn't accompanied her, cursed the kickers in town, cursed the horse, cursed Barbie for being bitten, cursed the buzzards, cursed the pasture, cursed the heat, and cursed the stupid idea of having a place outside town.

She thought about just leaving and just seeing what would happen. But what kind of a mother would she be if she did that?

Holding her stomach with one hand, she started sawing the knife back and forth again.

If she didn't look at the head and the rest of the body, it was kind of like cutting up a big roast. She put both hands on the knife and bore down.

Except that roasts weren't hairy. And roast didn't make the sickening popping sounds that the cartilage in the throat did.

She waited for her stomach to calm down again and attacked furiously. She tired quickly and stopped to catch her breath.

She was almost halfway through, she thought, but she couldn't tell for sure. She stood up to check and noticed that the buzzards had eased closer, like spoiled pets who stop for a moment after a reprimand and then begin again. She shouted at them, threw rocks at them, and drove them back a little farther.

She touched the horse's head with her foot and shoved. It didn't move very far. She felt her leg muscles pull when she shoved it a second time, but the nose moved out, turning the cut from a slit to an open wedge. The ground underneath was stained with blood and fluids. She retched and found her mouth dry. She was afraid if she ever went back into the house, she wouldn't finish the job. She stepped over the neck and resumed cutting.

She worked steadily, brushing the sweat off her forehead with her wrist. It was like stuffing envelopes for the Heart Fund or Muscular Dystrophy or whatever it was she volunteered to work on that year. You were supposed to feel good for helping, for doing your duty, and all it was was boring. Her clothes were already ruined, so she knelt and put her full weight into each downstroke and pulled on the upstrokes.

The knife grated against the neckbones and she stopped. It was like trying to cut a rock. How did she do chicken joints? She either wedged the knife in and twisted or she whammed down with the biggest knife she could find. She tried slipping the knife between two vertebrae but she couldn't force it.

She beat on the vertebrae, both hands on the knife. Meat scraps flew around her. One landed on her forehead, and she wiped it away, almost poking herself in the eye in her haste.

She found that she was crying, kneeling on all fours and crying. Then she was hiccuping and retching, and then she was vomiting coffee, eggs, and English muffins, her throat raw and burning.

She spat out the dregs of breakfast and started back toward the house. She washed her mouth out with the hose at the side of the house and marched into the garage. It took her a moment to find the ax, but when she did she yanked it off the floor and started back outside.

Holding the ax across her chest, she put each foot down as if she were stamping on some vile insect. At the horse's head she didn't think about taking a deep breath but did and brought the ax down with all her strength on the neck. She jerked the ax back up, clumsily, both hands on the end of the handle. She swung it in a wide arc, aimed for the same spot, and stepped sideways to brace herself for the blow. Her foot hit her own vomit, slipped, and she fell headlong across the horse's neck, the ax flying out of her hands.

She jumped up, repulsed. Breathing heavily, she spat the dust out of her mouth. She half-walked, half-ran to the ax, picked it up, and slammed it into the horse's neck as soon as she had her footing. Again and again she put all her force into the blow. Some hit the splintering vertebrae, some hit the flesh, splattering it in chunks. Even after the last white cord in the spine had severed, she continued slamming the axhead into the dirt between the severed head and the neck.

She leaned on the ax, panting, wiping the perspiration from her forehead. She let the ax fall and pulled the box over to the disembodied head still staring at the cloudless sky. She considered the problem for a while, then grabbed an ear in each hand. They were fuzzy and stiff. She heaved. The head was much heavier than she thought it would be. She heaved again, feeling her stomach muscles strain, and lifted the head off the ground. But it wasn't high enough, and she only hit the side of the box, knocking it away.

She heaved a third time, pulling the head up her leg, trying to lift it with her knee. She poised it over the open box and let it drop. She closed the lid and stood up.

She dusted herself off, erasing the line the horse's head had made up her leg. The buzzards had eased closer and stood in an ugly and studious circle around her.

She flung rocks at the birds. She grabbed the ax and ran at them ready to chop off their heads. She raced from one side of the circle to the other, screaming at them. Clumsy and slow as they were, they moved out of range. She threw the ax at one with all her might, but it fell short by a wide margin. She did not bother to retrieve it.

Her back muscles popped as she lifted up the box and started toward the house, staggering from time to time as she stepped on a rock. She put one last effort into the task and worked the box high enough to drop it into the car trunk.

She slammed the lid and sat panting on the bumper. She wiped her brow and flung her hand out, spattering the concrete floor with sweat. When her breathing became more regular, she went inside. She grabbed a can of Pearl Light out of the refrigerator and took a long drink. She shivered with the cold beer and the air-conditioned temperature and told herself she would be better outside until she cooled down.

Sipping the beer, she stood in the shade of the garage, her eyes squinted against the glare and watched another buzzard glide to a landing in the pasture. She shivered again but not with the cold.

It wasn't pretty, she told herself. The land wasn't the least bit pretty. It was hot and hard and life died on it and was eaten by other life. The land would burn your skin, wrinkle your face, and turn your hands into tools. People out here didn't care any more than they did anywhere else. She could break her leg and nobody would know. The house could burn down and no help could save it.

The only things that made you civilized were flush toilets and electricity. That was all. She followed the power line from the corner of the house until it disappeared in the cedars along the road. That one thin wire was the only thing that made the country livable, cooling the drinks, cooking the food, running the air conditioner, pumping the water.

She saw the wire running on through the cedars to join the other wires along the highway which ran into the co-op electric company. Wires were all along all the highways; they traced and followed all her journeys. They crossed and crowded each other, and she could follow them all the way to Houston, but Houston was nothing more than a bigger tangle of wires.

All along, she had been thinking of going the moment she finished her task. Now she found she wanted to stay. One place was like another. Besides, she had met the country as it was. She had done what needed to be done. Nobody had helped her. Nobody. Not her husband, not her child, not her neighbors, not the people you expected to help you. She was the one who had done the sickening work. Now she wished she had been braver as she did it. Surely she could have kept her stomach if she had tried a little harder.

It would be better to go, though. In another day the corpse would begin to rot and stink. When they returned there would be nothing in the pasture but a heap of bones. She would leave a message for Wilson to take the bay back to his place. Maybe he could drag the body to the far end of the pasture.

She finished the beer but didn't go back in immediately. She heard nothing but the wind in the cedars and liked the sound.

"What did you do with Bootsie's head?" Barbie asked as Estelle passed her on the way to clean up.

"It's in a box in the trunk," she said.

"Gross," Barbie said.

Estelle spun and pointed a finger straight into the child's face. "I am sick and tired of hearing that word! You say it one more time and I'm going to slap your face!"

Barbie didn't say anything else until they were on the other side of Rio Ancho, headed for San Antonio.

"Are we going home?" she asked.

Estelle had thought that after she left the head at the Public Health Offices she would reward herself with a shopping trip. Somehow, that no longer seemed attractive. Spending money was something anybody could do.

"Yes," she said. "We're going back to Houston."

She wasn't sure what she would find once she returned to Houston, but whatever it was, she felt ready for it.

1981

THOMAS ZIGAL
Orphan of the West

Rex Range is one of the biggest-hearted fellas I ever cinched saddles with. I was his sidekick in thirty-two Westerns before the War and might've cranked out thirty-two more if the studios hadn't decided to hang a new image on him—leatherneck war hero—to try and save him at the box office. Personally I think he went grazing in the wrong pasture when he traded in his Stetson for a camouflage helmet and started tromping around swampy back lots killing Jap extras from UCLA. But it did pick up his career a little, even if it left me high and dry and fighting for bit parts as the harmonica player in campfire scenes or the goofy deputy sheriff that gets his keys stole while he's snoozing.

When television first hit, Rex and his wife, Belle, teamed up for a comeback with their very own cowboy matinee show, and it was good to see the old sidewinder with smoking six guns once again, though in all the ballyhoo he somehow forgot to ask me to sidekick for him. (And lord knows how many times I broke that coyote out of jail with a rope and horse tied to the window bars.) But their show couldn't stand up against Roy and Hoppy and the like, so they got cut loose after a year. Lucky for them old Rex's brokers had bankrolled his money into aluminum and electronics some years before, 'cause at least him and Belle could retire down here on a big spread and build themselves a fancy place. And lucky for me too, 'cause one fine day I woke up on the floor of a bar and realized my old lady had left me, everybody in town was after me for bad checks I'd laid down at some card games, and I had a

"Orphan of the West" appeared in *Western Edge*, a short-story collection by Thomas Zigal (Calliope Press). Copyright © 1982 by Thomas Zigal.

189

drinking problem that wouldn't wash. So I borrowed a car and drove three days nonstop till I found them down here and collapsed on the doorstep at their mercy. And Rex Range took me in, god bless him, and cleaned me up and shaved me, and Belle fed me and prayed over me till I got my grip back and could sip a steady soup spoon like the best of 'em. I guess you could say they adopted me, just like they adopted all them kids over the years.

They was building the Rex Range Western Museum down the drive apiece, next to the highway, and Rex give me a job on the crew. I was the wrong side of forty at the time but still healthy as a steer once I stopped the drinking and got out into the sun. Rex must've seen I could outwork them school boys 'cause he made me foreman in no time, and I been the number-one straw boss of the whole shootin' match ever since. Yes sir, it was like old times again—like me and Rex jangling around our very own movie set, hero and sidekick, back in the saddle again.

In them days Belle had just took up strong with this church outfit that was giving out kids nobody else would mess with, and she and Rex ended up with two Indian brothers (sometimes I'd josh him about how many of their pappys he'd gunned down in his day) and a Mexican girl. They was good as gold to them children. Fed 'em, took 'em to church, bought 'em clothes, taught 'em right from wrong. And when they was old enough they sent 'em off to college. And I'm telling you right straight, every one of them rascals is happily married today and rolling in the sweet clover.

But that was only the beginning. I seen a whole parade of younguns come and go—Chinese, Filipinos, Czechs, some Polack Jews, and even a couple of Japs and Koreans. There was always a house full, all ages and colors, jabbering and carrying on from sunup to sundown. Old Rex did his best by 'em, I can tell you that. He took charge of the boys and showed 'em how to ride a horse and catch a baseball, and a couple of times a year he'd drag 'em along on a big hunt so they'd get a feel for the cold metal trigger of a rifle. When they was old enough he'd let 'em work in the Museum dusting the display cases of his holsters and brushing the hair on the stuffed horses he'd preserved from his movies. The brightest with figures, usually the Jews and one or two of the skinny little yellow kids, he'd let run the cash register and sell the souvenirs.

We had us a cowboy Shangri-la around here for so long it really knocked the dust out of my blanket when suddenly, here just about ten years ago, Belle's church council come out to check on some complaints. Said word had got back to 'em that Rex was being too familiar with one of the teenage colored girls, if you know what I mean. I didn't believe a damn word of it and told 'em so. Then the girl up and run off and got caught a couple of months later turning tricks down in New Orleans. And about the same time the oldest kid at home, some kind of Arab boy, stole a pair of silver spurs from the Museum and tried to hock 'em in Houston. We kept it out of the papers but couldn't do the same for his Puerto Rican brother that got busted for dope peddling that same year. Talk about rough shod. The press was poking around out here. The church was on our back. I kept telling Rex he was too old to still be raising a gaggle of youngsters. They was different now, I told him, a whole new bunch I didn't pretend to savvy and didn't think him or Belle did neither. He must've took my words as good medicine 'cause they up and sent back the smallest whippers to the church. Said they wasn't going to adopt any more. We rode out a couple of tough years with the high schoolers till they graduated and drifted off on their own. It was time for some long-overdue peace in the valley, let me tell you.

At first it was kind of lonesome but it didn't take us no time till we was all busy as jumper cables at a Mexican funeral. Rex and me and some of the hands was always over in Louisiana hunting duck or out in the Hill Country scaring up dove. Belle started up a Christian radio show out of Houston and it kept her occupied saving souls. Rex even decided to build another wing onto the Museum and fill it up with junk from his war pictures—his bayonettes and uniforms and even a by-god armored tank from one of them Jap films. I thought it would sour the idea of the Rex Range Western Museum but he didn't pay me no mind, and before you know it I was fighting the damn heat and dust (and at my age!) trying to ramrod them no-account young hands toward a two-by-four and a bag of cement. Hell, my patience was in more danger than my heart.

Then the damnedest thing happened. One of Rex's old cronies from our Hollywood days, some jasper that put up a lot of dough on Rex's pictures, got a wild hair when our boys started pulling out of Vietnam (Why we couldn't win that one, this old dog'll never know) and flew one of his big-ass planes over there and like some damn crazy hero started grabbing up Asian kids at an orphanage where the Communists were due to invade any minute. He whisked 'em back to the U.S. of A., and not a day after we saw it on the news was on the phone to Rex asking him to adopt a dozen or two.

I was dead-set against it. It'd been quiet for seven years on the ranch, and we was at an age when most folks were bouncing grandkids on their knees and collecting social security checks. But you should've saw Belle's eyes go all glassy when Rex told her. She stuck that little "I'm saved, thank Jesus" smile on her lips and I knew right then my word was no better than a ranch hand's. A radio show was no trade-off for a warm-blooded little boy. "Just one," she told old Rex. "We'll take just one."

His name was Duc and they brought him dressed in shorts, a dirty pajama shirt, and rubber sandals like he just come in from a marble game on the playground, like it only took 'em an hour to snatch him up and drop him off at our door. He was supposed to be fifteen but didn't look a day over twelve—a match stick of a kid with shaggy hair and a cold, hungry stare. The first thing Rex did was give him a bath and a haircut and find him some decent clothes out of the chests of hand-me-downs Belle'd never had the heart to throw away. I knew we was headed for some hard breaking in when the kid scrapped like a wild pony to keep his pajamas and sandals from the incinerator. But Rex was an old hand at dealing with ornery little colts like Duc.

We'd just finished the new wing of the Museum and was starting to move things in, so Rex put the kid to work pronto. Right off he seemed to shy back from all the crap—the cases of M1's and Brownings and that damn big tank—but I got him to watch me assemble a mortar and an old water-cooled machine gun without much guff. He just sat there on the floor with his legs crossed, staring with those hollow dark eyes at all the parts scattered around, giving me the once-over while I fidgeted with a bunch of Rex's greasy old toys. For a couple of work-days he wouldn't leave his spot on the floor and I didn't bother him to, but finally one morning I noticed he was walking around a little, snooping through the crates real cautious like. He seemed to take a shine to the dud grenades.

Long about chow time I looked around and couldn't see him no-where. I found him out back, messing around in the trash pile. He was digging through all the busted lumber and twisted wire and scraps of sheetrock and carpet, picking out special pieces of junk that caught his fancy and setting them aside in a neat little heap. He had him some long two-by-two's, a bucket of rusty nails, some worthless tin cans, and cracked glass jars. I laughed and asked him what he was going to do with all the garbage but he didn't comprendo. He just hunched his bony shoulders and stared at the ground till I took his hand and led him back to the house for some grub.

Belle figured to teach him English the way she did with the kids in the old days, but the little bugger would up and wander off in the middle of a lesson, sometimes disappear out into the pasture for a couple of hours before finally dragging his tail home. He didn't cotton to the primer-grade readers she'd put in front of him, but he loved to look at the pictures in magazines, especially pictures of his own people in some of the latest news magazines. He'd tear them out and take them to his room.

One evening Belle noticed that one of her fancy silver candlesticks was missing from the dining room buffet case. She was searching high and low for it, and when she passed Duc's room she could hear a bunch of mumbling gab coming from behind the closed door. She opened it to check on him and found the kid on his knees in front of a row of those magazine pictures, his head bowed low like he was praying, her favorite candle the only light in the room. Naturally she pitched a fit! Grabbed him up off the floor and eat him out for his pagan ways—tore up his pictures right in front of him. (She told me later they was pictures of old men sitting in front of huts or stooped in rice fields. Just old men with scraggly goatees, minding their own business.) The poor kid didn't know what to do but bolt out of the house. We spent half the night hunting for him by jeep light before we found him huddled asleep in the far pasture, pretty damn close to some nasty swamp marshes. Right then and there I told Belle she ought to be more tolerant of his ways, but she just looked at me like it wasn't no ranch hand's business.

Long about a week after that I was rocking out on the porch, listening to the breeze rustle through the treetops and enjoying the damp garden smells of late spring. A full moon lit up the lawn like a porch light, and I could see the white forms of cottontails skittering around down by the drive. I spit out my wad of Skoal and closed my eyes, hoping to catch some shut-eye before the late movie, a rerun of one of mine and Rex's old pictures. Just as I was drifting off I heard a noise from down by the Museum. The hands had been bellyaching that some of the tools was getting stole—a shovel and hammer and such—so I figured I'd better go have myself a look-see.

When I got closer I could hear the clatter of lumber and the rattling of cans coming from the trash pile. I picked me up a good head-thumping stick in case I'd need it and snuck around the side of the building till I could sharpen my sights. It was who I figured, his little head bobbing up and down as he grubbed through the junk. I giggled and called out his name, but as soon as I took the next step a sharp driving pain shot through the sole of my boot and I thought I'd been bit by a six-foot rattler. I screamed bloody murder and dropped my stick and buckled to my knees. The boy made tracks like a jumped fawn. I yelled for him to give me a hand but realized my words didn't mean a thing to him. When the ground stopped spinning and I came to my head a little, I reached down and real slow unlodged the board with the nail through it from my foot. It was a six-penny nail that stung as much yanking it out as it did going in. I was lucky it didn't ram straight on through the damn bone! I slung that board about a mile and slipped off my boot. I was bleeding, all right. But as I sat there in the dirt, trying to tie my sock around the wound, I could see clearly in the moonlight that that wasn't the only board I could've stepped on. There was an-other and another, a whole line of 'em in a neat pattern laid out from the building to the trash pile. And I'd bet each one of 'em had some nails in it, placed point up. And I'd bet they wasn't there by mistake.

I hobbled back to the house and showed Rex and Belle what hap-pened, and the old gal nearly busted a gut washing out the hole and dressing it up. She made me promise I'd drive into Houston the next day and get a shot. But when I told 'em I thought I'd walked into a booby trap they looked at each other like I'd eat some loco weed. It didn't help none when I took 'em out to the Museum bright and early the next morning to show 'em proof positive. Nothing was there on the ground behind the building! Not even my thumping stick! Sure, lots of boards with nails sticking out was scattered in the trash pile, but Rex reminded me that that was what the pile was for.

"You just strayed up too close to the trash," he said.

"Like hell I did," I said, but I let it go. And I never brought it up again.

When Belle finally opened her eyes and saw she wasn't making no headway with Duc, she hired a Vietnamese college girl, a cute little filly studying at one of the universities in Houston, to come out and teach the kid his three R's. They even loaned the girl a car to drive back and forth.

At first I didn't pay her no mind, but the more you was around her, the more she grew on you. She was skinny as a soup bone and flat-chested, but her hair was long and willowy and black as Uncle Dudley's boots. Her face was a peach and she smiled real pretty, almost in a naughty "I know something" way. And since I caught Rex staring at her real close a couple of times, I'd say the same thing was crossing his feeble old mind.

She seemed to be just what the doctor ordered. You could tell that the kid was tickled to speak his own lingo again. I saw him grin for the first time around her—not much of a grin, just a little something he'd been holding onto like a new dollar—but at least it told you he was alive.

The first thing she did was walk around the house giving him the name of things in English. That went on for days—him repeating words like he was trying to swallow 'em. They struck out on long walks through the pasture, naming grass and horses and trees, and some-times didn't beat a trail back till dusk. I told her to be careful out there and not go roaming through the swamp marshes 'cause of the snakes and such, and she told me they wouldn't.

All in all I could tell the kid was perking up. He was learning his table manners real proper and starting to say a few words. Pretty soon he got the hang of keeping his room half decent and didn't even buck at sweeping out the Museum no more. She had him singing songs like "Red River Valley" and "Home on the Range" before too long, and they was forever piddling with some kind of handcrafts. He was always making something out of them damn rusty cans he'd collected. And by the end of the summer Belle trusted the girl enough to let her drive Duc into Houston on the weekend to get a gander at what a real Ameri-can city was like. They'd be gone all day Saturday, sightseeing at the zoo and the parks and sometimes even take in a baseball game at the Dome. And on Sunday morning, rain or shine, Belle would have him next to her in church.

I think Rex must've got spurred by the girl's enthusiasm 'cause he finally started boning up on his fatherly duties. He introduced Duc to an old 410-gauge shotgun some of his other boys used to hunt with, and the three of us would mosey out to the shooting range every day for some practice. Said he wanted to get Duc primed for dove season. So we showed the little devil what a shell looked like—even cut one in half to let him see the powder—and how to load his barrel. The 410 didn't have much of a kick so he could handle it pretty fair. But after a few weeks he got bored with the shotgun and wanted to try Rex's 30-06. It was a hell of a rifle with a slick walnut stock and a scope you could spot a tick on a bull's ear at a hundred yards. Rex laughed and said, "Okay, son, but it's liable to knock your shoulder out its socket." Duc gritted his teeth and sighted his target and got kicked on his ass, but by damn if he didn't want to try it again! He give it three squeezes and managed to stay on his feet the third crack. Rex said, "That's enough punishment for one day," and we brought him home with a purple bruise the size of a baseball on his shoulder. Belle nearly took our scalps.

The kid was starting to fit in so good I was downright buffaloed by what happened one night about six months after we got him. Belle claims she was having one of her Jesus dreams and woke up knowing something was wrong. She went to check on him and found his bed empty and the window wide open, the screen unlatched. I heard her squawking all over the house and got up myself. Her and Rex was about to call out the posse but I managed to talk 'em out of it and got 'em to sit down and cool their heels. I told 'em I had a hunch he was just out for some air and would be back before morning, and not to get their feathers ruffled. Rex had a couple of stiff bourbons and decided to pack it in but Belle insisted on sitting in a chair by the kid's window till he came home. She must've give him a good shaking 'cause he was sullen as an old mule the whole next day and wouldn't raise his eyes to look at nobody, not even the girl when she drove in from Houston.

"I can't make any sense out of him," Belle told the girl. "Why'd he go and do a thing like that?"

"He says to walk in the night pleases his grandfathers," the girl said. "He thinks it is the will of heaven."

Rex fixed the bedroom window so it wouldn't raise more than six inches.

The girl stuck with educating him, and as the days rolled on she had nothing but blue chips to pile up on his progress. Said he'd be ready for the schoolroom with American kids by the next fall. Told us that on their trips to Houston he could order a Big Mac all by himself and count out the right change. And to clear away the bad air around some of the mistakes they'd made with him, Rex bought the boy his very own 30-06 with a mounted scope. I tell you, his little eyes lit up like a cat's in a room full of yarn. It was all we could do to pull him away from the shooting range to eat or do his chores at the Museum.

Now Thanksgiving's always the one day out of the year the kids and grandkids come back to pay their respects to Rex and Belle. We always put on a feed bag full of turkey and have a big whoopdeedo. But here the last few years the crowd's been thinning out. I guess everybody just naturally goes their own way after a certain time. Seems like this generation never did mind burning its bridges, anyhow. So it didn't surprise me when only three of the kids showed up with their broods— the Koreans, the Cubans, and the Jews. Belle pretended not to be disappointed and Rex cracked a few jokes about giving away all the leftovers to needy children in orphanages and I just filled up my plate a half dozen times and watched the football game on TV like everybody else. At first there was a lot of hoopla over Duc, how the kids was so happy to meet him, but after an hour or two he got ignored just like he was part of the family.

After the football game everybody got the notion to trot down and see the new wing of the Museum. Belle and some of the girls stayed at the house to clean up, so me and Rex was elected to give the tour. The grandkids went gahgah over the shiny brass medals and the camouflage uniforms and started climbing all over that old tank and makebelieving to shoot the tri-pod machine guns over in one corner. I was trying to round up a couple of the stragglers when I noticed something real peculiar. A rusty tin can resting on the glass top of the grenade display case. Before I could figure out what the hell it was doing there, one of the little Cuban boys wandered over and picked it up. I heard a loud shout from across the room and saw Duc hightailing it toward the kid, waving his hands and yelling, "No! No!" There was a bang like a cherry bomb and then a few seconds of quiet. The Cuban boy lay on his back on the carpet, covered in blood. Duc got to him first and helped him sit up, and the boy looked at his bloody hands and arms without a peep, like they really wasn't his. But by the time all the younguns started jabbering and huddling around, and his daddy and Rex reached him, he was bawling and squalling like a banshee. It took me a while to get my feet to shuffling and my stomach settled, but I finally made it over, and the first thing I did was shove that can away from the crowd with my boot and take a good look at it. It was crumpled up like a paper cup, and you could smell the gunpowder real heavy. I looked at Duc and he dropped his eyes.

Rex stood up and in a tough-guy Marine sergeant voice from his war pictures said, "What the hell is that damn thing and where'd it come from?"

I think he really knew the answer to that. He looked at me and I looked at Duc. In a trembly little voice, without raising his face, Duc said, "Is my prize." He glanced up and spread his skinny arms out and slowly moved in a circle to show he meant the whole Museum. "Is my prize for you," he said.

Rex didn't stop and think, he just backhanded the kid on the jaw and knocked him to the floor. "You little ape!" he said. "You coulda killed somebody!" He grabbed Duc by the shirt and dragged him to his feet. "Look at this!" he said, shoving Duc's face next to the blood-splattered Cuban boy now in his daddy's arms. "See what you done!" he poked his face closer. "See what the hell you done!"

Duc ripped free in one quick move, leaving a rag of shirt in Rex's hand, and shot to the door. "Stop him!" Rex shouted at me, but I was no match for speed. I just stared back at him and shook my head. The kid was gone. We needed to worry about the Cuban boy.

After a lot of hollering and crying and womanly panic back at the house, we finally got the boy's hands wrapped in a sheet, and Belle and the boy's folks dashed him off to the hospital in the station wagon. There was a lot of blood but I figured the boy'd keep all his fingers if he got a good surgeon. Me and Rex and the other grownups had just about settled the squallers down when up rode two of the hands at full gallop. They'd been out for a holiday ride when they saw Duc running lickety-split toward the marshes. They tried to stop him for his own good, but he hit the bushes like a jackrabbit and was lost in the cypresses before they could say anything, and they knew better than follow him into that bog with the horses.

"We better find that little fool before he hurts himself," Rex said. We rounded up three or four hands and raced Jeep and horses out to the edge of the swamp, where the boys had last seen him.

We spread out and trudged through the snarls of vines and palmettoes and the prickly undergrowth for a good hour, the mud squishing up on our boots, all kind of owls and herons flapping through the limbs overhead, and every now and then a crow cawing high above. I got switched in the face by just about every bramble in the county and had my hat knocked off a half dozen times and was just about to call it quits and go wait in the Jeep when one of the hands let out a whoop about fifty yards away. He kept on whooping till we got there one by one and stood around gape-mouthed at the craziest thing these old eyes have ever seen. It was kind of like a kid's clubhouse built out of bamboo stalks that was strung together by pieces of rope and baling wire. The roof was a patchwork of old carpet pieces I recognized from the Museum, and though it was sagging real bad from the dampness, it hadn't caved in yet.

Rex showed up muddy to his knees and in a real bad humor. "Is he in there?" he asked.

"Don't know," one of the hands said. "Thought we'd wait for you."

"Mighty considerate," Rex said. "Somebody crawl in there and see."

The only way to get in was through a hole dug under the bamboo like a dog would do. None of the hands was real eager to crawl in after what they'd heard about this afternoon, so Rex asked me to.

"I'm an old fat man," I said. "I can't hardly get my socks on in the morning."

Rex ordered the youngest hand to do it, and after a lot of bitching the fella finally got down on all fours and slipped on through. In about an eye's blink there was a loud crash and the breaking of glass. "Shit!" the hand yelled from inside.

"You all right?" Rex said.

When there wasn't no answer Rex give the word to tear out the wall. Everybody grabbed some bamboo and started yanking and straining, and it took five grown men a good ten minutes to rip down the side of the hut. The hand was okay; he was just befuddled at what was all around him. He'd fell through a rug covering a small dug-out place, kind of like a little cellar full of glass jars. The jars had dirt and some kind of roots in them. And we finally realized what went with all them tools we'd been missing. There was a pile of 'em in a corner, next to a mat of leaves.

Four or five two-by-two's from our trash pile held up the carpet roof like tent poles. At the far wall was a rickety table the kid had hammered together the best he could. It had a couple of storm candles on it like an altar and a faded page from a news magazine laid in between them. The page was a photograph of an old Vietnamese man smoking a long thin pipe.

"Belle'd have a hissy," Rex smirked.

We rummaged around for a few minutes and found another hole going who knows where. "You ain't getting me to crawl in *that* one," the young hand said. Then somebody outside yelled, "There he is!" and we ran out in time to see the little squirt pop out of a hole like a gopher about twenty yards away and shag into the brush.

"Let 'em go!" Rex said. "He'll wag his tail on home when he gets good 'n' hungry."

We checked out the hole he snaked out of and figured it for a tunnel all the way to the hut. We also run across a little garden plot he'd hoed and dug, but nothing had come up yet so we couldn't tell what he was growing.

"Okay, boys," Rex said, "let's tear 'er down and make tracks 'fore it gets dark on us."

The hands kicked the walls down and untied the bamboo. The two-by-two's keeled over and the carpet roof give in with a thud. I couldn't see no use in ramshackling the kid's playhouse so I folded my arms and watched, and every now and then shot old Rex the evil eye. He didn't seem to care. They busted up the little shrine and tore up the picture, and then smashed all the jars on the ground.

"You fellas done a real perty job," I told 'em when they'd finished and gathered up all the tools to take back. "Oughta be damn proud of yourself."

Duc didn't come home for supper and he wasn't home by pitch dark. Belle was beside herself with worry and took a pill, and Rex said if he wasn't back by morning he'd call the sheriff's department to help us look. He had a Jack Daniel's or two and hit the hay. I tried to sleep but couldn't. I kept thinking about the kid's homemade trophy gift for Rex's big trophy room and how much sense it made. The sight of all that blood was racing around in my head, and I couldn't help remembering the cold hard look on Duc's face when Rex hit him. I tossed and turned for a couple of hours before I finally give up and went to sit on the porch and have myself a dip.

Now if you've ever stood in a neighbor's yard and watched their house burn down or walked through the ashes of a charred barn you know there's a peculiar bitter odor, a smell I can't rightly describe, that you'll never forget as long as you live. It'll wake you from a deep snore. You can catch it on a wind gust sometimes when you're driving through a big city. It ain't like a trash fire or a barbecue; it's like the devil's own flesh smoldering in hell. I've only smelled it a couple of times in my life but I knew exactly what it was, sitting out there on the porch in the cool night air. At first I thought the house had touched off and I hobbled out onto the lawn to see what I could see. The house was dark and tight as a tick, so I scouted around and noticed a bright orange glow the size of a campfire down at the Museum.

By the time I got there the flames had blew out the glass and was leaping up through the roof. I thought I could smell burning horse hide, probably them stuffed stallions Rex was so proud of. The ranch bell was clanging up by the bunkhouse, and all the hands were rushing down the hill in their long johns like extras in some B Western. Pretty soon Rex was down, barking out orders about fire hoses, and Belle was scampering around in her housecoat trying to organize a bucket brigade. This may sound sick, but even after all the work I put into that place over the years, after all it meant to good old Rex, I didn't much give a damn what happened to it just then. It was never *my* place— something he let me know time and again. After all, I was just his sidekick.

The way I was feeling must've been sewed to my shirt sleeve 'cause Rex looked at me real hard once and said, "Come on, man, get the lead out!"

What I said had been bottled up in my head pretty near all evening. "You shouldn't've tore down his playhouse, Rex," I yelled above the fire's roar. "It wasn't hurting nothing!"

Rex looked at me like I'd just punched him in the stomach. He looked at me for a long time. Then he turned without a word and marched over to help with the hoses.

It took the fire trucks an hour to show up, and by that time everybody was soaking with sweat, smoked up, and tired as a preacher in a border town. I couldn't go another minute, and I don't think Rex or Belle was up to it neither. We let the firemen take over and straggled on back to the house like tongue-dragging hounds. And if there was any guessing about how the fire got started, if anybody was gun-shy about the plain truth, it was all cleared up once we went inside. While we was out fighting the fire the pantry had been raided and enough food to last a week was stole. The 30-06 and several boxes of shells were missing from the kid's room.

Yeah, the sheriff and his boys come out the next day and we all loaded up with enough hardware to wage a small war and went slopping through the swamp marshes to hunt the kid like he was in season. It was a disgusting wingding if I ever seen one, and I was along mostly to make sure no trigger-happy fool got carried away. We stayed out there till dark pulling the moss out of our face and getting our feet wet, and I knew it was time to call it a day when some of them young deputies started firing at each other by mistake. Real nervous outfit. But we didn't see hide nor hair of that little swamp rat. And it's been damn near two weeks now since the sheriff and every volunteer in the county's done drug that marsh every day like they had a net and come up empty. I keep telling 'em he ain't out there but they won't listen to me. I keep telling 'em where he is but they treat me like a snakebit cowpoke just in from the range.

We asked Duc's teacher why he'd got in so much trouble and she just give us some Oriental mumbo jumbo: "He is a son full of piety. He has followed the path of his grandfathers." I don't get her drift and I don't think nobody else around here does neither. Belle just sits around and wrings her hankie and prays and cries and prays some more. Rex don't even go out to the swamp with the sheriff no more—he rocks on the porch and sips his whiskey and talks about the good old days making pictures, when right was right and you could size up a varmint by the color of his hat. And me, every once in a while I'll wander down to what's left of the Rex Range Western Museum and kind of stir through the rubble. I'll find the buckle off a belt or a silver dollar or a blackened piece of holster. And I'll think about what I read in the paper about two people shot this week in Houston. Two people on the street gunned down by a sniper. Two people in two different parts of town, both hit by 30-06 slugs, probably the same weapon, they say. And I can jaw at the sheriff till I'm blue in the face and write all the letters I want to the Houston P.D. They still don't believe me when I tell 'em we snatched up the wrong bunch of orphans, and that we can't never again be sure about the refugees we take in. What if the big cities start running wild with snipers again, only this time they're not lunatics and fanatics but all the little Ducs we've tried to make a home for but failed? When I tell folks this they just walk away. They don't realize that the enemy has raised his little yellow head.

1982

HARRYETTE MULLEN
What Can't Be Measured

Whenever I go outside I can't help but see what's in the eyes of the black women whose houses line this street. They've seen me, a white woman, out cutting the grass when that "no-count" man of mine is laid up in the house with a whiskey bottle and ain't about to get behind this mower, and they don't try to hide what a joke I am to them. They can barely hold back the amused smiles that force apart the thick, dark lips to reveal their gapped teeth. They walk home from the market with collard greens waving out of a brown grocery sack, waddling down the street in run-over shoes, with stockings many shades too light rolled down and knotted above their knees. They smile to themselves, knowing that a white woman is no better off than they are.

I see how they smirk at me. The smug ones with working husbands, who make their men fat with their cooking, who swell up every year with another baby, and who sit out on their wooden front porches wearing flowered moomoos, pink sponge hair curlers, and dirty scuffed house shoes. With sweat rolling down their creased and greasy necks, they sit in rocking chairs shelling peas and sniffing the air for gossip. I know they talk about me among themselves. Sometimes I'll hear two of them snickering together, and catch them looking over at me as I cut the grass or tend my roses.

It must make them feel real good to think about me living over here on the East Side, to see me working, knowing my man is sitting on a bar stool in some joint down on Twelfth Street right now, or bending over a pool table, or sneaking out of some black bitch's back door. These women who stand together like solid black columns, who surround me like a forest of thick, dark trees; who are the pillars of their black holy roller church, where they go each Sunday to scream and stomp like they were back in the jungle—they are all laughing at me.

The other evil-eyed women—the sharp, sleek black women who sleep around like alley cats, who take money from men to buy their cheap, flashy clothes—they laugh at me too. Some of them look at me as if they know all about me, from what he's told them. Even the harsh black harpies whose ugly complaining voices have driven their men away are laughing at me for loving a black man, and living with him here on Poquita Street, just a few blocks from the projects, no better than a nigger.

I've left my own people and taken one of their men. That's how they see it; though I know they call him no-count, a low-down black man who lives off a white woman and lets her buy his liquor for him. Still he's one of them. He should belong to one of them instead of me, the one who stole him. They wonder why he'd want me—nothing much to look at, I know that myself. They must figure it's money: someone to support his drinking habit. And someone who'll take more shit off him than any of them would.

"Never catch *me* out choppin' down grass with a push mower while that no-good nigger cools his heels inside with a beer in his hand. Un—unnh! No ma'am, no sir!"

"And the way he run around chasing anything that got a hole. He done left her so many times now . . . I would'a shot the nigger dead long time ago if it was me he was skippin' out on."

"Girl, that nigger treat her worse than a dog."

Yes, I know how they talk. They don't make any secret of how they feel. These loudmouth black women will always say exactly what they think. But I've seen them with a split lip or a black eye from the husband who didn't appreciate hearing any static that particular night. The bruises don't show on them as bad as they do on me, but I know I'm not the only woman on this street who gets kicked like a dog.

They can talk all they like. I know that man loves me and will always come back to me. This is the first time he's stayed away more than a couple of weeks. We have our troubles: he just wakes up mean some days, seems like. When he gets like that I try to stay out of his way, but it's like he has to fight somebody. He always used to tell me he liked me soft, not like those hardheaded colored women. Quiet, where they are loud. So I tiptoe around him when he gets his habits on. Sometimes, though, it just seems like he has to fight me anyway. When he sees I won't fight him back, he leaves the house. Stays away a few days, but he always comes home. Always he shows up on my doorstep like a wandering old tomcat, hungry for a meal.

Those are the good times, when he's sweet to me, wanting to make up after being gone so long. Sure, he comes back with his pockets empty, and needing money for drinking, but it's always me he comes back to. I'm the one he needs when he finally comes home.

After he ran off the third time, I started keeping a bottle of something in the kitchen cabinet, up over the Frigidaire, for when he'd come back, to celebrate. I'll take little sips myself now and then, when it's getting on to evening and he still ain't back yet. Got so, with him gone for days on end, I'd finish the bottle and have to buy another one to keep on hand for him. Then when he'd come home I'd fry him up some chicken and we'd both get so drunk we'd roll into bed singing, and he'd want me so bad and love me so hard, we'd both forget about the whores he'd been with. He'd grab me and wrap his big, heavy black arms and legs around me and rock me back and forth for half the night.

When he's giving it to me, he's giving me all he's got. So I try to forget about all I was missing when he was gone. Just let him take all the hard edge off me, let my body turn soft in his arms. But I swear it's hard on me all those times he's gone, and me all alone, like now, on this street.

Every time I go outside, I catch the eye of one of those women. She's looking pleased with herself, thinking, "Maybe that wild nigger done run off for good this time and left the white woman flat. Maybe he decided he like that black pussy best of all."

While I am whiter in the places where the sun doesn't hit, around the breasts and backside, he is darker under his clothes. His skin is several shades of dark brown and black, and the narrow, dented cheeks of his butt are much blacker than the rest of him. His penis and balls are purple black. His whole body is smooth and almost hairless—nothing like Donald, who had curly blond hair all over his stomach and chest, spilling out of the V at the neck of his Coca-Cola uniform. Donald even had hair on his shoulders and back. Donald, my husband for ten years, who married me a week after I got my diploma from high school, and who serviced me as efficiently as he did his Coke machines: turn the key in the lock, open up, and grab the coins. He made the evening news when he lost control of the truck in that tight curve: smashed Coke bottles lying wicked and dangerous across the freeway; Donald pinned inside the truck and dead when they finally pried him out. What would he think if he knew that the income from the wash-ateria on Chicon Street is what Jake and I live on now? I bought the place with the insurance money.

I never meant to take him seriously when Jake courted me with flowers and music, bringing me charming bunches of handpicked blossoms, singing and playing his guitar for me while I mopped the concrete floor of the laundromat. But there was something loose and easy about him, the way he walked, his low sleepy voice, his gentle persistence, that made me decide to take him on. Finally I sold the trailer and moved in with him.

When we first got together Jake wanted to make love with the light on, so he could enjoy the contrast of his dark skin against my whiteness. I was embarrassed at first, since Donald and I had always done it in the dark. Jake licked my nipples and then let his wet tongue slide down my belly until he got his mouth between my legs. He scared me the first time he did it. It was something I'd never had done to me before, so it was like being a virgin a second time and losing it all over again. I felt like my whole body was stretched out like a tight piano wire, and he was a felt hammer hitting me hard, but soft. Not hard enough to make me snap and break apart; softer, just hard enough so that I could feel the music vibrating all through me, making me tremble all over. I was shaking and panting—coming harder than anything I'd ever felt before. It knocked the breath out of me, and I lay back trying to catch my breath when it was over. A warm feeling that began between my legs had spread all over my body until even my fingers and toes felt electric. Suddenly I was laughing. I'd never felt so good after making love.

"How'd I taste?"

He licked my thigh again and said, "Sweet, baby. You taste good and sweet. Like licking up pure white sugar. You're just as pink and white all over as a birthday cake. Yeah, baby, icing on a birthday cake."

Sugar pink roses on snowy frosting. The birthday cake with sixteen candles. That was when I turned sweet sixteen. Two years after that I was married to Donald. We lived in a trailer and he slid bottles into

Coke machines. When I was sweet sixteen I'd had five years of piano lessons. Piano lessons on Thursdays and helping out in my father's hardware store on Saturdays. Mass on Sundays. Sneaking into clubs at night with Donald, smoking cigarettes and acting grown. I wanted to be a singer. I wore white gloves and a beautiful lace mantilla when I sang at mass on Easter Sunday. My parents had wanted me to go to college and marry a doctor or a lawyer. When I married Donald right out of high school they were so angry they never spoke to me again. It's a good thing they're dead now.

That Sarah woman that lives next door watches me water the rose bushes in my front yard. She looks thirty-five but is so fat she could be younger. Take away the double chin, her skin is smooth and oily. Forehead unwrinkled, no hard creases around her mouth or tiny lines fanning out from the corners of her eyes. She's a gossip and a busybody and laughs a lot. But when she isn't laughing her face smoothes out— the laughing leaves no footprints on her face. Wait a minute, she must be older than thirty-five. She has a daughter twenty, and a grandchild. She hauls herself up from the old recliner rocker that's into its second life now, on her front porch. She sets her beer can down and comes over to "pour some tea" with me. Because she's so nosy she speaks to me more than any of the others do. I don't go into their houses, or invite them into mine. She's got to catch me out in the yard, like now, to start up a conversation.

"He ain't never been gone this long before, have he?"

"What have you been doing, marking the days on your calendar? You got nothing better to do than wonder about my private affairs?"

"Well, I don't know if you heard, but they sayin' Jake done took up with this young girl name Monique that sings with a band weekends over at Club Midnite. He tellin' people he done cut you loose, and she gonna be his woman from now on. But you know, some mens is just like them 'strike anywhere' matches. They'll rub up against anything to get they fire goin'. He taken' up with this young thing now, but he prob'ly be back pretty soon and forget all about her. You take up just where you left off. It's like my mama used to say: What can't be measured can't be missed."

But what if it *can* be measured, after all? That wouldn't be so hard to do. I could count the days to measure what I'm missing; mark black X's in rows across my calendar for the days I've spent alone. I could sit in a kitchen chair, letting my eyes slide back and forth from the brown burn spots on the formica tabletop to the calendar on the wall above the table. Count the cups of black coffee I drink alone, before I give in and unscrew the cap off the whiskey bottle. Measure the days that way. And the nights . . .

I could measure time on my hands, count the nights on my fingers. Pink fingertips curling gently, burrowing in the moist hair. The first touch so delicate it only tickles. So I move my finger harder, rub faster, stick it in as deep as it goes. I do it by candle light. The dark makes me feel lost sometimes, but the 75-watt bulb in the ceiling makes the room too bright and empty when I'm alone. But candles—didn't they use candles long ago to measure time? Hours measured as how long it takes a candle to burn down. A birthday cake with sixteen candles. A frosting of white with pink sugar roses. Candles on the altar at Sunday mass.

I have the Virgin Mary, all in blue, her white hands folded like a lily. All around her, on top of the dresser, a rainbow of saints in rich-colored robes. The dresser top has a starched lace crocheted cover, immaculate as any altar cloth, and all the candles burning in circles of tender warm glow. I lie in bed with my hand hidden under the chenille bedspread, and the whole room flickers with the soft golden halos of the saints.

Once Jake brought me a candle for Saint Martin de Porres. "I got you a black saint for your collection, from the Safeway. They had 'em on a shelf next to the pork 'n' beans." A wick held stiffly up in lilac-scented purple wax poured into a tall glass jar, with a painted decal on the side: an image of Saint Martin de Porres. "Now you got a black saint you can pray to."

When you do a penance, you can count your prayers on a rosary: fifteen Hail Mary's, thirty Our Father's. But I don't need to measure or count, since I can feel each day like a shovel scooping further down into my insides, digging a deeper hole in me. Exact measurements hollowed out of me, so that I know precisely, without having to count anything, how deep and how far down this loneliness goes.

I dug holes in the earth and planted rose bushes. Pink and white roses. I'll never forget how tender he was when we first started. I still shiver when I think of how he'd lift my hair with one hand and kiss the back of my neck. How his hand touching me was like creation. Like my body was coming alive for the first time. I live on the memory of that, wishing I could have that feeling back again.

Roses don't just open, they unwind. The petals spin slowly around the center, each one turning a soft pink cheek to the air, to be kissed. That's how they reveal their fragrance to the wind.

All those feelings he started up in me, that I never knew I had, so that even when the glory faded and there was pain instead—even the hurt got all mixed up in what I felt and remembered, and that became a part of what we shared. The memory transparent as a dream you strain to recall.

He is on his knees before me, smelling my rose. The one I keep between my thighs. I kneel in the garden, its fragrance of black earth making me want to sing. A thorn pricks my finger. I put it in my mouth to suck.

All the hurtful ugly things that happened between us got somehow wrapped around the sweetness like a hard rind around a delicate rare fruit. Like a flower garden completely surrounded with tangles of barbed wire.

There was a time we'd lie skin to skin in bed together in broad daylight, or stretched out under the bright ceiling light. "Look," he used to say "we're piano keys touching each other. You're the ivory, I'm the ebony." He liked the look of his hand on my breast, his smoke-black fingers lying with grooved knuckles against my whitest, softest skin. Now it seems he's lost his delight in the contrast of skins. His darkness deepening beside my white, my paleness starkly naked against his black.

I don't remember exactly when he began to turn off the light before we made love. The whole room suddenly black. Our bodies lost. Both of us fumbling, one toward the other. Maybe he began to think our opposite colors would keep our bodies always distinct and separate, even within the closest embrace. Turning off the light, I guess, was what he had to do to erase the boundary between our bodies, where black ended and white began.

Now he's gone off and left me, it may be forever this time. Gone to be with a woman whose body, meeting his, will be a color that shades and blends into one darkness: her body taking up the color again where his body leaves off. They'll make love in the light and create their own darkness.

Fat oily Sarah hasn't gone away yet. Her big feet stay planted in my yard. She looks at me like she's trying to read me, the way you try to read a far-off road sign, or a letter written in a baffling scrawl.

"You got something else to tell me?"

"It may be this other woman done put a fix on him. Don't know if that had occurred to you or not."

"A fix?"

"Yeah, you know. Could be she hoodooed him. She s'posed to be from Louisiana, and they say the women there is all raised up knowin' how to put spells and charms on men."

"You believe that nonsense?"

"Me, I don't know if I personally believe it myself, but I won't say it can't be done—just 'cause I don't mess with it my own self. You're talkin' to a church-goin' Christian—Baptist raised and born, but I've heard stories that make me wonder. Stories about men captured by them spells. I've even heard some of these women'll hire a root doctor to tie up a rival woman's womb if the man got her pregnant, to give her a hard labor. Or they'll make the woman go out of her mind, just to make sure she ain't no competition. All kinds of stories."

"That's exactly what it all sounds like to me: a bunch of stories."

CLUB MIDNITE. APPEARING FRI & SAT NITE: THE AF-RONIQUES FEATURING MONIQUE CHANSON. The girl is thin, nervous looking. She sits at a table in a dim corner, fiddling with one cigarette after another. Long tapered fingers with plum purple nails. She's pale yellowish, the color of bleached stubble in a harvested field. What's he want with her? I thought it was darkness he wanted. I thought he'd get one who looked fresh and plump, lusciously padded with soft flesh, with a high, round, rippling ass. Not some wispy high-yellow girl who looks as if when you touch her she'd crackle like cellophane.

She's got a dark mole on her cheek, I noticed when she sang in the spotlight. Was it real or penciled in? She might be the sort who would lean on an elbow in front of a mirror, twirling a tiny circle just so. Like an actress preparing for a role. It's obvious she plucks her eyebrows to thin high arches. Never could I imagine her paying off a musty old fortune-teller to perform secret rituals with hair and fingernails and menstrual blood.

Why would he leave me for this brittle hussy? This Creole sip of half-and-half, hardly darker than I am. This girl he himself would've called "the next best thing to white."

I might as well go on back home. Looks like he ain't going to show up here tonight.

They're singing a hymn to Mary, the Virgin, the *rosa sine spinas*, rose without thorns. I am not praying to get him back. I ask no favors of the black saint, who is deaf to my prayers. I pray, instead, to the Virgin Mary, who needed no help from a man to carry God in her belly. I pray to the Virgin for forgiveness for needing a man. I'm praying because I want to kill him. I am the rose with thorns, the flower with teeth. It's been years since I set foot in a church to pray. I've come now to confess my sins and be forgiven. Killing him wouldn't be worth it. I've just wasted eight years of my life with a nigger, that's all. Living on a nigger street being talked about by niggers.

At last I tracked him down: saw him in front of a barber shop, gettin' his shoes shined. He was wearing a brand new suit, and the shoes were new too. I asked him when he was coming back home.

"Woman, I've left you for good. I won't be coming back."

"You got to come back. What do you mean? You can't just walk out like that, without a word. You didn't even pack your stuff. You sneaked out on me, just like the low-down nigger you are."

"Woman, you're drunk, but I'm warning you now," looking around at the other men, "get your white ass out my face before I get mad and go upside your head."

"I remember when you couldn't get enough of this white ass, when you loved this white skin. Your sweet white sugar, that's what you said."

"Well, now when I look at you I don't see nothin sweet. I see a white bitch, that's all. I see you and I think of somethin' sick or dead. A dead fish floatin' belly-up in the water. You ain't got nothin' I want, woman, so go on home."

I tried to kill him. I had the knife in my purse, thinking I'd eventually run into him around that barber shop where he always hangs out to chew the fat with his cronies. I went at him with the knife, but the shoe-shine boy—actually a hard, wiry man—gripped my wrists and squeezed until the knife fell to the sidewalk. The other men ran out of the barber shop to watch; somebody took the knife away.

"Get lost now, before I decide to call the cops," the barber threatened. They all went inside and left me rubbing bruised wrists, with tears falling to the sidewalk.

After confession I still can't close my eyes. I take the bottle with me to bed, to nurse me to sleep. Should've been his blood on the sidewalk, not my tears. Red as agony, sudden as a scream—vivid drops from torn black skin, drying, turning black as the spot on her cheek. A small black spot spreading, growing bigger until the blackness fills up the room.

The bedroom is too dark. All the candles have burned out. It's so dark in here, too dark. When he started turning the light off before we started, we would both be black in the dark, the way all cats look the same in the dark.

I get out of bed, light a candle, and stare at the face that floats in the mirror, pale as the communion wafer I earned with my confession. My face could melt away like the wafer on my tongue. Her face would melt like butter in a hot skillet, leaving nothing but a penciled-in beauty mark, the blackest thing about her. It's the darkness that lasts and lasts, the night that covers everything. I stare at the watery mirror face, the face that looks like a dead face underwater. The face of someone who drowned. The face they all stare at with comic nigger eyes peeking out of minstrel show faces.

I can be as black as any of them. I've been living in the dark so long, surrounded by blackness, I've soaked it up like a sponge. No better than a nigger. I've seen it in their eyes. I've heard them whispering, "Worse than a dog, that's how he treats her."

"Bitch, get out of my face," he told me, sitting like a king on a throne, getting his shoes shined. I go to the closet, where all his old shoes are lined up in a row.

"Get out of here before I call the cops," the barber said. No better than a nigger. But it's nigger he wants, leaving me for her. I'm more nigger than she is, that nervous yellow wisp. He made me one, baptized me in the name of nigger and nigger and nigger. How can he hold her in his arms, brittle as she looks? In those strong black arms she'd snap in two. She can't take what he puts down. Not the way I can. Not like me. I've always taken it: the bad with the good. What can't be measured. The hate and love mingled together like bittersweetness. Going after him with a knife—it was what one of *them* might've done. It's not his blood I want, it's his heavy dark arms, his smooth shiny fingertips against my skin, his tongue like wet satin.

I want the roses blooming again for him between my thighs. The two of us together like music. The ebony and the ivory. The wire stretched taut, yet not breaking.

I'll be a nigger for him if he'll come love me again. I'll be more nigger than she'd ever want to be. If it's black pussy he wants, I'll be his black pussy, the way I was his white pussy, satisfying his sweet tooth. I'll be black and he'll want me again. In the back of the closet, behind the shoes, is what I'm looking for. So he liked the black beauty mark? Well, I'll go her one step better. I'll make myself black on the outside to match what I feel inside. No yellow-gal voodoo can stand up to this magic he's tasted here.

Sarah's little grandchild stares at me when I come out on my front porch, dragging a chair so I can sit and rock and watch for him to come back. The child can't understand how white skin can suddenly turn black, like hair turning gray overnight.

Even old Sarah won't understand. Sarah who said to me, "What can't be measured can't be missed." She's shaking her head, telling the little girl that their next door neighbor must be drunk again, or else lost her mind behind that no-good nigger man. "Lord have mercy, child, it look like she done painted her face with shoe polish."

Sarah won't know it goes much deeper than that. She won't understand that I've become a nigger through and through—that I've soaked up blackness in the marrow of my bones. She probably won't ever understand, even after Jake finds out my color has changed, and comes back home to be with me forever.

The roses will all be blooming when he gets here.

1984

NAOMI SHIHAB NYE

Pablo Tamayo

Pablo Tamayo is moving today, to stay with his brother-in-law on Nueces Street till he can find another house. "Don't worry so much," he told me over the fence. "I'm a beat-up man, my wife is an old lady, I always told you the roof was gonna fall."

That's wrong. He never mentioned the roof. He used to call on the telephone and say in a gruff voice, "Who's there?" as if I'd called him. When I stuttered, he'd laugh and say, "This is me, I'm standing on your roof," but he never mentioned it falling.

I want to give him eggs, a flannel shirt. I want to tell him this neighborhood will be a vacuum without him. To go back to the beginning, make a catalog of his utterances since the day we met over the bamboo that divides our yards. I was standing on a ladder with clippers, trying to tell the bamboo who was boss. In the next yard he stooped over a frizzy dog, murmuring Spanish consolations. He looked like he might once have been a wrestler. "So," he said, looking up. "You're pretty tall, I guess." I told him I was his new neighbor and he said he was my old one. He pointed, "Look at how I put this eyeball back in my dog."

Once his dog had a fight with a German shepherd. Pablo came running to find the eyeball dangling on its string. He called a doctor, the doctor said twenty dollars at least. "So I do it myself. Good job, no?" The eye was now glassy white. It looked like it had been put in backwards. "My dog goes with me to Junior's Lounge," he said, giggling.

You don't expect giggles from a man with tattoos. He told me Welcome to the Neighborhood, it's a Nice Neighborhood, I been here Forty, you know, Years. Throwing his head back when he spoke, like somebody proud and practiced, or kicking up dust, looking down like a kid, a brand-new kid.

Later I found myself wondering about him. What made this man act so happy? His house tilted, his wife had no teeth. We invited them for dinner, but they wouldn't come. "She don't like to chew without teeth in public." His car had not run in twenty weeks. Where was his history, what was his life?

"I was born in Mexico, like half the people in this town. They get born, they go north. Like birds or something." One night he showed me their wedding pictures. Such devastating changes the years make! From a shining silken couple, a future of roses, to a house of orange crates and dead newspapers, a shuffling duet of slippers and beans. "I love another girl first, her daddy was rich. He told her never marry a baker." His face goes dark for a moment. "Sometimes I still think of that. There was a rooster who rode on my shoulder but one day he changed, you know, he bit me on the leg." When Pablo speaks of the village in the mountains south of Monterrey, he stops smiling, as if those memories are a cathedral which can only be entered with a sober face.

The next day I ask him when he bought his house. "Aw, I never did. They wanted me to, in 1939. But I didn't like to pay so much money all at once, so I just keep payin' forty dollars a month till now." I want to shake him. Who is his landlord? "A bad, bad man. Once I had a good man but they change over the years. This guy, he won't fix the pipe, he won't paint the outside. I want to paint it, but he won't let me. What color do you think I could paint it?"

We stand back to examine the peeling boards.

"Beige."

Three days later he knocks at my door. "I just want to ask you. Is that the color of coffee with milk in it?"

His wife speaks no English and loves to wash. She wears a faded apron, veteran of a thousand washtubs. I can imagine her getting up in the mornings and going straight to her sewing machine. In a cage outside her back door lives a featherless bird named "Pobrecito." Pablo found it on Sweet Street, hobbling. She feeds it scraps of melon and bread.

Around her telephone she has pinned an arc of plastic lilies, post-

215

cards of saints, a rosary of black beads. Who is she hoping will call? If Jesus were to manifest for her in modern ways—¡Buenas dias! she would say. Mi casita, mi perrito, mi Pobrecito, mi Jesús. I have a garage sale and she buys my battered hiking boots. Where is she planning to go?

After much prodding, Pablo tells me they have three children. Two are in their fifties, live in Houston or somewhere, "Naw, I don't see them, they don't see me." One is twenty. Pablo and his wife are more than seventy so that means she had the boy when she was fifty, at least. I ask him about this and he says he guesses it's true. Months later I hear another story from the widow down the street. The twenty-year-old is a grandson. She says, "Pablo lies."

When the boy comes home he turns on rock-and-roll so loud the candles quiver on our piano. His hair is longer than my hair. Pablo says, "He had bad luck. Got married too young, seventeen, something like that, to a girl born north of the border. That means she's lazy. It's true. If a Mexican is born north of the border, her husband will walk the road of tears. So they broke up. Bad luck."

Months later, after numerous references to the road of tears, I ask Pablo for details. You mean to tell me all the smooth-faced innocent-hearted Mexican girls in local high schools are going to have husbands who walk the road of tears? C'mon Pablo, find your way out of that one. He looks at me, puzzled. And then his face cracks into its goofy grin. "I got it," he says. "You get a boat."

He asks what I do, why I'm always in this house chattering away on my typing machine. "I write things down," I say.

"Like what things?"

"Like little things that happen."

He looks around, shrugs. "I don't see nothin' happenin'." Then he goes indoors to make me a perfect pie. Pablo understands pie crust, for him poetry is the fluted edge of dough. And Pablo is the only one who will ever understand the delicate grammar of the engine of his car. There was no fuel pump in the city, he said dramatically, which would fit it. So he was building a contraption of wire and soup cans, like a child's telephone. He was going to communicate with his car.

One day, after nearly a month of tinkering, I heard the engine cough, choke, exhale a huge sigh. And there was Pablo passing my house, waving madly, his one-eyed dog perched in the back window. Ten minutes later he returned. There was a problem—the car could only go as far as the amount of gas the can would hold. But it *worked* now. That was the important thing, it worked. One night I dreamed that wings sprouted where the dented door handles were and Pablo went flying over the city, sending down lines of symbolic verse.

He said he would get another "Alamo seed" so I could have a tree like the one in his yard. He said he was tired of the mud out back, he had this plan for grass. "I used to drink more beers," he said, "than any man with a mouth." That was when he worked at the hotel, when he came home with cinnamon in his cuffs. Some days now he still journeyed out to work, dressed in a square white baker's shirt, to cafeterias or hospitals to "fill in" someone's absence. "I made 35 dozen doughnuts today," he'd say, folding his craggy hands, shaking his head. "I don't wanna be like the man who killed himself in your bathroom." This was news to me. *What man?*

Then Pablo looked worried, he'd slipped, he'd said too much. "Aw come on, I was joking, let's go hammer the fence, aye-yi-yi." He got shy sometimes, his words blurred. *What man?* And he told me his name. Howard Riley. Spoken slowly, How-ard Ri-ley, as if the name had grown longer in Pablo's head.

"He was an old man, kinda old, you know, oh what the hell, everybody's old. You're kinda old. He was old a little sooner than I was. He used to hit a golf ball in the yard, that end, this end, that end, this end. I hear this little tick, you know, like the clock, the little sound it made. But one day he went in your bathroom and shot his own head. Pow! (Finger to head.) I was at the bank. I came home with ten dollars and my wife, she said, Howard's dead. In Spanish, you know. So I went over to see him and he was gone already. They came in a car and took him. I just went to the bank! I used to think of him at night when the nuts fell on the roof. Tick, tick, tick."

"Why did he do it?"

A shrug. "I dunno. He was tired. He had nothin' else to do." Pablo stared down at his two big feet. "So let's go hammer the fence, I get the hammer, you get the nails."

Months later, on the same day I was watching him busy at work in his yard at 7 A.M., wearing a blue-and-white checkered jockey cap, dragging a tin pail of cilantro from one mud crease to the next, that day his faceless landlord appeared and told him they had two weeks to get gone. After forty-eight years, two weeks. Pablo came to me with the same expression my father had on the day he had to fire twelve

217

lifetime printers from his newspaper because they were being replaced by computers.

"We gotta move."

The little dog running in circles, sniffing the ground. Another fall, pecans splitting their dull-green pods in the grass. A pumpkin pie still warm in my hands. How many pies had Pablo given us? Maybe a hundred, maybe more. Lots of times we gave them away. We don't like pie too much. But we'd keep them out on the table a while, on a small pedestal, like a shrine.

"This one's good."

He'd always say it. "This one's good." Forget any other one. Pablo in the yard with a ragged tea towel on his arm, hands outstretched.

"What do you mean, move?"

His landlord wanted to build an office. I was yelling about zoning while his wife unpinned the rosary from its wall, felt the cool black beads move again in her fingers.

"You know, he might make a parking lot here where the Alamo tree is." This year the tree had had eighteen leaves. From that seed Pablo found in a gutter. We joked so much when it came up, ugly stick. Not one leaf for months. Then he put small twigs around it like a barricade, tied them with string, little red flags, and it started doing things. His voodoo tree. Smack in the center of the yard.

I wanted to meet this goddamn landlord immediately. Where had he gone? What kind of office? With filing cabinets and Dictaphones and secretary's shiny legs? Obviously they wouldn't fit in this tilt-a-whirl house, they'd flatten it out, 'doze it under. Pablo's crooked stove. The ancient valentine heart tacked to the porch. From whom to whom? Gruff voice. "Me to the lady."

He stood there in his yard which was slipping out from under him, he stood there with hips cocked, plaid shirt half-buttoned, his hair still full on his head, and said, "I wanna tell you somethin'." That always meant, come a little closer, put down your groceries. "You know this world we got here?" He motioned with his arms. "Lemme tell you, this world don't love us. It don't think about us or pray for us or miss us, you know that I mean? That's what I learned when my father died. I was a young man. I got up the next day and went outside, feelin' sick, my face still fat from cryin'. And there was the sky. Lookin' just the same. Dead or alive, it don't matter. Still the sky. So then I started lookin' around and there was still the flowers, still the bugs, I mean *the bugs,* who cares about bugs? My father was dead and the world didn't miss him. The world didn't know his name! Ventura—Morales—Tamayo—but *I knew it.* And I say to myself, That's all we got! I know it, the barber know it, so what? This don't make me feel more bad, you know, it make me feel—better. Aw, I dunno, I gotta go find a box."

Hours later he's coming down Sheridan Street pushing a box in front of him, a giant box, like the boxes washing machines come in. He's done this before. I never knew what he did with those boxes. They went in the door and disappeared. He doesn't have a fireplace. Inside his wife is taking down the sweaters. They have the smell of sunlight in them. She's had them out on those poles and ropes so many times they're a little confused today. Now they're going someplace else. She's shufflin' around and he's shufflin' around, taking down calendars, rolling up the years. God knows where the boy is when they need him. Pablo probably rolls up his "Marijuana Boogie" poster without even reading it.

Once he said, "When you die, you die."

"Oh yeah? That's very interesting."

Then we were laughing ridiculously on our two sides of the fence.

Can I translate this great philosophy so it applies to now? "When you move, you move." Simple. Throw up the hands. Still we're very upset in our house. The sky doesn't know it, but we know it. The news comes on the television. I go out back. There is no other news.

1983

PAT ELLIS TAYLOR

Leaping Leo

—when you're down and out in dallas
you are down and out
—fr. de dallas blues

S o in dallas leo is always working one place and I am working another, I get up in the morning while he's still in bed or after he's already gone to work, hours and days erratic working temporary jobs. I walk through the alley in back of our apartment house in the morning to gaston avenue to catch the bus to wherever kelly girl services say I should be going, the exhaust fumes flooding over the curbs and crashing in rush-hour waves against the darkening brick mix of apartments/tattoo-parlor/mex-tex-bars/and/fast-foods on both street sides. And leo coaxes the pick-up truck to his jobs, he's registered with manpower, atlas, and peak-load, he loads gatorade and drives a delivery route and makes electric circuit boards and sprays paint on pipes. And he comes home telling stories, you know how the newspaper said that street guy fell into downtown traffic and was killed? he tells me. Well, he didn't fall he was pushed, that's what one of the men down at atlas told me today. He was a pursesnatcher and the cops couldn't catch him, so they finally pushed him under the wheels. And he tells me where some of the men sleep, under the freeway, and where they told him to go on the highway to ask truckers for work unloading in town, little pieces of labor pool lore, who's hiring where, and how many at a time. He works for two or three days at a time, then lays off for two or three days, sitting around in the efficiency apartment, watching teevee in his shorts, drinking beers, letting the aluminum cans pile up in grocery bags under the kitchen window, writing poems about how workers hate working and

---

how he wishes he was alone and free and unencumbered and somewhere else.

In the evenings when I get off of work, sometimes leo and I walk
down gaston avenue to tom thumb supermarket which is a grocery
store like the neighborhood built in more peaceful, more affluent tree-
lined times for the sweet-stay-at-home-housewives who were our mothers who abandoned these city neighborhoods for the safer cleaner
north dallas suburbs. Now it is sticky-floor-broken-glass-crowded-
aisles, votive candles and mountain-pass cans of chile across from won-
ton wrappers, strong-smelling men in salvation army suits cruising
with grocery carts full of plastic-sacked beans and boxed rice, iron
bars between the store doors and the parking lot to keep the carts
from getting ripped off by grocery-bagged walkers. The store sits at
the end of a horse-shoe mall, but the dimestores and baby-knitting-
fabric shops which once must have lined the other two sides of the parking lot are long gone, windows boarded up, one corner ex-drugstore
now mario's lounge, black plywood across the window glass, low-riders
parked in front, young chicanos lounging against the chrome-nosed
hoods at night, mario's door open and loud music coming out. One night
at the supermarket check-out stand I am so happy to be off work for
the day, so happy to be with leo, who is holding my hand, I say isn't this
romantic, the two of us here checking out groceries, and leo looks at
me like I am crazy. You've got to be kidding, he says, no romanticism
left in leo anymore, he can see very clearly where he is, and it's no
place good.

Because the truth is that the landscapes of leo's memory/mind are
like a series of snapshots from a family album, there are rolling green
lawns of suburban homes and university campuses and country lots,
and there is a family standing together on the front steps of a tidy
home or in front of a tidy christmas tree or lined up on the sides of a
tidy turkey dinner: a small-boned beautiful angel-faced wife and two
angel-boy-babies calling him leo instead of daddy in the liberal uni-
tarian style, him pointing out nature to them in the ravines and hills of
the paradise of nuclear family life they are growing up in. So leo's
present reality dances across the stage in front of these green landscapes like a wino reeling his way through a montessori school, hey
where *are* we? Just where the hell are we? Wife, children, house and
car, all gone, university job finally taken away for all the scandal and
chaos which once kicked up like chicken feathers in a whing-a-ding

transformation from leo-the-professor to leo-the-man falling falling falling for a shady woman with teen-aged children (who is me) and po-etry as a way of life. And somehow or another it has all come to this: leo creating the plot of his own story from labor pool lounge to tom thumb barrio-market and seeing (incredibly!) himself in the faces of the other men there too old too poorly educated too alcoholic too sui-cidal too lonely to be anything like him, but there they are anyway, wheeling the aisles of tom thumb together at night and in the daytime sharing the same set of folding chairs.

Now if leo didn't love me, he could be a poet and live alone in a card-board box (like a man who lived somewhere up east leo read about in the dallas morning news) and then he wouldn't have to work very much at all, he could simply eat cheap mackerel and soda crackers and write poetry all day. Or if I were simply myself alone, then we could be gyp-sies together, we could ride the rails and hitchhike and explore deserts and mountains and meet south american shamen and learn universal secrets from listening to the grass sing across the canadian tundras and from kundalini-fucking in the dry bed of the rio grande. But I never seem to be myself alone, that sharp thin blade of a female-fantasy-companion fit for a gypsy-poet-man, I always seem instead to have these children always tying me to the world of work. And in dallas at first there is only one of these children, there is only morgani, who is a grown child and who works himself at a car wash bringing in one-third of the rent every month. But then there are two others, calling long-distance from el paso no longer wanting to live with their father, wanting to come for the school year to dallas and live with me. And I am a mother, born under the sign of mother, called by the name of mother and all of its variations wheeling off three children's developing tongues: the continuing chorus of all my adult years. So because of these children wanting to come, I think, well, we've got to be some-where, we've got to have a place to sleep at least, the word *we* no longer meaning leo and me, having wider and weightier implications.

So leo thinks maybe he will get a grant of money. But he doesn't. And then he thinks maybe someone rich will give him some money for the sake of poetry, but nobody does. And then he thinks maybe if we take off in the camper for two weeks in july for the annual-naked-hippie-rainbow-family-gathering we will get a revelation and some new kind of future other than temporary labor pools and dallas apartment-semi-migrant-neighborhoods will open up. And we do go to the rainbow-family-gathering all right. But it rains, we only have wet wood and don't know how to build a fire, we get diarrhea, the wind blows toilet paper from the shitter around our tent poles, the tent falls down around our ears. So we're back in dallas and poorer than we were before, and I start looking around for a bigger place with a lease that allows children because it's already august and the school year is about to begin and my children are coming.

So one day I tell leo, there is an apartment for rent just three doors down big enough for everybody, and leo says how much a month?

I say 325.

And he says utilities?

I say we pay them.

And he says well, that's over a hundred dollars more a month than what we're paying now.

But I say I'll pay more than you need to, to cover the kids.

Who'll pay the deposit? he says.

Oh, don't worry, I'll get it together, I lie-hope-wish-dream, because there's no more than fifty dollars in the envelope underneath the rug in the closet where I keep my money, and kelly services hasn't called me for work in over four days. Leo looks at me like he knows I am lying and he is mad-as-hell but he isn't saying anything, because he's seen again that I am not alone, even though I try every night to make him forget it by making him concentrate on that singular body under the covers, but the truth is always there below the surface: *leo is working in labor pools in dallas instead of crab-fishing on the acapulco-tibetan-desert-beach because the woman he has chosen is always shadowed by children not even his own.*

So it is toward the end of the summer to beat all summers, july murdering grass and shrubs, august murdering babies, old people stroking and dying, burnt-out trees like torches outside the apartment window dead-green and still. It is too hot to wear clothes so I am hanging around the apartment with nothing on but a white half-slip pulled up to my armpits. And in the corner of the kitchen is a pile of used carpet which someone brought home from a dumpster because it is perfectly good. So I lie down on top of that and look out the window at nothing like a floundered fish pining for my kids because they're so good and I'm so bad, singing that old bad mother song. And oh these kids, I am thinking, they've been through shit with me, I quit their bankrupt ad-agency boozing dad thinking for sure I could make something better for us all than that but where am I now, baby, where am I now? My arm is over my eyes listening to leo running bathwater on the other side of the wall, and I start to cry because I'm living in a two-room efficiency apartment in an east dallas neighborhood where the winos piss in the park bushes across from the elementary school and I don't have a job and I don't even have a place for my kids to stay. And I don't even have a place for them to stay! Oh I should have bought a pair of hose, I should have lacquered my fingernails and put my papers in a briefcase and finished my degree and copied my resume and stopped pretending to be a writer, and I should have married someone other than leo who would give me money anytime I asked for it, or stayed married to the children's dad who has become successful-sober-and-dull without me around, or I should have never moved to dallas I should have stayed in the country and gone to work in wills point for champion mobile homes or gotten a job at the local dairy queen dishing ice cream.

The front door opens, and it is morgani coming in from the car wash, he comes into the kitchen and opens the refrigerator but doesn't say anything to me like I am probably sleeping with my arm over my face. And thank god thank god, I am thinking, at least a little money coming in from morgani thank god for a grown son, oh, and I keep lying on that pile of carpet, not only am I not able to take care of my own children, I am not able to take care of myself. Here I am, I am thinking, no better than a fat-black-shawled peasant mother being taken care of by a grown son (and I am getting lower and lower)—how can this be when I am such a *smart* person? How can such a bright-young-looking-kind-of-woman-for-her-age, such a—I would even say—sometimes *sexy* woman—who at the same time writes funny things as well as serious things, someone who is sometimes somewhat of a female folklore scholar, how can such a charismatic person like myself be so down and out?

The telephone rings and leo answers it. He comes into the kitchen a few minutes later, and he looks his worst, his arms and legs look skinny, his hair looks stringy, when he looks at me I hear him saying you-limpbag-of-depression-and-doldrums-you-witch-bitch, and when I look at him he can hear me saying you moneyless-no-good-bummer-nonpoet-of-a-man . . . That was gray eagle on the telephone, he tells me, he's going to come over and drive us to his house so we can see some slides he took of the rainbow gathering. And I am thinking oh no oh no, not gray eagle, not the rainbow gathering why oh why did I ever go to the naked-hippie-rainbow-family-gathering this summer in west virginia, why did I let leo talk me into spending my money on that? So I don't say anything, I just lie there with my arm on my eyes.

Leo says so do you want to go?

And I say no.

He says I think you should go, I think you should get out of this apartment.

So I take my arm down but don't look at him, I look around for my shoes, I'll go I say, reaching around for the pants I had on which are somewhere.

Just then someone knocks at the door and morgani answers it, and it is my biker-brother who came passing through el paso on his way to dallas and gave one of my kids a ride. So I hug this particular kid, who is blonde and sixteen, and I tell him that he looks good, because he does, and we walk out of the kitchen into the other room and he says, so this is it, huh? And I say yes, this is it.

And he says well, where am I going to sleep?

And I wave to the floor and say here for right now.

He says where's the other kid going to sleep when she comes?

And I say, she's going to sleep here, too.

My biker-brother sits down on the couch, red beard frazzled, face red, leo brings him a beer, this city is already freaking me out, my biker-brother says, I don't see how you can stand living in the middle of the city. I called out to your house in the country first thinking you'd be there. Some other people had your number. They said they had people calling for you all the time.

Well we haven't been out there for a long time, I say. For one thing, our truck's on its last legs, so leo has only been using it to drive to jobs.

I don't know why you don't live out there anymore, my biker-brother says.

Well, we're not living out there because we ran out of money and there wasn't any work out there, I say.

Oh you could have worked if you wanted to, leo says.

Where? I ask him.

You never even asked around.

Well at any rate it certainly seemed to me that there wasn't any way to make a living there.

Someone is knocking on the door again, and this time it is gray eagle, leo introduces gray eagle to my biker-brother and they shake hands.

And on one side of the hand-shake is gray eagle whose beard is gray and whose cheeks are rosy from hippie vitality who lives by himself on bee pollen and rose hips (like leo himself might look if he were fifty and lived alone) and on the other side of the hand-shake is my biker-brother full of biker-blood-lust, his face already dark-red from homicidal city vibes. Leo asks my biker-brother if he wants to come and see slides of the rainbow gathering and my biker-brother says yes, and we leave the apartment with morgani and the other kid sharing a joint. We drive to gray eagle's ranch-style house with trimmed-up bushes in a quiet north dallas neighborhood. He sets up his carousel slide projector on a coffee table in the living room and starts projecting larger-than-lifesize photographs of two nude blonde women, one a well-preserved fortyish, the other in her teens. These are mother and daughter, he says, who came to dallas from new mexico and convoyed with me to the hippie rainbow gathering the rest of the way. I took these shots of them in the shower the night they were staying here. We were just goofing around.

Now that's quite a mother, my biker-brother says.

The older woman is lathering the younger woman's boobs for several slides in a row, then for several others the two of them change places.

I wouldn't mind some of that ass, my biker-brother says.

These are my rainbow sisters, gray eagle says like a gentle reprimand.

Jesus look at those tits, my biker-brother says.

Gray eagle picks up the pace, clicks through five or six fast glimpses of blonde pubic hair and smiles and stoops and bends. Then the blonde women are suddenly replaced with panoramas of nude women bathing in streams, hiking along forest trails holding hands, eating fruit, carrying babies, everyone looking free from the cities, from working, for the taking, for gray eagle or my biker-brother or leo, anyone who can claw through the screen. And my biker-brother is going crazy. He is drinking up gray eagle's red wine, he is talking cunt and tits, so gray eagle shuts off the slides and turns to him. If you're going to talk like that about the rainbow sisters, he says, I won't be able to show you the slides.

Leo has been sitting on the floor not saying anything drinking one long-neck lone star after another, but now he speaks up. Well you do show more photographs of nude women than you do nude men, he says, although maybe it's natural if you're a man to have that bias, and his words are thick but precise.

I want to see some more of the shower girlies, my biker-brother says.

The thing is, gray eagle says, these people let me take these photographs because they know me, they know I'd never hurt them in any way.

Oh I'd never hurt them either, my biker-brother says, oh maybe I'd want to fuck them but I wouldn't want to hurt them.

Well they know that we are like brother and sister, gray eagle says.

Or maybe I would only hurt them a little, my biker-brother says, if they hurt me or something like that.

Gray eagle turns off the slide projector. Well I guess it's time to take us back, I say. So we're back in the car, I sit in the front seat with gray eagle, leo and my biker-brother in the back seat, driving back the way we came, through the quiet winding streets of north dallas to the freeway back south toward downtown. Gray eagle tells me maybe I should write a story, maybe I should write something about women who work for the railroads and he could take the photographs and we could make some money collaborating that way, and a mercedes whizzes past us, and my biker-brother throws the driver a finger and yells fuck you! out the window at him. Then another car passes and he throws them a finger, too, and yells fuck you! fuck you! Then leo starts throwing fingers out the back window at the car behind us, I see him fluttering his fingers in and out of his ears, and gray eagle says or maybe we could do a story together about women who work for the highway department fixing roads. Leo is yelling you rich bastard! You rich filth! And gray eagle pulls up to the curb in front of our apartment, and my biker-brother says—Trisha stays calm through everything, she runs the show.

There is a pause, and then leo says yes she does run the show, doesn't she?

Then he slams out of the back of the car and runs up the apartment steps and disappears. My biker-brother gets out, he has a happy booze smile on his face and is swaying back and forth holding the last of a gallon bottle of red wine he took from gray eagle's house and one of gray eagle's glasses. I wave to gray eagle as he pulls away from the curb, my biker-brother puts his arm around me, I love you, he says, because you're always running the show.

When we walk into the apartment leo is throwing clothes books papers into a duffel bag. I am leaving here! he yells out when he hears the door open, and I never want to see any of your faces again! He walks out, slams the door. Morgani and the other kid are sitting on the couch watching teevee, hardly look up when leo walks out the door. Maybe we don't want to see him again either, morgani says.

Well he must love you, my biker-brother says. He probably left so that he wouldn't beat you up.

So leo walks out the apartment to gaston avenue where the buses run, but before he gets on a bus he walks down to mario's lounge and gets *really* drunk. And then afterward he gets his suitcases stolen while he's waiting for the bus. And he heads for austin where his ex-nurse-wife is living with the children which at least are his own. But I don't know any of this until he calls me the next night from the nurse-wife's phone. Why don't you come down to austin? he says. You could work kelly services down here. But I say no.

Then two days later he calls up again and he's now in galveston as a poet-in-the-schools living in a camper truck because he happened to walk into the right office at the right time. Why don't you come down to galveston? he says. But the ocean is behind him and the sea gulls are swooping down on his shoulders and back up and down again and calling, and the beach is all sand and no rocks, and leo is already dancing with the galveston dancers and singing to the blonde sisters who are not yet mothers in the galveston bars, leo unencumbered as light itself since gaston avenue took all his papers and clothes.

1982

PETER LA SALLE
Life in the Sun Belt

hen, in the early evening, the sky simply went purple out there on the West Texas desert. And the city, an oil boom town, ran right up to the desert, a pink flatness dotted with mesquite and yucca, spreading like some dreamt, dry ocean to the horizon.

The firm's sales offices were in a new white slab of high-rise owned by one of the oil companies. Brodeur, his double-knit sportjacket over one arm and his Samsonite briefcase in the other hand, stopped in the asphalt parking lot and stared at that enormous sky. The first white stars seemed too close to be real, flickering. In March, the evening breeze, so dry and with only a trace of fumes from the refineries, was already warm.

"Brode."

It was Stath. Stath was a mustached block at thirty-five, a Texan.

"Hey, Stath."

"I just wanted to tell you. We can take my car next week, and both put in for the mileage for that meeting in Waco. How's that?"

"Ah, fine, but I don't know if I'll be able to get away for the whole thing. I mean I might have to start a little later." He was lying.

"I'll go when you're ready. I think it would be a fine time for us to talk. I've been seeing a doctor." He smiled. He had sad, drooping eyes, and despite his lineman's bulk, he would always be a boy. "I found out something about my problem."

"Your problem?"

"What I told you about before."

"Of course. Sure, we might as well go over in one car." Brodeur set his briefcase down on the Granada's hood. "These evenings you get out here are really something, though, aren't they?"

"Purty."

"You saw, ah,—"

"No, not a psychiatrist. It's a heap simpler than that. But it's kind of complicated too. That drive will give us plenty of time for an old heart-to-heart."

"Of course."

Brodeur had bought a house in the city. He would have said, if he still were in Michigan, it was a new house in a new development. But that wasn't necessary. Just about everything was new in the West Texas city, except for the pocket on either side of the Texas Pacific railroad tracks and the old Route 80 beside that. There, most of the stores were either pawn shops or seedy cafeterias now; the Chicano ghetto was the same few unpaved red-dirt streets with dilapidated stucco shacks; and a half dozen of the original settlers' bungalows remained, black-leaved live oaks above them, in a part of the country where any leafy trees were rare.

The oil boom had brought new straight six-lane boulevards farther out to give plenty of room for expansion. They formed a perfect square that was gradually becoming lined with offices and shopping centers. In the last year, work was finished on a giant mall with a Montgomery Ward's on one end and a Woolco on the other. Also, the rather posh Desert Park had just opened with twelve quality retailers and pueblo modern architecture—shops stacked atop one another, little verandahs, blue-tinted glass, and the occasional touch of red-tile roofing here and there for accent. There were starts on three more high-rises, such as the one Brodeur worked out of, and those pools of massive parking lots everywhere, like black velvet fields, landscaped with islands of crushed white stone, in turn swirled with darker wood chips around shaggy-topped joshua and clawlike ocotillo.

Brodeur's house was brown brick with a streamlined, tar-and-pebble overhanging roof. It was overpriced at $61,000. But the real estate agent had assured Brodeur a year before when he bought it that everything in the area would go up another $10,000 as soon as bids on leases were in for the new petroleum fields. And it was true. That gain never could have happened in Michigan.

Brodeur had grown up there, in Saginaw. He attended Michigan State, met and pinned a girl from Delta Zeta, and was married in his senior year. He worked a sales route for Labott Pharmaceutical for ten years. He and his wife, Anne, lived in Lansing, had two boys, and though Brodeur spent more time than he really liked in the bleak Detroit neighborhoods keeping stocked the little drugstores with pink neon signs in the windows and bars over that glass because of all the break-ins, he was generally content in Michigan. Anne seemed to be, too. They saw many old friends from the university, and the ongoing sports contests of the Spartans in their green-and-white garb made for a good focal point for their social life, attending games and getting together afterward.

And then Labott Pharmaceutical simply folded. Brodeur began collecting unemployment benefits and registered with four placement agencies. He worked for less than two months as a shoe salesman in a Morse store in East Lansing, until he flatly decided that with a college degree and solid sales experience, he deserved to be doing more than kneeling down in front of a fat-legged woman and her kicking kid, with a metal measurer in one hand and a rubber-stinking tennis shoe in the other. He realized he would have to increase his options by agreeing to relocate, and after two interviews at an appliance company's home office in a Chicago suburb, he was offered a job. He stayed in a motel in that suburb for a month during an orientation course, and Anne got the household ready to move to the Southwest. The firm, at that time, hadn't said exactly where.

That was when Brodeur first met Larry Rich. Silver-haired Rich was already working out of Dallas, getting things ready for the firm's sales beef-up in the region. He talked individually with members of the training course in a conference room at the home office. There were just two fiberglass scoop chairs and sound-proofed walls.

"Are you a Wolverine fan?" Rich said. He wore an aqua leisure suit, his shirt collar pressed open. He was middle-aged and tanned.

"Actually, no."

"But here in your file it says you went to Michigan State." Brodeur smiled at that.

"U. of Michigan is the Wolverines. State is the Spartans."

231

"Spartans. Wolverines. What the hell. I'll bet you're a ball fan."

"To tell you the truth, I am."

"Yeah, that's just what I need," he said, looking at the dossier he held and talking more to himself than to Brodeur. He looked up, "Yes-sir-ree, no New Mexico or Arizona for you. I'm going to put you deep in the heart of my state. West Texas. And believe me, those folks out there are football-crazy. You'll have something to talk about with your buyers. And to be honest, it's a prime assignment. That's oil country."

At first, the weather alone was enough to dazzle Brodeur, Anne, and the boys. It was that terrible winter, and eating supper in their house that was so new the kitchen still smelled of the plastic in the Formica counter tops, they watched the national nightly news and its films of Buffalo, Cincinnati, and just about every other city up there. They wanted to empathize, but it was difficult even to muster up a sense of such severity when on the weekends Brodeur could play eighteen holes of golf and it was sixty-five degrees. Once on the news they saw pedestrians using ropes to tug themselves up Wabash Avenue in Chicago while the wind blew the snow horizontal. It was hilarious. They saw plows laboring on streets through depths higher than their revolving roof beacons. They saw a clip of men playing softball far out on Lake Erie's ice for a gag. They heard stories of poor old people freezing to a blue hardness when local gas companies cut off their supplies, and weirder stories still, like that about the man whose car stalled on an interstate in thirty-degree-below temperatures. He was dressed lightly, and he trudged to a nearby trailer home, where the resident refused to let him in. The motorist, screaming, eventually bashed down the door *and* the resident with an ax—and received two years in prison for it.

They were pleased to be in West Texas. Anne was learning to cook Mexican dishes, graduating from adding fresh vegetables to sauces and frijoles from the yellow-labeled Old El Paso brand cans, to actually starting from scratch with nothing but tortillas, jalapeño peppers, ground beef, and ordinary tomato sauce. The kids sent their old schoolmates in Michigan postcards with scenes of the chocolate-and-orange mountains of Big Bend National Park, which they hadn't visited yet, but which wasn't that far away either. In fact, when the summer came, the heat wasn't what they had expected. Sure, there were days when it was 105, but the humidity was nothing more than 10 percent, because the wind came straight up from the lunar plain of the Chihuahua Desert in Mexico. People had told them they wouldn't feel the heat. And that was true as well.

But maybe the dazzle had started to wear off. The schools were one problem. Brodeur's older son had eczema, and for a while he feigned some sort of a flu to stay home from junior high school. Anne had to go there herself to see what was causing his reluctance to attend, and it was the P.E. instructor, just out of Texas Tech, who finally figured that, admittedly, "Old Tim does get a little razzing when the boys have to change for gym class because his skin is so darn funny looking like that." Tim was a target of the Pokes, a gang of toughs in the junior high school who roamed the corridors in Western boots and cowboy hats, principally bent on making life miserable for the members of the school's marching band, though Tim, small for his age, proved a victim too.

And there were other things, both small and maybe bigger.

In July, after having lived there for six months, Brodeur suddenly noticed the litter. And once you noticed it, it seemed to mar everything—fluttering white shreds and bouncing aluminum cans pouring in an ongoing stream from the big American cars and the customized pickups, tumbling in slow motion across those acres of new parking lots to drift in piles against the chain-link fences or spread onto the desert. After a good blow, all the mesquite was decorated with the rags of paper napkins and cellophane. Maybe there was too much space and too much fast money. There was no need to be careful.

One morning, coming back to the city from his sales route, Brodeur saw his own tanned face in the Granada's oval rearview mirror. He said to himself, "There are no cemeteries in this town." It upset him terribly. It was a city of 150,000, and by then he had been living there a year, never noticing a cemetery. Where were people buried? He didn't go directly to the office building that morning. He raced the Granada from one end of the city to the other on those boulevards, from open desert to open desert.

And nothing.

Finally, he pulled into a Kerr-McGee station for no-lead, and he openly put the question to the leather-faced attendant. The man looked as if he might be a reformed bum, or a bum off the skids for a while, anyway. It was tough to get reliable help for such menial jobs, Brodeur knew, because of the money most anybody could make roughnecking in the fields. The man wasn't much older than Brodeur's thirty-two. But his teeth had gone. His blue eyes had that hungry dazzle bums' eyes often get. Country music crackled from a radio in the dingy station proper, the window of the cubbyhole stacked with a pyramid of cut-rate motor oil.

"That's what I mean," Brodeur said. "Where are the cemeteries?"

"Cemeteries. Well, there are cemeteries in the little towns."

"But what about all the people here? This city is big."

The attendant grinned with those rotted teeth. "Not much folk are from here. Makes sense that not much folk are going to die here, I figure. They all go away to die; maybe they just sort of crawls back to where it was they come from."

So, turning into his driveway that Friday evening after Stath had caught up with him in the parking lot, Brodeur didn't feel at all the flood of satisfaction he felt sometimes upon seeing that brown-brick ranch house with the overhanging roof on the street where most of the houses remained unfinished. (That was something else. Everywhere you looked there were new building starts on apartments and houses. All that clean plywood and pine framing gleaming in the blinding sun. Nothing would ever be finished, it seemed.) Getting out of the Granada and looking at the lawn of thick desert grass now yellow—the straw texture of it still amazed him—he didn't say to himself, "Well, the worst of it's over. I'm working. I'm giving them something. This is our house."

He felt, well, uneasy. That business about Stath. He didn't want to be in a car with Stath for over five hours going to Waco. In Waco, he didn't want to see Stath go into those paralyzing attacks of speechlessness that somehow, out of the proverbial blue, just started afflicting the man one day.

Stath was in trouble. Everybody in the office knew it.

"So, you see how glad I was to learn it wasn't something in my head," Stath said. "I read this book by a kid named Vonnegut. It was called *The Eden Express.*" Stath talked slowly, and very confidently with a smile, as they kept at an even fifty-five on Interstate 20. In the early morning glare, the oil pumps with their long snouted heads seemed to be nodding on either side of them, listening to Stath and agreeing, "Yes, yes."

"Kurt Vonnegut. I didn't think he was all that young."

"No, this is that Kurt Vonnegut's kid. A friend of Shelline's got it from a book club. Anyway, I read that. That poor boy tells about some real mental problems, and at least that gave me some relief. Because I knew then that if that's crazy I was safe. So then I saw a regular doctor, an M.D.—Pruitt."

Stath had one hand on the white plastic wheel of the hulking, late-sixties four-door Impala. (Brodeur knew that even if Stath was a do-it-your-self mechanic who had put two new engines in the car, and even if cars were slower in general to wear out in the warm dry climate, Stath should have something newer—just for appearances.) Stath stared straight ahead, and with the other hand, he slipped open the top lid on a dull-aluminum cake pan. Inside was a neatly sliced beef brisket, and with fingers as fat as panatellas, Stath probed the limp flaking stuff for a couple pieces, which he ate out of his hand.

"You sure you don't want me to put some of that between the bread you have," Brodeur suggested.

"No, this is just real fine as it is," Stath said, his full country-boy accent really taking over. "Mmmmmmm-mmmmm. That *is* good. But I will let you get me some of that Sanka. And there's a thermos of good regular instant all made up by Shelline for you too."

Stath explained more. This Dr. Pruitt had run tests for over a month on Stath. He finally delivered his diagnosis, which was "serious," as Stath emphasized, lowering his oxen-yoked eyebrows, but, "Not nearly as serious as finding out that I had some wires singed in my old haystack." It was a matter of low blood sugar, and it was causing Stath to lose his composure when he was in any slightly demanding situation, such as being in a group, and breathe as if he had just run a mile, jittering uncontrollably to the point, as was said, he couldn't even muster a voice.

At first, Stath had confided the problem to Brodeur in a bar in the city. That was when Brodeur originally learned about it. The bar was a typically flashy new place. There was an attempt at sophistication with what looked like murky oils of Indian maidens from a distance, though upon closer inspection they turned out to be mildly pornographic portrayals—puppy-snouted breasts cupped in hands beneath gossamer, and spreading bronze thighs. There was dark paneling and deep gold carpet, and Brodeur and Stath had stopped there to unwind after both finishing their sales reports at the office at about the same time.

Brodeur would never know why Stath chose him for such confidence, but he had always liked Stath. He liked that honest, country-boy something about him. Stath took a long belt on his iced bourbon.

"It happened in Lubbock today. I had to address a pack of them at a department store and I froze. It's true what they say about it. All the blood went out of me. My face was cold. I was dizzy, and I couldn't mutter a thing to them." He gripped the glass tightly, as if he would crunch it to make his point.

Brodeur naturally had told him then that the trouble was most likely simple nerves, but within a month of that, even the typing secretaries whispered stories of how Stath shook around them when he turned over reports. How he perpetually stammered. He probably could have gotten by for a while, Brodeur was sure, just on old account renewals. The overall business in the Sun Belt was so explosive that even a salesman who discovered he couldn't talk to people could get by.

"Eight times a day?" Brodeur now asked him in the car.

"That's right. Eight little meals."

Stath talked of his diet. He had to make certain something was always in his stomach to keep the blood manufacturing sugar and, so, ensure his composure. Hence the brisket. Also, nothing fried, and nothing acidic, such as regular coffee. And certainly no alcohol.

"I can't tell you how much the diet has changed me in the last week."

"Then you haven't had any trouble on your route?"

"I haven't been on my route this week. I've just been trying to get all my paper work in order with my reports for this meeting. Hell, though," he smiled, talking quite assuredly, relaxed, "if I don't feel a hundred percent better. I suppose this meeting will be the big test. But to be frank, I ain't worried."

"How about desserts?"

"Desserts. Now that's a strange one. You'd think that they contain sugar, but I'll be darned that it doesn't work that way. Somehow they just tend to cut down on what's in the blood. Re-versely proportional. Now, maybe if I had taken some of those biology courses instead of all that Bible at SMU, I would have found out about those things." He had it back, Brodeur could tell. He had the old salesman's zip, the way you windily apply what you are to what is being talked about to establish intimacy, for a generally friendly, even if it is phony, spiel.

They left the freeway after Big Spring, a picturesque town with a big church with twin spires and red-tiled roofs, and a lot of tall, slim cedars. They cut into the hilly brown land, over two-laned country roads on which the Impala's tires hummed, and toward Hillsboro where Stath's father lived. Actually, Brodeur himself often avoided the monotonous interstate freeways if he had time to spare on his route, and Stath had asked him beforehand if he minded, "If we swing by my daddy's place. I've been tinkering with this old lawn mower this winter, and I want to give it to him for this sweet little spot he just bought." Brodeur was all for the idea. He had driven Interstate 20 to Dallas too often for it to be even vaguely interesting, and, besides, they both agreed that the first day of the meeting—a conference of the Southwestern region's salesmen to assess the firm's area performance— wouldn't get into full swing until the afternoon. They could miss the opening luncheon.

In the hills, unlike in the desert, you could start to sense spring. There were more budding trees, going lime, and there was something as simple as normal green grass. Red-headed vultures sat hunch-backed on fence posts. There were unpainted dilapidated barns, and Stath ate the brisket, sipped the Sanka, and talked of growing up in a town not far from an intersection they braked for. The roads crossed at a right angle with an old Texaco station and one of those seedy, but somehow right, Texas Dairy Queens with yellow fluorescent lights under the jutting roof and bug-splattered windows. Stath's father was a retired Methodist minister who now kept himself busy repairing an old house he had bought in Hillsboro. He also occasionally drove up to Dallas to help out with clerical work at the Southern Methodist Head-quarters there. His wife had died a couple of years before.

Purple blossoms burst on the Texas mountain-laurel and the air smelled perfumey. Stath breathed it deeply.

"Why, I sure *do* feel good." He talked some more about his own brief career, only a year or so, in the Methodist ministry after he graduated from SMU. "I guess I wanted to follow in my daddy's footsteps, being an only son and all. But I soon learned, different people are different people."

Brodeur refused all of Stath's offers to stop so he, Brodeur, could get a decent meal. Then Brodeur must have dozed. When he woke, they were in the dusty caliche driveway of a small wood-framed place, a porched miniature Gothic idea for a house with tracery along the front peak. The house seemed something from another philosophy of the world. Stath's father, in clean khaki work clothes, had a bad eye covered by a cardboard insert replacing one lens of his eyeglasses.

They were there for a couple of hours. Stath's father conversed politely, quietly in that way old men get around their sons at some point when they start listening to them respectfully. It stung Brodeur to see it. Stath's father showed them the leaning garage that needed much work; the porch on which the planks had been replaced with concrete the workmen had poured just two days before; and the various rooms inside, only a couple of which had been refinished with fresh paint, carpeting to blanket the creaking floors, and clean floral-print slipcovers for the furniture. There was a bedroom, done in crisp blue and white, with floor-length windows in which the glass was old and distorting. Those windows were a wonderful touch. And Brodeur was taken in by the way the afternoon sunlight, visored by the porch ceiling freshly enameled a sky blue, fell in long parallelograms on the beige indoor-outdoor carpeting. Dust motes hung suspended, like the stars you see when you rub your own eyes.

It did something to Brodeur. It was like when he suddenly noticed that there were no cemeteries in the West Texas city where he lived, and when he drove wildly, and lost, around those new boulevards searching for one.

"Brode." It was Stath. He had caught Brodeur staring.

"Oh, yeah."

They sat in the cramped living room and drank coffee—Sanka for Stath—and talked. Stath's father asked a lot of questions about the lawn mower, and said he really didn't need it, to tell the truth. The one he had was fine. He and Stath talked of a house that reminded Stath of this house. They had lived there for just a few dimly remembered months in the early fifties when his father filled in at a congregation up by Texarkana. Stath's father talked more, and, discovering Brodeur was from Michigan, he told him about how he and two other preachers once went to Detroit on church business. "Grand. And we saw the giant tire and got a tour of the De Soto plant. I used that in sermons for I don't know how many years—life as a meaningless assembly line and all—until a lady at my last congregation finally spoke to me, gingerly, and said, 'Reverend, they just don't make De Sotos anymore.' I guess that was a sure sign I was getting too old to preach, too old for most anything."

238

"You're not old, Daddy. Why look at the energy you have to fix up this sweet little spot."

"It keeps me occupied."

By the time Stath and Brodeur got on the north-south freeway, Interstate 35, for the stretch down to Waco, it was late afternoon.

"Daddy trying to pretty up that big house. Hmmmmmm," said Stath. "You know why, don't you?"

"Keep himself busy, like you said."

"Nah, Daddy believes that someday, if I peddle me enough of these refrigerators, the firm is going to transfer me to Dallas. And Shelline and all of us can just move in, and I can commute. I suppose it could happen."

Brodeur knew then, quite clearly, that Stath was going to blow it at the meeting. And did he ever.

No more than ten minutes after they heaped their bags onto the beds with nubbed spreads at the Sheraton Motor Inn, it started at the cocktail session downstairs. They had already missed the afternoon's opening sales seminar. Waco was hot, a heat not like spring, but like summer. The evening was muggy. Ordering a Fresca on ice, which the bartender didn't have, and then a Diet Pepsi on ice, which he did, Stath had trouble steadying his hand, and it was an awkward moment when he caught Brodeur gawking at the palsied rattle there on the imitation-walnut bar top. Their eyes snagged.

Stath was truly greenish, rather than colorless, as he had described the condition to Brodeur before. His whole face seemed to pulsate, and sweat beaded on his forehead.

Rich, the district manager who had come up to Chicago to enlist Brodeur for the Southwestern office, waved them over. The conference room was cluttered with the latest models of the firm's ranges, refrigerators, compactors, and dishwashers, all in a new shade of yellow with burnt, antiqued edges, a combination that was being unveiled by the firm at this conference. Called "Old Ranchero," it promised to prove a top regional seller.

"The rest of the West Texas gang," silver-haired Rich said, pumping Brodeur's hand. More hellos followed, more handshakes, and Brodeur tried not to make Stath any more self-conscious than he was. But did the others see that petrified smile? Did anybody else notice Stath was unable to talk?

"Boys, now where was I?" Rich supplied a quick summary for the benefit of Brodeur and Stath. Then he continued with his story that had the others, including four Arizona salesmen, encouraging him on, telling him it was "Great!" and "Really too much," and just satisfiedly rocking on their heels, as if to say in a chorus, "You *got* to be kidding, Rich." The gist of it was that a well-known Fort Worth judge had an uncontrollable "thing" about the Dallas Cowboy cheerleaders, who perform at the football games. He tried to hire all of them, or maybe only five or six, at a thousand dollars each for a little session of "athletics" in his own Arlington mansion on an off-season Saturday afternoon. "When he couldn't get the real girls to come, why I'll be damned if that judicial old boy didn't just hire himself a handful of hookers, pretty as can be, and dress them up perfect-like in those little white shorts, white boots, and those blue halter contraptions, for a dose of real touch football there in his den. He was drunk as a fart when the cops showed after the neighbors complained about the racket, and the way I heard it, he kept mumbling as they dragged him away, 'But when you see them on TV, don't you always just want to undo those little belts on those little shorts?'" Rich's audience roared, to play up to him (understandably) more than for any other reason. Brodeur hadn't noticed Stath leave.

Brodeur found him back at the room where Brodeur went for a fast shower before the evening banquet and the scheduled talk afterward. Stath sat on his bed, his head in his meaty hands.

"I'm finished in this business. The jig is up. To think I believed it was a matter of a diet. That was some laugh, huh, Brode?" But Brodeur managed to talk him into coming over to that session after the dinner. A professor from the University of New Mexico was delivering a talk titled "Life in the Sun Belt." The air-conditioner was malfunctioning and Brodeur was sweating at the talk. The professor didn't look too professional. He wore a leisure suit, in this case pink, and body jewelry looped his baggy neck as if he were a walking, dime-store display rack for the stuff.

He ran through a list of statistics about population curves and trends. He wore a cheap toupee, and Brodeur wasn't listening, though he took satisfaction in having gotten Stath to show. To put in an appearance, if nothing else.

"Now, before I go into my interpretation of these figures, I'd like to

240

ask some of you folks, at random, just what the Sun Belt means to you. How can we draw conclusions from all these numbers, this surging growth?"

Brodeur almost knew ahead of time what would happen. Stath never had a chance.

"How about you, the burly gent with the mustache," the professor said. Stath said nothing. He flashed the frozen smile again. "That's right, you. What does the Sun Belt mean to you?"

The silence ached on like hours for Brodeur. The other faces had turned. Brodeur saw only Rich, and Rich was squinting, as if to say, "What the Hell?"

"Well, sir?" the professor repeated.

"V-v-v-v . . ."

"What?"

"V-v-v-v . . ."

"What?"

"V-v-v-v-v—"

"I'm not sure if I understand you. Now, the—"

"V-v-van Allen Belts."

"What?"

"V—" And then Stath's lips moved without a sound, if you didn't count the raspy wheeze surely deep in his pounding trachea.

"Maybe somebody else," the professor said, over the whispering.

Back in the room again afterward, Stath lost all control.

"I'm crazy. It's true. I'm looney as the day is long."

"Don't be ridiculous," Brodeur said.

"You're not listening. I'M CRAZY!"

"Hey, take it easy."

"I knew all along, and I knew this meeting would be the worst of it. Do you know why I lugged that goddamned lawn mower to my daddy's?"

"Take it easy."

"I just wanted to stall. I started shaking this morning in my garage. I needed a ploy to keep us out of this meeting. And now look what I did."

"Just sit down."

"I'm a *basket* case!"

"Ea-sy."

"HOW ABOUT THIS, WHAT IF I CRY? DID YOU EVER SEE

THAT? MY KID HAS, WHY NOT YOU TOO, BRODE. LOOK, I'LL
GET DOWN ON MY HANDS AND KNEES AND START CRYING
LIKE A LITTLE PUPPY!"

"STATH!"

"YOU'LL LOOK, YOU SUCKER. LOOO-OOOOOOK!" Rolled in a
fetal position on the floor, he did just that—whimpered like a puppy,
his hands flapping like little paws.

That night, the air-conditioner humming, Brodeur first had two
understandable-enough dreams. In one, a Dallas cheerleader with dol-
lish puckered lips and bobbed auburn hair stood in full regalia, asking
Brodeur to help her with, "This little old belt," with which she seemed
to be having trouble. In the second, Stath's father was saying what a
fine job the repaired lawn mower did, as he followed it around his back-
yard. Brodeur and Stath watched him contentedly. Again, those dreams
weren't all that strange. They were shreds of the day. When Brodeur
woke from the second, the sheets were damp with his perspiration.
The air-conditioner had kicked off, and in a T-shirt and slacks, Stath,
on the other bed, snored loudly. Out on the motel's walkway, a black
woman's shrill voice, peppered with profanity, yelled that somebody
had hurt her arm. She must have been one of the hookers with whom
the Arizona contingent had organized a party.

The third dream Brodeur probably wouldn't remember. It was more
vivid, but deeper too. In it, he was with his wife and two sons. They
wore beach or pool garb—swimsuits and sneakers—but they were out
in the country, trudging along a snow-covered knoll in winter. They
didn't talk to one another. They just pressed on through the white powder that was up to their knees, though, strangely, Brodeur, bare-
legged like that, couldn't feel the cold. Occasionally, one of them would
drop backward as if in slow motion to the snow, fanning the legs and
spreading the arms to leave an imprint of an angel, as children playing do.

They had left hundreds of such imprints already.

They were all sober-faced.

Yes, near-naked, they kept on, as if it was work they had to do.

Stath and Brodeur had attended the two sales seminars, and, surprising to Brodeur, Stath came for the final buffet at noon. He ate a

few of the jumbo Louisiana shrimp fanned out on a romaine-lettuce leaf, telling Brodeur shrimp surely was something allowed on his diet. He didn't say much at the table where they sat with the Arizona salesmen—they looked exhausted—but he did cover himself with some soft comment that he wasn't himself, and he must be coming down with "that flu that's around."

Also surprising to Brodeur, the next week, back in the West Texas city, it seemed as if Stath was once more comfortable and relaxed. Brodeur himself had been in El Paso most of the week, and he came back around noon on Thursday to see Stath sitting at his free-form desk. A yellow cardboard box of Church's fried chicken sat in front of him.

Brodeur looked in.

"How you doing, Stath?"

"Brode, mi amigo." He licked his fingers exaggeratedly. He grinned. "Smells awful, don't it? But I tell you, this Church's is the only fried chicken worth a damn. I mean have you really ever taken time to taste that Kentucky Fried? Now, they steam it, is what they do. Who ever heard of steaming a bird before you fry. I mean that's a secret recipe? Why don't they just piss on it too while they're at it." He laughed at his own wit. "Want a fry?" He held up the white paper french-fries pouch. "I've been so rushed getting down all my orders from when I was up in Lubbock yesterday, I didn't have time even to get my old carcass the hell out of here to a restaurant."

"How about your diet?"

"Well, that there was one sucker that didn't last long, did it?" He winked, and held up a bottle of Carta Blanca he had been holding beneath the desk.

Maybe that was all he had needed, Brodeur thought. That one good rant in Waco to get it out of his system.

But those couple of days in Waco had affected *Brodeur*. He had thought about it considerably while in El Paso that week. What he had concluded was that there was some genuine sense to Stath's reaction. He was sure of it. Maybe Stath didn't fully understand it himself, but Brodeur knew that Stath's speechlessness stemmed from the fact that he just couldn't take it anymore. It was Stath's realization that he couldn't go into those buyers' offices and play the game with a vinyl-covered catalog on his lap and a crummy repertoire of jokes ready to

243

fill the gaps when you got scared that the bald-headed oaf, let's say, wasn't going to buy, when you could hear the second hand on the electric clock on his desk buzzing around, and around, and around—

In truth, that was all Brodeur had thought about in El Paso.

And then, in the Desert Inn motel there the night before he returned, Brodeur sat on the bed that smelled of urine and cigarette smoke, and he watched a "Good Times" rerun. (He had seen the show maybe twice before. J.J. dates the boss' daughter in his advertising agency, and then suspects that that is the reason why he is getting so many prime assignments for agency art work.) Brodeur was drinking beer. He had a twelve-pack of Pearl, and he cooled the buff aluminum cans—with their printed scene of the hills around San Antonio—in the ice-water pitcher, two at a time. Maybe he *was* a little drunk, but more and more it made real sense. What he, what Stath, was doing with his life was sheer idiocy. "Good Times" gave away to another situation comedy, but Brodeur never noticed what the show was. The television almost wasn't there. He was trying to remember something, and—

"Van Allen Belts!"

He said it out loud. That was what Stath had stammered, and, again, maybe Stath didn't know what he was saying, but possibly this showed some insight, hinted at the more important. Brodeur was excited. He stamped around the motel room with his reflection stamping around in the opposite direction in the mirror above the blonde-wood dresser. He couldn't for the life of him recall exactly what Van Allen belts were. Finally, frenzied, he pushed his arms into his shirt, tugged on his suede loafers again, and drove until he found a newsstand near the campus of the El Paso branch of the University of Texas. The newsstand had paperbacks and a stack of Webster's dictionaries.

"A belt of intense ionizing radiation that surrounds the earth and the outer atmosphere." If they were belts, they pulled, Brodeur reasoned. *It was tugging them all away, and now Brodeur understood it.*

Brodeur was sure, and, drunk back in his room at the Desert Inn, he decided that he had had enough of Texas, enough of the Sun Belt. He had had enough of drumming and the rest of the nonsensical game, and he was on the verge of tears when he thought of himself, feeling bad for himself for having never really had much fun in life, with all the rush of going from school to marriage to a job. He felt bad for his wife, Anne, and he hated to think of her putting up with living in that city in the desert where admittedly she had no friends, but sticking to it because she thought the job was important to him. He felt bad for his sons, especially the older who had that eczema and who was taunted by those bullying corridor prowlers in their ten-gallon hats.

He had had *more* than enough. They would go back to Michigan, and it was as simple as that. Or at least it seemed so simple when Brodeur fell asleep, or maybe passed out drunk, in the motel. The television screen turned to an impressionist's canvas of a million dots pulsating to the off-the-air hiss.

Now, back in the city where he lived and where he saw Stath eating the fried chicken, it wasn't as clear. But Brodeur remained resigned to talk it over with Anne. There was no use putting themselves through it any longer for the sake of refrigerators and trash compactors. There had to be something more.

That evening, Brodeur arrived home to have Anne tell him that Rich had phoned twice the night before from Dallas.

"Rich? Why would he call here?"

"He said he'd get back to you tonight." The call came five minutes later.

"I was trying to pull you aside to talk in Waco," Rich said, "but everything was so rushed there." Brodeur listened, trying to put it all together.

The firm was making Brodeur a district sales manager. There would now be two sales districts in the Southwest. East Texas and Oklahoma in one. West Texas, New Mexico, and Arizona in the other. The West Texas city would be headquarters for the new district and Brodeur would head it up, in a capacity about equal to Rich's. Though the firm had considered setting up that headquarters in Arizona, the oil boom in West Texas dictated it should be there, even if it was close to Dallas and seemed to make for a lopsided concentration of power. Had Rich actually said it would mean a flat ten thousand dollars a year more? To start?

"It all sounds fine."

"Chicago likes the work you've been doing out there. They're all for you, Brode. You're organized. You've proven you're responsible too."

"Thanks."

Much talk followed about how Brodeur would have to go up to the Chicago suburb and the firm's home office, and how he would have to go through about a month and a half of additional managerial training. Brodeur kept thinking, "Had he actually said a flat *ten* thousand more?"

At first the proposal had come so fast, and he still wasn't sure of the figure, and—and before he knew it, they were talking of the operation as it stood then, and Brodeur was suggesting that they really should get rid of Stath.

"I thought I did detect something about him in Waco," Rich said. "I do know his sales are OK, though I must admit he probably doesn't fit the new image we want. That dirt-farmer style may have been all right before, but it's not too modern, now that I think of it."

"Dirt-farmer style?" And in a way, Brodeur had no idea why he was doing this. He could later justify it by reasoning that he knew he got the management job because he was a take-charge sort, and maybe he wanted to exhibit that dynamism right off the bat to Rich. But that was a lie. He just did it: "You haven't heard anything. I hate to talk about the guy, but let me tell you about what I had to put up with when I was with him in Waco. Let's just call it a puppy-dog story, and you judge for yourself."

"What?"

"Listen." And Brodeur told him.

Brodeur had his mental breakdown two months later in Chicago. Rich afterward would claim that the worst thing about the "whole mess" was that, because of "that crack-pot Brodeur," the firm had lost Stath. "And Stath, there was a decent salesman."

1983

DOUG CROWELL
Living in the Desert

What place is this? Why are we here?

In all directions, there is nothing to be seen. In a sense we are at the center, the center of the nothing which stretches in all directions. And yet, with nothing to be seen there can be nothing to define a radius—where does the nothing (if it does) end?—and with no radius there can be no center. We are unanchored, floating, an absent center floating in the desert, surrounded by nothing, linked to nothing, nowhere. In a book once I read: "And then there was geography. We were in the middle of the middle of nowhere, that terrain so flat and bare, suggestive of the end of recorded time, a splendid sense of remoteness firing my soul. It was easy to feel that back up there, where men spoke the name civilization in wistful tones, I was wanted for some terrible crime."

So why are we here? For answer: silence.

One of the things I like to do sometimes is go to the crowded shopping places and look at girls' crotches. This is much more complicated than it sounds. There is even a fine art to looking at crotches. Over the past few years I have gotten better at doing it. The thing is, I mean girls, not women. Twelve, thirteen, fourteen tops, eleven maybe, along in there. And they have to be with their mothers. This is essential. Because it's the mothers you're after, they're the ones you want to see you looking. Just any girl won't do, and this is where the art comes in. I've really improved, myself, in the last year. If the girl's too young, the mother won't react right, she'll just look at you like you're something filthy. And if the girl's too old, that mother won't react right either. She might look at you like you're something filthy then too, some do. But sometimes when the girl's too old, the mother'll look at you like you're dirt, not filthy but just dirt. In a way she'll be glad you're looking, she'll smile kind of, like she's saying, who are you, who you thinking you're looking at, you're nothing, and my daughter, young as she is, already knows that much, knows that you aren't worth the shoes she walks in. When the girl's too young, you've missed your point, but when she's too old it can be a real mistake. You can feel the anger rising when the mother looks at you that way, rising up inside you. And anger's no good, anger gets you nowhere, especially when you're living in the desert. I've seen sometimes what the anger's done to my pappa, to my mamma.

When the girl's just the right age though, then the power's yours. If anyone gets angry then, it's not you. The mother reacts just the way you want her to, and then you can smile at her, which sets her off again. This is where the art comes in, in picking out the girl who's just the right age. It's not the age itself, you know, it's what state they're in. And it is an art. I've gotten better at it, refined myself. I know. You want a girl who's just on the edge. Just on that edge. The blood is welling up inside her like the anger you don't want to feel, and it's about to come out. Or maybe it already has, but not for long, not for long or she'd be too old. One of the ones already too old. The mothers by then have come to terms. But when you get the girl who's just on the edge, everything works the way you want it to. The thing is, there aren't many right pairs walking around. The best times are the off nights, a Monday or a Thursday maybe. Weekends aren't much good at all, the shopping places are much too crowded then. No one has the time to look at you. You have to catch the mother's eye first of course, or the whole thing doesn't work. You spot a pair you feel is right, follow them a while to catch their rhythms, and then you put yourself in front of them. Here they come. You catch the mother's eye, her eye holds on yours a bit, and then you know you've got her. Then your eyes go right down to her daughter's crotch. You have to hold on the crotch a while, it's important. There's a chance you'll lose the mother if you hold too long, but you have to hold the crotch a bit, a simple glance won't do. So you hold on the crotch, and then it's back up to the mother's eyes. If her eyes are still there, and if the girl's just right, you've got her then. No expression, it's important not to have an expression. You just look at the mother's eyes, after looking at the daughter's crotch. Her eyes start to go then. She starts to wrinkle up inside, you can tell. And it's not you she's thinking about then, not whether you're filthy or dirt, it's her daughter she's thinking about, her daughter's crotch. You've got her, you've got the power then. There's times in my life when nothing pleases me more, makes me feel better, than finding a right pair at one of the shopping places. I always go have a few beers after, and feel the good feeling welling up inside me. Pleasure.

One of the hard things is when you lose interest in sex. I don't mean lose interest, but when you learn it doesn't mean anything. That's hard. It happened to me when I had sex with a woman I met in a movie theater one afternoon. I used to be interested in sex. I don't mean interested in it, but excited by it, by the idea of it. I would take real pleasure in trying to get a girl to say yes. But back then I thought it was hard to get a girl to say yes. I liked the idea that it was hard. And then one day a woman talked to me in a store and all of a sudden I asked her and she said yes. That was the first time it occurred to me that maybe it wasn't so hard to get a girl to say yes. I didn't know what to think. Over the next few months I began to ask more often and at what before would have seemed to me to be odd times. I got a lot of yes's, but even the no's were not bad no's. I began to wonder about things. Then one day I went to a movie in the afternoon. I bought a Coke at the stand in the lobby. A woman spoke to me, but I was thinking about other things. I went in and sat down. In a bit, the woman sat down a couple of seats away from me. I didn't say anything. She didn't either. After the movie she got up and walked on out. I stayed in my seat until everything went by on the screen, until the lights went up. I walked out into the lobby and then outside into the sun. I was walking to my car when the same woman pulled up beside me in her car. She asked me if I would have a coffee with her. I didn't want to, but I did. I don't know why, but I did. After coffee, she took me back to her house. When we got close, she told me to bend down, below the window level so no one could see me. I rode two or three blocks bent down like that. She had an automatic garage door opener, opened the door and drove inside, then closed the door. She chucked my chin then, and told me to get up and come on inside. Inside the house she led me to a small bedroom that felt like no one had lived there for a while. It was only a twin bed. The woman started taking her clothes off and told me to take mine off too. She didn't even turn the cover back. We fucked on the twin bed, on top of the covers. After we fucked, she went out and came back with two glasses of something white, with ice in it. It was a little like wine but it had ice in it. The woman talked, mainly about fucking and her husband and her women friends. I just sat there. She talked about fucking and my cock started to harden up a little. The woman poured what was left of her drink and ice onto my cock, and then she laughed at me. I was feeling funny things. She bent over and sucked on me a little bit, and then she wanted to fuck again. She got on top. After we fucked that time, she started to get dressed. I got dressed. She drove me back to my car. I had to bend down in the seat again, while we drove a few blocks away from her house. At my car, I got out of hers, and she said, You were a good fuck, and then she drove off. None of this was very good for me. It made me start to think about some things. Things haven't been right for me since.

My father never told me anything. Maybe he never knew anything to tell me, but I doubt it. My father lived in the desert all his life. It was written on his face, the desert was. You could see it in the way his ears burned, in the way his hair was blown, in the way his chin looked when he smiled, or tried to. There come times when I wonder what my father knew, wonder about the things he never told me.

I worked with a guy once named Delmont. He was a comical little guy, and I mean little. He was something of a runt, Delmont was, probably five-two tops, and he'd be lucky if he went featherweight. Wore glasses, had real short hair, funny ears. He was older than the rest of us, or most of us anyway. Delmont never talked much but he was friendly enough, took all the jokes he got in stride, even told a joke now and then. You can see the jokes, guys would ask him how his pineapple was, stuff like that. Not funny jokes, but work jokes. Delmont's best friend at work was another older guy, named Brown Brown, and I'm not kidding here. Brown Brown was his real name, we checked the files once, with money riding on it. Brown talked a whole lot more than Delmont did, always telling stories none of us believed. He didn't expect us to. Don't misunderstand me here: we all liked Brown's stories. He knew how to tell them. Now what I'm getting to is that every now and then Brown would make reference to Delmont and women. Brown would say how Delmont really went for the big tall strapping, lush and lovely types. And then Brown would say that the funny thing wasn't Delmont going for such a type of woman, but that most of those big tall women Delmont would put his eye on would also go for Delmont. Brown would shake his head then. Delmont's a big killer with the women, Brown would say. You should see some of the women he's been with, good-looking women, Brown would say, and Delmont here such a short one. Delmont never would say anything. We never believed all this talk about Delmont any more than we believed Brown's other stories. And Delmont never said anything one way or the other.

I didn't work long at that place, and, about a year after I left there, I ran into Brown and Delmont in a bar one night. Brown remembered me right away, and pulled me over to sit with them at their table. Delmont said howdy. Brown was about the same. We all started in to drinking, and after a while the women came back up again. Delmont's women. I had been wanting to ask. Tell him about your wife, Brown would say, and Delmont would look a little odd. I was a little bit surprised. I hadn't ever imagined Delmont married. I knew it was true too, by the way Delmont was acting. Tell him about your wife, Brown would say again. I never pressed. Brown went off once to talk to some girl he knew and Delmont looked around a bit and finally said, Brown talks too much sometimes. I didn't say anything. I was married though, Delmont said, almost two years. Yeah, I said. I was excited, but didn't show it. Delmont started talking a whole lot then. Maybe he was trying to beat Brown back, I don't know. It poured out of him. There came a point in his talking when I wasn't sure I wanted to hear any more. But I was in for the duration by then. I'd never seen or ever even thought of Delmont being like this. Delmont was talking away. Nothing could have stopped him.

There's a lot I'm not saying, but the story goes something like this. Brown's stories had been true, or partly true. Delmont did love the big, leggy, flashy women. Strip dancers is what that meant. Sometimes he'd have them, when he had the money, or wanted to spend it. These women fascinated Delmont, he could never have enough of looking at them, thinking about them. Then one time he fell in love, real love. Her name was April Dawn, and that was the only name he ever knew her by, even later on when they were married. He didn't know who she was. April Dawn was all he knew. She didn't pay much attention to him

251

at first, but he kept it up, Delmont was *in love.* Delmont didn't have much money but he didn't mind spending what he had on April. He couldn't have all of her he wanted, but he kept it up. After a while April Dawn started to notice him more, but all this was going on over two, three years. And Delmont just kept it up, kept it up. He wanted her, he was in love. Now, Delmont lived with his mother, his father was dead, and then his mother died and Delmont got the house and what money was left, not a lot but more than a little. And, in the meantime April Dawn had come around. Delmont's keeping it up had paid off. They got married. Delmont said the times after that were the best times in his life. He was happy. April Dawn kept on dancing. He'd go down to watch her and just about die from being happy while he watched her take her clothes off, knowing she was his. He liked the other guys looking at her. Sometimes she didn't come home for a while but she always came home; Delmont didn't care about that. He had what he wanted. April Dawn could do what she had to, was the way he looked at it. He didn't like it when the guys in the bar would make comments about his being with her, but she always changed the subject, so it never got him down. Delmont was a happy man, he had exactly what he wanted. And then April Dawn started going crazy on him, about a year and a half after they'd got married. She started yelling, screaming, breaking things. Sometimes she'd get on him, how short he was, how small, how he looked like a mouse. This hurt Delmont but he never said anything. He knew she was going through something. He just kept quiet. He knew April Dawn would do what she had to. She stayed crazy a long time. He knew she was going through something. Then he came home one day from work. April Dawn was lying naked in the bed, with a gun in her hand. I'm going to eat this gun and blow my brains out, she said to him. I'm going to eat this gun and blow my brains out. Delmont just kept quiet, didn't say anything. He knew April Dawn could work things out for herself. After a while she came out of the bedroom. Delmont was watching television. Come fuck me Delmont, she said, I want you to fuck me, come on. Delmont didn't want to, but he did what she said. She was April Dawn. He still loved her, crazy or not. After that she went off to her dancing job and he stayed home, watched television a little bit, then went to bed. Next thing he knew, he was waked up by a big blast right in his ear almost. April Dawn had blown the back of her head right off. April Dawn, his

252

one real love. I felt bad about it, Delmont told me, but it just wasn't any of my business. None of it was any of my business at all.

I came home one evening to silence in the house. My mamma didn't say anything. My pappa didn't say anything. Neither did the younger kids. This silence was odd. I didn't say anything either. When dinner came up, the silence continued. There were six of us around the table and not a word was said, not even passing words. Spoons and forks hit on plates. Glasses were set down against the table top. The occasional sound of chewing. All through dinner this silence kept up. After dinner I walked out the door. When I got back that night, the house was silent too, but this was because everyone was in bed by then. The next morning, people were talking again.

One night I went to a bar I had never been to before. I sat at the bar and ordered a bottle of beer. The bartender asked me if I wanted some of their free popcorn. I said sure. We've only been open a month, he said. Business is picking up. There were half a dozen people in the bar, all men. The bartender took a plastic serving basket and spent a lot of time placing a paper liner inside. He made two or three adjustments of the liner before he seemed satisfied. He filled the basket up, brought it over, and set it in front of me on the bar. This may be a little salty, he said, but it's eatable. My name's Robin, he said. His face was pock-marked bad, and he wore a little gold earring. His face looked mean but the rest of him didn't. He went on down the bar to get someone a beer. He didn't come back. I looked around, took a few sips of beer. The place was peculiar, in its tone, or something. There was an overlay of new, but the place had a real run-down air to it. There was a new carpet on the floor, but it already looked used, and there were so many seams in it it must have been put together out of scraps, or by a bad carpet man. The walls had new paint but it was a bad job and you could see the pockmarks underneath. The walls had seen better days. The bar stools were cheap, light and cheap. When I took a bite of popcorn, I almost gagged, it was so salty. You could eat it if you forced yourself. Everything about the bar seemed real amateur. After a while Robin came back down toward my end of the bar to make more popcorn. There was a plastic-topped popcorn-maker there, the kind you get in a discount store, or from a television ad. The oil was in a quart bottle and he used too much. The popcorn came from a jar. I remember thinking they had probably paid retail for it. I wondered how long it would take for the bar to go under. When the popcorn popped, Robin poured it into a big aluminum pan and stood shaking salt into it. It seemed like he shook salt for a minute or more. I think I got it right this time, he said. He looked over toward me. Yeah, I said, right. That batch there is a little salty, ain't it, he said. He smiled like he'd made a joke. It is, I said. Try some of this then, he said, and put a basket in front of me. He went on back down the bar. I tried the new popcorn. It was too salty too, maybe a little better than the last had been, but maybe I just knew what to expect by then. By the time I'd had two or three beers, more people had wandered into the place. You could almost hear a buzz of talk. Robin walked back and forth behind the bar, giving popcorn to people.

Once I was in an all-night restaurant. It was after midnight, and a loud-voiced man was telling jokes to the other people at his table. They did not seem to want to listen, they did not look comfortable. The jokes were dumb jokes. Everyone in the restaurant could hear the man. In fact, no one could not hear him. It was impossible not to hear the jokes he told. The man would tell a joke and laugh, tell a joke and laugh. He was rolling. What's the German word for virgin? Gudenteit, ha ha ha. I had a wife once—but then her husband came and took her back, ha ha ha. What's the Chinese word for sixty-nine? Tu Can Chu, ha ha ha. There was a real good-looking girl banging on my door at three o'clock this morning, she was just banging away, banging away on my door— so I finally got up out of bed and let her out, ha ha ha. What's the Russian word for syphilis? Rotchakakov, ha ha ha. Did you hear the one about . . . ? Ha ha ha. Did I ever tell you about the time . . . ? Ha ha ha. I drank a quick cup of coffee, and left the place. Behind me, the man was rolling, rolling on into the night with his jokes, there in a coffee shop in the desert.

One time I camped out in the desert for a week. I was alone. I got into my jeep, drove out of town on the highway, finally turned off the highway, off the road itself, and headed out into the desert. I went far enough to reach what might suit for a center: in all directions, there was nothing to be seen, nothing but desert. It is true what they say:

that the desert gets cold at night; that there is more animal life than you might think; that the desert is hard on a man. After something ran across my sleeping bag on my second night there, I no longer slept on the ground, but on the jeep's roof. I wish I could say that I had visions in the desert, but I didn't; I didn't even see a mirage. Perhaps because I was stationary, was not on the move, in search of water. I got cold at night. I got hot during the day. I ate less food than I usually do in a week, and drank more water. I wore long-sleeved shirts, and sunglasses. I wish I could say that I had a mystical experience in the desert, but I didn't. I spent my days mostly sitting, sometimes walking about, never going very far from the jeep. There were a few cactuses about, a few rocks, a few small animals. There were snakes and lizards, different kinds of birds. Once I saw a brown rabbit. Flies and gnats. No mules, no prospectors. The sun rose in the east, set in the west. It beat down in between. My hair turned a lighter shade, just in a week. I wore a hat during the hours either side of high noon, but there are people who will tell you I boiled my brains out there anyway, hat or no. I didn't read. I didn't think. I looked, and there was not much to see. Once I wondered how much wind it would take to make a cactus wave like a tree, gently waving in the wind. I wish I could tell you that I learned something special from my time in the desert, but I didn't. I found no gold, I saw none, I felt none, smelled none out. I did not test a gold coin with my teeth, did not hear it ring.

Once in our town an outsider, a rich gentleman farmer who had not lived there long, announced he was going to show us how to beat the desert. He got front-page coverage. Hydroponic farming, I think he called it. Liquid nutrients. Why pour water into the dry hole that the desert is? he naïvely asked. What return do you get on that? he asked. Liquid nutrients, he said, with a big smile on his face, are the answer. We knew he was wrong, but we allowed him his front-page space. We even wanted to believe him. Liquid nutrients. Big tanks filled with them. For a while there was a constant stream of visitors out to his experiment. His vegetables did grow, in those tanks, for a while, but in the end the desert did them in, as we had known it would. The desert can suck up other things than water. It takes much more than liquid nutrients to beat the desert. The man's hydroponic farming failed, but we had had a brief moment of *looking forward*, and we appreciated it.

The rich farmer stayed among us, his tanks dry, rusting, slowly disappearing in the steady sun. Like liquid nutrients. Not one of us ever disliked him for thinking he could come in and defeat our desert. We had all of us had our moments of delusion. We empathized.

This is the desert, we are here to go.

1984

WILLIAM HARRISON
Roller Ball Murder

The game, the game: here we go again. All glory to it, all things I am and own because of Roller Ball Murder.

Our team stands in a row, twenty of us in salute as the corporation hymn is played by the band. We view the hardwood oval track which offers us the bumps and rewards of mayhem: fifty yards long, thirty yards across the ends, high banked, and at the top of the walls the cannons which fire those frenzied twenty-pound balls—similar to bowling balls, made of ebonite—at velocities over three hundred miles an hour. The balls career around the track, eventually slowing and falling with diminishing centrifugal force, and as they go to ground or strike a player another volley fires. Here we are, our team: ten roller skaters, five motorbike riders, five runners (or clubbers). As the hymn plays, we stand erect and tough; eighty thousand sit watching in the stands and another two billion viewers around the world inspect the set of our jaws on multivision.

The runners, those bastards, slip into their heavy leather gloves and shoulder their lacrosselike paddles—with which they either catch the whizzing balls or bash the rest of us. The bikers ride high on the walls (beware, mates, that's where the cannon shots are too hot to handle) and swoop down to help the runners at opportune times. The skaters, those of us with the juice for it, protest: we clog the way, try to keep the runners from passing us and scoring points, and become the fodder in the brawl. So two teams of us, forty in all, go skating and running and biking around the track while the big balls are fired in the same direction as we move—always coming up behind us to scatter and maim us—and the object of the game, fans, as if you didn't know, is for the runners to pass all skaters on the opposing team, field a ball, and pass it to a biker for one point. Those bikers, by the way, may give the runners a lift—in which case those of us on skates have our hands full overturning 175cc motorbikes.

No rest periods, no substitute players. If you lose a man, your team plays short.

Today I turn my best side to the cameras. I'm Jonathan E, none other, and nobody passes me on the track. I'm the core of the Houston team and for the two hours of play—no rules, no penalties once the first cannon fires—I'll level any bastard runner who raises a paddle at me.

We move: immediately there are pileups of bikes, skaters, referees, and runners, all tangled and punching and scrambling when one of the balls zooms around the corner and belts us. I pick up momentum and heave an opposing skater into the infield at center ring; I'm brute speed today, driving, pushing up on the track, dodging a ball, hurtling downward beyond those bastard runners. Two runners do hand-to-hand combat and one gets his helmet knocked off in a blow which tears away half his face; the victor stands there too long admiring his work and gets wiped out by a biker who swoops down and flattens him. The crowd screams and I know the cameramen have it on an isolated shot and that viewers in Melbourne, Berlin, Rio, and L.A. are heaving with excitement in their easy chairs.

When an hour is gone I'm still wheeling along, naturally, though we have four team members out with broken parts, one rookie maybe dead, two bikes demolished. The other team, good old London, is worse off.

One of their motorbikes roars out of control, takes a hit from one of the balls, and bursts into flame. Wild cheering.

Cruising up next to their famous Jackie Magee, I time my punch. He turns in my direction, exposes the ugly snarl inside his helmet, and I take him out of action. In that tiniest instant, I feel his teeth and bone give way and the crowd screams approval. We have them now, we really have them, we do, and the score ends 7–2.

The years pass and the rules alter—always in favor of the greater crowd-pleasing carnage. I've been at this more than fifteen years, amazing, with only broken arms and collarbones to slow me down, and I'm not as spry as ever, but meaner—and no rookie, no matter how much in shape, can learn this slaughter unless he comes out and takes me on in the real thing.

But the rules. I hear of games in Manila, now, or in Barcelona with no time limits, men bashing each other until there are no more runners left, no way of scoring points. That's the coming thing. I hear of Roller Ball Murder played with mixed teams, men and women, wearing tear-away jerseys which add a little tit and vulnerable exposure to the action. Everything will happen. They'll change the rules until we skate on a slick of blood, we all know that.

Before this century began, before the Great Asian war of the 1990s, before the corporations replaced nationalism and the corporate police forces supplanted the world's armies, in the last days of American football and the World Cup in Europe, I was a tough young rookie who knew all the rewards of this game. Women: I had them all—even, pity, a good marriage once. I had so much money after my first trophies that I could buy houses and land and lakes beyond the huge cities where only the executive class was allowed. My photo, then, as now, was on the covers of magazines, so that my name and the name of the sport were one, and I was Jonathan E, no other, a survivor and much more in the bloodiest sport.

At the beginning I played for Oil Conglomerates, then those corporations became known as ENERGY; I've always played for the team here in Houston, they've given me everything.

"How're you feeling?" Mr. Bartholemew asks me. He's taking the head of ENERGY, one of the most powerful men in the world, and he talks to me like I'm his son.

"Feeling mean," I answer, so that he smiles.

He tells me they want to do a special on multivision about my career, lots of shots on the side screens showing my greatest plays, and the story of my life, how ENERGY takes in such orphans, gives them work and protection, and makes careers possible.

"Really feel mean, eh?" Mr. Bartholemew asks again, and I answer the same, not telling him all that's inside me because he would possibly misunderstand; not telling him that I'm tired of the long season, that I'm lonely and miss my wife, that I yearn for high, lost, important thoughts, and that maybe, just maybe, I've got a deep rupture in the soul.

An old buddy, Jim Cletus, comes by the ranch for the weekend. Mackie, my present girl, takes our dinners out of the freezer and turns the rays on them; not so domestic, that Mackie, but she has enormous breasts and a waist smaller than my thigh.

Cletus works as a judge now. At every game there are two referees—clowns, whose job it is to see nothing amiss—and the judge who records the points scored. Cletus is also on the International Rules Committee and tells me they are still considering several changes.

"A penalty for being lapped by your own team, for one thing," he tells us. "A damned simple penalty, too: they'll take off your helmet."

Mackie, bless her bosom, makes an O with her lips.

Cletus, once a runner for Toronto, fills up my oversized furniture and rests his hands on his bad knees.

"What else?" I ask him. "Or can you tell me?"

"Oh, just financial things. More bonuses for superior attacks. Bigger bonuses for being named World All-Star—which ought to be good news for you again. And, yeah, talk of reducing the two-month off-season. The viewers want more."

After dinner Cletus walks around the ranch with me. We trudge up the path of a hillside and the Texas countryside stretches before us. Pavilions of clouds.

"Did you ever think about death in your playing days?" I ask, knowing I'm a bit too pensive for old Clete.

"Never in the game itself," he answers proudly. "Off the track— yeah, sometimes I never thought about anything else."

We pause and take a good long look at the horizon.

"There's another thing going in the Rules Committee," he finally admits. "They're considering dropping the time limit—at least, god help us, Johnny, the suggestion has come up officially."

I like a place with rolling hills. Another of my houses is near Lyons in France, the hills similar to these although more lush, and I take my evening strolls there over an ancient battleground. The cities are too much, so large and uninhabitable that one has to have a business passport to enter such immensities as New York.

"Naturally I'm holding out for the time limit," Cletus goes on. "I've played, so I know a man's limits. Sometimes in that committee, Johnny, I feel like I'm the last moral man on earth sitting there and insisting that there should be a few rules."

The statistical nuances of Roller Ball Murder entertain the multitudes as much as any other aspect of the game. The greatest number of points scored in a single game: 81. The highest velocity of a ball when actually caught by a runner: 176 mph. Highest number of players put out of action in a single game by a single skater: 13—world's record by yours truly. Most deaths in a single contest: 9—Rome vs. Chicago, December 4, 2012.

The giant lighted boards circling above the track monitor our pace, record each separate fact of the slaughter, and we have millions of fans—strange, it always seemed to me—who never look directly at the action, but just study those statistics.

A multivision survey established this.

Before going to the stadium in Paris for our evening game, I stroll under the archways and along the Seine.

Some of the French fans call to me, waving and talking to my bodyguards as well, so I become oddly conscious of myself, conscious of my size and clothes and the way I walk. A curious moment.

I'm six foot three inches and weigh 255 pounds. My neck is 18½ inches. Fingers like a pianist. I wear my conservative pinstriped jump suit and the famous flat Spanish hat. I am 34 years old now, and when I grow old, I think, I'll look a lot like the poet Robert Graves.

The most powerful men in the world are the executives. They run the major corporations which fix prices, wages, and the general economy, and we all know they're crooked, that they have almost unlimited power and money, but I have considerable power and money myself and I'm still anxious. What can I possibly want, I ask myself, except, possibly, more knowledge?

I consider recent history—which is virtually all anyone remembers—and how the corporate wars ended, so that we settled into the Six Majors: ENERGY, TRANSPORT, FOOD, HOUSING, SERVICES, and LUXURY. Sometimes I forget who runs what—for instance, now that the universities are operated by the Majors (and provide the farm system for Roller Ball Murder), which Major runs them? SERVICES or LUXURY? Music is one of our biggest industries, but I can't remember who administers it. Narcotic research is now under FOOD, I know, though it used to be under LUXURY.

Anyway, I think I'll ask Mr. Bartholemew about knowledge. He's a man with a big view of the world, with values, with memory. My team flings itself into the void while his team harnesses the sun, taps the sea, finds new alloys, and is clearly just a hell of a lot more serious.

The Mexico City game has a new wrinkle: they've changed the shape of the ball on us.

Cletus didn't even warn me—perhaps he couldn't—but here we are playing with a ball not quite round, its center of gravity altered, so that it rumbles around the track in irregular patterns.

This particular game is bad enough because the bikers down here are getting wise to me; for years, since my reputation was established, bikers have always tried to take me out of a game early. But early in the game I'm wary and strong and I'll always gladly take on a biker— even since they put shields on the motorbikes so that we can't grab the handlebars. Now, though, these bastards know I'm getting older—still mean but slowing down, as the sports pages say about me—so they let me bash it out with the skaters and runners for as long as possible before sending the bikers after me. Knock out Jonathan E, they say, and you've beaten Houston; and that's right enough, but they haven't done it yet.

The fans down here, all low-class FOOD workers mostly, boil over as I manage to keep my cool—and the oblong ball, zigzagging around at lurching speeds, hopping two feet off the track at times, knocks out virtually their whole team. Finally, some of us catch their last runner/ clubber and beat him to a pulp, so that's it: no runners, no points. Those dumb FOOD workers file out of the stadium while we show off and score a few fancy and uncontested points. The score 37–4. I feel wonderful, like pure brute speed.

Mackie is gone—her mouth no longer makes an O around my villa or ranch—and in her place is the new one, Daphne. My Daphne is tall and English and likes photos—always wants to pose for me. Sometimes we get out our boxes of old pictures (mine as a player, mostly, and hers as a model) and look at ourselves, and it occurs to me that the photos spread out on the rug are the real us, our public and performing true selves, and the two of us here in the sitting room, Gaelic gray winter outside our window, aren't too real at all.

"Look at the muscles in your back!" Daphne says in amazement as she studies a shot of me at the California beach—and it's as though she never before noticed.

After the photos, I stroll out beyond the garden. The brown waving grass of the fields reminds me of Ella, my only wife, and of her soft long hair which made a tent over my face when we kissed.

I lecture to the ENERGY-sponsored rookie camp and tell them they can't possibly comprehend anything until they're out on the track getting belted.

My talk tonight concerns how to stop a biker who wants to run you down. "You can throw a shoulder right into the shield," I begin. "And that way it's you or him."

The rookies look at me as though I'm crazy.

"Or you can hit the deck, cover yourself, tense up, and let the bastard flip over your body," I go on, counting on my fingers for them and doing my best not to laugh. "Or you can feint, sidestep up hill, and kick him off the track—which takes some practice and timing."

None of them knows what to say. We're sitting in the infield grass, the track lighted, the stands empty, and their faces are filled with stupid awe. "Or if a biker comes at you with good speed and balance," I continue, "then naturally let the bastard by—even if he carries a runner. That runner, remember, has to dismount and field one of the new odd-shaped balls which isn't easy—and you can usually catch up."

The rookies begin to get a smug look on their faces when a biker bears down on me in the demonstration period.

Brute speed. I jump to one side, dodge the shield, grab the bastard's arm, and separate him from his machine in one movement. The bike skids away. The poor biker's shoulder is out of socket.

"Oh yeah," I say, getting back to my feet. "I forgot about that move."

Toward midseason when I see Mr. Bartholemew again he has been deposed as the chief executive at ENERGY. He is still very important, but lacks some of the old certainty; his mood is reflective, so that I decide to take this opportunity to talk about what's bothering me.

We lunch in Houston Tower, viewing an expanse of city. A nice Beef

Wellington and Burgundy. Daphne sits there like a stone, probably imagining that she's in a movie.

"Knowledge, ah, I see," Mr. Bartholemew replies in response to my topic. "What're you interested in, Jonathan? History? The arts?"

"Can I be personal with you?"

This makes him slightly uncomfortable. "Sure, naturally," he answers easily, and although Mr. Bartholemew isn't especially one to inspire confession I decide to blunder along.

"I began in the university," I remind him. "That was—let's see—more than seventeen years ago. In those days we still had books and I read some, quite a few, because I thought I might make an executive."

"Jonathan, believe me, I can guess what you're going to say," Mr. Bartholemew sighs, sipping the Burgundy and glancing at Daphne. "I'm one of the few with real regrets about what happened to the books. Everything is still on tapes, but it just isn't the same, is it? Nowadays only the computer specialists read the tapes and we're right back in the Middle Ages when only the monks could read the Latin script."

"Exactly," I answer, letting my beef go cold.

"Would you like me to assign you a specialist?"

"No, that's not exactly it."

"We have the great film libraries: you could get a permit to see anything you want. The Renaissance. Greek philosophers. I saw a nice summary film on the life and thought of Plato once."

"All I know," I say with hesitation, "is Roller Ball Murder."

"You don't want out of the game?" he asks warily.

"No, not at all. It's just that I want—god, Mr. Bartholemew, I don't know how to say it: I want *more*."

He offers a blank look.

"But not things in the world," I add. "More for *me*."

He heaves a great sigh, leans back, and allows the steward to refill his glass. Curiously, I know that he understands; he is a man of sixty, enormously wealthy, powerful in our most powerful executive class, and behind his eyes is the deep, weary, undeniable comprehension of the life he has lived.

"Knowledge," he tells me, "either converts to power or it converts to melancholy. Which could you possibly want, Jonathan? You *have* power. You have status and skill and the whole masculine dream many of us would like to have. And in Roller Ball Murder there's no room for melancholy, is there? In the game the mind exists for the body, to make a harmony of havoc, right? Do you want to change that? Do you want the mind to exist for itself alone? I don't think you actually want that, do you?"

"I really don't know," I admit.

"I'll get you some permits, Jonathan. You can see video films, learn something about reading tapes, if you want."

"I don't think I really *have* any power," I say, still groping.

"Oh, come on. What do *you* say about that?" he asks, turning to Daphne.

"He definitely has power," she answers with a wan smile.

Somehow the conversation drifts away from me; Daphne, on cue, like the good spy for the corporation she probably is, begins feeding Mr. Bartholemew lines and soon, oddly enough, we're discussing my upcoming game with Stockholm.

A hollow space begins to grow inside me, as though fire is eating out a hole. The conversation concerns the end of the season, the All-Star Game, records being set this year, but my disappointment—in what, exactly, I don't even know—begins to sicken me.

Mr. Bartholemew eventually asks what's wrong.

"The food," I answer. "Usually I have great digestion, but maybe not today."

In the locker room the dreary late-season pall takes us. We hardly speak among ourselves, now, and, like soldiers or gladiators sensing what lies ahead, we move around in these sickening surgical odors of the locker room.

Our last training and instruction this year concerns the delivery of deathblows to opposing players; no time now for the tolerant shoving and bumping of yesteryear. I consider that I possess two good weapons: because of my unusually good balance on skates, I can often shatter my opponent's knee with a kick; also, I have a good backhand blow to the ribs and heart, if, wheeling along side by side with some bastard, he raises an arm against me. If the new rules change removes a player's helmet, of course, that's death; as it is right now (there are rumors, rumors every day about what new version of RBM we'll have next) you go for the windpipe, the ribs or heart, the diaphragm, or anyplace you don't break your hand.

Our instructors are a pair of giddy Oriental gentlemen who have all sorts of anatomical solutions for us and show drawings of the human figure with nerve centers painted in pink.

"What you do is this," says Moonpie, in parody of these two. Moonpie is a fine skater in his fourth season and fancies himself an old-fashioned drawling Texan. "What you do is hit 'em on the jawbone and drive it up into their ganglia."

"Their *what*?" I ask, giving Moonpie a grin.

"Their goddamned *ganglia*. Bunch of nerves right here underneath the ear. Drive their jawbones into that mess of nerves and it'll ring their bells sure."

Daphne is gone now, too, and in this interim before another companion arrives, courtesy of all my friends and employers at ENERGY, Ella floats back into my dreams and daylight fantasies.

I was a corporation child, some executive's bastard boy, I always preferred to think, brought up in the Galveston section of the city. A big kid, naturally, athletic and strong—and this, according to my theory, gave me healthy mental genes, too, because I take it now that strong in body is strong in mind: a man with brute speed surely also has the capacity to mull over his life. Anyway, I married at age fifteen while I worked on the docks for Oil Conglomerates. Ella was a secretary, slim with long brown hair, and we managed to get permits to both marry and enter the university together. Her fellowship was in General Electronics—she was clever, give her that—and mine was in Roller Ball Murder. She fed me well that first year, so I put on thirty hard pounds and at night she soothed my bruises (was she a spy, too, I've sometimes wondered, whose job it was to prime the bull for the charge?) and perhaps it was because she was my first woman ever, eighteen years old, lovely, that I've never properly forgotten.

She left me for an executive, just packed up and went to Europe with him. Six years ago I saw them at a sports banquet where I was presented an award: there they were, smiling and being nice, and I asked them only one question, just one, "You two ever had children?" It gave me odd satisfaction that they had applied for a permit, but had been denied.

Ella, love; one does consider: did you beef me up and break my heart in some great design of corporate society?

There I was, whatever, angry and hurt. Beyond repair, I thought at the time. And the hand which stroked Ella soon dropped all the foes of Houston.

I take sad stock of myself in this quiet period before another woman arrives; I'm smart enough, I know that: I had to be to survive. Yet, I seem to know nothing—and can feel the hollow spaces in my own heart. Like one of those computer specialists, I have my own brutal technical know-how; I know what today means, what tomorrow likely holds, but maybe it's because the books are gone—Mr. Bartholemew was right, it's a shame they're transformed—that I feel so vacant. If I didn't remember my Ella—this I realize—I wouldn't even *want* to remember because it's love I'm recollecting as well as those old university days.

Recollect, sure: I read quite a few books that year with Ella and afterward, too, before turning professional in the game. Apart from all the volumes about how to get along in business, I read the history of the kings of England, that pillars of wisdom book by T. E. Lawrence, all the forlorn novels, some Rousseau, a bio of Thomas Jefferson, and other odd bits. On tapes now, all that, whirring away in a cool basement someplace.

The rules crumble once more.

At the Tokyo game, we discover that there will be three oblong balls in play at all times.

Some of our most experienced players are afraid to go out on the track. Then, after they're coaxed and threatened and finally consent to join the flow, they fake injury whenever they can and sprawl in the infield like rabbits. As for me, I play with greater abandon than ever and give the crowd its money's worth. The Tokyo skaters are either peering over their shoulders looking for approaching balls when I smash them, or, poor devils, they're looking for me when a ball takes them out of action.

One little bastard with a broken back flaps around for a moment like a fish, then shudders and dies.

Balls jump at us as though they have brains.

But fate carries me, as I somehow know it will; I'm a force field, a destroyer. I kick a biker into the path of a ball going at least two hundred miles an hour. I swerve around a pileup of bikes and skaters, ride high on the track, zoom down, and find a runner/clubber who panics and misses with a roundhouse swing of his paddle; without much ado, I belt him out of play with the almost certain knowledge—I've felt it before—that he's dead before he hits the infield.

One ball flips out of play soon after being fired from the cannon, jumps the railing, sails high, and plows into the spectators. Beautiful.

I take a hit from a ball, one of the three or four times I've ever been belted. The ball is riding low on the track when it catches me and I sprawl like a baby. One bastard runner comes after me, but one of our bikers chases him off. Then one of their skaters glides by and takes a shot at me, but I dig him in the groin and discourage him, too.

Down and hurting, I see Moonpie killed. They take off his helmet, working slowly—it's like slow motion and I'm writhing and cursing and unable to help—and open his mouth on the toe of some bastard skater's boot. Then they kick the back of his head and knock out all his teeth—which rattle downhill on the track. Then kick again and stomp: his brains this time. He drawls a last groaning good-bye while the cameras record it.

And later I'm up, pushing along once more, feeling bad, but knowing everyone else feels the same; I have that last surge of energy, the one I always get when I'm going good, and near the closing gun I manage a nice move: grabbing one of their runners with a headlock, I skate him off to limbo, bashing his face with my free fist, picking up speed until he drags behind like a dropped flag, and disposing of him in front of a ball which carries him off in a comic flop. Oh, god, god.

Before the All-Star Game, Cletus comes to me with the news I expect: this one will be a no-time-limit extravaganza in New York, every multivision set in the world tuned in. The bikes will be more high-powered, four oblong balls will be in play simultaneously, and the referees will blow the whistle on any sluggish player and remove his helmet as a penalty.

Cletus is apologetic.

"With those rules, no worry," I tell him. "It'll go no more than an hour and we'll all be dead."

We're at the Houston ranch on a Saturday afternoon, riding around in my electrocart viewing the Santa Gertrudis stock. This is probably the ultimate spectacle of my wealth: my own beef cattle in a day when only a few special members of the executive class have any meat to eat with the exception of mass-produced fish. Cletus is so impressed with my cattle that he keeps going on this afternoon and seems so pathetic to me, a judge who doesn't judge, the pawn of a committee, another feeble hulk of an old RBM player.

"You owe me a favor, Clete," I tell him.

"Anything," he answers, not looking me in the eyes.

I turn the cart up a lane beside my rustic rail fence, an archway of oak trees overhead and the early spring bluebonnets and daffodils sending up fragrances from the nearby fields. Far back in my thoughts is the awareness that I can't possibly last and that I'd like to be buried out here—burial is seldom allowed anymore, everyone just incinerated and scattered—to become the mulch of flowers.

"I want you to bring Ella to me," I tell him. "After all these years, yeah: that's what I want. You arrange it and don't give me any excuses, okay?"

We meet at the villa near Lyons in early June, only a week before the All-Star Game in New York, and I think she immediately reads something in my eyes which helps her to love me again. Of course I love her: I realize, seeing her, that I have only a vague recollection of being alive at all, and that was a long time ago, in another century of the heart when I had no identity except my name, when I was a simple dock worker, before I ever saw all the world's places or moved in the rumbling nightmares of Roller Ball Murder.

She kisses my fingers. "Oh," she says softly, and her face is filled with true wonder, "what's happened to you, Johnny?"

A few soft days. When our bodies aren't entwined in lovemaking, we try to remember and tell each other everything: the way we used to hold hands, how we fretted about receiving a marriage permit, how the books looked on our shelves in the old apartment in River Oaks. We strain, at times, trying to recollect the impossible; it's true that history is really gone, that we have no families or touchstones, that our short personal lives alone judge us, and I want to hear about her husband, the places they've lived, the furniture in her house, anything. I tell her, in turn, about all the women, about Mr. Bartholemew and Jim Cletus, about the ranch in the hills outside Houston.

Come to me, Ella. If I can remember us, I can recollect meaning and time.

It would be nice, I think, once, to imagine that she was taken away from me by some malevolent force in this awful age, but I know the truth of that: she went away, simply, because I wasn't enough back then, because those were the days before I yearned for anything, when I was beginning to live to play the game. But no matter. For a few days she sits on my bed and I touch her skin like a blind man groping back over the years.

On our last morning together she comes out in her traveling suit with her hair pulled up underneath a fur cap. The softness has faded from her voice and she smiles with efficiency, as if she has just come back to the practical world; I recall, briefly, this scene played out a thousand years ago when she explained that she was going away with her executive.

She plays like a biker, I decide; she rides up there high above the turmoil, decides when to swoop down, and makes a clean kill.

"Good-bye, Ella," I say, and she turns her head slightly away from my kiss so that I touch her fur cap with my lips.

"I'm glad I came," she says politely. "Good luck, Johnny."

New York is frenzied with what is about to happen.

The crowds throng into Energy Plaza, swarm the ticket offices at the stadium, and wherever I go people are reaching for my hands, pushing my bodyguards away, trying to touch my sleeve as though I'm some ancient religious figure, a seer or prophet.

Before the game begins I stand with my team as the corporation hymns are played. I'm brute speed today, I tell myself, trying to rev myself up; yet, adream in my thoughts, I'm a bit unconvinced.

A chorus of voices joins the band now as the music swells.

The game, the game, all glory to it, the music rings, and I can feel my lips move with the words, singing.

1973

Notes on the Authors

Bill Brett is a native Texan and former nearly everything: postmaster at Hull, Texas, where he lives, roughneck, driller, cowhand, truck driver, farmer, construction worker, what have you. He is also a writer and has published numerous stories and several books, including *The Stolen Steers: A Tale of the Big Thicket* (1977), *There Ain't No Such Animal and Other East Texas Tales* (1979), and *This Here's a Good'un* (1983).

Doug Crowell, born in Dallas in 1952, attended high school in Houston. He holds degrees from Rice and Johns Hopkins and the Ph.D. from SUNY-Buffalo. He lives in Lubbock and teaches creative writing at Texas Tech University. Over a dozen of his stories have been published. "Work" won the Texas Institute of Letters short story award in 1981.

James Crumley was born in Three Rivers, Texas, in 1939. Educated at Texas A&I and the University of Iowa, he currently lives in Missoula, Montana. His books include *One to Count Cadence* (1969), a war novel, and three novels about a boozy detective named Milo Milodragovitch: *The Wrong Case* (1975), *The Last Good Kiss* (1978), and *Dancing Bear* (1983). "Whores," a *Pushcart Prize* selection in 1978, holds a special place in Crumley's memory: "In 1973 I did an assignment for *Playboy*, a piece about Houston. It never ran. I didn't seem to have the right attitude about urban life and love. I wrote about alligators and cancer patients in the Hermann Park Zoo. But the editor who turned it down asked if I had any other ideas, something that wouldn't require any expense money. Since I had spent some of my youth sitting in bordertown whore houses, I thought I would do a thoughtful piece about the working girls and the afternoon drinking. The article became a

NOTES ON THE AUTHORS

story in the first sentence. I was pleased. Stories last longer than articles, mean more to me, and come closer to the truth than nonfiction."

Linda West Eckhardt, born in Dodge City, Kansas, in 1939, was raised at Hereford, Texas, in the Panhandle. She holds degrees from the University of Texas and San Francisco State University. Her writings include *The Only Texas Cookbook* (1982), two other cookbooks, and nearly a dozen short stories published in little magazines. She lives in Ashland, Oregon, and teaches creative writing part-time at Southern Oregon State College. Of "Christmas 1918: Sennicot Place" she says: "I've always thought this legend straight out of my own family to be revealing of Texas attitudes and beliefs about War, God, Pride, and false pride. I know this story by heart. My mother told it—she's the little girl in the story—more times than I can count."

Robert Flynn was born in Chillicothe, Texas, in 1932. He was educated at Baylor and is the author of a dozen short stories and three novels: *North to Yesterday* (1967), which won a Texas Institute of Letters award, *In the House of the Lord* (1969), and *The Sounds of Rescue, the Signs of Hope* (1970). He lives in San Antonio where he teaches creative writing at Trinity University. "The Savior of the Bees" grew out of childhood experience: "One of my jobs as a farm boy was keeping the water troughs clean. That meant picking out a lot of bees, although the wasps never seemed to drown." To Flynn, the incident began to take shape as "a boy's recognition of injustice and his inability to do much about it."

William Goyen was born in Trinity, Texas, in 1915. He took B.A. and M.A. degrees from Rice University. He has won many literary prizes and has an international reputation. His short stories were brought together in *The Collected Stories of William Goyen* (1975). His most celebrated novel, *The House of Breath* (1950), won a Texas Institute of Letters award. Goyen died in 1983.

A. C. Greene, born in Abilene, Texas, in 1923, has for many years been associated with the *Dallas Times Herald* as book review editor and columnist. He served as president of the Texas Institute of Letters, 1969–1971. His books include *A Personal Country* (1979), a memoir about West Texas, and *The Highland Park Woman* (1983), a collection of short stories. Greene lives in Dallas. He recalls how "The Girl at Cabe Ranch" started out as one thing and became something else: "In the late 1950s, doing research on some West Texas forts, I became fascinated by the beautiful Putnam ranch house, located near Camp Cooper and built in the nineteenth century by the notorious John Larn, who was assassinated by the thirteen men in yellow slickers while being held in the Albany [Texas] jail. At the time I thought of writing a ghost story, but twenty years later, when I actually got around to doing something, I'd completely forgotten the idea."

William Harrison is a native of Dallas, Texas, where he was born in 1933. He was educated at Texas Christian University and Vanderbilt. His works include *The Theologian* (1965), several other novels, and a collection of short fiction, *Roller Ball Murder and Other Stories* (1974). He also co-authored the script for the film *Rollerball*, which was based upon his story and starred James Caan. Harrison teaches creative writing at the University of Arkansas. "Roller Ball Murder" evolved from an idea and an incident: "I was reading and thinking about economics in that spring of 1973, deciding that just as nationalism grew out of feudalism so would corporate society grow out of nationalism. I still think so. Then I went to an Arkansas–Texas A&M basketball game where a fist fight erupted. I wrote the story in the next three weeks."

Dave Hickey was born in Fort Worth in 1940 and educated at Southern Methodist University, Texas Christian University, and the University of Texas. He wrote for the *Texas Observer* in the early 1960s and was executive editor of *Art in America* during the 1970s. He is the author of many short stories, most published in the sixties, after which he turned mainly to cultural and art criticism. His work has appeared in such publications as *Rolling Stone, Penthouse*, and the *Saturday Review*. Hickey has also written a number of songs that have been recorded by Nashville artists, such as Bobby Bare and Dr. Hook. Today Hickey is a free-lance writer living in Fort Worth. Legend has it that "I'm Bound to Follow the Longhorn Cows" grew out of a bet with a fellow student at the University of Texas Union. Somebody spotted a newspaper story about an old man who had been stranded in a bathtub and bet Hickey that he couldn't write a story about it. Hickey won.

Paul Horgan, born in Buffalo, New York, in 1903, has enjoyed a long and distinguished career as Southwestern novelist and historian. He has received two Pulitzer Prizes for history and the Bancroft Prize for history. Two of his novels are set in Texas: *Whitewater* (1970) and *Mexico Bay* (1982). His stories have been collected in *The Peach Stone: Stories from Four Decades* (1967). Three times he has won awards from the Texas Institute of Letters: *Great River* (1954), *Whitewater*

(1970), and *Lamy of Santa Fe* (1975). He is professor emeritus at Wesleyan University in Connecticut. "In Summer's Name" grew out of Horgan's life in the Southwest: "In the thirties I had a particular interest in observing the passionate, summer-heated revival tent meetings that came to town and my reflections concerning them I embodied in the character of the doctor-narrator, who was drawn after a retired man of medicine I knew and admired for his charm of mind and integrity of character. That, with impressions of the local youths and maidens, gave me the story."

Mary Gray Hughes is a Texas native, born in Brownsville in 1930. Her father, Hart Stilwell, was a well-known Texas journalist and novelist. She was educated at Columbia and Oxford, England. *The Calling*, a collection of short stories, appeared in 1980. "The Judge," which was reprinted in *Best American Short Stories 1972*, had its roots in both local and international happenings: "The Mexican's shack existed not far from my home in South Texas. I passed it twice daily going to and from school and a few times I saw inside. I was working on this story, which is as made-up as a story can be, in 1969 and 1970, and for me its other title was always 'Why We Are in Vietnam.'" Hughes lives in Evanston, Illinois.

William Humphrey, one of Texas' most distinguished authors, is a native of Clarksville, in extreme northeast Texas. Born in 1924, he attended college at Southern Methodist University and the University of Texas. Three of his books have won prizes from the Texas Institute of Letters: the novels *Home from the Hill* (1958) and *The Ordways* (1965) and the memoir *Farther Off from Heaven* (1977). He has also published two volumes of short stories: *The Last Husband and Other Stories* (1953) and *A Time and a Place: Stories* (1968). He resides in Hudson, New York, where he is at work on a novel about the Cherokees in Texas. "A Voice from the Woods" grew out of his Clarksville past: "Such a robbery happened in my town during my childhood (I was 12 years old). Otherwise the story is an invention."

Peter LaSalle was born in Providence, Rhode Island, in 1947. Holding degrees from Harvard and the University of Chicago, he is the author of *The Graves of Famous Writers and Other Stories* (1980) and *Strange Sunlight* (1984), a novel. He teaches creative writing at the University of Texas at Austin. One of his short stories was reprinted in *Best American Short Stories 1979*. "Life in the Sun Belt" owes its origins to a teaching job LaSalle accepted in 1976, when he came to a "brand-new university in a booming West Texas city." The move turned out to be fortunate, he says: "My fascination with the Sun Belt phenomenon was immediate. I sensed an almost dreamlike mood surrounding the eerie, and probably crazy, business of thousands and thousands of Americans suddenly migrating south for work toward the end of this century. It became one of my chief fictional concerns, first in this story, then—when I returned to Texas a few years later to live in Austin—in several others as well as in a novel."

Larry McMurtry, born in Wichita Falls in 1936, took degrees at North Texas State University and Rice University before devoting himself fulltime to writing. He is today Texas' best known author, both locally and nationally. Two of his novels have won prizes from the Texas Institute of Letters: *Horseman, Pass By* (1961) and *The Last Picture Show* (1966)—a co-winner. Four of his novels have been made into motion pictures. His most recent novel is *Lonesome Dove* (1985). McMurtry lives in Waterford, Virginia.

Vassar Miller, a Houston native, was born in 1924. She holds two degrees from the University of Houston. Widely anthologized and regarded by many as Texas' finest poet, she has three times won the poetry award of the Texas Institute of Letters: *Adam's Footprint* in 1956, *Wage War on Silence* in 1960, and *My Bones Being Wiser* in 1963. "Pact," she says, is "autobiographical in that the characters are based on actual people—the child is I, the father my father, the maid a Bohemian maid we had, or rather drawn from these real persons."

Harryette Mullen, an Alabama native born in 1953, grew up in Fort Worth and graduated from the University of Texas with a B.A. degree. She published a volume of poems, *Tree Tall Woman*, in 1981. She was also a Dobie Paisano Fellow that year. Currently she lives in Santa Cruz, California, where she is completing a doctorate at the University of California–Santa Cruz.

Amado Muro was born Chester Seltzer, in Cleveland, Ohio, in 1915. His father was a powerful newspaperman in Cleveland. During World War II, Seltzer served several years in federal prison because he refused to kill anybody on order of the state. Seltzer criss-crossed the United States on freight trains and worked for a number of newspapers. In the 1940s, in El Paso, he married a native of Chihuahua City, Mexico, Amada Muro, from whom he took the pen name under which he wrote short stories and sketches for such journals as the *Arizona Quarterly* and the *Southwest Review*. Several of his stories were cited over the years in *Best American Short Stories*. He was one of the first newspaper editorial writers in the country to take a strong stand against American involvement in Vietnam. Seltzer died in 1971.

Naomi Shihab Nye was born in St. Louis in 1952. She received her education at Trinity University in San Antonio, where she resides when she isn't traveling extensively. She has published several volumes of verse, including *Different Ways to Pray* (1980) and *Hugging the Jukebox*, co-winner of the poetry award of the Texas Institute of Letters in 1982. Nye says that Pablo Tamayo "is based on a very real person in my downtown San Antonio neighborhood. I worked for over a year on this story, trying to find his 'voice' on the page, till one day the page finally started talking back." "Pablo Tamayo" was cited among the year's best work in the *Pushcart Prize* anthology for 1984.

Carolyn Osborn, born in Nashville, Tennessee, in 1934, attended high school in Gatesville, Texas, and earned two degrees from the University of Texas. She has published two collections of stories, *A Horse of Another Color* (1977) and *The Fields of Memory* (1984). One of her stories, "The Accidental Trip to Jamaica," shared the short story award of the Texas Institute of Letters in 1978. She lives in Austin.

William A. Owens was born in Pin Hook, in northeast Texas, in 1905. He took two degrees from Southern Methodist University and a Ph.D. from the State University of Iowa. He taught at Columbia University for many years. His works include an impressive range of autobiography, folklore studies, and fiction. *This Stubborn Soil* won the Texas Institute of Letters award for 1966, as did *Walking on Borrowed Land* in 1954. Owens lives in Nyack, New York. He recalls how "Hangerman John" lives in his memory: "The first part of 'Hangerman John' was drawn from a childhood experience. The setting and characters were my Lamar County home and family. The murder of the peddler was about as I wrote it. This morning in Nyack, New York, I recall all too well the sound of the gun and his dying cries for help. The factual ends about there. The distortion allowed to fiction writers accounts for much of the last part of the story, a distortion created out of recollections in maturity."

Hughes Rudd, a familiar face from television news broadcasts, was born in Wichita, Kansas, in 1921 but was raised in San Antonio and Waco. For many years he served as a CBS News correspondent, including a stint as bureau chief in Moscow, 1955–1966, and in Central Europe, 1966–1974. He also anchored CBS Morning News for a time.

He has published one collection of stories and sketches, *My Escape from the CIA and Other Improbable Events* (1966). Currently he works for ABC and lives in McLean, Virginia. According to Rudd, "'The Shores of Schizophrenia' is pretty much straight reportage: my class at Dean Highland grade school in Waco *did* take insane field trips like that one year, and the teacher *did* abscond with our little savings fund."

R. E. Smith was born in Holyoke, Massachusetts, in 1943. He holds degrees from Harding College and the University of Oregon and the Ph.D. from the University of Missouri-Columbia. He has several family connections in Texas, where he has spent considerable time off and on over the years. Smith lives in West Lafayette, Indiana, and teaches in the Department of Communications at Purdue University. "The Gift Horse's Mouth," which was anthologized in *The Best American Short Stories 1982*, has its origins in hear-say: "All the time I was working on the story, I thought the source was a story my wife had told me after one of our summer visits to Texas. I had the whole thing happening to some anonymous person living around Bandera. After the story was published, I discovered the incidents had taken place around Dallas and the source of the original story was my sister-in-law. A friend of hers had been caught in similar circumstances."

Pat Ellis Taylor, born in Bryan, Texas, in 1941, holds two degrees from the University of Texas at El Paso. She has published an oral history, *Border Healing Woman: The Story of Jewel Babb* (1981), and a collection of stories, *Afoot in a Field of Men* (1983). Most of her stories, including "Leaping Leo," are intensely autobiographical. She resides in Austin where she co-owns a used book store and writes.

Thomas Zigal, born in Galveston in 1948, grew up in Texas City. He was educated at the University of Texas and Stanford University. Author of a novel, *Playland* (1982), and a collection of stories, *Western Edge* (1982), Zigal won the short story award of the Texas Institute of Letters in 1983 for a story called "Curios." He lives in Austin and is co-editor of publications at the Humanities Research Center. "Orphan of the West" had a gradual genesis: "I had long felt that the story of Roy and Dale and the adoption of all those kids from different countries was somehow the perfect metaphor for American imperialism. And then during the final pullout of American troops from Saigon, I read in the newspaper that some wealthy American had dashed to Vietnam in his private jumbo plane to 'rescue' the children in a nearby orphanage that was soon to be 'overrun by the Communists.' He wanted to save them from a life of certain misery, so he evacuated them in his plane and brought them back to America. 'Orphan of the West' seems to me to be a possible consequence, via literary fantasy, of such an action and attitude."

www.ingramcontent.com/pod-product-compliance
Lightning Source LLC
Chambersburg PA
CBHW031206020726
47499CB00002B/508